IGLOO

David Stephens

PublishAmerica
Baltimore

First printing

At the specific preference of the author, PublishAmerica allowed this work to remain exactly as the author intended, verbatim, without editorial input.

ISBN: 1-4241-3355-6
PUBLISHED BY PUBLISHAMERICA, LLLP
www.publishamerica.com
Baltimore

Printed in the United States of America

From *David Stephens*:

Due to ill health, the last few years have been far from easy for me and my family, but through their endless support for which I am eternally grateful and the tremendous effort of my editor Katja Banik, I have been able to transform Igloo from an idea in my mind to reality on paper. I sincerely hope you enjoy reading it as much as I've enjoyed writing it.

One

"Wake up Jerry, it's time to wake up," Jerry heard being repeated in the sound of his girlfriend's voice as if she were making a feeble effort to get him out of bed. As his eyes slowly opened, he realised it was still dark outside and Jerry proceeded to stretch out his arm from under his warm duvet in an attempt to switch off the alarm clock he had only recently built. Projected on the wall beside the bed was the time, which, whilst squinting through eyes that would rather remain closed; he made out to be 4.45am. Whilst slowly gaining consciousness in his penthouse of a new luxury apartment block built in a well to do suburb of North West London, thoughts started to rush through Jerry's head. "What am I doing? Why did I agree to go away for so long? What can I possibly learn? What will they expect from me?" Desperately trying to acclimatise to the fresh February morning air, the questions continued to cause a stir in his mind. "What about Rochelle, will she wait for me as she promised? What will happen to my business?" All were questions he had asked himself many times over during the last three months, since agreeing to go along with this crazy idea. "How did I get tangled up in this? I must be mad!"

He called out "Lights" and the voice recognition system he had designed, built and installed when he bought the apartment, immediately reacted by switching on the bedroom lights. Jerry sat up for a moment before swinging his legs around and over the side of the bed, whilst trying to muster all his energy considering he was still half asleep, finally making it to a standing position. He looked around the bedroom, his suitcase lying in the far corner, still open, waiting for the few remaining items he still needed to pack. He had booked a minicab to collect him at six-thirty for the forty-five minute ride to London's Heathrow airport, allowing him sufficient time to complete everything before the taxi arrived. The flight on Israel's national airline EL AL wasn't due to depart until eleven-fifteen that morning, but since 9/11, passengers had to check in at least three hours prior to the published take-off time to allow for the intensive security measures the airline carried out. Jerry had endured them before, when he was a child, his parents having taken him to Israel, a top of the list holiday destination for many young Jewish families and he could still remember the endless security questions: "Why were they going to Israel? Who packed the bags?" And so on. A vision then sprang to mind as he recalled watching the humiliation of some travellers as their cases were opened and searched by EL AL security personnel in full view of the other passengers, with clothes and other personal possessions being removed from the cases and placed in piles beside them on the tables. With the contents hastily thrown back into the cases, the luggage was then passed through an x-ray machine, with the security officers examining each item whilst watching the embarrassment of their owners.

Jerry would also have to endure the two things he most loathed in life; waiting and wasting time. Sitting in an airport lounge for several hours with nothing to do other than counting away the minutes until departure, definitely fell into both these categories. What made matters worse, it would be followed by a further five and a half hours in the aircraft, the only comfort being a good book as Jerry could never concentrate on the in-flight films. Whenever flying, he normally arrived at the airport within the hour for international flights and even closer to departure time on the occasional internal flights he took. On this particular occasion he had been advised to arrive at least three hours prior to departure and felt compelled to comply, particularly since nothing was the same following the eleventh September incidents in America.

Jerry made his way to the bathroom, still wondering if he had made the correct decision, although he knew it was far too late to back out now. He had spent the last couple of months preparing for the trip, both mentally and physically, as well as ensuring to the best of his ability that the business would continue to flourish during his absence under the leadership of Rochelle, who was not only his girlfriend but also his business partner.

Having showered and shaved, he carefully placed the items he needed from the bathroom into his wash bag and zipped it closed. Jerry then took the bag, placed it beside the suitcase en-route to the kitchen where he commanded the voice activation system to switch the television onto channel one by calling out "TV one," while making himself tea and toast. Flicking from channel to channel, he listened to the news headlines, being much the same as he had heard the previous evening. As usual there was no earth-shattering news story, so he listened to some item about a recent study carried out showing that the proportion of multiple births in England and Wales had increased by twenty percent in the last decade, something obviously dug out by a desperate producer having to fill their time slot. It being of no interest to Jerry whatsoever, he looked down the hallway towards the front door for the daily newspaper normally lying on the mat beneath the letterbox by the time he ate breakfast, but nothing was there. Thinking momentarily, he remembered it wasn't simply because it was too early, which it probably was, but more so, due to the fact Rochelle had cancelled them for the period he would be away.

Before returning to his bedroom, Jerry finished his breakfast and washed up rather than filling the dishwasher. He dressed in jeans, a clean white shirt and a dark blue jumper he had left aside for travelling in, finished packing the remaining items and then, with his full body weight resting on the soft top, struggled to close and lock the very large suitcase.

Dawn was beginning to break and Jerry ordered "Open curtains" to the system that controlled them. He had recently modified it by adding a light sensor and timing device. These changes enabled the motor to open the curtains at a preset time in the morning, although it contained what Jerry termed ‘fuzzy logic’ in that it randomly varied the time by up to twenty minutes either side of what was set. Closing the curtains used similar logic, but instead of being time based, the trigger was darkness, the closure being varied on a random basis up to forty-five minutes following dusk. Jerry shouted “Lights” and the bedroom light switched off. The program he used to control his curtains was similar to that which he had written for his lights, randomly switching them on and off after dark, whenever the intruder alarm was fully armed, a signal to the system that the penthouse was empty. This was to create the appearance to anyone watching from outside that the place was occupied.

Looking at his watch, Jerry couldn’t believe he was ready with sufficient time to make a last check of his emails. Only junk had arrived since his previous download just before going to bed five hours earlier. As he announced “TV off,” the entry phone for the main entrance buzzed. Although Jerry knew it could only be his cab driver, he still asked the question and waited for the reply before saying “Top floor,” then pressed the button to open the door. He unlocked and opened his apartment door, ordered the alarm to set and after hearing the synthesised voice confirmation that the apartment was fully protected against unauthorised entry, he pulled the front door shut having shoved his suitcase and bags into the hallway just as the driver stepped out of the lift.

“Door lock,” Jerry announced, and when the confirmation had been given, which appeared to the stunned driver as if the door was talking, Jerry motioned to him to pick up the case and lead the way.

Two

It had all started when Jerry was in his final year at Westfield College some three years earlier, one of the many colleges making up the University of London. Having enrolled on a computing and electronics degree course, he spent most of his time either online to various secure servers to which he should not have been able to gain access, or in the electronics lab designing, building and writing the software for numerous gadgets, never mentioning them to anyone. All these devices were then stored in cardboard cartons filling every cupboard in his bedroom.

Dismantling, fixing and re-assembling electronic and analogue watches from a very early age, Jerry built his first IBM compatible personal computer at the age of thirteen, but had been programming micro processors and building electronic devices from as far back as he could remember. His introduction to developing software and building computerised gadgets started on very old microprocessors including Sinclair ZX Spectrum's, Commodore Amiga's and Atari's, all of which his father managed to obtain cheaply as they were already many years out of date. For his Bar Mitzvah, the thirteenth birthday of a Jewish boy when he becomes a man in the eyes of his religion, his parents agreed to finance all the parts he required to build a high specification personal computer with whatever peripherals he wanted. From then on his bedroom was constantly full of electronic components and reams of computer printouts spread across the floor.

Besides the ordeal of having to endure school during the day, the only other places he ever frequented were his two favourite stores which specialised in electronic gadgets and parts, namely Tandy and Maplin. Both shops were short bus journeys from his home, but as far as Jerry was concerned, these trips were lengthy distractions for him. He far preferred to use his father's credit card and order components from these stores in addition to other reputable companies, either by email or over the telephone. In the two school years before starting university, Jerry financed his passion by writing code for electronic game companies, just managing to find time to complete the minimum amount of schoolwork whilst carrying out his paid assignments.

What had suddenly attracted the attention of his college lecturers and tutors to Jerry was not the fact he was so studious, but the content of his thesis titled, 'Electronic Data Security Systems—How to Infiltrate and Protect Computer Networks.' Although it was not uncommon for students to try and hack into various computer systems, only the most intelligent of them really understood how to infiltrate them without luck playing a strong part, doing so leaving no sign of infiltration on the target systems whatsoever. His thesis demonstrated that Jerry understood the structure of data packets and how they travel between computers and peripherals across private and public networks, allowing him to remain the hidden intruder at all times. The emphasis was not directed towards causing mayhem or any criminal action; it was used as a means to demonstrate the vulnerability of servers connected to the public network and ways to dramatically improve their security. He summarised an idea of his, whereby significantly improved defences could be applied to systems containing confidential information, such as government organisations and e-commerce web sites specialising in selling products, particularly those offering electronic downloads, such as computer software and music, items that make up the majority of electronic theft.

On returning from the Christmas vacation in the final year of his Bachelor of Science degree course, he was summoned to meet with one of his lecturers, a Dr Fog, who specialised in micro switching circuitry design, a topic that interested Jerry since he had learnt that the technology formed the heart of any electronic decision making device. Dr Fog's lectures had focussed on designing the basis of central processor units or CPUs as they are commonly referred to, the key component of any data processing unit, examining past, present and future silicon chips. Jerry's interest in the subject was far from building yet another CPU; he had become fascinated in one particular project that Dr Fog's department was working on. It was the design of a very powerful, yet minute in physical size, decision-making chip that remembered all the millions of solutions it had ever calculated, thereby making it appear to be self learning. The intention was for it to become the heart of a cybernoid, a robot which in time would carry out the mundane household chores.

Jerry was asked to explain why he had failed to complete his assigned coursework by the due date, which was before the Christmas recess. This was nothing new for him since despite being recognised as a very bright student, Jerry was also renowned for doing his own thing rather than following the curriculum. If the truth were told, his understanding of computer systems and their interconnectivity was already far greater than that of many of his lecturers, including those that taught the subject.

He had always thought highly of Dr Fog, one of the few lecturers Jerry respected for his knowledge. For the first time in what was nearly three years at the college, he was questioned about his online work and electronic projects. Dr Fog appeared to be showing a genuine interest in Jerry's obsessive activities and his desire to develop his knowledge as far as he possibly could. Once he had given the latest excuse, the discussion led to what Jerry wished to do after graduation. Judging by the reaction of Dr Fog as Jerry gave his reply, he could immediately tell that the answer was not the one Dr Fog had anticipated.

Jerry realised the meeting had been planned to offer him a position within Dr Fog's postgraduate research team whilst he studied for his Masters degree. Continuing one's education to a higher degree was considered normal for a student of Jerry's calibre and his response had therefore come as a shock. Jerry explained he wanted to start profiting from what he had learnt, looking at forming a technology-consulting boutique specialising in electronic data security. On hearing this, Dr Fog quickly concluded the meeting, finishing off by offering Jerry the opportunity to use him as a sounding board at any time, adding, "If you think I can be of any assistance, please don't hesitate to ask. My door will always be open to you and I will endeavour to do everything I can to assist you in whatever you decide to do."

It wasn't until Jerry put the last full stop on his final examination paper that he decided to take Dr Fog up on his offer. As most students left the examination hall and made their way to the main exit, Jerry went off in search of his new found mentor. Reaching his office, Jerry could hear Dr Fog's voice through the door, although he was unable to make out what was being said. He proceeded to knock loudly and waited for a response. Finally the door opened and a short grey haired man with a surprised look on his face was standing in the opening.

"I wasn't expecting to see you again," said Dr Fog.

"Nor I you," replied Jerry. "But I'm taking you up on your offer. You said I could chat with you at any time and you would do your best to assist me," he continued. "Well, here I am. Do you have a few minutes? I realise I haven't made an appointment."

Dr Fog beckoned Jerry to one of the well-worn dark brown leather two-seater couches, closed the door and sat in the facing armchair.

"How were your exams?" Dr Fog asked.

"A doddle," Jerry flippantly replied. "But that's not why I'm here. As we discussed a few months ago, I've spent most of my time researching how one can really secure electronic data, a subject that has become a significant issue for governments and corporations alike. My thesis was on the very subject as you're aware. However, I feel that I can only put onto paper a very small part of the knowledge I've gained over the last three years or so." Jerry paused for a moment collecting his thoughts. Without giving Dr Fog time to ask why, he continued: "Rumours circulating the campus grapevine suggests you're involved with a number of large commercial organisations outside of University, the type I believe would be prime potential customers for me, until that is, I could demonstrate to governments how secure I can make them." Whilst speaking, Jerry watched Dr Fog's body language, trying to determine if he was really interested, or whether his thoughts were elsewhere. "At the same time," he continued, "I'm also concerned that many governments may take a very different view of the technology I've developed and try to block the sale of it in some way, since what I have, would, whilst assisting in their internal security, make it near to impossible for them to eavesdrop on electronic traffic." Again Jerry looked for some reaction from Dr Fog who appeared to be listening intently whilst allowing Jerry to finish uninterrupted, so he continued. "Before you ask, at this stage I'm not prepared to reveal my methods of securing the data to you or anyone else for that matter, suffice it to say I have carried out numerous tests and can assure and demonstrate to you it really does work," Jerry said with confidence. "What I need, if you really want to help as you offered when we last met, are introductions to some of the corporations you are involved with. One sale should provide sufficient funds to get me properly started. Could you do that for me?"

Dr Fog had listened patiently to his former student, having ample time to consider his reply before Jerry had even finished: "Slow down Jerry, we need to take this step by step." He tried to calm Jerry who had become quite excited whilst speaking about it. "Firstly, I don't know what you mean by 'rumours circulating the campus grapevine' as you call it. Yes, of course I have contacts in commerce, as do many of my colleagues in the university." He started to explain: "My postgraduate research team undertake projects for a number of companies, that's how we obtain much of our funding. I'm very fortunate that the expertise of my team is currently in great demand by integrated circuit manufacturers. But that's where it starts and ends. My department, which you could have been a part of if you recall, is invariably considered to be our client's research and development facilities, or an extension of them, for want of a better description. We contract for a given project and endeavour to complete it to the best of our ability for which we receive payment. I don't have personal contacts at the level I believe would be needed to get you through the door and furthermore, even if I did, I would certainly have to have at least some information to sufficiently excite the right people for you to get as far as saying 'hello'. These people are inundated with offers and proposals every day."

Jerry wasn't taken aback so easily and inquired: "Are you saying that you can't help me, or you maybe able to assist me if I were to disclose the specific details to you?"

"At least give me something to work with, then I can mention it to the project managers I deal with, passing on your documentation to provide them with at least an inkling into your offering. That would place them in a position to know if it were something that maybe of interest to their company. If they were not the people to make such a decision, they would certainly be able to point you in the right direction. But you must have something to show them, you certainly can't just walk in, tell them you're able to install a system that will protect their data, it will cost them whatever, please sign on the dotted line. It just doesn't work that way however good your product is, that's one thing I can unfortunately guarantee," Dr Fog said, trying not to be condescending towards Jerry.

"Of course I realise I have to demonstrate the system. I never for one moment thought otherwise. I've been working hard on building a prototype for that purpose. I'm able to demonstrate the system works across a local area network and can assure you it is something that has to be seen to be believed. I can't describe the solution on paper without divulging to some extent the manner in which I'm achieving the results and as soon as I do that, I would immediately be digging holes in the system. Surely you of all people appreciate that?" Jerry replied without hesitation.

"Look, Jerry, leave it with me and I will see what I can do, no promises though. Have you applied to protect the system, patents and so forth?" Dr Fog responded after contemplating the information for several minutes.

"I've looked into protection, but would need to provide very detailed specifications of the system and how it operates, including listings of code, drawings of the electronic circuits and so on. I feel all I would be doing is shouting my mouth off to all and sundry. Reading the requirements of what has to be submitted, I believe I'd be providing the tools to crack open the system to every Tom, Dick and Harry, almost inviting them to have a go. Don't get me wrong, it's not that simple to break, but why provide any assistance whatsoever? With respect, it's not the same as developing a microchip device that you don't want people to copy. Security is all about keeping one step ahead of your potential intruder and some hackers as I'm sure you're aware, are very devious."

Dr Fog stood up and went to shake Jerry's hand. "It's coming up to holiday time so a lot of people will be away. Send me at least something on paper that I can use. Then give me a few weeks to discuss the idea with my contacts and we'll see where we're at." Taking his mobile phone from his desk, Dr Fog pressed some keys on the keypad and then showed the display to Jerry. "This is the best number to reach me on over the holidays. I keep it switched on most of the time." Jerry copied the number into his palm pilot.

"And this is my number. If you need to ask me anything, or you get a positive response, please don't hesitate to call me," Jerry said after putting away his palm and handing Dr Fog a business card with his name and number printed in bright blue embossed glossy ink, something reminiscent of a prestigious Mayfair or Knightsbridge address. "I appreciate your help," Jerry murmured as he opened the door.

He then made his way back to the main exit and joined the last of the stragglers leaving the building from an exam they had just completed. As he walked away from the main college building and across the courtyard towards the Finchley Road in the bright June sunshine, Jerry felt vulnerable, a feeling he had never experienced before. His future no longer depended on others, it was now entirely in his hands. There could be no more hiding in one of the college computer rooms or electronic labs. He was thankful for being able to work from his parent's home for a while, where over the last couple of years he had built a sophisticated computer network which had almost taken over the whole house, much to his mother's annoyance. She would regularly moan that her home looked more like a computer centre, with cables pinned to almost every skirting board, a number of boxes screwed to various walls and computers on almost all flat surfaces. In every direction you looked, in every room there was some piece of technology buzzing away, or broken up into several components. "She will just have to put up with it for a little longer," he thought to himself.

Jerry spent the next few days trying to put together a descriptive document of his system as requested by Dr Fog. After numerous attempts he felt he just couldn't get the correct words down on paper in a way that would interest a potential customer, or was not giving away too much technical information on how it worked. Due to the time he spent in the computer suite and electronic labs, he had no time available to take modules in business studies or media communications, or for that matter any other subject that may have provided him with tips on how to proceed. Seeing his frustration one evening, his mother attempted to offer some ideas, all of which Jerry shot down very quickly.

"You know who could possibly help you?" she suddenly said excitedly.

"If I knew someone do you think I would have spent the last week, day and night, sitting here achieving absolutely nothing?" he replied in a frustrated tone, "So who?"

His mum smiled: "Rochelle, Belinda's daughter."

"Rochelle who? Belinda who?" Jerry shouted, as if he were reprimanding his mother for trying to annoy him.

She tapped his forehead as if to knock his memory into place whilst ignoring his ranting: "Remember Belinda, your dad's second cousin. I'm sure the last time we met with her and her husband Paul at some function or other, she was bragging about their daughter just being appointed marketing manager, or something similar, for a multi national company. It was supposedly a major achievement since she had not long before completed her degree and was allegedly very young to obtain such a highly rated position. I'm sure it was her, let me make some calls," his mother said.

"If she has a job as good as you're implying, I can't believe for one moment she'd be interested in helping with this. Look mum, Jerry said having calmed down. "I know you are only trying to help, but from what I do know, generally speaking the principles of marketing are to communicate the benefits of a product and why it's better than the competition. This is normally achieved by bragging about its features and cost benefits, precisely the opposite of what I wish to do here," Jerry tried to explain. "I'm certainly not going to produce a document that details the features of my system and how it works and what's more, I'm not prepared to discount the price. It's good, no, it's brilliant," he said excitedly as he continued "And it's not going to be cheap. I have no need to compete with other products, as far as I'm aware, there is nothing quite like it on the market at the moment. By only stating it protects electronic data far better than any existing product, it makes it harder for potential competitors as well as hackers to copy or crack it, keeping me at least one step ahead and thereby allowing me to sell the solution at a premium."

"Let me talk to her, you've nothing to lose," his mother said after Jerry had finished.

"Okay, you win as usual," Jerry replied with a deep sigh adding, "My apologies for raising my voice earlier."

Three

It was 6.50pm when the doorbell rang. Believing it to be Rochelle, Jerry ran down the stairs from his bedroom as fast as he could, desperately trying to beat his mother to the front door, in an attempt to save him the embarrassment he was sure to endure if she were to get there first. Being a typical Jewish mother, he knew that despite all the nagging about the mess his project made of her home, she idolised him and boasted to everyone that her son was a genius. Worse still, she was always on at him about his obsession for computers and that he should concentrate at least some of his effort on finding a nice girl. Despite her hundred percent failure rate, she still took every opportunity that arose to try to match make him.

As he opened the door, a quiet yet confident voice enquired, "Jerry?" in such a manner as if checking she was at the correct address. Jerry felt his head nod to confirm, as if it were no longer under his control, he suddenly became too embarrassed to speak. The very attractive girl standing in front of him continued, "I'm sorry, I'm a few minutes early, not as much traffic as I anticipated."

Mustering all his concentration he sort of stuttered as he felt himself blush. "You must be Rochelle, come on in. Yes, I'm Jerry." He was not used to being in the presence of any girl and to be welcoming such a pretty blonde-haired female into his house, for whatever reason, was proving to be a very awkward situation for him. "How am I going to discuss the project with her?" he thought to himself. "Surely she can see me blushing from embarrassment and yet appears to be unperturbed." As she followed him into the living room, he realised she was probably more than used to being in the company of boys, looking as she did. Clearing that thought from his mind he managed to mumble, "I'm sorry that my mum dragged you over here, but you know what mothers are like, always thinking they know best," although he had no idea how far she had travelled.

"Don't worry, my mother's exactly the same, it must run in the family," she said jokingly. "Wow!" she exclaimed on entering the living room and seeing the myriad of machines. "Do you think you have enough computers in here?" Rochelle asked.

"It's what I do, well, sort of," Jerry replied.

"I heard you're more than a bit of a wiz on these things. I use them, but I'm certainly no more than your typical computer user, spending the same amount of time talking to the company's help desk people as I do actually being productive with them," she said smiling. "How come we've never been introduced before at family functions or anything?" she asked Jerry in an attempt to ease his embarrassment.

Jerry started mumbling again, "From what mum has said, I think we're distant relatives. We've probably been at the same family parties, but have never been introduced to each other; you know what it's like." Jerry paused for a moment. "Can I get you something to drink?" he asked, suddenly remembering his manners. He couldn't help thinking how good-looking she was and although his friends nicknamed him Geek and until now he had certainly never been interested in girls whatsoever, or for that matter socialising with members of either sex, on this occasion he couldn't avoid noticing how gorgeous she looked.

Rochelle smiled at him looking at her. Whilst doing so he noticed she didn't seem to use much makeup, she was naturally beautiful, the kind of girl he thought his friends would call a real stunner. "Thanks," Rochelle's voice interrupted his thoughts. "Orange juice would be great."

"Coming up," said Jerry's mother, appearing in the open doorway to the living room. "And what would you like to drink, Jerry?"

"A can of Coke, please mum," he answered and after a short pause where he was staring into thin air, he sat down on the couch at the opposite end to where Rochelle had already made herself comfortable. He managed to manoeuvre himself into a position where he was facing her without having to continually twist and turn, but at the same time was far enough to feel safe.

"So what do you do? Mum says you're a marketing manager for a major company," Jerry opened with, trying to regain some composure.

"It sounds far better than it actually is. I'm one of several marketing managers for a company called Milky Way. They are an Australian organisation, manufacturing a range of confectionary, fairly big in the Southern Hemisphere and now trying to break into the Northern one, particularly Europe and America. They are second to Nestle in both Australia and New Zealand and looking to give them and Cadbury's a run for their money here as well. I have a couple of people that report to me and I in turn report to the Vice President of Communications. I've only been in the job for six months so its early days and certainly nothing to write home about just yet." She stopped for a sip of orange juice and Jerry took the opportunity of her pause to say "Thanks mum," in such a way as to ask her to leave the room. She took the hint, closing the door behind her.

Rochelle continued: "So that's me, but I didn't come here to talk about myself other than to allow you to determine if I have the skill set you require if I decide I'm interested in the project. I've been led to believe you have an interesting story to tell, but your mother didn't say very much to mine about what you are actually doing when they spoke on the phone. All I know is what I said before, you allegedly know your way around computers, you build all sorts of electronic gizmos and over the last few years you have completed several contract jobs for game publishers. The only other point your mother made was that you are expected to get a first class degree with honours and if you don't, she will demand a re-mark. It's all very interesting, but tell me, where am I needed?" she finally asked in a manner and stature as if she were interviewing him for a job which made Jerry feel even more uncomfortable.

"Before I start, please don't feel obliged to help me just because we're related," then he drank some coke and looked at his glass as if he had never seen one before, only to avoid her ice blue eyes watching him very carefully. He tried to justify himself: "This idea of talking to you was mum's, not mine. I honestly would understand if you're not interested. I don't even know if what I require is actually possible to produce within the parameters I'll insist on," he said, beginning to relax a little and regaining some composure.

"Don't worry," Rochelle replied appearing completely at ease. "As you'll find out very quickly if we do start working together, I'm not one to hold back on speaking my thoughts and whilst we're on the subject, if I can assist you in any way whatsoever, it's certainly not going to be a freebie. I live by my talent, whether I'm using it between nine to five Monday to Friday, or outside of those hours," she said, making sure there was to be no misunderstanding in the terms between them right from the beginning.

"Okay," Jerry replied. "Let's first see if you're interested. If you are, we can discuss the finer details." He carried on, "I'm not really sure where to start, I haven't had to explain the project to anyone before, only ever having to answer to myself. I suppose a brief background would be the best place to begin," he said to himself aloud so that Rochelle understood where he was coming from. "As you stated, I know my way around a computer, both hardware and software. I've always been interested in electronics and communications. For at least five years, I think it was when I started sixth form; my interest has been focussed towards electronic data security. I taught myself to hack into allegedly secure computer systems, not to cause trouble or boast how good I am, it was merely to see how well protected they really are. If an amateur or school kid can infiltrate them, what do you think a professional hacker could do?" He posed the question but didn't wait for an answer, immediately continuing, "I've never left any signs of my infiltration, I haven't boasted in any of the hackers' chat rooms or on their electronic notice boards, never have and still don't go to them. Hacking into systems has been for research purposes only, for me and me alone. Please stop me if I'm going too fast for you, or you don't understand anything I'm talking about," he suddenly thought he should add.

"I'm with you so far, part of my degree was using the web as a marketing tool and that included keeping data secure, so I do have a little knowledge of the subject. I have heard of hackers' chat rooms and web sites so nothing new there," Rochelle replied, taking the opportunity of Jerry's pause.

He continued: "That's great. Okay, I have written algorithms or code capable of getting me through network security systems and I quickly learnt to identify the type of security implemented, thereby allowing me to infiltrate other systems employing the same protection without having to do much additional work each time and ensuring I don't trigger alarms by mistake." He paused momentarily. "Then wireless networks started to evolve in a fairly big way, their rapid growth partially due to the vast increase in the usage of notebooks and the upsurge in the adoption of hot desking." Not sure whether Rochelle was familiar with the term, Jerry, in his usual manner of trying to explain everything to the 'nth' degree continued. "Hot desking is where a number of people share the same desk space, since they spend the majority of their time either on the road or working from home. It saves companies paying unnecessary expensive rents as they are able to manage in smaller buildings. The scheme has therefore been adopted by a significant number of major organisations where their employees only occasionally require office facilities."

Having explained the commercial reasoning, he then proceeded to explain the technical details. "With wireless networks, there is no need for cables lying around loose on the floor waiting to be plugged into the travelling notebook computers, which occasionally cause hardware failures due to spikes of static electricity, besides being a serious health and safety issue with people sustaining injury by tripping over them. Wireless networks avoid the need for cables altogether. A wireless adapter installed in the computer sends and receives data using an inbuilt transmitter and receiver in a similar way that a mobile phone handles voice traffic. I'll come back to mobile wireless access using 3G and wireless Hot Spots in a moment," he slipped in before continuing,

"The adapter connects to the network through an Access Point, the name given to the data transmitting and receiving device connected to the main infrastructure by cable, each one capable of supporting many computers simultaneously at speeds similar to conventional cable connections. As Jerry explained it, he pointed to a white box in the top far corner of the wall Rochelle was facing so she could get an idea of what they looked like.

"Anyone with an ounce of knowledge can pick up the signal and connect to the infrastructure, thereby gaining access to the network and data. Someone could be gathering a company's electronic information in this way whilst sitting in a car parked in a street completely out of sight and entirely unknown to anyone within the company. And if you think that's bad, it gets worse. Remember the billions of pounds the UK government earned from the mobile phone operators for 3G licenses?" Jerry asked, this time waiting for a reply.

"If you're referring to the auctions that took place a while back, then yes I do remember. I'm also aware that the mobile phone operators have more recently complained they substantially overpaid for the licenses and are having trouble recovering the fees from their subscribers," Rochelle answered.

Jerry picked up the conversation again, excited that Rochelle had some knowledge of the communication industry. "Well, besides sending nice photos of friends doing stupid things no one is really interested in, or speaking on mobile video phones, the real benefit of the technology is for companies to operate much larger wireless networks. Using 3G, the three hundred metre or so limit for connecting through an access point disappears. Fast data transfer can take place wherever there is mobile network coverage and of course with roaming, that means it is international. With 3G and the rapid growth of hot spots and the trials of city-wide, wireless connections which will compete against 3G, systems and data will shortly be able to be accessed from almost anywhere in the world. The problem that exists today is companies have not really modified their data security to take into account that their information is suddenly all around us. It has never been difficult to infiltrate networks, especially if one knows what to do, just look at the number of malware or malicious software reported so frequently on the news. These various forms of viruses, with other similar breeches of security and privacy causes havoc and huge disruption to companies and the general public almost every day, but now with widespread wireless connectivity, systems can be infiltrated far more easily and silently than ever before."

Rochelle interrupted Jerry's flow: "I said I speak my mind so here I go. I'm no way at your level with any of this, but am I not correct in thinking systems today operate using something termed 'hundred and twenty eight bit encryption', not that I understand what it means other than it's meant to be more secure?"

"Yes, you're right," Jerry told her. "One two eight bit encryption has been around for several years although it has not been widely implemented and even where it is in use alongside a good firewall, it takes me about ten minutes to crack, that includes writing an algorithm on the basis I haven't come across the firewall before, something which is now quite unlikely. If I wanted to, I could break into and amend the data sent between Washington and the US troops operating in the Middle East and the data transmitted to the munitions being deployed there. For that matter it could be any government and any army. Can you imagine if al-Qaeda gained the ability to do that? And no, I'm not up for sale to the highest bidder before you get the wrong idea." Jerry paused to sip some coke.

"Keep going," Rochelle said. "You still have my full attention."

"Without being accused of being modest, I'm good. I know that. My lecturers asked me questions rather than the other way around, but I'm sure I'm not alone. There must be thousands of computer gurus with the ability to listen in, steal, or alter data that doesn't belong to them. Industrial espionage, a war, or other military campaigns, politicians and governments, anyone and everyone are susceptible to serious infiltration and the consequences that could ensue. We just have to look at the US for a very simple example of electronic data manipulation and the damage it can cause. If you recall not long ago, the web site of a candidate standing in the presidential election was changed without his team's knowledge, the alteration being far from favourable, raising a number of questions regarding the individual's integrity and thereby possibly influencing the public vote," Jerry mentioned, thinking it would serve as a good illustration. "If you're still interested when we finish tonight, I'll give you a copy of my thesis; it goes into a fair amount of detail on the subject and will allow you to appreciate the scale of the problem. It makes good bedtime reading," he added jokingly. "Anyway, I've developed a solution that without any modifications being required to servers or workstations connected to a network, whether locally or across a wide area connection, provides dramatically improved security to wireless as well as fixed wire systems. I won't say it's impossible to illegally penetrate since I don't believe it's ever possible to provide one hundred per cent protection to anything, despite the representations made in marketing blurb to the contrary and I'm not just referring to computers. However, even having designed and built this system; I have as yet not been able to break into a server protected by it as long as it's maintained correctly, merely a matter of changing batteries when advised. I can easily demonstrate it works." Jerry stopped at this point, hoping Rochelle would want to view the system in operation.

"Of course I'd like to see it working, but I'm still unsure as to what you want from me. It sounds like your product should sell itself," Rochelle commented, trying to get Jerry to say in his own words what she had deduced very quickly, almost as soon as Jerry started speaking. She needed him to understand that success isn't just based on the product itself; it's as much the way the benefits of the product are communicated to others. It was immediately evident that effective communication was a skill Jerry didn't posses. Once this was appreciated, often a difficult concept for technical people to comprehend, he would then realise the value her contribution would make.

Jerry knew he had to tell Rochelle about his discussion with Dr Fog, something he hadn't originally planned to do. "At university I had a lecturer who thought I'd stay on and do a Master's degree whilst working as part of his micro electronics research team. I discussed with him the opportunity of commercialising this project, selling it to his contacts, only to be asked for documentation to pass onto prospective customers. He advised me that no one would even consider discussing it without first seeing something on paper. I've spent the whole of last week, almost twenty-four hours a day, every day, trying to produce a document and all I have to show for my time is a blank sheet of paper. Where I did manage to get words down in black and white, all they did was shout out the methodology I'm using, allowing anyone to replicate it. I've never been so unproductive," he finished in a subdued tone.

Rochelle didn't seem to find this a problem: "So you want me to put a teaser together?" she asked enthusiastically.

"Teaser?" Jerry repeated as a question, never having heard the term before.

"Oh sorry," Rochelle apologised. "It's my turn to use technical jargon. A teaser is simply a short document, no more than a couple of pages, describing your product or service in a way that excites the reader sufficiently to create an appetite for more information. In this case the 'more' would be a demonstration."

"In a word, I suppose yes. That's of course if you want to, and feel you can," Jerry replied.

"Before I answer those questions, could I see what you have?" Rochelle finally asked to Jerry's delight.

"Of course you can, that's if you don't mind coming up to my bedroom?" Jerry enquired, suddenly becoming rather embarrassed again.

"Not at all," Rochelle said with a lovely smile and a sparkle in her eye. She noticed his embarrassment confirming her initial suspicion that Jerry had little if any experience with girls, unlike herself who had been interested in boys from an early age, already having a number of relatively serious relationships under her belt.

She followed him up the stairs where she couldn't fail to notice the many cables neatly attached to the skirting boards. "Why, if you have a wireless network do you need all these cables? And how come your parents don't mind you turning their home into a computer centre?" she asked as they made their way to his room.

Jerry quickly replied, "I need to experiment and test on all types of connections. And who say's they don't mind me taking over their home as they put it. I certainly haven't had an easy ride with all this kit, most of the time they give me so much grief I've considered throwing in the towel on several occasions. Whilst at university the continual moan was 'Why do I need all this stuff here? Surely I could use the university's facilities' and now it's changed to 'Why don't I rent an office?', which once I get going is at the very top of my list of things to do," he answered Rochelle somewhat abruptly, immediately realising he had made a mistake and wishing he could turn back the clock by a few minutes. After all it wasn't her fault, it was just the thought of the subject which made his blood boil, being the cause of almost every argument with his mother over the last three years. He hoped Rochelle wouldn't delve further into it.

As she stepped into Jerry's room, Rochelle had the feeling of entering a different world. The curtains were half drawn and she quickly counted nine screens around the place, all displaying different, constantly changing information, none recognisable to her. There were also countless computer boxes, some proudly showing their innards, others fully cased, most humming with various coloured indicators glowing. The room was scattered with small black boxes that appeared to be in clusters of three or four, evenly spread around the floor. Spaghetti junction was an accurate way of describing the tangled web of cables that created a second carpet. In the far corner was his bed, but even that appeared to look more like a desk, completely covered in computer printouts, spare cables and equipment.

"You surely don't sleep in here?" she suggested.

"Not often," Jerry admitted, looking in the direction of his bed. "I doze off in this chair occasionally and that keeps me going most of the time. When I really want to sleep, I kip on the couch downstairs. I could use my sister's room since she's now at university, but on the odd occasion I have, the girl goes berserk when she finds out."

"Have you seen a shrink recently?" Rochelle asked jokingly.

Jerry chose to ignore the question since he couldn't think of a suitable humorous answer that would impress her. Instead he requested her to: "Think of a computer system you want me to infiltrate and retrieve data from."

Rochelle thought for a moment or two. "What about the company I work for? See if you can find the ingredients and recipe for Choc-O-Bar, that's their best seller and they keep the details secret," she paused. "And whilst you're there, you can remind me of my salary."

Jerry seemed disappointed with her choice. "Are you sure?" he asked. "I was thinking along the lines of the Police National Computer, the FBI or the CIA. Something you'd expect to be really secure," Jerry said, anticipating her to try and push him to his limits, something he would have done had the situation been reversed.

"Yes, I'm sure. You've probably hacked into each of those a hundred times. You try and get me the information I asked," Rochelle replied with a slight tone to her voice indicating he shouldn't have questioned her.

Jerry sat at one of the screens, his fingers immediately playing with the keyboard. Rochelle stood mesmerized, watching the ever-changing monitor whilst Jerry continued to tap away at the keys, but not like an experienced touch typist using specific fingers for particular characters. His was far more of a high speed, right-handed two or three fingered process, with the occasional support from a finger or two of the redundant left hand to carry out specific functions such as pressing the Shift and Tab keys. He also manoeuvred the mouse far faster than she had ever seen anyone do before. Within a few minutes, a laser printer sitting on a shelf behind her sprang to life. Three sheets spurted from it as Jerry spun his chair around to retrieve them. He quickly glanced at the pages before handing them to Rochelle as he returned to face the screen.

Each page was headed Choc-O-Bar and below the large bold print were the complete ingredients followed by a detailed recipe of precisely how they are mixed. "Fifty thousand pounds per annum," he said pointing to one section of the screen, which had a number of windows open.

Maximising each of the windows in turn, Rochelle viewed the offer letter sent following her third interview, her payroll record, a summary of a recent review carried out by her boss, the Choc-O-Bar recipe, the printed version still held tightly in her hand. As if that were not enough, she could also see the company's monthly management accounts and her email account. "With my skills fifty thousand pounds is nothing, I should be earning several times that amount at the very least," was her only comment, trying to justify the amount being paid to a recent graduate. She finally looked away from the screen and back at Jerry, for some reason her brain had started calculating she couldn't be more than a year older than him. "I can't believe this. I regularly have problems connecting to various web sites and people frequently complain that emails they send to me are often returned to them, particularly when they have files attached. I'm continuously told by the help desk boys it's due to the firewall," she informed Jerry, surprised at how easily he obtained the information.

Jerry's attention had returned to the screen. "I'm into both the UK network and the servers in Australia. The recipe is on the Australian side, as is your email and the management accounts. The payroll and personnel files are from the UK system," he informed her as if it was common knowledge.

Quickly checking her watch, "That took you less than five minutes. Now show me how it can be protected," Rochelle said after pondering over the screen for several minutes.

"Obviously I can't show you on the Milky Way's system, but let's move to one of my servers. Can you see those three little black boxes to the right of the scanner over there with the green light emitting diodes or LEDs glowing?" Jerry asked whilst pointing to the boxes.

"Yes," Rochelle replied beginning to become impatient, having seen for the first time how easy it was to hack into protected networks, trying to calculate the value of a product that could resolve the issue.

"The green LEDs show the status of the boxes, either on or off. Just below each LED is a small black switch. Press the switch once on each box, the green glow should disappear," Jerry said in a manner requesting Rochelle to carry out the task for him.

Rochelle switched each of the units off. "Pull up that chair and watch this screen," he said indicating a second typists chair in the room overloaded with papers, which she carefully placed on the floor. Once he was happy Rochelle was concentrating on the screen, Jerry showed her how to list the contents of various files. "Now you do it," he suggested as he moved the keyboard and mouse closer to her. She repeated the strokes exactly as he had, with the identical information being displayed. "We have hacked into one of the servers in this room. Coincidentally, I'm running a similar firewall to the one protecting Milky Way's network," he mentioned. "If we move to the workstation here" and he rolled the chair a few feet to be beside another screen and keyboard, Rochelle following, he continued. "We are now working on a PC authorised by the firewall which also has a small program running in the background whilst the machine is on. We can call up the same files as before using Microsoft Word or any other suitable application. Here, this is probably a more familiar display to you." He opened one of the files that Rochelle has listed moments earlier on the first screen, into Word.

"Yep, I certainly recognise that layout. May I quickly make a change to the file? I could then see what comes up when I open it on the other computer," Rochelle suggested.

"That's precisely what I was about to ask you to do," Jerry replied and gestured to her to continue. Rochelle typed a couple of sentences about the weather and finished off with her name, the date and time before saving the file. Using her feet, she pushed the chair back to the first screen, forcing it over several cables and then listed the file as he had initially shown her. The amendments were visible on the screen.

"We will now turn the boxes on again," Jerry said as he moved over to them and pressed the switch on each case causing the green LEDs to glow, indicating they were in an active state. "Now try and list your file," he requested. Rochelle tried to no avail; it was as if the computer was dead. Without Jerry mentioning a word, she returned to the second screen, the one with the special software and managed to open the file in Word with no problem adding a further couple of lines before saving the modified file. Before returning to the first screen, she tried listing the file in the same manner as on the first computer, to find it worked perfectly. Attempting the same task on the initial screen, she was still unable to obtain a response. Jerry turned the black boxes off once more and asked Rochelle to make a further attempt to view the data. To his relief, from both machines she was able to access the original text and the sentences she had added.

"I guess that proves it works assuming you did nothing more than you said."

"Oh, the trust," Jerry responded with a smile, gaining confidence in himself. "I'll leave the room without touching anything; you know how to turn the boxes on and off. You try it without me being in here."

"That's fair," Rochelle quickly replied, beginning to appreciate what she had just witnessed. "It will prove you weren't doing anything whilst my back was turned."

Jerry ignored the comment and opening the bedroom door, "Call me in when you're finished, I'll be just outside the room."

Rochelle repeated the sequence several times, on each occasion changing the status of the boxes to prove to herself Jerry wasn't cheating, at least not to the best of her knowledge, something she accepted was limited in this field. However, her logic and the minimal knowledge she did posses led her to believe there was no trickery at play. Before recalling Jerry to report her findings, Rochelle spent several minutes contemplating the potential of what she had just witnessed. Recollecting the modules taken on various elements of computing as part of her Marketing and Communications degree, she compared her experience of data security to the trial successfully completed minutes earlier. Thinking she may know of one or two people who maybe interested in seeing it, she finally asked Jerry to return.

"So, are we ready to talk terms?" he asked once she had finished confirming the results.

"Please ask your Doc friend to hold off for a week or two before speaking to anyone. There is someone I want to discuss it with first whom I believe will be able to confirm or refute the viability and potential opportunity of your system. I may even be able to persuade him to be your first customer, but for being a test site and possibly an important referral, he probably won't pay what its worth, but it will get us started."

"Us?" Jerry repeated as a question, baffled by its use.

"Yes us. We will agree the details later, but if I introduce the organisation that orders the first installation, it's us," she told him, realising that a further explanation was required. "I know several guys who were a couple of years above me at university that took the same or similar courses to the one I followed. They each joined start-up internet projects on finishing their degrees, seeing an opportunity and grabbing it, in the most part, initially giving their time in return for part ownership of the company. Since then, they have all made fortunes when their respective organisations' have either become listed on the Stock Exchange, or where the company has been bought by another, in all instances at seriously silly valuations. I'll be perfectly honest with you; I wish I'd been available at that time as I would have been at the front of the queue to jump at such an opportunity which only comes once in a lifetime, if you're lucky." She looked at Jerry making sure he fully comprehended what she was saying, feeling it important he did so in order to be able to justify the terms she was going to state.

"This could be my opportunity; I can see the potential although as I said, I will of course need to confirm the concept with a third party. As long as an independent assessment is favourable, I'm prepared to take a gamble on it and give up the Milky Way to work full time with you in an effort to make the most of the potential of this project. You said yourself earlier this evening, you have wasted your time trying to produce the sales material. I like what I have seen so far and if everything is confirmed, which I have no doubt it will be, then I'll take a punt on it. I don't think you have the funds to pay me at the moment, you have seen what I earn, so yes, it's very much us."

Without any hint, she changed the subject to the task in hand, as if nothing had been mentioned that might have given Jerry something fairly major to consider. "Can you please bullet point for me by tomorrow afternoon what you are happy to say about the product, including its USP. I don't want any comparisons to existing products, it will only prompt more 'how' questions that I appreciate you wish to avoid. Email them to me at rochelle.levy@mhhost.com." She then asked, "Are you happy to work on a Saturday?"

"I work everyday. If you are asking me if we are religious and keep the Jewish Sabbath, then the answer is no. We are what I suppose you would call a traditional Jewish family rather than an Orthodox one. We keep the very religious festivals, like the New Year and Day of Atonement. We also keep Friday nights in as far as the whole family stay in and eat together. That's about the extent of our Judaism." Jerry paused, having realised she had mentioned another term he hadn't heard of before. "Excuse my ignorance, but what does USP mean?" he asked sheepishly whilst still trying to get his head around her comment of becoming a partner in his baby, which she seemed to just slip into the conversation as though it had been a natural comment to make.

"Oh sorry, more marketing jargon again, I'm worse than you," Rochelle laughed. "It's an acronym for unique selling point," continuing, "It's the term used to explain, 'what makes this product different from its competitors?' But as I just said, don't give me any comparisons, just the key features of the offering." In an effort to make general chit-chat between them, she once again changed the subject, picking up on Jerry's explanation of his religious observances. "By the sound of it, your family is probably very similar to mine when it comes to religion, except we don't really do the Friday night thing like you. Is it okay if I come round Saturday morning then, say nine-thirty, to really get started?"

"You don't beat about the bush do you?" Jerry replied, somewhat satisfied with his evening's performance in as far as it had certainly appeared he had managed to gain her interest in the idea. He knew he had some serious thinking to do regarding the partnership scheme of hers and decided it was probably best to wait and see what else she had to say on the subject, in particular what split she had in mind. He decided to wait rather than jump in feet first sounding very negative, thereby putting her off providing him with the skills he knew he desperately needed and felt she could offer.

Seeing he had become preoccupied in thought and assuming it related to her wanting part of the business, she stated: "I did warn you at the very beginning of the evening I speak my mind. I also advised you

I don't work for nothing," Rochelle reminded him.

"Depending on the terms you're thinking of, yes, Saturday is fine," he finally replied, believing it would at least progress things slightly further.

"Don't worry," Rochelle said in a placid voice. "I know we'll come to an amicable agreement. I came this evening with no preconceived ideas so let me think the details through tomorrow. Meanwhile, can you make some space around here for me to work? And don't forget that email," she said seeing the drastic change in his reaction to her since she'd mentioned the term 'us'. To an extent, Rochelle thought she understood why he felt as he did and desperately tried to take his mind off worrying about losing everything to her, which was not her intention. "I think we should leave it there for now," she continued to say. "Time is pushing on and I need to get going. Here's my card, it has my mobile number and I've written my personal email address on the back. You can call me anytime, but please only send emails to my personal address and not to Milky Way." Rochelle finished saying, as she handed Jerry her business card.

"Thanks," Jerry replied, taking the card from her, not thinking to give her one of his. "See you Saturday morning then," he repeated whilst still in deep thought over the partnership thing. As he was about to make his way downstairs he remembered to give her a copy of his thesis. "It's probably worth you having a quick glance through this," he said as he handed it to her. Taking it, she followed him down the stairs. Saying goodbye to his parents she left, with Jerry watching as she drove off in what looked like a brand new BMW.

At 3:15am, some five hours after Rochelle had shaken his world with the use of one short word, Jerry sent her the requested email and then managed to doze off in front of his screens as he often did.

Four

Jerry woke unusually late the following morning, his mother being careful not to disturb him. When he finally entered the world of the living just before ten-thirty, he proceeded to eat a late breakfast and peruse the daily paper. His approach to the day was completely different to his normal attitude. As a rule, he either hurried his breakfast or skipped it altogether, always in a rush to continue his work. Today he was happy to sit at the table, sipping what now had to be a cold cup of tea whilst reviewing yesterday's news stories. He had mixed feelings intertwined together; excitement, frustration and apprehension. He was overjoyed that Rochelle's initial reaction was so positive to the extent of wanting a piece of the action, prepared to quit a well paid secure job for it, if he heard correctly. She might even have a potential customer waiting in the wings. What was eating away at him was the long wait until the following morning, some thirty-six hours after she'd left with such zeal, before they were to meet again and Jerry was concerned her enthusiasm would evaporate before then. He wanted to pick up the phone just to say something like: "Hi, it's me, Jerry, any further thoughts on last night?" From the tone of her reply, he felt he would be able to determine whether her excitement remained at the same level, or she was going off the idea, either way at least he would know where he stood. As much as he wanted too, Jerry knew he would never be able to pluck up the courage to do it.

From what he could remember, this day stood out as being the only one where he could not face working. Until now, the only days he's ever taken off since starting the project have been the Jewish New Year and Day of Atonement, the two most religious days in the Jewish calendar when his parents forbid him from working whilst he lived under their roof. On tender hooks, he spent much of the day trying to watch TV, finding it difficult to concentrate on any programme. Knowing his mother would start an inquisition, Jerry decided to summarise the meeting with Rochelle for his parents over dinner that evening, the perfect time to do so since it was Friday, the traditional weekly Jewish feast, normally eaten when the men return from synagogue having brought in the Sabbath. Although neither Jerry nor his father went to synagogue on a Friday night, the tradition of the evening meal was kept, it being the one night of the week the family ate together. Most weekends Jerry's sister returned home from university in Manchester to join them, enduring a five hour journey to do so and always bringing her mother a present for the Sabbath; a bag full of her dirty washing.

Having lit the candles and recited the prayers over the glass of wine and special religious bread, all part of the Sabbath ritual, they sat down to what was always an excellent meal. Having finished the bowl of piping hot chicken soup, often referred to as Jewish penicillin, whilst his mother served the main course of roast chicken accompanied by potato and vegetables, Jerry chose to relate the previous evening's events summing-up the overview they both gave, Rochelle's comments on the project, her reaction to the demonstration and finishing with her proposition on moving forward and his reaction to it. His parents listened without comment until he had finished, his father confirming Jerry had made the correct decision in waiting for Rochelle to state her terms, adding in his opinion it was a good idea for her to be given an interest in the project in lieu of salary as long as the percentage was reasonable. His mother's only comment was: "She seems a lovely girl," adding, "And intelligent too," from which Jerry knew precisely what was brewing in her head. His sister Judith remained silent, knowing any comment she made would only be considered antagonistic; she had often voiced her opinion on her brother's obsession.

Whilst speaking, Jerry admitted to himself he was upset Rochelle hadn't called during the day, if only to confirm receipt of his email, all he wanted was some reassurance. Then he thought, "No news is good news." At least the hours were ticking away and it would only be a few more until he hoped the blue BMW 3 series would park outside the house and from it a striking girl would emerge. Still unable to work, Jerry spent the night sleeping on the living room couch. Rising early the following morning, following breakfast and a shower, he managed to tidy his room and make space for Rochelle.

As promised, just before 9:30am, from behind an upstairs curtain Jerry watched the BMW being parked. Relieved she had arrived, he rushed downstairs to open the door. Rochelle breezed in carrying a briefcase in one hand, her other holding a mobile phone to her ear. She smiled at Jerry and without muttering a word, headed straight upstairs to his bedroom, placing her bag on the worktop where Jerry had cleared a space. Finishing the call she pulled up a chair and motioned for Jerry to sit along side her.

"Sorry about that," Rochelle said, whilst pressing the end call button on the phone and placing it on the worktop before opening her case. She removed a blue tinted, semi transparent plastic envelope file with the letters 'IGLOO' written in thick bold black letters in the top left hand corner. The file contained a number of sheets of paper which Rochelle handed to Jerry, each headed with the same five letters. "There should be two copies of everything, a set for each of us."

"What do the letters I, G, L, O, O stand for?" asked Jerry, calling out each letter individually in a perplexed tone.

Keen to assure Jerry she is completely focussed on making the project a success and that she had already spent time on it, Rochelle answered, "The first thing we need is an identity," in a relaxed manner. "On the assumption you haven't considered a name; I tried to find something that would conjure up an image that describes what we have without giving anything away, as you requested. After spending considerable time playing around with ideas, trying to think of something that has synergy with the project, I finally came up with an

Igloo." Wanting to ask for a coffee, but deciding to hold off until she had finished, she explained, "An Igloo is a shelter which protects its inhabitants and their belongings in harsh environments, leaving everyone else out in the cold. I believe our product is not dissimilar in function to an Igloo; it's a shelter to protect an organisation and its electronic data in harsh environments. Anyone without our system will be left out in the cold to defend themselves against bad elements. The other evening you went to great lengths to instil upon me the fact that an organisation's electronic data contains its owner's innermost secrets and is therefore a very valuable and possibly sensitive possession. Bearing this in mind, it finally dawned on me you have created a virtual or electronic Igloo."

An eerie silence consumed the room whilst Rochelle allowed Jerry time to mull over her idea. She knew before arriving she would have her work cut out in selling the various items to him and it was just a matter of waiting for a reaction as he played mental games with the first. She could understand it being difficult for Jerry, a complete stranger coming along and having stretched lateral thinking to it's extremities in conjuring up such an obscure name. If that wasn't enough, she was about to take a share of his idea to boot. It was something he would need time to dwell on.

Finally Jerry looked up from the five characters that had been the focus of his concentration since being handed the sheets several minutes earlier. Turning to look at Rochelle, he repeated "Igloo" several times in a monotone, as if in a deep trance. "Igloo," he said once again, but this time as though it meant the world to him. "Igloo" he repeated once more, quickly followed by "You really are quite good at this, aren't you?" his face suddenly alight with joy. "I like the name, it certainly grows on you," he told her with excitement and then went straight onto ask, "So, what else do we have here?" glancing down at the bundle of papers.

Rochelle took her set of papers and flicked through them stopping on a page close to the bottom of the pile. Looking at it she said, "As promised, I took a first hit at producing a short teaser to give to people. I'm nowhere near finished, but it's probably at a stage where we should review it together to ensure I'm on the right track." Whilst Jerry started to read the teaser, Rochelle returned to the top page. "Don't go through it yet, we'll do it together," she said and then referring him to the top sheet continued, "These first few pages are a draft of a standard shareholder agreement to which I've made some minor amendments. I propose a seventy thirty split in your favour if I introduce the first order providing the necessary funds to set up the business in a professional manner, at which time I'll leave Milky Way. I appreciate you have dedicated the last few years to this project, but you must understand I'll still be taking a substantial risk and therefore believe thirty percent is a fair reflection of that risk. We also need to agree our salaries which I think should be equal and initially based on what the company can afford to pay us each month, once we have the funds. I have to give Milky Way four weeks notice, but I have some holiday due, so it shouldn't be more than a fortnight from handing in my notice until I'm able to work with you full time, but I will of course work evenings and weekends until then."

Rochelle continued in her corporate mode, "Take the agreement to a solicitor, you'll find it's very fair. I believe that by combining our skills we can both do well from this little idea of yours and you know someone with my skills is needed to turn the project into a commercial success. For me, well I've already told you, I'll be taking a huge risk in leaving a secure job, but I'm convinced there is a real opportunity here and I want to be in on the ground floor. After all, I have seen the benefits of such a gamble as I mentioned the other evening." She paused for a moment before adding, "I also feel we'll have a lot of fun developing the business together and know I'll enjoy making the decisions with you which will influence our future. That's not in most job specifications that I receive, but is something I have always dreamt of."

On hearing her terms, Jerry knew that waiting for her to open the bidding was the correct thing to do. At least he was now aware of her expectations. The fact she was a woman, and a very pretty one at that, was a major disadvantage to him in trying to negotiate a deal, due entirely to his shyness and embarrassment. "That's on the assumption her terms weren't merely a set of demands," he thought to himself.

"Thirty percent," he kept thinking, repeating the number in his head time after time.

Rochelle saw that Jerry was once again in deep thought. "What's up?" she asked in an upbeat, carefree manner.

Jerry looked at her with an expression of disbelief. "And you really believe you're worth thirty percent of everything I earn? This is my idea, my project, my effort, you do remember that?" he said, with an element of shock. "I thought you were going to try and help me, not rob me," he then stated as an after thought, regretting it as soon as he had said the words.

Rochelle was fully prepared for this discussion. The order of proceedings so far this morning had been premeditated to give her a subconscious advantage for this debate, certain Jerry would not simply agree to her terms without putting up a good fight. At the same time she was adamant she was not going to budge, prepared to walk away if he didn't accept them. She felt thirty percent was very reasonable taking into account her abilities and tried to explain her reasoning to Jerry. "If you were to finance this through investors, a venture capital fund or some other similar financial institution, I can assure you that in today's market they would take the major chunk of the company and provide very little if any practical assistance other than cash. I'll only get my thirty percent if I introduce the first order." She paused for a moment for Jerry to appreciate what she was saying, "It's obvious to me that technically you're a genius, but you know yourself you can't make this project, your idea, the success it deserves on your own. I can and want to help you, but there needs to be the incentive in it for me as well. I really do believe I'm being very fair with the split. So it's not as you said before, thirty percent of what you earn, it's thirty percent of what we earn!"

Jerry listened intently to her every word "When do I need to make a decision?" he asked.

"You can take as long as you like, I obviously won't do any additional work until you've decided," she replied knowing he was eager to progress things quickly, as was she.

"From the way you've spoken, I don't suppose we could settle on a smaller share for you, I accept that you deserve something?" he asked, knowing it to be a stupid question as soon as he said it. Negotiations were not his forte.

"I've said my piece; I've already come up with a name you like and put together a few words. I have even provisionally organised a demonstration for next week," she slipped in as an additional incentive. "They're my terms, take it or leave it," she stated assertively, preparing to pack away her things.

"Okay, Okay. You win. Thirty percent and equal earnings," Jerry finally gave in. "I'll take your papers to a solicitor as you suggest."

Relieved the negotiation had been a lot easier than she anticipated, Rochelle held out her hand to shake his, "Let's make this happen, partner," she said with a refreshing smile. "Now we need to get on with the real work," she continued. "Firstly a coffee would go down well, white, no sugar please."

"Oh, I'm sorry," Jerry replied, his mind still thinking about the thirty percent, annoyed with himself for giving in so easily. "I'll go and sort it for you." He immediately ran downstairs to the kitchen where his mother and Judith were finishing breakfast. He persuaded his mother to make a coffee for Rochelle and tea for himself, which he carried back to the room on a tray, breaking the golden rule of no food or drinks to be consumed there.

If there was any doubt in Jerry's mind as to there being an impending demonstration, it was dispelled very quickly. "Some time next week can you do a similar demonstration to the one you gave me the other evening? Before you answer, please consider carefully since it needs to take place in an office, not this room." Rochelle asked, as if the morning started when Jerry walked in with the tray.

Trying to forget he had just given up thirty percent of everything, Jerry could already see a few long sleepless nights ahead of him: "I'll have to do some work on the black boxes to enable them to be switched remotely, probably via the Internet; they need to remain in here attached to the servers. Managing them across the Internet will compromise the protection they provide, but I suppose it's only for demonstration purposes." He thought aloud. "Yes, as long as we have access to an unrestricted Internet connection then I can do something for you pretty quickly. Leave it with me, I'll come up with something," he replied with excitement, seeing that things were already starting to move in the right direction.

"Now, let's look at the teaser," Rochelle suggested. They both reviewed the bullet points she had produced from the email Jerry sent the previous morning; thinking carefully about each one, Jerry checking it passed his criteria. By the time they had finished, twelve had been struck out, leaving twenty-one. "I think we need a little more detail to make it finger licking good," she announced. "And I need to work on the format. A series of bullet points won't create the interest we're after, at least not these bullet points!" She removed her laptop computer from the briefcase and went to hand Jerry the plug of the power adapter.

"Over there," he said as he pointed to an empty power socket on the wall.

"Do I need to use my dial-up Internet account or have you an always on internet connection here?" she asked. "My machine has WiFi and an RJ45 connection in addition to an internal modem."

Jerry was once again impressed with her apparent knowledge of computing, or at the very least she was aware of the correct terminology. He knew manufacturers listed WiFi on their specification sheets to inform prospective buyers their products had built in wireless connectivity enabling them to talk to access points and other WiFi enabled systems without the need to purchase any additional adapters, but he wasn't sure how many people actually understood what it meant. It occurred to him she had already understood wireless networks before his long-winded explanation the other night and he could kick himself for not asking first. Even more encouraging to Jerry was her comfortable use of the term RJ45 connection, the standard connection used in a wired local network environment. This indicated she really was aware of the difference between computers connected to networks by cable as opposed to wireless connected systems. "Had she mentioned something about taking a number of computer related modules as part of her degree course?" he asked himself, not sure of the answer. He really must listen to others when they speak.

"Pass your machine over and I'll configure your WiFi to one of my access points. The Internet will be much faster than your modem connection and won't cost for the online time. I have a leased line connection, which is similar to broadband except much faster and the same speed in both directions, so you may as well make use of it. I'll also give you access to an admin server so you can use the printers and disk storage to save your files, or at least back them up," he said, beckoning her to pass the notebook to him.

A minute later Rochelle was able to connect to the web. She noticed Jerry had named the connection IGLOO, which brought a small grin to her face. He immediately started working on modifying his little boxes to enable them to be managed via the Internet whilst she continued to work on the teaser.

At around 1pm, Rochelle turned to Jerry. "Let's get a bite to eat. What's quick and simple around here?"

"Pizza," was the first thing Jerry could think of. While saying it, he immediately wished he'd had a little more experience with women and had taken his time to answer, thinking before he spoke. "Why did I not say something like 'I know a really good little Italian restaurant not far away,'" he thought, knowing it to be quite intimate with a good selection of wines, not that he was a drinker. He had been many times with his parents to celebrate birthdays and anniversaries. "If we went there, maybe I could get to know her a little better, socially as well as for business. That's if my brain doesn't blank out on me from embarrassment." Since first meeting her, Jerry dreamt of something more than just a business relationship, perhaps that's why he was so embarrassed whenever she spoke to him about anything unrelated to work, where he now viewed her as a colleague, her gender being irrelevant. He had no idea how to approach such a situation; the only certainty was that suggesting a Pizza wasn't going to help him in his endeavours whatsoever.

"Fine, are you ready to go?" he heard her say.

Having already missed one opportunity, he couldn't believe he was saying, "I don't normally do lunch whilst I'm working." It was as though he were watching himself in a slapstick comedy.

Fortunately, Rochelle wasn't interested in his excuse. "You do as from now. Come on, I won't take no for an answer. It's on me, don't worry."

Facing the opposite direction from Rochelle so she couldn't see his embarrassment, Jerry switched off the soldering iron and like a lamb being herded, followed her downstairs. They walked in silence the few minutes around the corner to a Pizza Express located at the beginning of the High Street, where a table for two was quickly prepared.

After ordering, Rochelle asked Jerry to tell her a little about himself. He wasn't sure what to say, he was shy and far from at ease being in the company of a girl, let alone one so beautiful as her. He tried his hardest to talk, but Rochelle had to keep prompting him. After listening to Jerry for a while she gave him a short overview of her background from childhood upward. One of Rochelle's attributes immediately apparent to Jerry was her confidence and he wished he could be the same.

They finished their Pizzas and Rochelle settled the bill as promised. The topic of conversation as they walked back to the house was of various family members they both knew, although Rochelle did most of the talking.

The remainder of the afternoon was spent concentrating on their individual tasks until Rochelle finally broke the silence at around five-thirty, "I need to leave soon; I'm out tonight, are you okay to continue tomorrow morning?"

"Yes, sure, same time?" Jerry enquired.

"Traffic should be light so say between nine-thirty and ten. I'll get in touch with some local estate agents and see if I can find a flat nearer here, which will dramatically reduce my travel time. In the meantime I'll ask mum if I can move back there for a while until I find somewhere, on the assumption I'll be leaving Milky Way shortly. I only moved out to Reading since it was taking me well over an hour commuting every morning and evening and that was on good days, although now I'm not sure I could live back home again. Mike, my boyfriend I mentioned over lunch will be more than happy he doesn't have to schlep to Reading, but probably won't be quite so amused when he realises we lose our privacy."

Jerry felt he needed to know but didn't get a chance to ask earlier, "How serious is it between the two of you?"

Rochelle didn't seem to mind the directness of his question and was happy to explain, "We've been together as a couple for about six months, but have known each other for a couple of years. What about you? I don't remember you mentioning any girls in your life."

"That's simply because there haven't been any," he said, embarrassed once again. "I've always been too busy playing with machines and I'm sure there aren't many girls who would be prepared to compete with a computer for my attention on a Saturday night."

Rochelle couldn't accept his reasoning, "That's probably true, I certainly wouldn't. I'm a strong believer in working hard, what you get out of something is invariably proportional to the effort invested. At the same time I also think that it's very important to take time out of work and enjoy oneself, ideally with a person you want to be with. When returning to work after a break, however short it may be, one is normally far more productive. Didn't you notice a difference stopping for lunch?"

"Possibly, I don't really know. Go on, have a good time tonight and I'll see you in the morning," Jerry said, trying to give her a cheerful goodbye even though he'd rather she stayed a little longer, not so she could complete the work, simply because he enjoyed having her around despite his embarrassment.

Rochelle stood up, unplugged her computer and packed everything away in her briefcase.

"You can leave your case here if you want," Jerry offered.

"Thanks, but no thanks. I prefer having it with me. I'm sure you know what I mean." She finished collecting her papers together. "Don't stop. I can see myself out if it's alright with you?"

"Great. See you tomorrow then," Jerry replied.

As Rochelle made her way down the stairs, Jerry heard her speaking on the phone, "I'm running a little late. Collect me from the flat at eight-fifteen. We'll get a bite to eat first then go to the late screening. Sorry, darling..."

"Where does she put all these meals whilst maintaining a perfect figure," Jerry pondered. "She's just had a Pizza for lunch and is immediately calling her boyfriend to arrange another restaurant meal."

He then heard the front door being closed and with it couldn't help feeling just a hint of jealousy. His friends, the few he had, were correct, he really was a geek, always having been far more interested in computers than anything else, particularly girls and he was so shy which made matters worse. Even when he had met a girl he liked, he could never pluck up the courage to ask her out. Until now it had never bothered him, even when his friends bragged about their conquests and relationships and yet at this moment he felt a void in his stomach for the first time.

Jerry tried hard to put this thought out of his mind and concentrate on the matter in hand. He had a long night ahead, wishing to be in a position to do a dummy run of the demonstration with Rochelle in the morning, allowing him sufficient time to practice and make it slick before the real thing. Other thoughts then began to circulate around his head. "Had spending the day with what was now the girl of his dreams affected his concentration, or was it the excitement of the project moving forward that was confusing him?" Whichever it was, he couldn't remember who he would be demonstrating too. "How could she have possibly interested an organisation so quickly, without really knowing much about the project? Or was it only to get the independent confirmation she spoke about the other evening?" She didn't say and Jerry realised he had never actually asked the question. "What inspired her to come up with the name 'IGLOO'?" a name that was growing on him as each hour passed. New thoughts kept entering his head: "Thirty percent of the company; is that really realistic? If she thought she was that good, why didn't she ask for more? Should I have agreed so quickly to her terms? Did she expect me to haggle? Would she have settled for less? How can she be so confident in getting the first order? Should I ask dad about a solicitor now, or wait and see what happens? I don't want to waste money unnecessarily. What should I tell mum and dad? Should I tell Dr Fog to hold off as she suggested, or let him carry on? She is cute. Come on, pull yourself together, you have work to do."

Jerry finally managed to focus his concentration on the electronics and programming of the boxes and the hours started to race by. He thought he had only recently heard his parents go to bed; his father sticking his head around the door of Jerry's room on route to his own bedroom, telling him to get some sleep, as was his habit. Now Jerry could hear the birds chirping outside the window and through the partially open curtains, could see the golden yellow glow of the morning sun easing its way up into the sky from behind the distant tall buildings that help make up the City of London.

He had worked through the night non-stop, but wasn't tired in the least. If anything, he now felt somewhat invigorated, a sensation he had missed for some time. The excitement was mixed with a little disappointment; progress with the modifications was slower than he had anticipated. Fortunately, there were still a few hours remaining before Rochelle's arrival, to sort out some of the technical issues he was encountering.

Jerry went downstairs to the kitchen and made himself breakfast, then returned to his bedroom and continued to work. Before he knew it, the doorbell rang and he heard his father greeting Rochelle. She made her way up to his room, removed her file and computer from her briefcase, powered up and continued with her work with only the quietest of "Good morning's."

"Did you have an enjoyable evening?" Jerry enquired, trying to make conversation.

Her response was simple, "Fab thanks, a really good time. How did you get on?" she then asked.

Jerry knew Rochelle was referring to work rather than his social life and answered accordingly, "Progressing slowly, I'm hoping to have something to show you by the end of the day, what time are you planning on leaving?"

"I need to leave around five or so; a friend is making a barbeque. You are welcome to join us if you wish. I'm sure it would do you the world of good to get out once in a while and meet new people," Rochelle suggested in a friendly tone.

Once again, before he could stop what he was saying, Jerry had replied with, "I don't think so, besides let's see where I get to with this."

"You'd be really welcome, I mean that, I'm not just saying it," Rochelle repeated, almost pleading with him.

This was his chance, an opportunity to change his mind and say yes. He cleared his mind of everything and concentrated on the three letters; Y, E, S, trying self-hypnosis. Finally, confident in being able to reply he began: "Thanks, but as I said, let's see how far I've progressed by then." He couldn't believe those words left his lips; somehow he just seemed to lose control of what he was saying. He wanted to beat himself up, he was so angry for being unable to give the response he really wanted too.

Rochelle said no more about it and the room went silent apart from the continual tapping of the keys on the keyboards and the occasional sound made by Jerry rummaging through small drawers full of electronic components. By mid afternoon progress had started to be made on the hardware and code. After confirming with Rochelle that the dial up modem in her computer was configured correctly, he gave her a modem cable with one end already connected into a telephone socket. Once she had plugged the other side into her computer, he asked her to disable the Igloo connection and reconnect to the internet using the modem. Rochelle clicked on the Icon that dialled her Internet Service Provider, AOL, a service which she was generally happy with. After the usual warbling sounds the machine went quiet. Looking over Rochelle's shoulder at the task bar on the bottom of her screen, Jerry could see that the connection had been made.

"Watch this," he said as he tilted the machine towards him and took over the keyboard, opening a number of windows on the screen and jumping from one to the other. He placed a CD into the drive on the side of the machine and ran an install application from it before removing the disk. "That's the client side, nine kilobytes, it'll never be noticed in today's world of large file computing," he said to her as he logged into his network with a user name Rochelle. "Don't worry, I set you up as a user yesterday if you recall when I gave you access to my local services. The prompt for a name and password now is because the server realises your computer is not currently connected directly to my network, whereas before it was automatically recognised on the local connection." As he continued to tap away at her keyboard, Jerry gave her a quick explanation of how computers which are not continuously connected to the internet are given temporary addresses rather than fixed addresses, allowing there to be sufficient unique addresses for every machine simultaneously connected to the internet. "Here is the file you were playing with the other day," he finally said, pointing to a window that had Word running with the file open. Selecting one of the other windows, he typed a number of commands. "Watch the green LEDs on the boxes over there." And as he spoke, each one extinguished. "Keep watching them," he said excitedly and moments later they were re-kindled, one by one. "We can now turn the boxes on and off remotely and can therefore do the demonstration from anywhere we have Internet access," he said happily. "I suggest we initially prove we have access to a system, amending files whilst the protection is switched off. We then switch the system on and access the files we amended, repeating the process as many times as necessary, basically what you did the other evening. I'll create a web page to access these commands which will look a lot better. We will have to explain that it works on wireless as well as hard wired systems, protecting servers and workstations."

"What happens if someone forgets to run the client software?" Rochelle asked.

Jerry explained: "If the software isn't installed, or it's removed for some reason, the user will not be able to see the network and therefore fail to gain access to it, as if they were not authorised to access the system, which in fact they wouldn't be. In the demonstration I'll basically simulate what you did the other night when you kept swapping machines." Jerry paused to think through his statement, never before had he analysed it so simply, which suddenly gave him another idea. "A machine protected by this system can't even be pinged; a function to test if a specific device exists on a network, particularly the Internet. With an idea racing through his brain, he asked, "Have you heard of Denial of Service attacks?"

Rochelle thought for a moment, "Didn't Hotmail suffer one a

couple of years ago? I think I've heard of other major web sites also suffering from such attacks."

"I can't remember precisely when it was, but yes, Hotmail was a famous one. Well, it's always been said that it's impossible to completely protect from that type of attack, but thinking it through, we could use a slightly modified version of the system to do so," Jerry informed her excitedly. "I'll try to include something in the demonstration; it's a major fear for anyone with a public website."

After confirming for her own satisfaction that everything worked as she had seen the previous Thursday evening, Rochelle said: "I'll storyboard a demonstration and email it to you tomorrow sometime. Please learn it, practice as often as you can. If you think anything can be simplified or improved, all the better." She was looking at her diary on her handheld Palm Pilot, "I'll come over on Tuesday evening when you'll go through the demonstration as though I was the decision maker of the largest company in the world," she said. "Unfortunately I'm not quite as fast with my words as you are with the technology, at least not to deliver the message we want whilst keeping within your parameters, but I'm getting there and I hope to have something for you to look at tomorrow evening, failing that, certainly by the time we meet on Tuesday. This is probably a good time to break for the day, you going to come to the barbeque?" she asked Jerry again.

In his excitement, Jerry had completely forgotten about it, but remembering what happened earlier, felt he wasn't ready for things like that just yet; it would only serve to make a fool of himself. "I think I'll take a rain check this time, I still have a fair amount of tidying up to do with the electronics and code for the boxes. I just wanted you to see we can demonstrate from anywhere. I'm assuming you understood that by using the dial up modem on your computer, you were in effect accessing the network from outside the house and not internally via a direct connection."

Rochelle noticed that even a simple question relating to a social activity made Jerry uncomfortable and he needed to redirect the conversation back to the project. Not having the knowledge of a therapist, she believed he was using it as a virtual hiding place, in this case to save him risking further embarrassment. However, she felt obliged to answer his question. “Yes, I did appreciate we were off your network when connecting through my AOL account. The reason for creating a storyboard to follow is to ensure we don’t forget any points when we do the demonstration. I would rather push to use their PC not ours to prove there are no tricks, so it might be worth taking an external modem with us. If all goes well on Tuesday evening, I’ll confirm with my contact on Wednesday that we’ll be in a position to carry out a demonstration for him on Thursday. It’ll probably be up in town if that’s okay?”

“Wherever, it doesn’t matter,” Jerry replied, the demonstration being furthest from his mind at this precise moment. He was thinking how he so wanted to accompany her to the barbeque, realising it was now too late to change his mind even if he could pluck up the courage to do so.

Rochelle packed her belongings into her briefcase and as she was making her way out of the room reminded Jerry, “Arrange for a solicitor to look over the agreement this week.” She ran down the stairs and through the front door, Jerry watching her making a phone call on the way.

Five

Jerry tidied up the technology to enable a slicker demonstration to be given. Having considered how the solution would be implemented in a commercial environment, he made various modifications which he intended to mention during the presentation. These included remote access to the black boxes via the internet, for which he created a simple screen allowing the boxes to be switched on and off with the ability to display the current status. He made a note to mention a live system would only show the battery status, the ability to switch the boxes off would not exist. Jerry then simplified the process to list a set of files and in the hope of leaving nothing to chance he set-up a duplicate system, connecting it to the internet using a basic dial up telephone connection rather than his leased line, in case either the fixed connection failed, or the main server crashed. All he had to do on the day was remember to open the dial-up connection before leaving home. Finally, he made sure he had several copies of the client application on both floppy disk and CD, to install on a computer if he wasn't able to use his own, which despite what Rochelle had said, was his preferred option.

An email from Rochelle arrived in his mailbox at lunchtime and he opened it with trepidation.

"*Jerry,*

Hope you have managed to sort out the issues you had, I have every faith in you.

Attached is storyboard as discussed. If you have any questions regarding it, please let me know, otherwise start practising!

Still working on the teaser – sorry, but I'm sure it will be worth the wait.

You should have joined us last night. Everyone had a great time. Next time I won't take no for an answer so prepare yourself.

I'll check in with you later this afternoon for an update of your progress.

Regards,

Roch"

Jerry opened the attachment that contained a forty-slide PowerPoint presentation. He flicked through each slide making sure he understood the sequence and message Rochelle was trying to portray. It looked as though it would work and he started to run through it as a demonstration, slide by slide, reading aloud his lines. He felt extremely stupid. "Is this what actors go through? Surely not," he thought to himself. "But she really is into this project, that's for sure. This must have taken several hours to prepare."

At 4pm his mobile rang displaying a number he didn't immediately recognise.

"Jerry, its Roch. Thought I'd just give you a quick bell and make sure you're okay. I sent you the storyboard earlier, did you get it?"

"Yes, I'm working on it as we talk. I've also managed to reduce the number of screens for the demonstration. I think you'll be happier with them now," he replied, thinking how he liked the name Roch, it suited her.

"Excellent. I have provisionally confirmed Thursday at 11am. It will be here at Milky Way's offices in Reading, I hope that's okay with you?" she asked.

"Yes, as long as you give me directions. I take it the customer is Milky Way. That's cheating a bit, don't you think?" Jerry said with a smirk, although an order is an order, he didn't really care where it came from.

Rochelle quickly responded: "As it happens Milky Way is a second prospect. They have agreed for their office to be used for the demonstration which they want to see, but I promise that the organisation I referred to yesterday is not Milky Way, as you will find out on Thursday."

"So who is the other company then?" Jerry asked.

"I'm afraid you'll have to wait until Thursday," was the only response from Rochelle.

"Why the secrecy?" Jerry asked.

"No secrecy, just be patient," Rochelle responded, giving nothing away.

Jerry tried once more: "Why can't you tell me who the main prospect is? I thought we were partners."

"We are partners. But I'm sorry; you'll just have to wait. I've been asked by my contact not to name them at this point. I'll call you tomorrow. If you need to talk before then you have my number and can call me anytime. By the way, I've checked how quickly I could leave here. If I handed in my notice today, I would leave at the end of next week, ten working days. So make sure you have a really slick demonstration because I'm ready to go," she informed him.

Jerry said, "Something tells me we're going to get on well together. I admire people who make up their mind about something and go for it. And you are certainly proving you fall into that category. Thank you for your faith in me, I won't let you down."

"Don't worry, I won't let you. I need to go now; someone's waiting to see me. Call if you need anything, otherwise we'll catch up in the morning and I'm with you tomorrow evening anyway, as early as I can make it," she said and before Jerry could get the words out to say goodbye, the line went dead.

Jerry continued to practice the demonstration until the early hours of the morning, then, having had several hours sleep on the couch, woke and carried on rehearsing it for most of Tuesday. Rochelle arrived at 5:30pm, managing to leave the office early in an attempt to miss the rush hour.

"Well, show me what you're made of partner," Rochelle breezed in saying, with a fresh smile. Jerry spent the next thirty minutes doing a perfect demonstration. “Fantastic!” she exclaimed. “Far better than I ever imagined, the screens are tremendous too. All they are missing is a logo.”

“That’s because we don’t have one,” Jerry replied.

“We’ll that’s where you maybe wrong,” she said opening her briefcase and removing her PC. After powering up the machine she displayed a page of nine images. “I started with a picture of an Igloo and finished with an ice pick,” she said, quickly scrolling through the pages. Many of the icons consisted of the name in a variety of fonts with an illustration of an Igloo, whilst others were just the name in various typographical styles. A final batch was the name in the same fonts, but substituting an ice pick for the letter ‘I’ in the name, some with a picture of an igloo, others without.

“There are six screens, fifty-four logos in total. I think two or three work well, but before I tell you my preferences, you tell me which if any, you think would work for us,” Rochelle said.

Jerry’s eyes scanned the images. He viewed each page from the first to the last and then reversed back through them. “Not bad, I’ve already told you the name works for me, but the igloo, I don’t think so. I must admit the ice pick replacing the ‘I’ does look quite effective, particularly the one with the diamond handle and the letters in what looks like frosted metal,” Jerry stated, once he was satisfied he had examined them all properly.

Rochelle replied, “I’m glad you said that,” as she loaded a single image of the word IGLOO that took up the whole screen with the ‘I’ being formed from the diamond handled ice pick.

“I bet you had a large image of each logo,” Jerry said teasingly.

“Check if you wish,” Rochelle immediately replied, but Jerry declined the offer.

“Is it difficult to add the logo to your web pages?” Rochelle asked.

“Not really, it shouldn’t take too long to do. Email it to me and I’ll add it to my ever-growing list,” Jerry reassured her, thinking it was going to be yet another sleepless night.

She then opened a Word document that looked like a page from a magazine. “Read this, mark any changes you feel are required,” she said whilst turning the notebook to allow Jerry to use the keyboard more comfortably.

He read it and re-read it. Besides making a couple of very minor amendments "It's brilliant, says everything and yet says nothing and so readable," Jerry said in a somewhat surprised tone. "And they say blondes are thick," he finished with, beginning to feel more confident in Rochelle's company.

Rochelle replied without hesitation, "There are exceptions to every rule. You should know that, being a scientist! Seriously though, I'll email you the file, but don't give it to anyone yet. When we do distribute it electronically, it should only be in an Acrobat 'pdf' format which makes it difficult for anyone to amend."

"I'm happy with that," Jerry responded. "I've an application which converts document files to pdf's so it's not a problem for me." He told her reassuringly.

"Tomorrow I'll confirm the appointment for the demonstration with both prospects. We'll probably have to do the presentation twice, one for each, so I'd imagine we'll finish about one-thirty. Now let's go and celebrate with a meal, what do you fancy?" Rochelle asked.

"I'm not fussed, if you want to stay fairly local there's an Italian, Chinese, Turkish, Indian, Pizza which you know and of course Kosher," he rattled off. He wanted to recommend the Italian, but still couldn't bring himself to suggest it.

"Let's go for Italian then," Rochelle said and as she spoke the words she saw a glow appear across Jerry's face that she had not seen until now.

Six

Jerry arrived at the Milky Way's offices forty-five minutes earlier than originally planned, having called Rochelle whilst en-route to inform her he would be early. He wanted to allow himself sufficient time to connect everything and carry out a full run through of the demonstration on his own, to ensure everything worked properly, having time to deal with any issues.

He entered the modern brick building through the large glass doors and headed straight for the reception desk where two girls were sitting in front of computer screens wearing headsets connected to their telephone systems. One was reading a magazine, the other filing her nails. As he approached, the girl reading looked up at him in an enquiring manner as if he should know what to say. Jerry gave his name and stated he had a meeting with Rochelle Levy. While he was signing the visitor's book as requested, the receptionist called through to Rochelle having found her telephone extension on the computer monitor in front of her. Jerry was impressed as the system she used was state-of-the-art touch screen. Following a short telephone conversation, Jerry was issued with a nametag he had just watched being printed on a small purpose built printer and placed in a plastic holder by the receptionist. He was then directed to the waiting area to the right of the reception desk, the two areas separated by a glass partition creating a very modern appearance. In it were a number of large leather tub chairs and two huge flat screen televisions, one either side of the room, showing Australian TV adverts for Milky Way products. Scattered around the area were small coffee tables with industry magazines and information on Milky Way neatly placed on each. There were two other men in the room and Jerry wondered if either of them were the person he was due to meet. Looking at the clock mounted on the wall at the far end of the room, he believed it was probably too early for them to have arrived.

After a short wait which Jerry spent watching the adverts many times over, his attention was caught by a tall man with short fair hair and dressed in a dark pin striped suite, exiting a lift and walking over to the reception desk. Having chatted with the girls for a few moments, he made his way towards the room where Jerry was sitting. As he walked through the open doorway, he called out "Jerry Freedman" in a stark Australian accent. Jerry immediately stood up, grabbing his bulging briefcase which contained his notebook computer, a number of CDs and floppy disks, a modem as Rochelle had suggested, an assortment of connecting cables and everything else he thought might be needed for the demonstration.

"I'm Peter," the man informed Jerry. "Rochelle asked me to show you to a meeting room to prepare for a demonstration. She says she'll be with you shortly, you've arrived a little earlier than expected and she is still in another meeting." Whilst speaking, he held out his right hand to shake Jerry's. Before Jerry had a chance to respond, Peter asked, "Have reception issued you with a nametag?" in a manner as if he knew they had, he immediately continued: "Please, for security reasons you must wear the badge in a position where it is visible at all times."

For some reason Jerry had not carried out the receptionist's request and found himself still holding the card in his hand. He hoped Peter's initial opinion of him was not one of an absent-minded blundering professor, as his mother often referred to him as, in situations similar to this. He promptly clipped it to his jacket which he'd taken out of mothballs for the occasion.

Jerry felt uncomfortable in a tie and jacket, but thought he ought to dress smartly thinking his normal attire of worn jeans and T-shirt wouldn't be suitable for the occasion. "If you're ready we can go up,"

Peter said and started to walk towards the lift. They took the elevator to level three and when the doors opened Jerry could see from the overall appearance that the corridor ahead of him consisted solely of meeting rooms. The floor was covered with a thick plush blue carpet and the walls were constructed from sheets of opaque glass from floor to ceiling on both sides. At irregular intervals, large wooden doors, again reaching from floor to ceiling broke the large expanse of glass, which, as Jerry looked properly, he could see was double-glazed. Between the two panes were narrow blinds with the controls positioned on the inside of each room. Jerry presumed the blinds were to shut out prying eyes, although as they started to walk along the corridor he noticed many were not positioned in such a way to prevent this.

Peter led Jerry into a room; home to a large oval, highly polished wooden table which he assumed was made from Beech wood judging by its creamy brown colour. Precisely positioned around the table were eight black leather chairs. In the middle of the table sat a large conference phone, its shape resembling a miniature alien spacecraft. In the far corner of the room, opposite the door, stood a camera on a motorized tripod which Jerry quickly realised must be part of a video conferencing suite and strategically located in the middle of the longest wall was a large flat LCD screen with speakers attached to each side. The cables disappeared into the wall, but Jerry assumed they somehow connected to the conferencing system. He also believed it was probably possible to use it as a large computer screen. His thoughts were then interrupted.

"We can pull in one of our PCs if you wish, or you can connect up your own notebook," Peter suggested in an enquiring tone, assuming the bulk of Jerry's briefcase was his laptop computer.

"Whichever," Jerry replied, "I'm happy to use my notebook if it's more convenient for you. All I'll need is a power socket, access to the Internet that bypasses your firewall and the video connector for the screen on the wall," Jerry said, whilst removing the notebook from his case.

"I'm sure you'll find everything in the recessed floor compartment under the table. You just need to lift up the flap," Peter replied, pointing to a covered compartment located in the floor, positioned almost centrally in the room under the table, with a cable protruding from it. Jerry followed the wire with his eyes and noted the other end was plugged into the phone on the table. "You're probably best to use the available telephone socket and a modem for your Internet access, that way you're guaranteed to avoid any firewall filtering. There should also be a remote control for the screen in there somewhere. I'll leave you to it, but if you need anything don't hesitate to call me, I'm on extension two, two, seven, one." That said he left the room.

Jerry set everything up and checked it worked properly. He was confident with his script and what he had to do, but decided it was worth taking the time to go through the complete demonstration once more to ensure he made no mistakes. As Rochelle had said the other day, a lot was resting on his performance this morning. Just as he was finishing, Rochelle and Peter entered the room.

"I believe you've already met Peter. He's responsible for the Milky Way's computer network around the world," she said without even as much as a good morning. "Peter and I have been friends for several years, in fact it was Peter that suggested I apply for a job here," she told Jerry. "Since he is the most knowledgeable person I know when it comes to computers, I asked if he would be prepared to carry out a technical evaluation of your system. To give him an idea of what it was, I talked him through the demonstration you gave me last week to which his initial reaction was that there was no way you could have accessed his infrastructure without him knowing, so I showed him the printouts you gave me."

Peter cut in, "I'm sure you can imagine my reaction when I looked at information I've never been allowed to access." Changing the subject completely, Peter asked, "Rochelle, have you organised drinks yet?"

"I was waiting for Leon to arrive before I ordered refreshments, he was meant to be the first demonstration this morning and you were second on the list." The way Rochelle spoke, it was as though Peter knew Leon. "Since Leon's late and time's pressing on, why don't we change the order and start with you, if you don't mind being a guinea pig?" Rochelle asked with a slight grin across her face.

"Not at all, I have a fairly easy day, but please organise some coffees, I haven't had anything to drink since first thing this morning," Peter informed her.

"Jerry, drink?" Rochelle asked.

"Tea, please." Jerry answered, looking at her as if she should have known. Rochelle stretched over the table and keyed in an extension on the conference phone.

"Catering," was the immediate response heard by all through the grey, multi directional speakers.

"Hi, can we please have a pot of coffee for two, tea for one, a bottle each of sparkling and still water, three glasses and biscuits in room three eleven," Rochelle called out fairly loudly in the direction of the spacecraft.

"Be with you shortly," was the response.

Rochelle responded with a "Thanks," and then having to reach across the table again, she pressed a button to clear the call. Jerry couldn't help but notice her fantastic figure as she did so.

"First of all," Peter started, "Could you please tell me how you managed to break through our firewall?" and without pausing, continued, "Rochelle tells me it took less than five minutes and as far as I'm aware, that was without any preparation. By that I mean you had no idea what system Rochelle was going to ask you to hack into," he stated as he went to seat himself on a chair opposite the screen.

"You're correct Peter," Jerry replied. "I had absolutely no idea what Rochelle was going to select and I'd certainly never heard of Milky Way before she mentioned it," he continued. "As I'm sure you'll agree there is no such thing as a hundred percent protection of anything. If someone is committed to breaking into the Bank of England they'll succeed. They could stick explosives around the building, take people at gunpoint stating they'll detonate the charges or shoot the hostages if their demands were not met. If a person or group is so intent on achieving an objective, they'll do it with absolutely nothing anyone can do to prevent them; an excellent example is 9/11. Al-Qaeda wanted to attack the USA at her heart and despite all the security measures the

Americans have in place, the terrorists succeeded, apparently with ease. Where there's a will there's a way." Jerry paused for a moment trying to read Peter's body language, not being sure how far to go on the subject. "The trick is to try and make an attack as difficult as possible, in your case deterring a would-be assailant from your network, with a little luck they'll attempt to infiltrate an easier target. The term 'totally impregnable' just doesn't exist. Firewalls provide a single line of security, but that's it, they are just one line of protection." He then posed the question, "I trust I'm correct in assuming you run anti virus applications on all your servers and workstations?"

Peter quickly answered, "Yes, of course we do and the virus patterns are set to update automatically."

Jerry acknowledged Peter's answer and carried on, "Why have you implemented separate anti virus measures when you have a perfectly good firewall?" Before Peter could reply he continued, "It's another line of defence because you realise consciously or sub-consciously, that weaknesses exist in your firewall." He paused on hearing a knock on the door and following a short delay, a waitress brought in the refreshments Rochelle had ordered. Jerry waited for the drinks to be poured and the waitress to leave before saying. "In theory a firewall will only allow authorised users through, but emails from almost anyone are allowed to reach the inbox of the intended recipient, which are inside the supposedly secure network. As we all know from experience, many emails contain attachments which are allowed through with the body of the email." Jerry paused for a moment to take a sip of tea. He glanced at Rochelle and then focussed back on Peter before continuing. "You may have configured your protection to filter out and block 'exe' and other executable type files attached to the emails, knowing such attachments could possibly contain nasty code. However, most organisations invariably allow 'zip' and other compressed and uncompressed formats through."

Once again Jerry paused to quench his thirst. "Well, the bad news is that most types of files can be disguised thereby enabling naughty files to pass through the firewall unhindered. You therefore implement an anti virus system in the hope that any rogue file that does manage to fool the security system will be detected by the anti virus application." Realising he was probably speaking on the subject for far too long, Jerry couldn't find a way to break the flow so carried on, "Today's anti virus systems are very good, but generally work using technology which checks each file for sequences already known to be viruses. Code that shows no such tell tell signs will unfortunately remain undetected. Without going into further detail, I managed to infiltrate your system by sending an email to the postmaster address, a default email account, one of a few that are used on almost every mail server. Attached to the email was a disguised file, an application with the task of obtaining and reporting all the information I needed to gain access without being detected. From there on in it was simple. Once inside your network, I could do whatever I wanted since the servers believed I was the System or Super User, which basically are the machines internal users'. Gaining access by inserting applications via emails is only one of many ways in which systems can be infiltrated, normally the simplest and quickest, but it requires a valid master email address." Jerry stopped to make sure he had not lost Peter, having tried to keep the explanation as simple as possible whilst at the same time careful not to give anything away.

With no questions or comments from either Peter or Rochelle, Jerry felt it was time to move on. "Now let me show you how you can better protect your network. The demonstration is going to be in two parts. Firstly, I'll infiltrate my network which is running a firewall, but with the special protection system switched off. You must remember what I said earlier, I'm not replacing conventional firewall technology whatsoever and I'm certainly not advocating that systems will no longer need to have them, I'm simply adding a further line of defence, one which I think you'll agree after seeing the demonstration is a lot better than anything currently available," Jerry said with confidence as he started to run through the demonstration like a true professional. After finishing the first stage, Jerry talked through the action of switching on the Igloo system and continued with the second part. Rochelle remained silent throughout.

"Very impressive," Peter remarked once Jerry had finished. "Now can you show me the demonstration again, but without the firewall running?"

"Just give me a minute to switch it off," Jerry requested, it was the one question he had not anticipated. Fortunately he was able to remotely access the machines in his room as if he was sitting beside them and after a short pause during which he typed away on the keyboard without saying a word, Jerry was ready to run through the demonstration again, as requested.

"But there is no difference," Peter observed once Jerry had finished.

"No apparent difference, you're right. The system I've built doesn't operate on filtering access the way a firewall does. However, I'll repeat again, I certainly don't recommend losing any form of defence. The more barricades in place, the harder it becomes to break through them," Jerry reminded him.

"You've convinced me it works, which is what Rochelle asked me to assess. What would such a solution cost?" asked Peter.

Jerry quickly glanced at Rochelle looking for inspiration since cost was the one area they had not yet discussed. Although she was reasonably confident of being able to sell to Leon, Peter's interest took her by surprise, she hadn't believed the demonstration would be sufficiently persuasive to prompt such a question. Jerry started to explain, "It very much depends on your system's architecture. The more external points of access the greater the cost. What I mean by points of access are for example: authorised PC users connected by cable being one point of access; each hub, switch, bridge and wireless access point connecting a group of PCs being treated as separate ones. Every server on the network is another point." Jerry paused again, being very aware of what Rochelle had tried to drum into him over the last couple of days in as far as holding the attention of everyone in the room. He thought for a minute and then started to speak again. "The more areas that need securing, the more units are required and therefore the greater the cost. I suppose a good analogy would be a burglar alarm for a building, every door and window is an access point into the building and therefore requires detection equipment. The greater the number of such entry points the higher the cost, the maths is simple."

Jerry could see Peter understood the concept, so continued, "No hardware is required on any of the workstations, they just run a very small application, nine kilobytes to be precise, which can be distributed electronically if required. Furthermore, unlike firewalls, my system doesn't require any additional servers. The only hardware required are small boxes connected at strategic points within the core infrastructure." As Jerry spoke he removed from his briefcase a spare black box he brought with him as a sample and handed it to Peter. "Besides the magic circuitry, the box contains two batteries to provide the power it needs. You can also see there is a small LED on the front. When connected to a network, the LED glows green whilst the batteries remain charged and flashes red when either of the batteries begins to run low, thus alerting you to the need to change them. The flash rate defines which battery requires changing, a slow single intermittent flash signifies battery one, a sequence of two rapid flashes then a pause confirms its battery two. The second battery provides the power when the first is being swapped out and vice versa to ensure protection is never compromised. A web based screen can be provided for the devices to be monitored remotely, similar to the one I used to switch them on and off during the demonstration, clearly identifying the battery that requires changing. Obviously there will be no functionality to turn the units off," Jerry said before finishing his cup of tea, which was now cold.

"I understand the principle you're using to cost an installation after that detailed explanation, but I still need at least some idea of a figure, say for a basic network with four servers. The first running a web server, the second being an internal file server, a firewall and a machine acting as a backup and monitoring device. Every user has access to the Internet," Peter quickly added.

"How do the users connect? In other words; how many access points?" Jerry asked.

"There are two, thirty-two port switches and a wireless access point which can connect another sixty-four PC's in addition to the router providing access to and from the Internet," answered Peter.

"Look, Peter, to be honest Jerry and I haven't yet discussed pricing,"

Rochelle interrupted, trying to take the pressure off Jerry who she could see was struggling and getting hung up on unnecessary detail. Remembering some of her university lectures, "If you supply Jerry with a network diagram," she looked at Jerry for confirmation she was saying the correct thing, "I'm sure he'll be happy to prepare a full proposal."

"Rochelle," Peter looked at her, "I like what I've just seen and I currently have a budget to enhance our computer security," he announced. "And that was before you spoke to me the other day. However, being honest, the budget is limited so I need to know whether I can consider this system. If it helps, I'd be more than happy to be used as a referral site and could provide quotes for your marketing, anything you want within reason. What I'm not so keen to provide is a layout of our infrastructure," Peter stated, watching for a reaction from Rochelle.

Jerry caught Peter's attention once again by suggesting, "I understand where you're coming from and I'd be happy to sign a Non-Disclosure Agreement or any other similar document you wish, protecting you from me divulging the information to anyone else. Surely you understand that without seeing the layout of your network there's absolutely no way I can determine what's required and therefore the cost."

At that moment Rochelle's mobile rang which brought an immediate halt to the conversation. It was reception informing her that Leon had finally arrived. Checking her watch, she commented to anyone listening. "Not bad for him, only ninety minutes late," referring to Leon and then looking at Peter she told him, "Let me talk to Jerry after we finish the next demonstration and I'll catch up with you on cost. Are you around all day?" She asked.

"Yes, you should find me either in my office or in the computer room," he answered, then standing said, "It was nice to meet you Jerry and well done. I think you have a super product and opportunity. I hope we can reach a position whereby Milky Way can benefit from it sooner rather than later. Rochelle, please make sure you definitely meet up with me later," and with that Peter left the room.

"I'll go down and fetch Leon, you sort yourself out. I think you did fantastically well, just repeat the same for Leon please," she asked whilst walking through the open doorway.

Seven

A short chubby man with balding grey hair and a small beard followed Rochelle into the meeting room, his most outstanding feature being his acute acne which made his facial skin flake badly. The sports jacket he was wearing was speckled with what looked to be flour, but Jerry realised it must have been dandruff. He figured the man to be well into his fifties if not older, although he had never been good at judging people's ages.

On entering the room, the man spoke in a stern, husky voice, "I'm Leon and you must be Jerry. My apologies for being late, I was unfortunately delayed in the office although a message was left on Rochelle's voicemail which she apparently hasn't picked up yet. I trust the hold-up hasn't inconvenienced you too much." Leon looked at the table as if deciding where to sit. "I've heard a lot about you, all good I hasten to add." Whilst Leon was talking, Jerry managed to give him the customary handshake. "I specifically asked Rochelle not to mention who I represent for reasons that will shortly become abundantly clear and I apologise for any anxiety this secrecy may have caused." Having made his decision Leon finally sat down, coincidentally in the same seat as Peter had vacated. Before continuing, he allowed Rochelle to call catering to replenish the refreshments.

"I act for the Anything and Everything Group," Leon said whilst concentrating his attention on Jerry whom must have had a look about him saying "Who the hell are they?" since Leon added, "A&E Stores," in a tone easily translated to mean, "surely you have heard of A&E Stores." Without being perturbed he continued, "a name I'm sure you're familiar with," which Jerry was. "Besides their large chain of retail outlets they also own a significant financial services business." Leon paused for a moment to consider the best way to progress the meeting. Although it was supposedly Jerry's presentation, Leon had taken control of events from the moment he stepped into the room. "Look, there's absolutely no point in playing games here, there just isn't the time and so before you start your demonstration I'll give you a brief explanation of the situation. What I'm about to tell you is extremely sensitive. Without going through the formalities at this stage, I will assume you'll treat everything we discuss today as strictly confidential and not repeat a word to anyone." Leon stopped talking once again, waiting for confirmation from both Rochelle and Jerry.

Satisfied with a verbal "Yes" from Rochelle and an affirmative nod from Jerry who was almost dumbstruck by Leon's abrupt manner, he continued. "Over the last few weeks A&E have suffered a number of very serious security breaches affecting their computer systems, compromising many of their servers. We are not sure whether the assailant is an individual or a group, however, for the sake of this conference we'll assume it's a person working alone. The perpetrator has managed to infiltrate the network with apparent ease, even with what had been considered to be very tight security in place, managing to gain access and amend, or in some cases delete beyond recovery, some of the most confidential information held by the company, including sensitive and personal data on the financial status of many of its customers." Leon continued to stare at Jerry as if in a competition to see who would blink first. "It is also thought that much of the remaining data held has been copied, but at this time there is simply no way of really knowing quite what. If customers from the financial services division, a shareholder, or the press, ever found out about these violations, the company could literally be destroyed. I have been charged with the task of finding a way to protect the infrastructure from further infiltration." He paused for a moment, then added, "I presume you now appreciate the concern for absolute discretion."

There was a knock on the door interrupting Leon's flow and moments later a waitress entered the room carrying a tray with the refreshments Rochelle had ordered. Leon waited for her to finish pouring the drinks and leave, watching the door close behind her before continuing. "I think I have sufficiently briefed you on the situation, the only additional point worth mentioning is A&E is prepared to consider any viable solution which can provide the required protection. It goes without saying that a speedy implementation is necessary and I'm afraid there is no time whatsoever to wait for software to be written or completed. On that point I understand your product is new, but I'm assuming it's finished and ready to be installed. Is that correct?"

"Yes sir," were the only two words Jerry could manage, still captivated by this elderly person sitting opposite him.

"Good," replied Leon, "If a solution is in place before news of these attacks ever become public and it will at some point in time, of that I have no doubt, A&E would be able to dismiss the comments as vicious and scandalous rumours started by it's competitors. So, Mr Freedman, if you believe your system will resolve the problem, let's see what you have, if not, we should pack up now rather than waste any more time," he finally finished, still looking Jerry in the eye.

Jerry wasn't quite sure whether to answer or ignore the comment and launch straight into his fourth demonstration of the day, including the practice and repeats. He had practised so often he could now do it in his sleep. Whilst deciding he heard, "I think you'll be pleasantly surprised," in a very sweet and innocent voice, sounding like a young girl handing in a project to her teacher. As Rochelle ended the sentence, she gave Jerry the nod to continue.

Feeling somewhat relieved that Rochelle had jumped into save him, Jerry confidently took Leon through each stage of the demonstration. Once finished, having repeated everything a second time whilst Leon carefully watched, he felt as if it was his best performance to date.

Leon allowed Jerry time to compose himself before announcing: "It looks as if Rochelle was correct and that you may well have something worth investigating in more detail," and without further ado he took his mobile phone from his jacket pocket and pressed a series of buttons.

"Leon here, check if all the boys can make tomorrow 11am, I'll hold," he said in the same brusque tone he had used throughout the meeting to whoever had answered his call. "Excuse me for one moment," Leon said, directing the comment towards Jerry and Rochelle as an afterthought.

Taking advantage of Leon being preoccupied on his telephone conversation, Jerry whispered to Rochelle, "He's a little rude, don't you think? Surely he doesn't expect us to drop everything for him and be available at eleven tomorrow, when he hasn't even had the courtesy to ask us before arranging his end?"

"Shush," she whispered back, placing her finger over her lips to signify that he should remain silent.

Listening intently to the person on the other end of the call, Leon finally said: "Righteo," before disconnecting the line. To Jerry, Leon's face appeared red as though he was angry about something or someone, but his manner had certainly not changed. "As you probably heard, I would like you to repeat the demonstration for my colleagues at eleven o'clock tomorrow morning. I hope you can make it," he sort of enquired.

Jerry glanced at Rochelle, his look silently asking permission to refuse, for no other reason than to show Leon they are not so desperate as to jump to his beckon call, but quickly thought better of it. "I can probably rearrange things although it is short notice," he answered pointedly.

Leon took Jerry's response to be a yes. "Rochelle, I think you ought to be there as well otherwise Jerry may feel somewhat outnumbered. Can you take a day's leave from here?"

"I'm sure something can be organised. Perhaps we should say half past ten to give Jerry time to set up," Rochelle suggested, not wishing to aid Jerry in trying to educate Leon. She had known him too long and knew he would never change, although on reflection she could see Jerry's point of view.

"That's settled then, I'll organise entry for you. When you arrive, report to the reception desk and ask for me, your names will be there which should avoid unnecessary delays in getting through security which seems to get tighter by the hour. Am I correct in thinking you've been there before, Rochelle?" Leon asked.

"Yes, several times," she replied.

"Well, I won't keep either of you any longer," Leon said as he stood up. "Please remember, not a word to anyone."

Jerry followed Leon to a standing position and as he did so, said, "I look forward to meeting you again tomorrow. Thank you for your time." But Leon ignored Jerry as if he no longer existed.

As she reached to open the door for Leon, Rochelle suggested to Jerry, "Tidy your belongings whilst I see Leon out and we'll have a quick chat when I return, if you've have a few minutes before you shoot off."

Having escorted Leon to the foyer since no visitor was allowed to roam the building unaccompanied, Rochelle returned to the meeting room choosing to sit directly opposite Jerry. Knowing he would be eager to hear her comments she exclaimed excitedly, "You were fantastic, I couldn't have asked for better demonstrations and a display of knowledge pitched perfectly," pausing momentarily to think, "Except for the whisper at the end, that's a definite no no for the future. I've known Leon a long time and that's him, he'll never change. He has always been very short with people and assumes other humans were placed on Earth for the sole purpose of working for him one way or another. I sincerely hope you get the opportunity to work with him long enough to not notice it, if you get my drift, but I am sorry, I should have warned you beforehand, I just didn't think about it. Having said that, he's very good natured, nothing is too much trouble for him." Seeing that Jerry had learnt his lesson she moved on, "Now, let's quickly discuss both opportunities and of course the pricing structure. By the way, with two sales under my belt my percentage of the company increases," she said with a grin.

Without waiting for Jerry to respond, Rochelle informed him: "A&E are desperate for a solution and my gut feeling is that we have an excellent chance of winning the contract if you manage to convince the powers that be tomorrow, as you did with Leon just now and he's no push over. As I walked him to reception we had a brief chat where I learnt that what you showed him was the best he's seen by a long way. He thinks that if the IT people like it tomorrow and we're in a position to install quickly, we have a good chance of walking away with a contract. What's more, Leon has a number of similar contacts which he will introduce to us if we successfully deliver on this one, the only down side is that he'll be watching you like a hawk." Jerry wasn't sure which parts were actually discussed as opposed to the assumptions Rochelle had made, but before he had a chance to clarify anything, she carried on, "Now let's quickly look at the pricing structure. Besides your time which I want to leave out of the equation for a moment since I'm interested in our potential cash loss if we fail to fix the hole as it were, what will be the actual cost we incur?" she asked. "Does it really depend on the number of points of access to the system?" Rochelle quickly added, looking directly into his eyes. As she did so, Jerry couldn't help but notice how bright, clear and seductive her eyes were as his in turn locked on hers. Appearing not to notice Jerry's stare, she said, "I've avoided this discussion until now since I've appreciated your reluctance to divulge the modus operandi. I hope you realise I'm totally committed to the project and that we have reached the point where I need to have a greater understanding as to what's involved in implementing a system, both parts and cost," she said praying he was starting to feel more comfortable with her being involved. "And I hope you trust me enough to bring me into your confidence," she said, trying to gauge his thoughts.

Jerry, managing to refocus on what Rochelle was saying rather than her looks, responded without hesitation, "I'll keep it simple since there's no middle ground, just two extremes, basic or highly technical. The system utilises a number of components which, when combined together provide the level of protection you've witnessed." He started feeling surprisingly comfortable in explaining it to her. "Besides a small application that runs continuously in background on every client device that accesses the network, the little nine kilobyte algorithm I've spoken about several times, we have a similar version that sits on each server. A unique identifier is allocated to each organisation which is hard coded into both these programs before we ship, but beside the nominal cost of a CD and the time which doesn't interest you, there is no additional cost to produce as many copies as needed," he told her trying to avoid geek talk whilst rubbing in the time element. "However, as you've probably guessed, the real magic takes place in the black boxes. The server and client software continuously talk to the boxes to confirm access, a task undertaken by a raft of network specific information added to every data packet at a very low layer of its structure, thereby not affecting the user's data itself. I'm sure you've absolutely no idea what I'm talking about so I'll stop there on how it works for the moment and we'll look at what happens as it were." Jerry said in a half serious tone.

"Very simply, access to a server fitted with one of our boxes will fail from a workstation not sending data packets with the information expected by the units, as you've seen," he said as a preamble. "Since the software in the boxes use similar code, the main cost is in their construction. Each of the test devices have been built individually, which in itself is a time consuming task. A production model needs to be assembled, being a modified version of what we currently use since they won't require the switches, just LEDs. Having the ability to remotely view the battery status via a web page as discussed with Peter, I think is an excellent idea and I want to implement it in the next version. Other improvements such as enabling the boxes to be flash upgraded, allowing us to easily upgrade with modified code as we release it should also be applied. Reading your thoughts," he said with a grin, "You think I'm digressing again, but on this occasion I'm not, I'm just trying to consider the variance in component costs to cater for these amendments. The cost of production on the current basis is around one hundred pounds for the components and each unit takes about half a day to build. Before you get hung up on a girly thing, I'm aware they don't exactly look elegant and whilst making changes, it probably makes sense to source a more ergonomic and stylish case." Jerry thought for a couple of moments before carrying on. "However, continuing to build them manually will save on what I'm sure would be a significant investment on tooling and will also allow us to carry on making modifications we deem necessary without any tooling constraints. Unless the volumes become substantial, I can see no reason to stop manual construction. We could benefit by having the circuit boards etched by machine since they would be more reliable as well as speeding up the process and we still keep the ability to make circuit amendments manually on them. We could probably find a school leaver or possibly even a student looking to earn a bit of extra pocket money to assemble everything we need built," he said thoughtfully.

Rochelle took advantage of Jerry's pause to repeat her previous question he had successfully managed to ignore. "Do you really need a box on every access point, as you call them?"

Jerry had purposely ignored the question the first time round, but was now a little upset with her tone; it was as if she didn't quite believe him. He decided to answer the question in an appropriate manner ensuring there could be no misunderstanding whatsoever. "Every connection to each server requires a box, which includes other servers on the same network in addition to other access devices, exactly as I explained to Peter." He hesitated, not sure whether to leave it there or continue, although it didn't take him long to decide. "I specifically designed the system in this way, not so we could earn more by supplying unnecessary boxes, the whole methodology requires protecting each individual link rather than creating perimeter security the way a firewall does. The advantage we gain by adopting this method is that even if an intruder manages to infiltrate a single server in a multi server environment, access is still prevented to the remaining infrastructure. This puts an end to server hopping, which if you recall is precisely how I managed to obtain the information from the Milky Way computers for you last week, jumping between the Australian and UK servers."

"Have you given any thought to pricing?" Rochelle asked after she had finished scribbling her notes, paying no attention to Jerry's attitude.

Jerry was once again slightly irritated with Rochelle's insinuation. "Of course I've thought about it. Surely that was evident from my response to Peter's question on the subject," he said quite abruptly, starting to sound like Leon. Suddenly, realising she wasn't trying to catch him out he began to calm down. "I'm sorry I didn't mean to get annoyed with you," he continued with sincerity. "My thoughts were along the lines of a server charge in the region of twenty five thousand pounds with an additional ten thousand pounds for each black box. Therefore a typical medium size installation, being six servers, a router and four hubs of one kind or another providing access to around a hundred users would cost in the order of two hundred thousand pounds." Making out he had quickly calculated the sum for her in his head. Before Rochelle could comment, Jerry took over again, "Another method I considered would be to charge based on the number of workstations or access devices connected to the network by electronically counting each live connection, something that would be fairly simple to implement. The per user charge would be around two thousand pounds therefore the price would be the same for a typical mid size network whichever way we priced it," he finished, feeling quite satisfied with himself being able to prove Rochelle had misjudged him.

Rochelle, having listened to Jerry without interrupting, felt that something had to be said to clear the air and put an end to Jerry's aggression towards her, despite his apology. She did appreciate he was probably quite exhausted, possibly contributing to his continual over reaction to many of her comments, besides the underlying factor of realising she was going to close a deal and thereby take a considerable chunk of his company. "Before we continue there's something I think needs to be said," she started. Jerry looked at her in total confusion. "I didn't intend to upset you just now and I appreciate your apology. We're meant to be a team with one objective, not two individuals with personal agenda's, so please don't read something which doesn't exist into everything I say, I'm not trying to have a go at you all the time, I promise. I'm doing my very best to try and help you to turn a project which started life as a hobby into a professional, creditable outfit." She gave him a lovely smile before eating the one remaining biscuit from the plate, giving Jerry a chance to comment. He didn't.

"Thank you for letting me get that of my chest, now let's continue.

Before you say anything, please just hear me out on this," she almost pleaded with him. "I've undertaken a small amount of competitive research looking at the products we would be competing against and I'm sure you're aware, the figure you've just mentioned is significantly higher than everything being sold today," she said, then placed her finger over her lip to keep Jerry quiet, knowing full well she had just shown a red rag to a bull. She wasted no time in adding, "Before you argue, I agree with you, there really is no real comparison and I've spoken with fifteen resellers around the country and three in the United States." She was obviously beginning to learn how to approach issues with him since this was the first time he had not immediately started to defend himself, believing she is trying to criticise him with each comment she makes and assuming she is constantly trying to be confrontational. Rochelle knew his attitude wasn't intentional, he was simply trying to protect his baby, having been the only person involved since its inception several years ago and now, for better or worse, someone else was stepping on his territory. She hoped that over time his feelings would mellow as she continued with her appraisal. "All the same, we don't want to out price ourselves before we start, particularly since our installation costs are minimal. Using the information you and Peter have given today, the cost to us in implementing a system here would be less that a thousand pounds in addition of course to your time. The only people I'd imagine you could get to hand over the sort of fee you're after at this stage of our development are those that have suffered serious attacks such as A&E. They are far more likely to consider it to be a cheap price to pay compared to the alternative that Leon mentioned. I can't believe companies similar in size to Milky Way would consider paying anything close to that sort of figure and they are most likely to be our best prospects in the early days. We already have a great opportunity here if we're sensible about it. Coming to an understanding with Peter will give us a jump-start, whatever transpires from tomorrow. The more clients we can boast early on in our history, the easier it becomes to convince other organisations, including large multinationals, to deal with us, each one further enhancing our credibility. After all, there are only a handful of players in the market." She felt she had sufficiently smoothed the way to mentioning a figure for what she thought could be extracted from Peter. "I would guess Milky Way would be prepared to pay about thirty five thousand pounds." As she quoted the figure, her immediate reaction was to run for cover as if she had just thrown a grenade into a building and was now waiting for the blast.

Jerry was unable to hide his obvious disappointment, but the anticipated outburst never came. "I'm about to say something which I can't believe I've even given brain time to, so you had better listen carefully since it's unlikely to be repeated," he said in a monotone. "It's your call from now on. I'm giving you full responsibility for everything to do with sales, so it's entirely up to you to pull off the best deal you think possible with Peter and everyone else. I'll tell you what it will cost to build and a guesstimate of the time based upon a network diagram and you then calculate the selling price. I'm sure you'll quickly come up with some form of consistent formula. It will give me more time to focus my attention on delivering the best possible solution starting now with designing the production model."

Jerry had managed to reverse the roles, this time it took Rochelle a moment to appreciate the words that had come from his lips. After some thought she replied, "Okay, I accept the role on the proviso that you allow me to bounce my thoughts by you and that you don't get upset over the price I finalise on any particular transaction."

"I accept both provisions. If you tell me it's the best we can achieve and you believe it's worth doing I'll not argue with you. I'm happy to give you sole discretion, at least within reason." To Rochelle, Jerry suddenly seemed a new man. "To be honest I'm very excited. I truly believe you've done fantastically well to get us this far so quickly, even if neither of them signs on the dotted line. All I ask from you is that you bear in mind I want to remain ahead of the competition because that's where our technology is; I think you can see that from the reactions of both Peter and Leon today. I understand it may make certain people baulk and possibly even turn to a cheaper product, but the way to demonstrate to the world that we really do have something a little bit special is to reflect it in the price. Rolls Royce doesn't compete against

Ford, why should we compete with the handful of network security offerings being sold today? In my eyes it's a similar comparison, we have the Rolls Royce of digital security solutions and I feel that our price should reflect it," he said in a very convincing manner. "We also need to recoup the research and development costs to date and of course to fund the ongoing work as we certainly can't afford to stand still, I hope you're aware of that."

Noticing and pleased that Jerry had referred to the project as 'us' and 'our' all day, Rochelle replied, "You're absolutely correct in everything you've said, but as I've just pointed out, we have to be sensible on the price at this stage. It's important for us to close deals to demonstrate our superiority and then we'll be able to slowly hike up the price. The Milky Way network isn't that big." She said as if she knew. "Look, I really don't want to lose these two deals because we're being greedy. If we can't do the job that's one thing, but not on price at this stage, I hope you agree with me."

She looked at Jerry who was preparing to leave; satisfied she would do her very best. "I'll come over this evening and we can discuss it further and we must plan our strategy for tomorrow." Finishing her lecture she added, "I maybe a little later than usual, I've two days work to catch up on here before I can walk out the door since I'm now away tomorrow and I've hardly done anything for them today. I also want to try and agree a deal with Peter and I need a chat with my boss."

Jerry's final words as he closed his case were: "Catch you later then. I've said everything I want to on pricing, it's your responsibility from now on."

"Hang on," she called to him as he was opening the door, "I need to show you out." Before leaving the office with Jerry, Rochelle left a message on Peter's voicemail telling him that she was ready to discuss a deal.

Eight

Rochelle arrived at Jerry's just before seven-thirty and his mother was quick to open the front door. Knowing two demonstrations had been arranged for that day, she was eager to discover whether there had been interest from either organisation, not having asked Jerry on his return since he was pre-occupied in thought and she had learnt several years earlier, whenever he had that particular look about him, any attempt at communication was treated as an irrelevant interruption and ignored. She asked Rochelle half jokingly, "Well, can we move all this rubbish out to an office yet?"

Realising Jerry had not mentioned anything, Rochelle looked at Jerry's mother trying desperately hard to hide her excitement and in a very subdued voice replied, "I think we can slowly start packing," but by the time the sentence was completed she was unable to disguise her euphoria. Mrs Freedman's reaction was typical of any Jewish mother, she hugged and kissed Rochelle.

Finally managing to disengage herself from his mother's embrace, Rochelle started to make her way up the staircase to Jerry's bedroom. Not having heard the doorbell, he had left what he was doing to investigate the cause of the commotion and met Rochelle at the top of the stairs. She immediately gave him the thumbs up signal followed by the now familiar finger over the lips caution, knowing he was well versed in its meaning. The only words Jerry's mother heard from upstairs were them saying "Good evening," to each other, before disappearing behind a closed bedroom door.

Seeing her excitement and having heard the uproar as she arrived, Jerry couldn't wait to say, "I assume it went well with Peter then."

"Are you asking me whether I own thirty percent of Igloo yet?" She asked, teasing him.

"Stop mucking around," Jerry pleaded. "Please just tell me how it went," he begged again, beginning to feel quite anxious. He wasn't in the mood for being teased; there was far too much work to be getting on with.

"We had a good discussion and he gave me his opinion of your demonstration to help us in the future. It's valuable criticism so please don't get upset with me when I repeat his comments," Rochelle stated.

"First tell me what you agreed on price?" Jerry asked once more. "I'm interested in his view of my performance, but that won't pay the bills whereas cash would settle one or two of them." Jerry informed her, trying to lighten up a little, knowing she had already agreed he would get the first ten thousand pounds to compensate for what he had laid out to get to where he had.

"We finally managed to agree a price and he confirmed our first order, promising to raise the official paperwork tomorrow. You won't be over the moon with the fee, but I wasn't too upset with the final outcome, particularly since the deal includes other forms of important support as well. I'll explain everything in a moment, but let's go through things in order. His remarks on the demonstration are valid, particularly as we have another one in a few hours time," Rochelle reminded him, intent on Jerry gaining the most from the day's experience. Before Jerry could comment further, she started, "He said the actual demonstration was excellent, the only criticism being; you mustn't get into long winded explanations when answering questions, just keep everything short and to the point," Rochelle recounted. "He went onto say in so doing; the important details and points you are trying to make will get across and be remembered, rather than lost in a cloud of waffle which is of no interest to anyone. His advice is to focus on the terrific online demonstration fielding any questions at the end, since most are actually answered during it." Relieved she had managed to complete the task without interruption; she was ready to inform him of the terms of the deal, having drunk a mouthful of water from a bottle she brought with her.

"We agreed that Milky Way will trial the system on their UK network and if that goes well they'll implement in Australia followed by other countries as the infrastructure is built. Initially the trial will be treated as a beta test, reporting any errors and difficulties they encounter and working with us to resolve them, something I believe will be very useful since you haven't yet implemented it in a live commercial situation. He is also more than happy to be a referral site, speaking to prospects on our behalf and provide any interviews and statements we feel would be useful for our PR, advertising and sales material." Looking at Jerry, Rochelle was aware that her summary omitted the only detail he was really interested in, although leaving it until last was unintentional.

Jerry was rapidly losing his patience, "Besides all the assistance Peter will give us, you said there was a cash element to it. Will I ever get to know how much?" Jerry could not hold back from asking, not appreciating and certainly not interested in the commercial benefits of the support Peter had offered at this moment in time. "Or was it such a paltry amount it's not worth mentioning?" His annoyance now very noticeable in the tone adopted.

"For the configuration that Peter used as his example this morning, which is basically the structure of their UK platform, we will receive fifty thousand pounds. That's fifteen thousand more than I anticipated and trust it meets with your approval," she finally announced, beaming with delight. "I estimated that it will cost us less than five thousand pounds including time, thereby deducing it wasn't a bad start for us."

Rochelle could sense the sudden relief in Jerry's voice as he spoke. "I told you earlier you're responsible for the commercial side of things, if you consider fifty thousand a good deal, then so do I. I'm certainly ten thousand five hundred pounds happier than the amount you quoted this morning," he said without thinking.

"Ten thousand five hundred pounds?" Rochelle repeated questioningly.

"Yes, that's my share after deducting your 30%" Jerry replied smiling.

The two of them sat looking at each other for a moment, both lost for words, absorbed by the reality of concluding their first transaction and making the transition from what sounded like a good idea into a trading entity. Rochelle finally broke the silence, "We've just left the starting block. I hope this is the first of very many orders, but there is a lot of work to do to make the most of this opportunity and converting it into a real success. Despite you telling me it's my responsibility, I still want to agree a formal charging structure with you for tomorrow's meeting; the finger in the air method used today with Peter would certainly be laughed at. If I understood Leon correctly, we're meeting with the Big Wigs and we need to handle ourselves in a very professional manner. That's why I felt it important to pass on Peter's comments, providing us with the best possible chance of convincing A&E to go with us."

Jerry had not heard anything Rochelle had said after the price she'd agreed with Peter; his thoughts were once again concentrated on her, trying to think how he could show her his elation. He was desperate to throw his arms around her and give her a kiss, but knew he would be unable to pluck up sufficient courage to do so, only managing to say, "You have lipstick on your cheek which looks very much like my mother's."

"She kissed me when I came in," Rochelle replied, quickly looking for her vanity mirror to deal with the blemish. "I had to fight her off once she realised we had some success today," her voice still full of excitement. Rochelle imagined she was experiencing a similar feeling to that of a new mum having just given birth, Igloo being her newly born baby which came to life when Peter confirmed the deal. "We urgently need to formalise the company, open a bank account and so on, including sorting out the shares. You haven't mentioned seeing a solicitor yet, should I assume you haven't?" she asked.

Rochelle's question brought a sheepish look to Jerry's face, one that almost any girl would find cute and Rochelle was no different. "I've been somewhat preoccupied this week perfecting the demonstration," he said covering up the real reason, but then added as an after thought.

"And to be perfectly honest it sort of slipped my mind," since he realised there should be no secrets between them, although he purposely omitted to mention the initial reason of not wanting to spend money until he could see things progressing.

"I fully understand, I know you've had a lot to keep you occupied this week, but don't think things are going to get easier," Rochelle stated. "There are certain things we can't put off now, this being one of them. We need to register a company before we can open a bank account. I have already purchased the internet domain igloo-uk.com. To protect us both we should have a shareholder's agreement in place along the lines I gave you the other day. If it helps, my sister is a trainee commercial solicitor and I have a good accountant, but I don't want you to think I'm taking over, so if you know anyone then I'd be happy to use them."

Jerry thought for a moment. "I know dad has an accountant since he often moans about the charges and I'm sure he must have a solicitor as well."

"Your dad's a doctor isn't he?" Rochelle asked, but before Jerry had a chance to confirm, she continued, "I'm sure even if he doesn't have a solicitor his surgery will, so by all means ask him."

"I promise I will as soon as we're finished here," Jerry said reassuringly.

Rochelle had one more piece of news for him but was unsure how to tell him, finally deciding the best way was to build up to it rather than just come straight out with it. "You really were fabulous today. If you can repeat the performance as well tomorrow, if not improve on it, we could really be on the brink of something very exciting," she said. Leaning over, she kissed him on the cheek which immediately made him blush. "I can see I have my work cut out with you Mr Freedman, that's for sure!" She thought out loud. "I'm sorry, I didn't mean to embarrass you, I'm just very happy and excited," she said after seeing his reaction and decided to just announce her final bit of news as casually as possible. "After all, he should be expecting it," she reassured herself. Aloud she said, "Oh, and by the way, I handed in my notice before I left the office this evening."

Jerry sat there partially stunned, having completely forgotten about Rochelle leaving Milky Way and working full time with him and it was the last thing he expected to hear at this moment. "It's certainly been an eventful day that's for sure, one that may well have changed my life," he reflected. "I've made my first sale and immediately become responsible for feeding two mouths rather than just mine." That thought sent a shudder down his spine. "There isn't the room for us both to work here all the time so we'll need to sort something out I suppose," he quietly muttered, before stating: "You praised me, but it was your contact and your deal, I merely proved the technology worked. You really have earned your thirty percent of the company today." Whilst his mind was still on the kiss she gave him, although he wished it had been more than just a peck on the cheek.

The next couple of hours were spent discussing the pricing structure, Jerry continually reminding Rochelle it was up to her, but she felt, despite understanding the principles involved, it wouldn't be right for her to create the structure without his input. They finally managed to agree on a simple method to cost an installation, with the price tag of a typical medium sized network, using Jerry's measure, not being too far away from the figure he had originally anticipated. "Let's go and talk to my father," Jerry suggested as Rochelle packed away her belongings.

The two of them made their way downstairs to the living room where Jerry's parents were engrossed watching the evening news. As they reached the open doorway, Jerry stopped and called out; "Dad, can we have a quick word please?"

"Of course you can, come in both of you." As they walked through the door Jerry's father said, "Please sit down Rochelle, make yourself comfortable," while removing some medical journals from one of the armchairs to make more room for her, leaving Jerry to perch himself on the arm of the settee. "What can I do for you both?" Mr Freedman asked, hiding the fact that he had already been briefed by his wife with everything she knew.

Jerry looked at Rochelle who silently gestured it would be better for Jerry to ask the question. "We have closed our first deal today and have been asked back for a second meeting tomorrow by another interested organisation," he started. "We therefore need to quickly put our house in order in as far as getting a company and everything else that goes with it." He continued, "Rochelle wants to make sure we do everything properly and suggests we get an accountant and solicitor. She has her own contacts but thought it maybe better if we know of anyone. Do you?" he asked directly.

"Firstly let me say how delighted I am with your news," he said looking at both of them, continuing, "You are absolutely correct Rochelle, you must do everything properly. If you'll give me a moment please," he asked as he stood up from the armchair that only he was allowed to sit in and made his way to the kitchen.

He returned a minute or two later with an address book in his hand. Sitting back down in his chair he flicked through the well-worn pages. Jerry remembered he had bought his father an electronic organiser as a birthday present, but Mr Freedman had refused to give up his pen and paper system. Whenever questioned why he never used the organiser, the same response was always given. "My pages have never crashed when I needed to find an address urgently," referring to a single occasion when he asked Jerry for some information several years ago, the one time his Palm Pilot failed him. "Here we go," he continued, "My accountant is part of a medium size practice, he is the partner that specialises in the medical profession, but I'm sure he would have a colleague with the knowledge you require. I have always found him very good and nothing is ever too much trouble for the practice, even if they are a little on the expensive side. I can give him a call tomorrow and ask, if you wish."

Rochelle replied for them both. "If you don't mind Mr Freedman, I think that would be very helpful."

"Please call me Richard. We don't stand on ceremony in this house," he told Rochelle. "Now for solicitors," he muttered, continuing his search through the little book before eventually stopping and after a short pause, stated: "Again, I have only had dealings with the partner specialising in medical issues although the practice has a number of solicitors in various disciplines. I haven't had the need to speak with them for some time so it maybe better if you take down the number and call them yourselves. You can mention that the surgery and I are both clients." Richard read out the number adding, "The partner I have dealt with is a Ronnie Jenkins."

Rochelle quickly pulled out her electronic organiser and scribbled down the name and number. "I'll try and give them a call tomorrow at some point," she said thanking Jerry's father.

"It maybe a good idea for the two of you to also meet with your contacts' Rochelle and then make a decision who you feel most comfortable with," Richard suggested.

Rochelle confirmed she thought it to be a good strategy. She also announced, "We will start to look for an office next week," although her comment was really intended for Mrs Freedman's benefit. "I assume you would prefer it somewhere local to save travelling into town every day," she said to Jerry who was now quite relaxed.

Rochelle stood up having looked at her watch. "It's getting late and I had an early start this morning so I'm going to have to leave, I'll be here around eight-thirty tomorrow morning," she said looking at Jerry. "That will give us a chance to go over anything before we leave. I'm staying at my parents tonight so I haven't got that far to drive."

"Before you go," Jerry's mother perked up. "Why don't you stay for dinner tomorrow evening? We make a traditional Friday night and Jerry's sister comes home from university," his mother asked Rochelle.

"That would be lovely thanks," Rochelle answered. "But you must be fed up with me being here all the time."

"Not at all, particularly after today's news," his mother replied.

Jerry walked Rochelle to the front door. As she opened it she stopped for a moment. Jerry wanted to take advantage of the situation that had just presented itself and willed himself to give her another kiss, even if it was only on her cheek, but as usual he just froze. He heard her call out "goodnight" to his parents and then she left.

Nine

There were nine suits seated around the large table when Jerry and Rochelle were directed into the boardroom. Once the pair were settled, Leon opened the meeting by apologising for the change in schedule, resulting in their being no set-up time prior to starting. "Knowing you were arriving earlier than the time fixed yesterday, my colleagues decided to bring forward the meeting rather than wait until after you had set up your demonstration, but there is no need to worry since our IT guys here will make sure you're sorted properly," he informed them both.

Leon continued by doing a quick round robin of the people invited to the forum, six men and three women. The boys, as Leon had labelled them yesterday were; the Chief Executive, the Head of Security, the Head of Information Services, the Head of Communications, a senior manager within the Information Services department, the Chief Financial Officer, the Managing Director of Financial Services and the Head of A&E's Legal team, the last three being female and of course Leon himself. He finished by introducing Jerry and Rochelle.

Rochelle quickly realised everyone that mattered within A&E had been assembled in the room and prayed Jerry had come to the same conclusion. The only one that seemed out of place as far as Rochelle was concerned was the company solicitor.

"I understand you have already been briefed by Leon and you appreciate everything we discuss during this meeting is confidential," the Chief Executive wasted no time in saying, as soon as Leon had finished. Sitting at the far end of the table beside the Head of Communications, he appeared to be a fairly tall man with dark hair, slightly balding. His face was long, narrow and clean shaven and he wore a black pin striped suit. All in all, Jerry visualised him as being a typical City Gent, imagining him strolling into the office each morning wearing a bowler hat, carrying an umbrella in one hand and a briefcase in the other. "We have taken the liberty of preparing a basic confidentiality agreement. Susan, if you would be kind enough to do the honours and quickly run through the details for Jerry and Rochelle, they can sign it and we can then move on," he requested, gesturing to the head of the legal team, a tall brunette with lightly tanned skin. From her stern face, Jerry assumed Susan was probably in her mid forties, although with a good covering of make-up one would probably believe she was somewhat younger. Dressed in a white blouse and a matching dark blue suit with her hair just reaching her shoulders, it was evident Susan was highly respected within the assembled team where she had absolutely no problem in holding her own.

Having completed the formalities as if they had been rehearsed, the IS manager made his way to where Jerry and Rochelle were sitting and crouching between them, he quietly spoke to Jerry. After a short discussion, Jerry handed the manager a CD he removed from his briefcase. With it, the manager walked over to one of the wooden cabinets lining each of the walls of the boardroom whilst a waitress, who had suddenly appeared from nowhere, served drinks and sandwiches.

A minute or so later a projector slowly descended a couple of feet below the level of the ceiling, having appeared as if by magic through an opening created by one of the white tiles parting from its neighbours, allowing the projector through from where it obviously lived when not in use. Two large cabinet doors constructed from the same wood as the rest of the furniture in the room, which Jerry identified as mahogany, then started to slide apart under their own power. When closed, the doors met in the centre of the wall which the projector was pointed at and once open, a large wall mounted screen was revealed. When everything had locked in place, the projector came to life throwing a powerful bright white light onto the screen. The display quickly changed to the Windows XP logo as the room lights dimmed. The IS manager loaded Jerry's disk as he had been instructed and then took a wireless keyboard and mouse over to Jerry, placing them on the table in front of him. Confirming the waitress had left the room, the Chief Executive announced, primarily for the benefit of Rochelle and Jerry who were sitting directly opposite him, "The floor is all yours, you have our full attention."

While everyone positioned themselves to be able to watch the screen in comfort, Jerry loaded the computer's browser and connected to the Internet, praying to himself everything was in full working order. He spent the next hour running through the demonstration, his being the only voice to be heard throughout. Everyone was completely engrossed in what they were seeing and hearing. The only other sounds to be heard in the room were the faint hum of the projector and the light tap of the keys on the keyboard as Jerry did his thing.

"Well, I think we have seen enough," the Chief Executive finally announced to Jerry's relief once he had completed the third run through. After a number of questions had been answered as directly as Jerry was able, remembering Peter's comment, the Chief Executive asked, "Would the two of you please be kind enough to allow us time to discuss what we have just seen?"

"Of course," Rochelle replied starting to stand up, quickly followed by Jerry who had just felt a light knock on his shin to notify him to follow suit. The Chief Executive called for his PA who entered the room as they both reached the door having collected their belongings together. No one else made any attempt to leave the table and she decided against walking around to each person to shake their hands, assuming Leon would be in touch with her either during the afternoon or early the following week. She also felt it an inappropriate time to ask how long it would take them to come to a decision.

As she was about to say "Thank you" and "goodbye" to them all, she heard the Chief Executive asking to his PA, "Please take these good people to the director's lounge and organise refreshments for them.

Can you also arrange a table for six in the restaurant for lunch? I assume that meets with your approval?" he asked looking at Rochelle, probably thinking to himself how good she would look modelling their ladies wear, rather than having a job selling some technology product.

Stunned for a moment, Rochelle quickly recovered replying, "We can stay as long as necessary and lunch sounds great."

They were shown to a plush lounge further along the corridor from the boardroom. Sitting on a table covered by a starched white tablecloth that dropped to the ground was a coffee percolator producing an exotic aroma that permeated the room and adjacent to that was a hot water dispenser. Next to the two machines were a bowl full of various tea bags, another of sugar cubes, plenty of cups, saucers, glasses, plates, spoons and several trays of freshly made sandwiches, biscuits and pastries. At the far end of the table, sitting on the floor was a glass-fronted fridge packed full of cold drinks. "Help yourself to whatever you want. I'm just through there," the PA pointed to one of the open doors that led off from the lounge. "Just shout if you need anything," she said walking into her office.

Rochelle placed her index finger over her lips and then picked up a daily newspaper for Jerry to read and an A&E clothing magazine to help her pass the time. She poured a coffee for herself and removed a can of coke from the fridge, passing it to Jerry with a glass tumbler, a couple of pastries and a small selection of biscuits she placed on a plate. Rochelle sat in silence opposite Jerry in a soft leather armchair. Whilst waiting, the only voice occasionally heard was that of the PA speaking on the phone, since they had both switched their mobile phones off prior to entering the meeting and had not yet switched them on again. Several cups of coffee and ninety minutes later, the PA entered the lounge from her office. "They have asked for you to rejoin them," she said, and beckoned the two to follow her back to the boardroom.

"Rochelle, Jerry, please take your seats. We apologise for having taken so long," the Chief Executive said. "The last hour or so have been spent discussing nothing other than whether we believe your solution could resolve our current problems." He stated in a very matter of fact tone. "To be perfectly frank, I know very little about computers and therefore have to be guided by my colleagues whose knowledge of the subject is far greater than mine." There was a short pause in his dialogue whilst he filled a glass with sparkling water from a bottle sitting on the table and took a few sips. "Having said that and without disrespect to anyone sitting around this table, or for that matter within the company, if our knowledge was greater still, maybe we would not be in the compromising position in which we now find ourselves." His tone appeared to taper off as if he were reciting a tale of horrors and from his attitude Jerry assumed the following statement would be A&E were not interested in pursuing the project any further.

Starting the next sentence far more positively, the Chief Executive continued, "From what we witnessed earlier during your excellent demonstration and the responses to our questions, we strongly believe you probably have a far better grasp of how to deal with our problem than we have. It is also our general consensus your solution is by far the best we have seen and could possibly provide us with the protection we require. I can assure you we have seen a fair number of potential solutions over the last couple of weeks so you certainly have something to be proud of. However, our concern in dealing with Igloo is simply that you have no track record by way of existing installations and if we were to move forward with your product we would be taking one hell of a risk." He paused to allow them to appreciate the predicament the company faced.

Never having participated in such a high level meeting, Jerry found the environment daunting. It was as though no one would even attempt to speak unless given permission by the Chief Executive to do so and when he paused for whatever reason other than allowing someone to say a word, silence prevailed. He continued, "As I'm sure you understand we find ourselves in the unenviable position of having our back up against a wall. I would like us to discuss costs over lunch, but in order to do that I need to implement some form of protection for the company ensuring we don't just throw money down the drain." The Chief Executive said making nothing of it. "To that end we have come up with a formula I hope you can accept. If we are able to reach an understanding now, Susan will draft a contract whilst we finalise the details. We could then sign the paperwork before you leave and start on Monday."

Jerry felt both exhilarated and worried at the same time, he was about to receive what he realised could amount to a substantial payment for his efforts over the last couple of years, which in his mind immediately changed everything, particularly removing any excuses for failure. He tried recalling how he had felt about the Milky Way deal and decided he hadn't had the same apprehension when Rochelle confirmed the details. "Was this because the meeting with Peter was far more relaxed and informal?" he wondered. Whatever the case he was more than confident in his ability to perform.

The Chief Executive carried on, "We've discussed amongst ourselves the terms I'm about to propose and we're in unanimous agreement they are fair for both our organisations bearing in mind our respective positions," he continued, watching Jerry and Rochelle very carefully. "They are also designed to confirm the confidence you have in providing us with a satisfactory solution to resolve our current situation and ensure that moving forward we don't find ourselves in a similar predicament again."

Without giving any opportunity for a response, he called upon Susan to detail the terms by which A&E would be happy to proceed. Susan carefully explained each point and Rochelle scribbled them down on a pad which had been provided to each attendee. Jerry couldn't remain focussed on what was being said, it sounded like any other lecture he sat through at university and was relieved in having Rochelle with him. As he watched Susan it occurred to him she was at home sitting on the board of a large organisation, she was obviously very intelligent and highly knowledgeable in her subject, appearing relaxed but confident whilst speaking, maintaining everyone's attention precisely as her Chief Executive. Jerry could see Rochelle in Susan; all that was lacking was some practical experience.

Jerry finally managed to tune back into the meeting. "The conditions we are looking at are quite simple," Susan was saying, "A&E will immediately remit an agreed amount to Igloo covering all direct costs. You will implement the solution in a manner you determine after consultation with the necessary parties on our side. All relevant personnel and systems you need access too will be made available as quickly as possible." She frequently paused allowing Rochelle to keep up with her. "Following initial testing, A&E will submit a further instalment, again the amount to be agreed today and following successful operation for three months, we will settle the balance." She paused once more before saying, "We have also taken on board the comment you made during the demonstration relating to the cost being dependent on the design of our infrastructure. Over lunch you will be given an overview of our network to allow an estimate of the cost to be made. If it transpires later on, as the project progresses, you underestimated; we will add the difference to the final balance thereby ensuring you're not out of pocket. If on the other hand you overestimated, you'll be able to keep the difference since it's unlikely you'd advise us if such a situation materialised." Susan tried to assess a reaction having completed the first section which was all very much in Igloo's favour, before progressing to the part which provided the protection A&E were looking for. "If however you fail to solve our problem in a reasonable time scale, a period to be agreed, you'll simply return all payments made by us."

The Chief Executive took over before anything further could be said. "Would the two of you like time to discuss it in private? If so, you can use my office, being the door adjacent to my PA."

Rochelle answered before Jerry had a chance to open his mouth. "I think it would be useful if we could just have a few minutes to consider your terms." She and Jerry then stood up and headed out of the door towards the lounge in silence.

"Well?" she asked having closed the office door.

"We don't have a choice, do we?" was Jerry's response. "Not if we want the order," he answered excitedly, confident in his ability and dismissing any situation whereby the funds would need to be refunded.

Undeterred by his assurances, Rochelle wanted to ensure she had not misunderstood any of the information obtained over the last twenty-four hours. "Am I correct in assuming we can use the same boxes for any client?" Rochelle asked.

"Absolutely correct," Jerry answered without a moment's thought.

"Then we only have your time at risk," she said considering the worst-case scenario. "If that's the position, I'm going to propose in the unlikely event we fail to resolve the problem, we keep a nominal fee to cover our out of pocket expenses and a minimal amount of time. I'll suggest the figure is a percentage of the amount paid." Checking again, "Surely if we reached the second payment, wouldn't testing have been successful?"

This time Jerry thought before he replied. "To be honest I'm not sure how clued up they are on this. Testing will demonstrate that attempts to infiltrate the system are thwarted, but it doesn't mean the existing attacker will also be excluded from gaining access since the current perpetrator may already have built in a back door which we would need to search for and destroy. Code could have been implanted which continues to forward data by email without further intervention by the hacker. They're the sort of things I'd do." Jerry stopped to make sure he hadn't lost Rochelle. "I'll mention this over lunch since we can possibly charge a separate fee for checking and cleansing the system, you will charge that quite simply on an hourly rate which we can discount since we're already working on the infrastructure, say a hundred pounds an hour," he said, pleased with himself.

"The bit I can't get my head around is how A&E could possibly think they would be in a position to sign off after only three months. I'd have thought they would need to give it substantially longer before announcing they were completely free from system violations." He paused again, still thinking. "What I believe it implies is these attacks are very frequent, probably the reason for their desperation." Having covered everything he could think of, "I've done my bit, it's your show now, do whatever you can."

"No problem partner, let's go into battle," Rochelle stated, smiling and with a determined attitude she marched along the corridor, back to the boardroom with Jerry in tow.

After Jerry had seated himself, Rochelle took the silent room as her queue. "We've discussed your proposition and agree your terms are generally pretty fair," she announced brimming with confidence. "However, I hope you'll appreciate and assist in the one minor issue we have." Everyone listened intently, Jerry comparing Rochelle's performance to Susan's. "We'll undoubtedly incur expenses and will have to focus almost all our attention to this project. Since we are only a small operation, the one thing we cannot afford is to lose our out of pocket expenses, which on a project of this magnitude could be quite substantial relative to our size. Furthermore, we would lose the ability to take on another project we have been asked to consider if the client is not prepared to deviate from their schedule. We would therefore accept a contract as Susan suggested with a clause stating that in the unlikely event that you prove we have failed in protecting your network from future infiltrations, a percentage of any payments you have made to us to that date will be retained to cover some of the expenses we would have sustained to that time, the percentage to be agreed today." Feeling quite happy with herself she glanced at everyone in turn finishing with Jerry who gave her a supportive wink.

The Chief Executive also worked his way around the assembled gathering, one by one, silently asking for their comment and receiving a nod of agreement from each. "You drive a hard bargain Miss Levy," he finally said. "As long as the percentage is sensible, I think we can live with your amendment." Then, moving his attention from Rochelle, he continued. "Susan, please go and do your magic," before announcing to everyone, "Ladies and Gentlemen thank you for your time." For the first time that morning other voices could be heard emanating from the room. Walking towards Jerry, the Chief Executive, looking somewhat relieved, called out to him, "You've earned lunch today, let's have something to eat and sort out the price." He then gathered a small group together from those in the meeting and led them to the restaurant reserved for directors and their guests.

Following lunch, Susan placed the necessary figures into the basic agreement she had prepared as requested and having reviewed it, neither Rochelle nor Jerry could find any reason for failing to sign it. By three thirty, both parties had put their respective signatures to it at which time the Chief Financial Officer promised the first instalment would be made the following Monday when Jerry would start work.

With the formalities completed, a handful of people from the IS team met with Jerry for an hour or so in the director's lounge to discuss the manner by which they were going to implement the protection, while Rochelle spent the time catching up on the numerous calls and messages she had received.

When they finally arrived back at Jerry's home shortly after six-thirty that afternoon, Rochelle noticed her parent's car parked close by.

"I invited your parents and sister for dinner Rochelle, I trust you don't mind," Jerry's mother informed her once they were through the front door.

"No, not at all," Rochelle answered back, not sure why the invitation for dinner had been extended to include her parents and sister, turning it into a family affair.

"So how did it go?" Jerry's mother couldn't wait to ask.

"Rather than repeat ourselves a million times, we'll tell everyone over dinner," Rochelle replied. They had agreed in the car that nothing would be said until they were eating. After bringing in the Jewish Sabbath, the eight of them sat down for the traditional Friday night feast.

"Three hundred and fifty thousand pounds initial contract in addition to a small consultancy fee to resolve an existing issue, although there are a couple of conditions attached," Rochelle suddenly announced excitedly as she was finishing her bowl of chicken soup. She sounded similar to a child that had just been given a brand new toy. Despite the obvious jubilation she decided to keep everyone on the edge of their seats by continuing, "Let me finish my soup and I'll tell you a little more about it." One thing Jerry had observed many times about Rochelle was how much she enjoyed teasing people. He couldn't help but smile to himself in admiration, at the same time fighting his mouth to keep his lips tightly shut whilst everyone turned their attention to him in the hope he would be first to spill the beans. As the main course was served, Rochelle casually chatted through the basic details, careful not to mention the client other than to say it was a household name. Jerry remained silent, grinning like a Cheshire cat throughout, he was so thrilled at what he and Rochelle had achieved in the week.

Rochelle's father took his prompt as soon as his eldest daughter had stopped talking. "I believe these two kids and they are still kids as far as I'm concerned, have done fantastically well. To close two significant orders with a combined value of over four hundred thousand pounds I think is tremendous and a performance that the most professional and mature sales person would be more than satisfied with," he said proudly.

"And you have concluded these deals in such a short time!" Richard cut in as though he had planned everything in advance with Rochelle's father, alternating sentences. "What's more amazing, the two of you have only been working together for eight days. One small order so quickly could be considered beginner's luck, but two major ones," he paused at that point allowing the full extent of their achievements to sink in for everyone. "Well, all I can say is, there must be a tremendous amount of knowledge and skill between both of you, something I never doubted in you Jerry." He then finished with the Yiddish word for congratulations, "Mazeltov to you both."

Rochelle's father took the floor once more. "I'd like to propose a toast," he said whilst filling his glass with champagne he had bought on the way over to celebrate the Milky Way order and continued. "Rochelle, Jerry and Igloo."

Although no one could be labelled a drinker, by the end of the evening the eight of them had managed to think up sufficient toasts to consume six bottles of champagne, which was every bottle that could be found in the Freedman's house.

Ten

Jerry spent his weekend designing and building the production version of the black box, managing to make it easier and faster to construct. In the process he included the necessary amendments to both hardware and software enabling the unit to be upgraded remotely, the status monitored via the web and to be accessed on several unique internet or static addresses. The additional addresses would provide flexibility when used in large corporations, the idea having come from suggestions during the meeting with the technical people at A&E. He also found a more aesthetically pleasing case.

From Monday through to Wednesday, Jerry worked on the A&E project, visiting both their head office in London and the central computing facility in Birmingham, resulting in a highly detailed plan of their UK platform being produced by the end of the three days, a far more detailed document than had existed until then. The contract between the two companies only specified the UK network, but Jerry had been told if he were successful, contracts would follow for the solution to be implemented on their systems in both Central Europe and North America.

Whilst working through the system, it didn't take Jerry long to locate the nasty as he referred to it, installed by the hackers. Managing to disassemble the code, a task far simpler than he'd expected, Jerry was able to confirm all A&E data files were being forwarded to another computer and found the Internet address of the recipient machine.

Using his online contacts made over the last few years, he knew it would be possible to locate the bricks and mortar address from the information without having to go to the authorities and alerting the world of their situation. Discussing the find with Leon and other A&E decision makers, Jerry managed to convince them not to take any action until he had fully installed the protection. "Any move before we have everything in place would only signal the attackers we are onto them," he explained to the top brass. "And without adequate protection it could result in disastrous consequences with further, far more aggressive measures taken against you," he added, finally gaining unanimous agreement.

Whilst Jerry was concentrating his efforts on the technical details, Rochelle organised the administration. She had arranged the formation of the company, booked meetings with the various professional advisors and banks and provided customer service in as far as keeping in contact with the clients on a non-technical level, providing an ear for any concerns. The rest of her time was taken up with flat and office hunting, whilst doing a hand-over of her job at Milky Way.

Jerry met with Peter the following day at Milky Way's offices, where together they produced a detailed network plan, similar to what he had produced for A&E, Peter finally accepting its necessity.

Following the meeting with Peter, Jerry arranged to catch up with Rochelle, meeting face to face for the first time since the previous Friday, although they were communicating several times a day by either phone or email. Rochelle handed Jerry every document that required his signature or some other kind of input from him, carefully explaining each one and he duly completed them accordingly. She had already dealt with many on her own, ensuring copies had been kept. She flicked through the correspondence file she had created, giving Jerry a brief overview of everything in progress or completed. As they were tidying up, Rochelle casually informed him, "Tomorrow is my last day here and I move out of my flat this weekend, back with my parents until I find somewhere else, but at least it'll be a lot closer to you. I suppose you're going to be too busy to help schlep?" she sort of commented.

Jerry was well versed in the Yiddish term Schlep since his mother often used it when wanting his assistance in carrying things for her. Jerry didn't have to put any thought into an excuse, "You know I'd love to help, but I'm sure you don't need reminding we are contracted to deliver on two large projects with only me to do the work," he replied with a sort of boyish smirk on his face, Rochelle knowing it was just a good excuse since he thoroughly enjoyed the work. "Speaking of which," he said, having thought for a second or two, "I've been wondering whether I should ask Dr Fog if we could use his lab to build the boxes. Officially the university is closed, still on summer vacation, so I wouldn't be interfering with studies. The vapour from the epoxy needed to seal the number of units required for both projects would probably keep my parents high for months. What do you think?"

Rochelle considered the idea. "It's certainly worth asking the question," she said without showing too much interest. "Have you spoken to the good doctor since stopping him from discussing the idea with his contacts?"

Jerry suddenly realised with all the excitement he'd forgotten to call Dr Fog and mumbled, "No, I don't believe I have," whilst praying his face wasn't saying any more.

Rochelle carried on as if she had not heard Jerry's reply. "Do you realise in just four days we officially start working full time together," she was excited, looking forward to the prospect. "Please, don't forget you'll need to take time out for several meetings I've arranged, you do know that, don't you?" she reminded him. "So make sure you don't double book any client trips. Here's a list of the arrangements, I haven't added anything new since the last email on the subject yesterday." Whilst speaking she handed Jerry a neatly typed list. Aware how disorganised he was in everything except technical things, she offered: "To help you, I'd be happy to manage your diary." Before he had a chance to answer, Rochelle continued with another statement, despite feeling it maybe misinterpreted and once again considered by him to be confrontational. "I'd also like to learn to carry out the demonstrations myself, taking some of the pressure off you. I already have a couple of other prospects in mind and it's important to start building an order book." She was speaking the truth, but didn't think Jerry would believe her, thinking the request was simply to muscle in even further on his territory, something furthest from her mind.

Jerry smiled. "Don't worry, I realise your suggestions are for the good of the company and I'd welcome you managing my diary if you think you have the time. What's more, I'd love you to take care of the demonstrations; I'm really bogged down with getting these projects out of the way and could think of nothing better than to have others lined up behind them. I know as well as you do all that acting isn't me, as much as you've tried to make me feel great about how well I've done, but to do them you'll need to be able to speak the pseudo technical chat." There was relief in Jerry's voice since things were quickly getting on top of him. "You should know I really do have confidence in you and if we continue to develop at a fraction of the speed we've started, I certainly won't have the time for the sales stuff anyway. I'm sure if I quickly take you through the commands, with a bit of practice you'll be far better at presenting it than I would ever be, so book some time in my diary next week for me to show you," he said grinning, following which he looked at his watch, "Is that the time? I must get going now, loads to do." As he stood up to leave he asked, "By the way, when are Milky Way coughing up with some cash? I have a lot of parts to buy."

Rochelle removed a purse from her handbag and pulled out a cheque for fifty eight thousand, seven hundred and fifty pounds payable to Igloo Ltd. "Looks good, doesn't it?" she stated proudly.

"I assume the extra is the tax rather than a bonus," Jerry replied, spotting the additional amount. "But it's not as good as this," he took the A&E cheque from his wallet, also payable to Igloo for the handsome sum of one hundred thousand pounds.

Rochelle handed Jerry the cheque she was holding, "We must get the bank sorted soonest. You keep it, after all most of it is yours," she said smiling. "Go home now, I'll see you at your place bright and early on Monday morning, although I'm sure we'll talk at least a hundred times before then. Remember, if you feel an onset of boredom come over you this weekend you know where to find me, an extra pair of hands certainly won't go amiss." She then opened the meeting room door and looked along the hallway in both directions before announcing, "Peter doesn't appear to be around so I better see you out." Having walked Jerry to reception, she watched him leave.

Arriving home late that evening, Jerry immediately started work reviewing both plans, determining the requirements for each organisation and calculating the number of TAUs needed to obtain maximum protection for each client. A TAU was the new name Rochelle had given to the black boxes, an acronym for Traffic Access Unit, which in her opinion was a far more professional term than referring to them as black boxes, particularly since the new cases were no longer black plastic. They were manufactured from brushed aluminium in an expensive looking silver grey colour.

Over the following weeks, Igloo changed from what sounded like a good idea into a fully functioning professional outfit with an office and attached workshop in Borehamwood, some fifteen miles north west of the centre of London. The premises were reasonably smart but relatively inexpensive, in a self contained unit probably built just after the Second World War and beginning to show its age. Although there was plenty of room for growth, it was rented on a revolving six-month lease, which enabled Igloo to move relatively easily if it looked that they were going to out grow it.

Rochelle found a flat to rent in Edgware, five miles from the office and was only too pleased to move out from her parents. It was somewhat smaller than the one she had given up in Reading, with the rent being half as much again. The old flat had plenty of room for Mike to leave his belongings for the occasions he stayed over, but there was now hardly enough space for her own wardrobe and she had been forced to leave a lot of her personal possessions, including clothes, at her parent's home. Rochelle was not overly bothered about Mike's items, having hardly seen him since moving out of Reading and becoming engrossed in Igloo. They frequently spoke on the phone and regularly made dates. However she found herself cancelling more often than not, due to last minute work or meetings and it didn't take her long to realise she wasn't really missing him. "Yes, he was a nice guy, good-looking, great physique and never short of a word or two to say," she thought to herself. He worked in logistics, but Rochelle always thought he lacked the motivation for success. Mike was more than satisfied with being one of the boys, never wanting to take on any additional responsibility no matter what and that, as far as Rochelle was concerned, was a huge clash in their personalities.

Eleven

Igloo had two very satisfied clients on their books and two further clients had signed contracts, with five additional proposals under evaluation. Rochelle quickly became as fluent as Jerry in carrying out the demonstrations and the work which had started in Dr Fogs laboratory had migrated to Igloo's own workshop, as did a couple of his post graduate researchers. Fortunately Dr Fog was thrilled by Jerry's success as opposed to being annoyed at having his people poached. Happiest of all was Jerry's mother, despite the tears of joy she shed when the reality finally sank in that Igloo and Jerry in particular, would no longer be working from her house. Despite the moans and groans relating to her home looking more like a computer centre, privately she enjoyed having Jerry around all day. To ease the trauma, Rochelle suggested the company pay for decorating the house, since the walls and skirting looked like Emmenthal Cheese by the time the cables and boxes had been removed.

Jerry spent much of his time training the ever growing technical team to handle pre-sales support, calculating the requirements of a system, building TAU's, teaching clients to connect and configure correctly, which on the whole was a very simple task, providing customer support when required and of course assisting in research and development.

Rochelle managed the sales team which had grown to three people excluding her within six months, looked after the marketing and public relations and had successfully recruited a receptionist, a general manager and a part time financial controller, whilst Jerry concentrated most of his efforts on developing the product to fulfil the requirements of other markets. When not in the office or workshop, Jerry spent most of his time at home continuing to work on the system, having kept a small network in his bedroom.

As the name Igloo became known within the industry, Dr Fog started to recommend a few of his contacts, one being the Ministry of Defence. To begin with a small contract was signed, but it had the potential based on performance, to grow into a multi million pound transaction over the following four years. A&E kept true to their word and rolled out the Igloo solution on their systems in Europe and North America, whilst Milky Way implemented the protection on their head office system in Sydney.

Although Igloo remained a relatively small headcount for the amount of business being transacted, they were rapidly growing a portfolio of very prestigious clients.

Rochelle created what quickly became known as Rogue's Gallery on the main wall in the reception area by displaying the logos of all their clients, a gallery which over a relatively short period of time could not help but impress even the most cynical prospects that visited them.

The first anniversary of Igloo's official start seemed to be upon them very quickly and Rochelle suggested they throw a party for the team, clients and the more serious prospects they were in negotiation with. "We could use our existing clients as an extended sales force by introducing them to our prospects." She suggested to Jerry late one afternoon as they were both preparing to leave for the day. "I appreciate most companies do their utmost to keep existing clients away from potential customers and when asked for references, are very careful which clients are used. I don't believe we have anything to worry about." She continued, "I'm convinced all our clients would speak positively about us, I can't think of one who doesn't sing our praises, except for the price of course. If we're clever about this, it could be very successful and elevate our standing in the market still further."

"You're just looking for an excuse to party, I know you. What's more, you know I'm not a party animal," Jerry replied once he had listened to her idea.

"Not even for the good of the company?" she said with her most convincing look that Jerry couldn't resist, turning his legs to butter even more so than usual.

He very sheepishly replied, "You'll have to teach me to party. Go on then look into it," not believing he had mentioned anything about teaching him. He did notice and was very pleased he couldn't feel himself blush and wondered if this was the start of getting over his embarrassment problem.

Within three weeks Rochelle had booked the ballroom of the Hilton Hotel in London's Park Lane and organised the menu. For entertainment she considered herself extremely fortunate as her favourite and a very popular Jewish American comedian would by chance be in London and available on the day. She knew virtually everyone she had invited would appreciate Jackie Mason's jokes, even though they were sometimes very close to the knuckle, but that was all part of his humour. The office had mailed out over two hundred invitations for the affair and Rochelle was progressing in compiling a multi media presentation, which both she and Jerry would deliver to their guests during the evening.

A few days before the big night, just as they were both about to leave the office, Rochelle whispered to Jerry, "Let's go and buy you some party clothes, you can't turn up at you own company's function dressed in dreary old rags."

"I'm sure I can find something in my wardrobe to wear," Jerry replied, nowhere near as quietly.

"I bet I can find something far more suitable and make you look dapper for a change. Come on, let's go and have some fun, you deserve it after all the work you've put in over this last year, let alone all the previous years," she sort of pleaded with him. "Please, it'll make me happy, I'll even pay. I know you're saving up for a place of your own." She paused then repeated, "Come on it'll be fun, I promise."

"Okay, I give in," he eventually said, shocked he had agreed to go shopping in the first place, something he never really did and what's more, with her. He was certain the excitement was embossed across his face. “Where do you suggest we go?” he asked, following with, “But I’ll pay. Thanks for the offer though.”

She looked at her watch, “If we go to Brent Cross which is only five minutes down the road, we should just have enough time since they’re open until 8pm and there is always plenty of choice. Drop your car off at your parents, I’ll drive the rest of the way as its silly taking two cars,” she stated.

They spent a little over an hour, until the shopping centre closed, mooching around and in the process bought a dinner suit, shirt and bow tie for the party, two lounge suits, three smart pairs of trousers, two pairs of jeans, five coloured shirts with three ties, six smart T-shirts, three jumpers and two pairs of shoes. Keeping to her word, Rochelle paid for everything. “I won’t embarrass you with underwear,” she said smiling.

“Why did you pay? You needn’t have done,” Jerry asked whilst silently acknowledging he had probably just enjoyed the best hour of his life. He desperately wanted to kiss her, but still couldn’t bring himself to do so.

“Because I wanted too, I probably had more fun than you. I love shopping, whether for me or someone else. Now, let’s go and grab a bite to eat,” Rochelle virtually demanded. “There’s a good little restaurant just round the corner.”

They had an excellent meal whilst Rochelle ran Jerry through the plans for the party, in particular his part of the presentation. She also explained what she expected of him in terms of mingling with the guests. Throughout the meal she sensed that Jerry’s mind seemed to be elsewhere, but didn’t know why and for once it was she that was completely focussed on work, trying to ensure the success of the party, so chose not to question him.

They walked the short distance back to where Rochelle had parked her car, Jerry willing himself so hard to hold her hand, but the closest he could get was brushing the back of his against hers on several occasions. She then dropped him off at home, handing him the collection of bags from the boot of her car and then drove back to her flat.

Twelve

Having locked her front door and feeling content with her evening activities, Rochelle prepared to take a shower. As usual, before doing anything else she checked the voicemail on her mobile phone. There was one message waiting and as per the familiar audio instruction, she pressed the number two to listen.

"Ever since you started work with that relative of yours, I never get to see you. You always use an excuse of work, work, and more work and when it's not work it's that stupid club of yours you've never included me in. I recall a time when you started with Igloo, you told me how all the guy does was work, he has no social life whatsoever and if I remember correctly you called him an asshole for being like that. I believe you said something along the lines of life is about living and he should learn to live. Have you taught him?" Rochelle knew exactly where the message was leading, but felt she should continue listening. "In the last month we have seen each other three times and you have stood me up on thirteen occasions. Just tell me we're finished, don't keep building up my hopes and then trashing them hours later. That's not fair! I'm sure you wouldn't take kindly to it if the situation was reversed and I am not prepared to tolerate it either." The tone was somewhat aggressive at this point, but still Rochelle felt compelled to hear the message through to the end. "Unless I hear from you by 9pm this evening, interpret this message as it was nice knowing you and I wish you luck for your future, a future without me." Once finished,

Rochelle heard the message time stamp and realised it had been left whilst she was busy buying clothes for another man and had obviously not heard the phone ring.

Her immediate thought was: "Wow Mikey," as she had affectionately named him fairly early on in their relationship. "You really are one upset chap." Looking at her watch she continued, "It's now ten-thirty. Maybe I should call and apologise?" she contemplated. "No, we'll have one almighty argument which will only make things even worse. I promise I'll call in the morning and discuss everything," she told herself.

Having placed the phone on her dressing table she showered, her thoughts continually jumping between the shopping spree, Mikey and Igloo's party. She switched the television on and with a glass of sparkling water, climbed into bed, making herself snug under her duvet, cuddling her furry teddy whilst watching a romantic film until she drifted off to sleep.

The following day was busy for everyone in the office. Rochelle had to submit the final numbers to the caterer and the table plan needed to be completed, so she organised the whole team to devote the day to a massive ring around. With the buzz of activity and adrenalin rush, she completely forgot about the promise she made to herself the previous evening. Suddenly, at 3pm she remembered and tapped out Mike's number on her telephone handset.

After a couple of rings the phone was answered. "Hi, you're speaking to Mike's mobile. If you want Mike, please give me the message and I'll do my best to remember to pass it on, otherwise I'm happy for you to chat with me, I'm a great listener."

Rochelle was only half concentrating on the call, but the message that Mike had used for many months always annoyed her. "Mike, it's me, Rochelle and you still have your stupid voicemail message." She recorded on the machine, almost shouting at it. "Look, I picked up your call last night, but it was late and I was too tired to call you straight back. I'm busy tonight and tomorrow. We have the Igloo party I told you about, so I'll catch up with you on Friday." With that said, she cut the call.

After replacing the phone in its handset, she sat for several minutes staring into space, just pondering. She realised the voicemail Mike left the previous evening hadn't really bothered her, nor the fact they'd not seen each other for ages whilst remembering on the last occasion they were together, neither had much to say to the other. The thought entered her mind that maybe it really was over between them and she no longer had any feelings towards him. To further that idea she noticed the message she had just left hadn't even finished with 'Love you darling', her standard sign-off. Before concentrating her mind back to the task in hand, that being to contact the remaining names on the list in front of her, Rochelle made a mental note that Mike had to be told properly their relationship was over, although she did still want to remain friends. Having sorted out that issue, she banished all further thoughts about him from her head.

Besides Jerry who left the office at around 7pm, the only person in the company Rochelle had not roped into assisting in phoning all the invitees, everyone stayed until the job was finished which was well after nine-thirty. They left together having finally spoken to almost everyone who had not replied to an invitation and finalising the arrangements for the following day where it was agreed the office would close at around 4pm to allow everyone time to freshen up and change before the evening. One of the team would need to spend the afternoon at the hotel to set up the presentation equipment and Rochelle had arranged a freebie room for the night so they could store their belongings and change at the hotel if necessary.

The reception was due to start at 6.30pm, but Rochelle was ready and waiting for her guests at six with the majority of the Igloo team. Guests started arriving at around six-fifteen, an hour before dinner was to be called, allowing fifteen minutes for everyone to be seated in the adjoining ballroom for dinner to commence promptly at 7.30pm.

"Where's Jerry?" she kept being asked by staff as well as guests as the time crept ever closer to seven o'clock. Finally, a little after seven, Jerry entered the now very noisy reception room looking like a lost sheep. Rochelle, spotting him as soon as he walked through the door, approached him from behind making him jump when she tapped him on the shoulder saying "Nice of you to join us, or are you a gate crasher?"

Jerry didn't take long to think of an appropriate answer: "I happened to be walking past this hotel and overheard a couple of police officers standing outside saying that there was a free meal going, so naturally I thought I'd take a look." He was amazed at how many people had turned up and it was the first time he appreciated just how far they had come in the past year. "Quite a few guests I don't recognise," he commented, having taken a quick glance around the over packed reception room.

Rochelle had started to worry that his shyness had finally got the better of him and was relieved the real star of the show had eventually arrived and in good humour. "I would describe it as a lot of potential business here," and responding to his comment about the Police, she informed him: "Security is tight because we have several government ministers, both British and from overseas. By the way you look real dapper," and she gave him a peck on the cheek. As she did so, she felt butterflies in her stomach. "Ummmmm," she thought to herself. "Haven't had that feeling for a long time," and watching Jerry, she saw him start to blush. Jerry wanted to tell her he thought she looked stunning, but just couldn't bring himself to do so.

After what seemed like ages to Jerry, but in reality was only a few minutes and precisely on time, the Master of Ceremony called for dinner to be served and the guests slowly moved to the adjacent dining room. Rochelle had arranged the table plan ensuring there were members of the Igloo team and at least two representatives from existing clients on each table seated between the prospects wherever possible.

The chefs did Rochelle proud, the menu being a great success as was the choice of wine judging by the amount consumed. Whilst the after dinner coffee was being served, Rochelle was called to the podium. The lights in the hall dimmed and a spotlight focussed on her. A large rear projection screen which had been displaying the Igloo logo throughout the evening, momentarily switched to a bright white glare and then to the start of the multi media presentation she had prepared.

As the hall went quiet for the first time that evening, Rochelle started the presentation, maintaining everyone's attention throughout. Finishing her part, she waited patiently as Jerry was called to the podium.

"Thank you Rochelle," he started, as per the script she had given him before deviating, "I really don't know how we've managed to achieve everything Rochelle has just recounted in only twelve months from a standing start. Having said that, I'm not sure if she's been a help or a hindrance," he said grinning. "I know she certainly distracts all the guys in the office from their work with her great looks," then asked the audience, "Is that how she's managed to close so many deals so quickly? Does she exchange a seductive smile and a flutter of the eye lids for a signature on an order form?" Whilst everyone was laughing he turned to face her, continuing, "Seriously, I must admit she is a very talented girl, a great marketeer and sales woman, without whom Igloo would certainly not be where it is today." At that point the hall broke into a round of applause during which Jerry whispered to her: "My turn to embarrass you." Somehow he managed to pluck up the courage and follow his words with a kiss on her lips in front of everyone, praying that no one could see how nervous and embarrassed he was. Public speaking was nothing compared with what he had just brought himself to do and he was rightly proud of himself for finally carrying it off. Rochelle was more than surprised, but delighted to receive the kiss, being the only person in the room that understood just what it took for Jerry to accomplish it, particularly as it was so public. She hoped and prayed the rest of the evening would go as she planned and her heart desired. When the hall finally quietened down, Jerry continued the presentation precisely as Rochelle had prepared it.

Once Jerry had finished and the applause subsided, the Master of Ceremonies handed the reigns to the comedian, Jackie Mason. Jerry spent the rest of the evening continuing to mingle with the guests as Rochelle had instructed him to do.

The last of the guests left the hall at around 12:30am and the team quickly packed away all their belongings, dismantled the presentation system and loaded everything into their cars. "Good night and thank you," Rochelle and Jerry were saying as each member of their staff left, Rochelle reminding them they needn't be in the office until ten-thirty that morning. Finally, only Rochelle and Jerry remained, sitting together at a table. Rochelle glanced through the paperwork the team had handed her, a mixture of orders and enquiries taken during the evening. "You know Jez," she started, "We've already picked up seven good orders from tonight. I think this will turn out to be one of my best marketing ideas yet and you performed brilliantly, see, you can do it!" she told him triumphantly.

Jerry was busy dwelling on the fact that Rochelle had called him Jez, hoping it to be a display of affection. It was the first time she had called him anything other than Jerry. "It was all you, I just came along for the ride," he said. "And now I'm totally exhausted."

Rochelle slowly leant over towards him, stopping close enough for him to feel her breath on his face, then whispered, "We have a room reserved upstairs, why don't we take advantage of it and stay the night?" Without waiting for an answer, she collected the papers together, took hold of his hand and led him from the banqueting hall to the lifts servicing the bedroom floors. Having pressed the button for the tenth, she nudged up against him. "It's been a good year so far, the best of my life," she said quietly. "Even breaking up with Mike," at which point she remembered officially she hadn't done so, although as far as she was concerned the relationship was well and truly over. Her head moved towards his and they kissed until the bell rang and the doors opened. Arm in arm, they slowly walked along the corridor until they reached the bedroom.

With the entry card still in her hand from opening the door, she whispered reassuringly in his ear, "Don't worry, I'll lead," as he heard his exit block behind him.

Sitting on the dressing table were two glasses and an ice bucket containing a chilled bottle of champagne ordered by Rochelle during the evening. Trying to remain as relaxed as possible, Jerry opened the bottle and filled the two glasses.

In between sips of champagne and kissing, they slowly undressed each other. Jerry felt he had to tell Rochelle: "You are the first girl I have ever looked at and wanted from that first day I met you," he whispered in her ear before kissing her again and then went on, "I've been wanting to ask you out on a date ever since, but have always been too shy and was never really sure where you stood with Mike." It seemed to take Jerry ages to complete each sentence. "What I said this evening was true, I did find it difficult to concentrate when you were around me and even more so when I knew you were with him," he finally managed to tell her.

Rochelle whispered: "We're together now, we're a good team in business and we're going to be a great team in love. I must admit that I've often thought about being with you too."

Those were the last interpretable sounds heard until Jerry's watch woke them both with its buzz at 6.30am the following day. "Good morning," Rochelle said sprightly. "I'm not sure if I told you last night, but that was the best night I've ever had, or was it a dream?" She then rolled over onto him, slowly put him inside her and they made passionate love again.

"I feel like going back to sleep," Jerry said as Rochelle finally got out of bed and opened the curtains to let the daylight in. The street ten floors below was already bustling with people on their way to work and both the north and south carriageways of Park Lane were hardly moving due to the volume of rush hour traffic.

"You can't, we have a business to run, remember?" Rochelle informed him.

"Oh yes, I almost forgot since I was lost in that dream of yours," Jerry replied with a look of content across his face.

"It was for real darling," she whispered, having sat beside him on the edge of the bed. "But perhaps also a dream come true," she added, giving him another kiss on the lips before standing up, her perfectly shaped naked body in front of him to be in awe of, before she slowly made her way towards the bathroom. "You're lucky; I held onto a pair of trousers and a T-shirt from our shopping spree the other day, which means we can go straight to the office without questions being asked," she called out from the bathroom.

"So this was pre-meditated?" Jerry suggested to her.

"As if," she called out, stepping into the shower. "And you didn't realise you were missing anything?" she asked him, but heard no answer.

After several minutes of listening to the running water, Jerry heard Rochelle's voice cry out, "Come here quickly, Jerry," as if she was in some sort of trouble.

Thinking Rochelle had an accident, Jerry jumped out of bed and dashed to the bathroom. "Come here," she called again in anguish and as Jerry got closer to the shower she grabbed hold of him and pulled him in.

"As if," he repeated quietly in her ear as the water rained down on them both.

Thirteen

Whilst driving to the office Rochelle punched the speed dial for Mike's mobile and waited for the ring tone, hoping she wouldn't get his voicemail this time. She hadn't rehearsed, or even given any further thought to the conversation, but was conscious of her end goal. Mike finally answered and Rochelle saw a mental vision of him with the phone pressed firmly against his ear.

"Mike, it's me, have you got a minute?" Rochelle asked.

"I suppose so," he replied, although it was easy to detect the reluctance in his voice.

"Look Mike, I'd really like to do this face to face but I'm so busy. The party last night was a huge success." She paused for a moment to concentrate on an idiot trying to overtake her in a dangerous place, right on a bend in the road.

Mike took the opportunity to congratulate her. "I'm pleased for you," he said, referring to the party. "I think you have a great opportunity in Igloo and realise you need to devote a huge amount of time to it. I truly wish you luck with it."

"As you know I always speak my mind and today is going to be no different," Rochelle stated, trying to keep to the subject. She was being careful not to get side tracked by responding to Mike's comment regarding Igloo, knowing once on the subject it would be difficult for her to get back to the matter in hand. Rochelle knew it was a common trick of Mike's to lead the conversation in a direction he wants, if he thought he didn't like where it was heading. "Since you left the message the other evening I've been thinking and I need to share my feelings with you."

"Do you?" Mike interrupted flippantly. He was upset that his attempt to get Rochelle to talk about Igloo, knowing once started she couldn't stop talking about it, had failed.

Rochelle continued, "There are lots of ways I could approach this and I'm not sure which route to take. You know what it's about."

"Please just say what you want to say Rochelle. Don't play games, I've had enough of them from you recently," Mike almost shouted.

"I know I've been engrossed in work lately and each time I've felt bad letting you down at the last minute having confirmed arrangements, but it really wasn't intentional and that's the truth," Rochelle tried telling him.

"So why did you agree to see me when you knew you wouldn't be able too? You could simply have told me you were busy and suggested I see some friends, rather than leaving me with nothing to do except watch TV. But that's not what this is all about, is it?" Mike replied, still with anger in his tone.

Rochelle thought for a moment. Without giving a direct answer, "I've become obsessed with Igloo, I realise that now, but I've had to put everything into it to stand any chance of making it a success. I knew when I started it would take up a lot of my time and I mentioned this to you when I talked about quitting Milky Way. Whenever I sat at my desk late at night I'd think about you. I thought there were only two loves in my life, you and Igloo," she told him before having to pause as the telephone line started crackling badly.

Mike pounced on the opportunity to ask, "What do you mean by 'You thought there were only two loves in your life'?"

"I don't know. Please let me finish," she begged him. "If you knew me the way you kept telling me you did, you should have understood I'd throw myself into making Igloo a winner. You know I have ambitions and I'm driven by success. Then you left that idiotic message, an ultimatum. My immediate reaction to it was, 'If that's how you feel, well it doesn't bode well for our future, does it?'" She waited for an answer, but on this occasion Mike remained silent. "As I've said, we held our anniversary party last night and I had a couple of drinks." She paused, quickly considering how best to say the next part without upsetting Mike too much. "I don't know if it was the alcohol or what, but suddenly there was another guy vying for my attention. I'm being honest with you Mike, I'm not trying to hurt you," she said with her voice tapering off towards the end of the sentence.

"But you are hurting me!" Mike replied, not making it any easier for Rochelle. "Are you sure it was only yesterday, out of the blue, you realised you had feelings for another person? I'm assuming it was mutual and you responded positively to the attention he was paying you," he asked in an ironic tone.

Rochelle wiped a tear from her cheek; she hadn't thought this would be quite as difficult as it was becoming. Never before had she found it so hard to end a relationship. "Yesterday was the first time I expressed how my heart felt about this person and as you know, I've never been one to suppress my feelings," she replied trying to make some sense out of everything. She had liked Jerry for a while, finding him cute in a funny sort of way and often wondered what he was really like. Until yesterday though, she had never visualised herself jumping into bed or getting involved in a relationship with him, he just wasn't her type, or so she thought. Analysing the situation, she normally went for tall, fit, confident, handsome guys that dressed well and continually pampered her. With her good looks and charisma she never had trouble finding men that met all her criteria, but Jerry didn't get a tick in any of the boxes, he was the complete opposite.

"Are you telling me that in one day this person managed to sweep you off your feet? He must be one hell of a guy," Mike commented.

"I did ask you to let me finish," she reminded him before continuing what she was saying. "When I heard your message I was angry, maybe at myself for letting us drag on, I don't know. I admit we've had some good times together, but I really can't see us ending up as a couple, we have completely different ideals in life." Pausing again, she wasn't sure quite how to finish. Mike remained silent this time, believing there was more to come. "As far as being an item is concerned, it's definitely over now. You implied that in the message you left me and I think it's for the best. But I really want to have you as a friend, can we agree to that?" She all of a sudden pleaded, realising she really didn't want to lose her ex-boyfriend completely. There was now a constant stream of tears running down her face, making her eyes blurry and therefore difficult to drive, so she stopped the car at the first convenient place.

Mike had heard enough. "I'm not going to ask you who he is, I can probably guess, but I do love you, or at least I did when I was seeing you. I've almost forgotten what you look like, let alone anything else. It's obvious our relationship isn't working for you, otherwise you wouldn't have treated me the way you have over the last few months." He wasn't interested in any excuses, just the facts as he had seen them. "We have known each other for about four years and I believe there is still something special between us, so to answer your question, yes, let's remain friends, I'd like that a lot. But please give me some time to digest this, despite my message I didn't think things were that bad between us, I left that message at the end of a bad day," he told her, wondering if there was still the slightest chance of turning things around. "It sounds like you've already made your mind up. I don't suppose there's anything I can do to help you change it back again?" This time it was Mike doing the pleading.

Rochelle could feel his pain and realised just how unfair she had been over the previous few months. Despite her preaching, she had fallen into the workaholic trap she had mocked a year earlier. Knowing for some time work excited her more than Mike, she now realised steps should have been taken earlier to end the relationship. "I suppose you could say I've used you and that's probably the truth. But I didn't do it intentionally, I promise you," she uttered between tears.

The one thing that Mike couldn't handle were girls crying and realising there was little point in continuing any type of rational discussion with Rochelle whilst she was in this state, he wanted to end the conversation. "Rochelle," he called, "I accept what you're saying and I believe you're right. It's for the best. You take care of yourself and I do wish you luck. You can call me whenever you want, I'll be there for you."

Rochelle had managed to stop the tears and felt relieved Mike had acknowledged things for what they were, or at least she tried to convince herself he had. "Likewise, you have my numbers, I've always been a shoulder for you to lean on, even before we were a couple and I'll continue to be there for you." She managed to blurt out. "This really is for the best though. Please take care of yourself and I'll catch up with you soon. Goodbye."

Taking the time to regain her composure, she wiped her face once more and having checked her mascara had not smudged, she completed the last couple of miles to the office content in the knowledge she had done the right thing.

Fourteen

During the following months both the business and their personal relationship continued to develop. In the office, Jerry concentrated on migrating the solution to other devices not originally contemplated, following requests from customers. His main attention was developing a viable solution to secure voice traffic, particularly wireless communications, including conventional telephone and two-way digital radio. Unlike the network security systems, the products Igloo started to launch in this sector were substantially cheaper than existing scrambling devices and allowed conventional communication products to be used as opposed to purchasing specialised units. This resulted in being inundated with enquiries from police authorities and the military from many countries, besides a large number of commercial organisations. The remainder of Jerry's time was utilised in servicing bespoke requests, where an existing product could be modified to fit a particular purpose for a client.

With the ever-increasing volume of work, the Igloo team continued to grow and they were finally forced to find larger premises. Eventually, an almost purpose built modern unit in Watford was found, about twenty miles from the centre of London and just a few miles further north of where they had been based in Borehamwood.

Since Jerry and Rochelle were spending more and more nights together cramped in her small flat, they decided it was probably time for him to officially move out of his parent's home. Rochelle had remained in the flat she had originally rented in Edgware, mainly due to lack of time in finding a larger one. Together they started to search for a place for Jerry, but he wasn't sure if it was a bachelor pad he was looking for, or something more suitable for them both.

Rochelle had managed to slightly change Jerry's attitude to life since being together in a relationship. He now spent a little less time working and was with Rochelle whenever they were both free, joining her when she went out with friends and spending intimate time together, just the two of them alone like most couples in love. Apart from her large circle of friends, Rochelle's other social interest was a club she was involved in, although it was the one topic of conversation that was taboo with all her boyfriends despite them knowing of its existence. Jerry never really had many friends and those he did, he quickly lost contact with except for a very old school mate who he talked to weekly, more down to the friend making the effort and Rochelle who got on very well with his wife when they finally met.

One Saturday evening in late July, whilst enjoying an evening picnic with a group of Rochelle's friends sitting on the grass in the grounds of Kenwood, listening to Beethoven being performed as part of the 'Concert In The Park' season, Jerry heard his name being whispered. Although the voice was quiet, the tone was somewhat questioning and one he had grown to expect would immediately be followed by a request for something or other. "My club is having its annual barbecue in a couple of weeks, a Sunday brunch. I'd really like you to join me."

Jerry was surprised by Rochelle's request since he had become accustomed to her making all their social arrangements without ever consulting him, not that he minded. "What's come over you? You have always kept that club of yours a secret from me. Is your next line going to be a marriage proposal?" he quietly asked so as not to disturb anyone sitting close by.

"Stop it," she said giggling whilst giving him a friendly nudge in the chest with her elbow. "But who knows what the future holds?" she continued to say with her lovely bright smile.

"You don't normally ask me when you want us to go somewhere, your usual line is 'We are going to such n such', so why the change of heart?" he whispered in her ear, taking the opportunity of giving it an affectionate nibble.

Rochelle answered: "As you know the club has always been my world, somewhere I can escape too from the rest of my life and at the same time help others. I know you've been careful never to question me about it for which I'm very appreciative." She paused to drink a sip of wine. "I think I'm now ready to bring you in on it, no more secrets. It's a huge leap of faith for me, I've never done this before and I suppose by asking you I'm confirming my feelings. Who knows, you maybe right about the next question, let's wait and see," she said in a very soothing tone.

Without hesitation Jerry replied: "If you want me to be there, of course I will. I don't care where we go as long as we're together. I enjoy being with you all the time, you know that don't you?"

"I do," she said and followed the reply with a passionate kiss.

Jerry managed to murmur, "I really have fallen in love with you," when he was finally able to catch some air.

"Me too," she replied and then thrust her tongue back in his mouth for another kiss to remember.

Fifteen

Due to the number of cars parked along the road, Jerry and Rochelle parked some five minutes walk away. Arriving at the white walled mansion they saw a passageway either side of the building and a sign showing both led to the garden at the rear of the house. Selecting the one on the left, they followed it through the black wrought iron, six-foot high gate into the large expanse of green. Jerry's first reaction was a feeling of being in a country estate rather than a dwelling located just a few miles north west of what is known as Central London in the expensive suburb of St. John's Wood. The garden must have been at least half an acre in size, built on two levels to take into account a gentle slope. The lower level furthest from the house consisted predominantly of a well-kept lawn and flowerbeds. A magnificent man-made waterfall leading to a pond filled with large Koi fish made up the centre piece, covered by a fine, almost undetectable netting over it to protect the valuable fish from predators.

The first part of the upper level, several steps above the lower, was a crazy paved terrace, a patio constructed from small. multi-coloured paving stones of varying shapes and sizes starting from the back of the house and reaching about thirty feet from the building. Doors from what appeared to be the dining room, lounge, living room and kitchen opened onto it. A large outdoor swimming pool and all the associated paraphernalia had been built at the end of the terrace, on the right hand side of the house, whilst the remaining upper garden consisted of another well kept lawn and flower beds. Along the left hand border was a small stream that fed the waterfall and Jerry realised that the water must be continually pumped from the lower garden to the upper. The effect was outstanding. The barbecue was set up on the patio near the swimming pool and a number of garden tables and chairs were spread around the whole garden.

Watching the guests, Jerry was surprised by the vast range in age group. Never being a club person himself, he assumed the participants would generally be of the same age; that's how it was at the clubs his parents and school friends tried to persuade him to attend when he was a young kid. Here there were people ranging in age from what he guessed must have been late teens through to some looking as though they were old enough to be drawing their pensions. He estimated about sixty-five people were in the garden and Jerry couldn't fail to notice two faces that he immediately recognised, faces he certainly wasn't expecting to see. "What are Peter and Leon doing here?" he asked Rochelle.

"They are both members, that's how I came to know them, in fact Leon runs the club."

Jerry thought for a moment before commenting: "Maybe I've been very naive for not asking before, but what exactly do you do at this club? I always thought of it as being some sort of social gathering, although I know you've occasionally mentioned it's to help the community." As Jerry asked, Leon made his way over to them.

Leon went to shake Jerry's hand and said, "It's great to see you both. Please go and help yourselves to food and drink."

Rochelle quietly mentioned to Leon, "Jerry wants to know what we do. I think you're probably the best person to explain it to him," she suggested. "I'll fetch some food for you Jerry, why don't you both find somewhere quiet to chat? Leon, anything I can get you?" she asked.

"No thanks, I've already eaten." Leon answered her. "Jerry, why don't we go inside and have a talk?" he asked as if Jerry had not heard Rochelle mention anything, the only other explanation being there was something to hide. They entered the mansion through a set of glass patio doors leading to a large living room, where a number of settees and armchairs appeared as if they were strategically positioned to form cosy groups. The room was empty other than the two of them, everyone being outside enjoying the early afternoon sunshine, some were even swimming. Leon gestured to Jerry to be seated and facing him with a serious tone, he started, “I’m sure you have heard about the continual threats to the Jewish community, both here and in other countries,” pausing for a response.

Jerry answered, “I suppose I do occasionally read about it.”

Leon continued, “So far we have been relatively lucky here in the UK. The authorities are fighting racism which has helped our community tremendously. They are also against the far right and left, in fact all radical factions, groups that are notoriously against the Jewish people. Because of this we have suffered fewer attacks than our brethren in other European countries, although with the continual conflict in the Middle East, the threat of international terrorism is continually increasing both generally and in particular against us as a specific community. We as an organisation work with the police and other government bodies to monitor the situation as well as providing security for Jewish events, allowing our people to carry on their day to day affairs without fear of attack.” He paused again wiping his brow with a clean handkerchief. “Our members give up some of their free time to do this on a voluntary basis and get-togethers such as this barbecue are the way that the community, through the main communal charities that we provide protection for, say thank you to our volunteers and their partners for giving up their time and for doing such valuable work.”

Jerry took the opportunity of another pause to ask “And Roch? What does she do? I can’t see her facing up to a skinhead or gunman unless she plans to show a bit of thigh to distract them.” he said, also in a serious tone.

“You’d be surprised,” Leon informed Jerry. “She knows exactly how to take care of herself if the need arises. She also puts together our research and presentation material, turning it into very readable documents which are then sent to members of both the British as well as the Israeli government. The Home Secretary is amongst many on her distribution list. You're very lucky to have her as both your friend and business partner. You take good care of her," he sort of ordered Jerry.

At that moment Rochelle walked into the room with two plates piled high with burgers, sausages, lamb chops and chicken wings with plastic cutlery and napkins in tow.

Seeing Rochelle, Jerry asked Leon, "Why do you think she has suddenly introduced me to this club," ensuring she could hear.

Leon thought for a moment not wishing to cause any friction between him and Rochelle. "Honestly," he asked whilst turning to glance at Rochelle. On seeing her nod he continued, "Because I asked her too. In the five years she's been involved with us, she has always kept this part of her life a secret from her other friends." He told Jerry as though it had been rehearsed with Rochelle. "Some of our younger volunteers use it as a social forum, besides the good work they do and I've been privileged to see many great friendships flourish. In other cases, particularly with our more mature members, couples use the club as a common interest. Rochelle for her own reasons has treated it as something separate to the rest of her life and I've been keen for some time for her to change that idea and open it up to you." Leon stopped to gauge Jerry's reaction. "I was overjoyed when she confirmed you would join us today, as I said before, this is a thank you to partners as well as the volunteers." Once again he looked at Rochelle, "I hope I've given you a satisfactory explanation. If you wish to become involved I'd be only too pleased, you have my number. All I would ask of you today is that you continue to support Rochelle in her efforts to assist us, rather than try and take her away."

Jerry didn't hesitate before replying, ensuring Rochelle could hear: "She has my support in everything she does, she knows that. I'm just a little hurt having things kept secret from me. Who knows, maybe I'd been interested in helping, after all it sounds as if it's only a slightly different angle to what I do every day," he smiled.

"I'm sorry, Jez," Rochelle said with her eyes beginning to moisten, standing behind his chair out of view. Having put the plates down on a nearby coffee table she continued, "I didn't mean to deceive you. On numerous occasions I thought about asking you to come along. If you recall, I even suggested you join us at last year's barbecue just after we first met. But it's different now, I no longer want any part of my life separate from you," she said sniffling. "If you want to become involved, a shared interest outside of work then I'd be happy, but I wouldn't force you into anything you didn't want to do. I really hope this doesn't affect either of our relationships, personal or professional," at which point she folded her arms around his neck and bent over him, kissing the top of his head. "There are so many things we do well together, one of them being the way in which we have managed to keep business separate from our personal lives. People say it's very difficult for a couple to work together harmoniously, but we have managed very successfully and I don't want this to come between us. I love you Jez." With that, she could hold off no longer and the tears started gushing from her eyes and down her golden cheeks.

As Jerry lightly swung Rochelle around to the front of the armchair she fell on top of him. He spoke again, specifically addressing Rochelle. "To put you right, I seem to recall our personal relationship kicked off by us not keeping business and pleasure apart, but you have my word that this won't come between us and furthermore you have my support in continuing. All I ask is that you don't leave me out of any part of your life again." Wiping her tears with his handkerchief he finished with, "I love you too."

Leon, pleased an argument had been averted, suggested "Now you two love birds, eat up and go and socialise outside with everyone else," and he walked off winking an eye at Rochelle.

Having rinsed her face and eaten, Rochelle spent the rest of the afternoon showing Jerry off to her friends until he reminded her they had arranged to view an apartment at 5pm. They quickly said their goodbyes and departed.

Sixteen

On arrival at the building site in Stanmore, they parked on a muddy path which Jerry assumed at some point would become the driveway and holding hands made their way to the wooden pre-fabricated hut acting as the sales office. On entering, Jerry said to the young man sitting at one of the two desks, "I have a viewing appointment to see the penthouse."

The salesman looked at the couple and then down at his diary, then back up again, "Mr and Mrs Freedman?" he finally asked with a look about him that seemed to say, "This is another waste of time."

"Yes that's us," Jerry replied smiling at Rochelle whilst tightening his grip on her hand as if to say "You're mine."

Having removed a set of keys from a cabinet behind him, the salesman, wearing a smart brown pair of trousers and a short sleeved beige shirt with the top couple of buttons undone, started to walk out of the hut saying, "If you wish to follow me I'll take you up."

They took their time looking around the penthouse, consisting of three bedrooms each with en-suite bathrooms, two large reception rooms, kitchen diner, study, guest cloakroom and a balcony overlooking a park. "The penthouse comes complete with a central door entry system as you saw when we came in, central station combined intruder and fire alarm, fully fitted kitchen with washing machine, dishwasher, fridge, freezer, microwave, electric oven and a trash compactor that extracts your rubbish into the main garbage bins downstairs." The salesman stopped as Rochelle stepped onto the balcony and took in the view of an almost never-ending expanse of green that made up Stanmore Common. When she returned to the living room he continued, "There's an independent heating and cooling system providing warm air in the winter and air conditioning in the summer and the bathrooms will all be fully tiled. The underground garage is being completed which will have an electric sliding gate securing it, and of course there's the elevator. At this stage we can decorate the apartment however you wish." He thought for a moment before concluding, "That's about it." His demeanour suggested he wished he were somewhere other than working on this warm, sunny, Sunday afternoon.

After a few more minutes of looking around, each step they took echoing on the wooden floorboards in the empty rooms, Jerry went back to the would-be living room where the salesman was standing. "We're first time cash buyers, not part of a chain and no waiting around for mortgages, so we can buy immediately. What deal can you offer us?" he asked.

The salesman's face brightened as he realised this couple could be more serious than he originally anticipated. "It's being advertised for five hundred and ninety five thousand pounds. If you sign today, I'll let it go for five hundred and seventy five thousand," he told them, offering what he considered to be a substantial discount to flush out precisely how serious and able they were.

Jerry informed the salesman of the obvious, although he knew the reference was to a deposit and not contracts, but he felt like being pedantic. "You know we can't sign without our solicitor reviewing the paperwork." He paused for a moment. "Just give us a couple of minutes please," and he led Rochelle into one of the bedroom's. "What do you think, do you like it?" he asked her.

Rochelle took her time in answering. "I think it has huge potential. It's the best we've seen."

Jerry then reminded her, "And the most expensive, but I concur with you. It's in a good area as well. If I can push him down a bit more on the price do you think we should go for it?" he asked her, his face having that irresistible baby look that she loved.

Realising it would be a major financial transaction for them both, having decided they would buy something together, she pondered before answering. "All we stand to lose is the hundred pound deposit if we sign now. Yes, why not? Let's go for it!" She exclaimed before giving him a quick kiss. "Good luck and let's see how my negotiation skills have rubbed off on you," she added as they walked out of the bedroom to discuss it with the salesman who had patiently waited for them.

Finding him standing in the kitchen, Jerry started his speech; "You want to make a sale today." Not waiting for a reply, "And we'd like to buy something today, but this apartment, as nice as it is, is in my opinion a little overpriced." Jerry then asked Rochelle for his chequebook and she removed it from her handbag as planned. "Who's the holding deposit made payable too?" he asked the salesman as she handed him a pen.

"Deven Homes plc," the salesman replied.

Jerry, tongue-in-cheek replied, "Five hundred thousand pounds and it's sold."

In an excited tone the salesman told him, "I can't let it go for that, the apartments downstairs are selling for four hundred and fifty thousand pounds and this is almost twice the size."

Jerry asked, "How much is the deposit?"

"One hundred pounds," the salesman quickly stated, not quite sure what Jerry was up too.

Jerry started to write Deven Homes plc on the cheque and as if on stage he called out each letter individually as he wrote it, followed by each word as it was completed, before proceeding to the next. He then repeated the chore with the amount and removed the cheque from the book having written the details on the corresponding stub.

He held it out to the salesman and in the well-known style from the TV Millionaire show said, "I want to give you this for five hundred and twenty five thousand pounds." The salesman hesitated, looked at the cheque, looked at Jerry, then Rochelle who gave him her most seductive smile. He then looked back at the cheque that Jerry was offering him.

As if he were not sure he was making the correct decision, but keen to sell the penthouse, the salesman hesitantly replied, “You have yourselves a deal. We need to go down to the office and sort out the paperwork.” Having locked the front door, the three of them returned to the hut where they spent the next thirty minutes going through all the necessary documents, with Jerry providing their solicitor’s details after checking with Rochelle the various additional on-going service charges were acceptable.

Walking back to the car he turned to Rochelle saying, “I guess you’re going to enjoy furnishing it.”

“You know me and shopping! When can I start?” she quickly asked with her face beaming with joy. As Jerry opened the car door for her, she threw her arms around his neck and kissed him. “I love you, darling,” she said, as she got into the car. “Let’s go home and celebrate.”

Seventeen

The penthouse was completed and between the two of them, another small fortune was spent fitting it out, Jerry converting whatever he could into state of the art devices. He built a central computer that controlled much of the standard electrics and electronics. What could be was voice activated; recognising his, Rochelle's and both sets of parents' voice patterns. He linked everything he could think of into the automated system, including the lights, heating and cooling system, alarm, door locks, electric curtains, televisions, video and DVD recorders, even the cooker, hob and microwave. The computer was connected to a telephone line enabling the devices to be controlled from anywhere, verbally commanding the system by dialling a telephone number, in addition to using the Internet to manage every appliance. There was now no excuse for ever missing a favourite TV programme, burning a meal, or entering a dark apartment irrelevant of the time they planned to get home. A finger print module, a device Jerry planned to further develop, provided additional security. He had also made plans to power some of the systems from natural or self generated sources rather than from the national grid, installing a number of solar power cells on the roof of the block in preparation.

Rochelle concentrated her efforts on the more mundane items including all the furniture, crockery and cutlery, lighting, carpets, bedding, in fact everything needed to live in the apartment. Things were really going well between her and Jerry and she kept meaning to give up her flat and move in properly, but she just never seemed to get around to it. However, most of her time was spent at the penthouse and the majority of her wardrobe lived there. The only time Rochelle stayed at her flat was if either had an early morning start, so as not to disturb the other.

Both Leon and Dr Fog continued to introduce clients to Igloo, several of which were far from the normal bread and butter mainstay of the company for which organisations around the world were signing orders for every day and for which they had become renowned. Jerry found several of these unique contracts interesting and something he enjoyed getting his teeth into, successfully completing each one. By the end of the second year of trading, Rochelle's Rogues Gallery occupied two large walls with an order book continuing to grow daily. The name Igloo was becoming synonymous with data security solutions in the same way Mercedes was synonymous with high quality reliable cars.

One evening, whilst Jerry was working in the study and Rochelle was busy preparing dinner in the kitchen, she called out to him, "I had a call from Leon today."

"So what did he have to say for himself, I thought you speak to him most days anyway, don't you?" Jerry yelled back so she could hear him.

Rochelle, not wishing to discuss the conversation at a sound level in excess of a hundred decibels, quickly finished in the kitchen and went to join Jerry in the study. "Dinner will be ready in a few minutes," she said, as she sat astride his lap, face to face. "It was you he asked about, which was strange in itself," she said, picking up on the conversation regarding Leon's call whilst slowly unbuttoning Jerry's shirt. Before he had a chance to pass comment, Rochelle continued, "Sometime over the next few days he wants to take you to the Israeli Embassy. He asked me how you were fixed for time," she said quietly while her fingers were walking over his now exposed chest. "I told him you have a fair amount of work on, but you were around so could probably do something at relatively short notice."

Jerry, starting to be aroused by Rochelle's actions just managed to ask, "Why did he speak to you and not me directly? Is he scared of me all of a sudden?"

"I don't know. That's what's so peculiar about it. He could have simply called your secretary and made an appointment. He didn't tell me what it was about either and to be honest I was rather busy at the time and never thought to ask. I suppose I assumed he was going to introduce them as a client." She continued, "It's only now I have thought about it, if that's his intention, he knows I, or someone from sales attend the initial meetings before we bring in technical people, particularly you." She kissed his chest and started to undo his trouser belt. "I'm just warning you that I have vibes it isn't necessarily work related, but before you have a go at me, I honestly don't know anything about it," she told him, the words being spoken in a protective tone. "Having said that, I do recall him mentioning something about special visitors as he loves to call them, coming over for a few days and maybe I'm subconsciously linking the two together. The comment must have been at the beginning of last week or the week before, but I didn't take much notice since I wasn't involved. I maybe completely wrong darling and even if I'm right, I still don't know why he wants you to meet with them, or why the meeting is at the embassy."

Jerry, having removed Rochelle's top and unfastened her bra, was more interested in making love than pondering over Leon's call. He whispered into her ear, "Thanks for the warning, when I know I'll tell you if your intuition is still tuned correctly, or whether I have to tweak it in any way, or should I just fine tune it now, before dinner?"

"What happened to that shy young man I met and fell in love with?" she asked in a very seductive tone. Before Jerry had a chance to answer, "You've been too busy to even look at me, let alone touch me over the last few days, so maybe I'll allow you to quickly give me the once over now whilst dinner is cooking," she continued to say as she pushed down his trousers.

Eighteen

Jerry's phone rang just after nine the following morning. "Jerry," he heard in a tone as if to confirm who had answered the call, but almost before Jerry could say a word the caller continued, "Its Leon. I have some friends over here that I would love you to meet. Are you free around one o'clock today for a couple of hours or so, although I suppose including travelling time, it's probably the best part of the afternoon we're talking about?" he asked in his usual abrupt manner Jerry now took to be Leon's style and not just blatant rudeness as he had first thought.

"If it's that important I can juggle one or two things around to free myself this afternoon," he replied without mentioning Rochelle's comment the previous evening.

Before Jerry actually confirmed it, he heard Leon say, "Good, see you at one then," and the line went dead.

"You can always count on a good conversation with Leon," Jerry thought to himself as his mind pondered the discussion he had with Rochelle, wondering who the special visitors were and why it was so important to meet them immediately that everything else had to be changed to fit in.

At one on the dot Jerry's mobile rang, it was Leon again. "I'm outside your office, I'll wait for you in the car to save parking, please be as quick as you can," and in Leon's normal fashion the line went dead before Jerry had a chance to say hello, goodbye, or even ask what the meeting was about. In an attempt to be prepared for any eventuality, Jerry thought he would take a complete sales pack consisting of a glossy folder with a large Igloo logo making up the front cover. Inside it contained a number of product sheets, one for each device in the Igloo portfolio, listing the technical specifications and examples of the way various customers have implemented the solutions, including a number of case studies. The final sheet explained the bespoke or special projects' service that Igloo provided. Normally only the relevant enclosures would be inserted, but since Jerry had no idea what would be required, he decided to take all of them with him. In addition to the literature, he also grabbed a fresh notepad and pen and of course his laptop computer which was like his shadow, going everywhere he went. Packing everything in his briefcase, Jerry checked that a power chord and spare battery were in one of the side pockets before running out of the office calling out, "See you later darling," as he breezed past Rochelle's open door, catching a fleeting glimpse of her sitting at her desk deeply engrossed in papers.

The first five minutes of the journey were made in silence, neither Leon nor Jerry uttering a word. Leon finally broke the tranquillity. "There are four visitors from Israel staying at the embassy for a couple of days and they have expressed a desire to meet with you. Two work for the Mossad and the other two are with Shin Bet. They each hold senior positions within their respective organisations and are in the UK for a meeting on terrorism between the CIA, MI5, MI6 and Scotland Yard's Anti Terrorist Branch."

Jerry thought about the two groups Leon named. "I've heard of the Mossad, that's the Israeli Intelligence agency I believe, but what or who is Shin Bet, besides being two letters in the Hebrew alphabet?" he asked trying to demonstrate he remembered something from his days at Sunday school many years ago.

"Both organisations are very similar and work closely with each other. Shin Bet is responsible for internal affairs, that being within the borders of Israel, whereas Mossad operates internationally, outside of Israel. The best comparison I suppose is probably MI5 and MI6. When people talk about Israel's Secret Service, they normally refer to

Mossad, that's the organisation most people have heard of," he answered. "Before you ask, I have no idea what they wish to discuss with you and it's been made quite clear to me that neither I nor my main embassy contact, someone quite senior in the rankings, are invited to the meeting. I can only assume the subject is of a sensitive nature. I'm merely acting as your chauffeur for the afternoon," he said smiling, which Jerry thought was the first time he had ever seen Leon with anything other than a worried look on his face. "I have a few things to do at the embassy whilst I'm there and will wait for you and bring you back."

Having slowly made their way through the heavy London traffic, Leon turned into the private road in which the Israeli embassy was located, coming to a halt at the security barrier manned by what looked like a commercial security firm. Parked in front of a white wooden hut on the public side of the barrier was a red police car, but looking through the windscreen Jerry could not see its occupants inside. Turning his attention to the hut positioned adjacent to the barrier, through the window Jerry could easily make out two uniformed police officers carrying what looked to him like sub machine guns. Their eyes followed one of the security guards who had emerged from the door at the side of the hut and was now approaching Leon's car. As he came close, Leon opened his window. "What can I do for you two gentlemen?" the guard asked.

"This is Jerry Freedman, he has an appointment with Chaim at the Embassy of Israel and I'm Leon Cohen meeting Jerome Stein," Leon replied whilst Jerry watched him hand over some kind of identity card. The security guard ran his finger down what must have been a list fastened to the clipboard he was holding in his left hand and then looked at the ID card, took another glimpse at Leon and gave a nod in the direction of the security hut. One of the police officers walked towards the car with the other still watching intently through the window. The officer stood alongside the security guard, peered inside the vehicle as if examining the back and front and then asked Leon to open the boot and bonnet, which he achieved by pulling two separate levers beside his chair on the floor rather than having to leave the comfort of the driver's seat. Having used a mirror to check the underside of the car, the police officer obviously satisfied, allowed the security guard to return Leon's ID and signalled for the barrier to be raised, allowing Leon to drive through.

The road had the appearance of being well maintained as one would expect for a private road in Kensington, trees lining both sides, almost hiding the large buildings behind them. Having driven about three quarters of the way along the road, Leon parked the car, stopping just short of the yellow 'No Parking' cones placed outside what could only be the Embassy of Israel with the blue and white flag of Israel above the large wooden doorway, blowing proudly in the light breeze.

"Is the security at the entrance to the road just because of Israel's embassy, or are there other high risk buildings here?" Jerry asked Leon.

"Ever since I can remember there has been a barrier. The police arrived after a car bomb destroyed part of the embassy several years ago. Many of the buildings along here are embassies belonging to various countries, there are a few corporate head offices and of course an entrance to Kensington Palace, so I suppose you could say that the road warrants its own security."

They walked up the pathway towards the large blue wooden recessed door from where Jerry could clearly hear the flutter of the flag above him. Leon approached the security window to the right of the door which was at an angle of about forty-five degrees and spoke to the individual on the other side of it. From what Jerry could see and overhear, the person had a Mediterranean appearance and spoke impeccable English, although Jerry had a strong feeling he was not a local boy. However, from the conversation it appeared as if he knew Leon fairly well and Jerry heard his name mentioned several times. After a delay of what seemed like ages, although was probably only a matter of minutes, there was a loud buzz. On hearing the tone Jerry started to push open the front door which turned out to be somewhat heavier than it looked, due entirely to the armoured plating it was constructed from.

They entered a small octagonal shaped entrance hall, which beside the door they had just entered through had only one other exit being a corridor leading deeper into the building. From almost opposite the entrance they had come through, the passageway led from the octagon at a fairly sharp angle to the right. Jerry judged it was probably just wide enough for two people to stand adjacent to each other and peering down it, estimated it was no longer than about fifteen metres. At the far end was what seemed to be a solid wall with a security camera fitted to it just below the ceiling, pointing in the direction of the front door and Jerry assumed it provided an excellent image of everyone entering the corridor. The floor had been constructed from wooden slats and the walls were made from large sheets of glass with a hint of pale blue colouring through them. With no alternative, Jerry followed Leon along the passageway to another security window built into the wall on the right hand side, close to the far end of the corridor and unseen from the entrance due to the clever use of angles. Here, two Israeli security personnel whose English was far from fluent, subjected both Jerry and Leon to separate interrogations, asking the nature of their visit. It was obvious to Jerry that Leon was well known to both officers and yet they were both being treated alike, as if neither were known, nor had been invited, but rather having just walked off the street. Their briefcases were opened and physically searched before being passed through what Jerry assumed to be an x-ray machine, after which they were returned to their respective owner.

Finally Jerry heard a quiet hum from behind him and looking over his shoulder he could see a glass door sliding open, recessing into the wall. As the entrance widened, it exposed another small, square lobby. Jerry followed Leon through the doorway into the vestibule, despite their exit being blocked by yet another door. The opening they had just passed through began to close and when sealed, the door in front of them slowly opened revealing a large lounge.

As they took their first steps into the room, Jerry could not help but notice two more security officers standing opposite each other, both with black earpieces connected to two-way radios hanging from their trouser belts. The officers appeared to be spending much of their time watching the lonely individual sitting on one of the many armchairs in the room. "Take a seat," the security officer nearest Jerry commanded,

"Someone will come down for you shortly."

There was a wooden staircase to the right of the room which led up to an open balcony overlooking the waiting area, with nothing more than a black, mock Tudor wooden handrail to prevent someone from falling over. Leon chose to sit facing the balcony, giving him sight of the 'T' junction it helped form, with a corridor continuing from the top of the stairs, to the left from where Leon had sat and another at ninety degrees to the staircase, opposite where he was sitting. This position gave Leon site of everyone approaching the staircase. Jerry sat in the chair beside him.

"I take it that all the walls here are made from two way glass?" Jerry whispered to Leon.

"And it's all armour plated," Leon replied. "It was given this modern look following the bombing, this part of the building sustaining the majority of the damage."

Moments later an elderly man appeared at the balcony, leaned over the banister and called down to Leon who immediately stood up, informed Jerry he would see him later, then proceeded to make his way up the staircase.

Not long after, the only other person still sitting in the room was collected, leaving Jerry and the two security officers alone. Finally a young woman with well tanned skin walked across the balcony and down the stairs towards him. "You must be Jerry Freedman, please come with me," she requested in what Jerry assumed to be an Israeli accent. He followed her up the staircase, across the balcony, along a corridor where he noticed the flooring had changed from the highly polished wood surface to a well-worn dark blue carpet and the walls looked as though they could do with a fresh coat of paint. As he reached another smaller lounge the girl asked: "Please just wait here a moment," whilst she knocked three times in rapid succession on one of the doors that led off the lounge. Jerry heard a quiet click and the woman opened the door. "Please go through," she beckoned and once inside, the door closed behind him and he again heard the quiet click of the door automatically locking.

Six men were sitting around the table looking as if they were approaching, if not already in their sixties. There were a further two unoccupied seats and Jerry was asked to take one. The man on Jerry's right offered refreshments from a tray sitting in the middle of the table. The room was dimly lit and the air had a stagnant smoke filled atmosphere about it. From the walls hung a number of large paintings, including a set of all the Presidents of Israel, others of various Israeli landmarks, the largest being an oil of the famous Western Wall. The table looked to Jerry as though it was made from solid Oak, but it had certainly seen better days and an Israeli flag attached to a wooden pole was standing in a corner.

"We have been monitoring your activities with interest," the same man started after Jerry accepted a cup of tea. "We know your girlfriend does a lot to help Leon, particularly in using her writing skills, producing papers promoting the community and its issues, many of which have found their way to the very highest levels of government here and in Israel. We would now like to benefit from your knowledge and skills." He spoke slowly and precisely. Jerry couldn't help admiring how the man came straight to the point rather than skirting around it for ages. "I must clarify there is no obligation on your part to assist us, but I would ask you to listen to what we have to say before making your decision. This meeting is not a job interview and what's more, if you do agree to help us, it will be as a volunteer with only valid expenses refunded to you." He stopped talking, providing Jerry with a chance to comment or ask questions, whilst he took the opportunity to moisten his mouth by drinking water from a glass sitting on the table in front of him. "We want you to work with us because you want too, not because we are forcing or financially rewarding you. Your reward will be far greater than any compensation we could ever give you, that being the personal satisfaction of having helped others and accomplished some good for the Jewish community," quickly adding, "Your community," making sure that Jerry understood he and his family were included in it. "I want to ensure you understand what I'm saying to avoid any disagreements on the subject in the future."

Jerry confirmed his understanding very simply; "In a nutshell, you want my time for free."

"My friends' around the table will explain how you could assist us, but please appreciate their English is not as good as mine, so if there is anything you don't understand please stop us," and with that he handed over to the person opposite him.

As he was about to speak Jerry cut in, "Before you start I have a question." The man looked at Jerry as if he was being rude to interject, but Jerry ignored him and continued. "You said you've been watching me for some time. How have you been doing that? Have you placed bugs in my apartment or office, or worse still, miniature cameras? And why?"

The man sitting directly opposite Jerry, probably the oldest present, seemed unfazed by the question. "Although I'm sure you have read and heard many stories about the Mossad in your national media, from books or even films, ninety-nine percent is, should we say inaccurate. Although many of the special devices James Bond and other special agents use do exist, I assure you that placing them in locations where they become useful tools is a lot harder in real life than on screen, resulting in them invariably not being utilised as film makers would have the public believe, so please don't be paranoid," he informed Jerry. "Monitoring was the term used by my colleague, not watching and there is a very big difference. For example, you have to file your company accounts and these accounts are available to everyone, so we can see very easily how you have performed as an organisation. Nothing sinister there I think you would agree?" He waited for an answer.

"I agree with you on that score," Jerry answered. "But the way it was said I felt more than just Igloo's financial status was being referred to."

The same man followed on, "We have a few common friends, Leon for instance being one of them. Has he not recommended your company to a number of organisations that have become clients of yours?" Jerry was asked.

"The way you phrased that question implies you know he has," Jerry replied.

The speaker continued in broken English taking the time to ensure he was using the correct words. "If you recall it was his contact which really got Igloo started in the first place and I can tell you the early success you achieved was no coincidence. We heard about your project and certain people in Israel believed your idea had significant potential in a number of areas which as a nation we could benefit from. A decision was taken to ensure you would succeed in progressing it from an idea into reality, a task requiring financial support. For obvious reasons we could not be seen to be directly involved in backing you and therefore had to find a more creative way to achieve our objective, one that could never be traced back to us." Jerry tried to cast his memory back to when he started working on the project, through his introduction to Rochelle and then their first few clients, whilst he continued to remain silent, listening to these allegations about himself and his company. "We had attempted to recruit you whilst you were developing your idea at university, but unfortunately failed to do so. We believe we were exceptionally lucky to have a second opportunity, something that rarely occurs in our business."

There was a short break in the discussion to allow Jerry time to appreciate what he had heard, the Israelis aware he probably had numerous questions he knew better than to ask. They were also very conscious of the fact it wouldn't take him long to deduce the answers for himself. Jerry was about to say, "So you infiltrated the A&E system and then pointed them in my direction via Leon," but chose to keep quiet.

Seeing his brain working away and in an attempt to stop him delving too deeply into how they could possibly have carried out such an act, the person on Jerry's right decided to continue with the original discussion. "We have been a little rude by not thanking you for taking the time to meet with us today, it is often the Israeli mentality to expect things of people for which I apologise."

"I suppose I don't get to know your names either," Jerry said, a comment really meant as a question rather than a statement.

"My apologies, of course you can," the same person replied. "Let's start with Zvi on your left and moving clockwise we have Samuel, Shimon, Avraham, Yitzhak and I'm Chaim. He continued, "We're in London for a conference on international terrorism, or more accurately, terrorism derived from the Middle East conflict under the banner of religion," Chaim carried on. "We believe, having analysed data from many sources, that it is irrelevant how the Israeli government proceeds in regards to giving land back to the Palestinians or anyone else, it will not stop terrorism either within Israel or international attacks carried out under the same banner." He then went on to explain, "There are people who want all Jews eradicated; they are of a similar mindset to Hitler. We also believe they, like Hitler, won't stop there, they'll change some words replacing Jews with Capitalists and so their crusade will continue. We have unfortunately started to witness such acts including the atrocity of 9/11, the night club attack on the island of Bali, the horrific train bombing in Madrid and of course the explosions in several hotels in the Egyptian Red Sea resort, to mention just a few."

As though it had been rehearsed, Chaim handed over to Yitzhak. Jerry remembered Zvi was about to say something before he had been interrupted and the subject changed, but it would appear the group of six had forgotten. "We have infiltrated a number of terror cells making up part of the international terrorist network both within Israel and in the Palestinian regions. In some cases, organisations have successfully been penetrated above the level of the operational cells and we are receiving more data than ever before, sharing it with our colleagues both here and in the United States," Yitzhak rattled off in his best English. "Because of the volume of information we are now receiving, a number of concerns have arisen, including maintaining the level of flow, keeping it and our gatherers secure and validating its accuracy. Much of what we receive are snippets of conversations that have been overheard, which unfortunately include ego trips and dreams told to impress a listener," Yitzhak finally finished with.

"Many of these groups have the ability to make 9/11 seem like a minor train derailment," continued Avraham in a much slower and calmer manner. "We know that several have access to sophisticated munitions, much of it from the old Soviet Union, but some being supplied from the West, allegedly inadvertently. We also have reason to believe they are now sourcing from communist Asia as well." He paused for a moment or two, making sure Jerry was listening. "Unlike many of the claims referring to the weapons of mass destruction in Iraq, we have no problem in demonstrating the abilities of some of these organisations." As he was speaking he lifted some blank sheets of paper from a bundle sitting on the table, exposing a number of photographs of what Jerry believed to be satellite images of desert regions. In the pictures were several open wooden crates containing what looked like missiles, something quickly confirmed by Avraham. "These missiles have both nuclear and chemical warheads available for them." As Avraham continued to speak, Jerry was handed a further set of photographs taken from the ground. The images in this second set were of badly shelled and dilapidated buildings, but clearly visible inside the flimsy structures were more crates with what Jerry thought to be familiar yellow markings on the outside of them, he just couldn't remember what it inferred. In the photographs, some of the crates were open as if to prove they contained the warheads that Avraham was speaking about.

"These images could be anywhere," Jerry stated, having spent a good few minutes studying them, whilst not wishing to question the experience of any of the men sitting around the table.

Avraham, the apparent specialist in this domain, took it upon himself to respond. "You're right to be sceptical, particularly after the way President Bush had maintained the pressure on the UN inspectors in Iraq with nothing being found. Unfortunately we have lost many informers and agents in obtaining this data and associated intelligence, which alone demonstrates the reliability of the information. Not only have our people taken enormous risks to acquire it, others have gone to great lengths in an attempt to prevent us from receiving it," he slowly explained. "In terms of the content of the photographs, any intelligence officer who specialises in the region will be able to confirm the images are locations in the West Bank and Gaza. We also know that allied forces operating in Afghanistan and Algeria have made similar finds over the last few months or so." He took his handkerchief from a pocket and wiped his forehead, where beads of perspiration had formed and were beginning to run down his face like tears as if he were crying.

Whilst still clutching the handkerchief in his hand, Avraham continued, “Besides the smaller munitions which are only a serious threat to the region, we have identified the existence of a number of inter-continental ballistic missiles placing the West at risk. We recently obtained data leading us to believe a number of individuals are being trained to operate such missiles, following which they will be placed in active terrorist cells. This is a turnaround in the modus operandi of several terror organisations in the fight they call the Jihad, who until now have concentrated their efforts on attacks that have relied on their operatives believing they would become martyrs if they sacrificed their lives for the cause, taking as many innocent victims with them.” He paused to wipe his forehead again. “If our intelligence is correct and the people at the top of such groups start advocating the use of bombs activated remotely, by timing devices, or delivered by missiles, with the ability to deploy them as nuclear or chemical bombs, all of a sudden they have the capability of causing unimaginable carnage and destruction anywhere in the world, with very little the security forces can do to prevent it. Devices could be planted weeks, months, even years before they were to be triggered, bringing life as we know it to a standstill from fear alone. You’re sufficiently intelligent to draw your own conclusions.”

Jerry detected something very morbid in the tone of the last few words Avraham spoke. Not knowing quite why, he responded in a similar fashion. “I can understand why you told me your concerns over the security of passing information, that’s what I deal with every day as you are well aware, although my data is always in electronic format,” he said, then raising his tone slightly, “Why not just come to me like any other customer?” he asked.

Chaim took Jerry’s question as his cue. “We weren’t really thinking about data security, more in terms of helping us to maintain the amount of data we receive. Before you ask, please allow us to explain.” Jerry was even more confused. The afternoon had already been a revelation for him and they still had more surprises to throw his way. “We know your solution has been implemented by the legitimate fronts of at least two terrorist units, since we were behind the introduction of these organisations to you.”

Jerry was intrigued. "Was there no end to their ability to manipulate sales for him?" he wondered to himself. "Which clients are they?" he asked in a concerned way, not sure if he had really understood what had been said and beginning to believe he had made a huge blunder somewhere and was about to feel the repercussions. His brain was running so fast with everything he'd found out over the last hour, added to the language problem, it wouldn't have surprised him if he misinterpreted something important.

Almost before Jerry had finished asking, Zvi, whom until now had remained silent throughout the meeting, content at studying Jerry's reaction, provided the answer, PreTekt and Kasar."

Jerry thought for a minute, "If I recall correctly, they were both introduced to us by Dr Fog."

Zvi, still watching Jerry like a Hawk replied. "That's correct. We were confident you would not question a personal recommendation from Dr Fog who has a very well kept secret which I trust we can rely on you maintaining." Zvi asked Jerry and waited for an acknowledgement before continuing. "Dr Fog was raised in a children's village in Israel called Boys Town Jerusalem. Boys Town is an educational campus that specialises is teaching technology, its students mainly coming from deprived backgrounds."

Somewhat surprised that Dr Fog was involved with the Israelis, Jerry asked, "What was he doing in Israel? I know he's not Jewish."

Zvi, rather annoyed that Jerry had interrupted him again explained, "You don't have to be Jewish to live in Israel, in fact a significant proportion of the population is not Jewish," he said firmly. "But we digress. Unfortunately both Dr Fog's parents perished in the holocaust for assisting Jews and many of those saved by them wanted to return something to the young orphan. A small group arranged for him to be given a place at Boys Town where he excelled. Thankful for being given a start in life and wanting to return something back to the country that had provided him with an opportunity for a future, in addition to having aspirations to continue the job his parents had started and felt so strongly about, to the extent of making the ultimate sacrifice, he approached us. He has been working for Mossad ever since. The companies I mentioned are fronts for large terrorist groups. We believe you may have other clients active in the world of terrorism recommended by those just mentioned, fearful of the Americans listening in on them."

Jerry, still very much on the defensive told the six, "We don't hide our client list from anyone, in fact it's quite the reverse, we actively promote the names of our customers and I'm sure if Leon had asked Rochelle for a list of all our clients she would have happily obliged, or has she already?"

"We haven't requested it although I admit the thought had crossed our minds, but we decided to approach you directly. It maybe hard for you to believe, but we value Rochelle's efforts for Leon and didn't wish to place additional, unnecessary strain on her relationship with you. We heard about the discussion that took place at the Thank You barbecue," Chaim said. "And I wish to make it very clear, Rochelle had no involvement in anything, or was even aware of our activities when she joined forces with you and that still remains the case today. Her mentioning you to Leon was nothing other than chance, she was hoping the club would be her first sale," he said using it as a further example of the monitoring that took place and reassuring him of Rochelle's innocence in all this. The last thing they needed at this stage was friction or mistrust between Jerry and Rochelle.

Jerry, ignoring the comment regarding Rochelle, was now quite confused. "Why make it more difficult for yourselves by encouraging these groups to secure their data? The Igloo system makes it almost impossible for you to eavesdrop, or have you found a way to compromise my technology."

Shimon decided to respond to the question, "We have tried on many occasions to crack your system, but so far we remain unsuccessful. You've developed a good product; my boys have managed to hack into every network they've attempted, other than those that have implemented your solution. We thought we were almost there on the A&E network a few months ago, but that turned out to be unwarranted premature excitement. You actually deserve the success you have achieved, I just sometimes wonder what would have happened if we didn't give you that early kick start." He stared at Jerry whilst complimenting him, Jerry taking the praise in his stride, something Shimon found reassuring, slightly concerned that success may have made Jerry over confident and therefore unsuitable for what they had in mind. "To answer your question, we encouraged them to protect their systems in the hope we would be able to bring you on board. I'll explain why in a minute. You probably think we approached things back to front and you would be correct in thinking so, however, an opportunity presented itself and it was felt it had to be taken. Unfortunately life doesn't always pan out the way one would hope. As was said earlier, since we invariably only get one bite of a cherry in this game, we decided to risk it and grasp the opportunity. If we manage to physically infiltrate their operations and by that I mean an inside man, we would learn a great deal more than we ever could from eavesdropping," he finished in a very positive tone.

"A mole?" Jerry enquired, remembering the spy books he used to read and films he loved watching as a boy.

"Not quite, but along those lines. We were hoping you would be happy to use your relationship with these organisations to obtain information for us," he said very casually. "Dr Fog has been our main contact to date, but he has gone as far as he possibly can without breaking his cover and we now need someone who can really get close to the top people," Samuel replied.

Until now Jerry was unable to identify the role they wanted him to take, but it was all quickly becoming abundantly clear to him. The problem was he certainly didn't believe he was 'mole' material. Desperately trying to conjure up words that were locked away in his innermost memory from his childhood, he laughed, "And you're expecting me to play the part of the spook, I'm no '007'. I wouldn't know where to start."

In a more upbeat tone and pleased Jerry had finally understood them, Samuel replied, "The success of your business is down to espionage, whether you call it that or not, you are living in that world every day, you've even admitted it. The only difference is you currently supply solutions to protect against infiltrators. To be able to do that successfully you had to become one yourself, so you have and possibly still are on the other side, admittedly for educational purposes, or so you have always maintained, however facts are facts. All we are asking is that you swap electronic circuits and code for ears and mouth."

Jerry was annoyed at the insinuation but chose to ignore it for the time being, focussing entirely on Samuel's reasoning. "Not quite the same is it?" he replied.

"Oh, I think it is when you look at the overall picture, but don't worry, we'll train you so that you have all the tools and skills required to carry out the task and at the same time teach you how to look after yourself should things ever not go quite as planned," Shimon assured him.

Once again Jerry was upset. From nowhere they were now talking about things going wrong. "If it was simply a matter of swapping electronic circuits and code for ears and mouth, what could possibly go wrong that needed special training?" he asked himself. Before anyone could say another word, he shouted, "Stop right there! Firstly, so far I've agreed to absolutely nothing, so don't start running away with yourselves," he told them. "And even if I had, what do you mean by 'to protect myself in case things don't go quite right?'" slightly quietening his voice as the sentence progressed.

Looking around the room Zvi nodded to the others signalling he would respond. "We haven't assumed you said yes to anything and my apologies if it sounded that way, something I'm sure is merely due to our poor use of English. What we were trying to tell you is we have your safety paramount in our minds and it would be grossly unfair of us to put you in a position which, compared to your daily job, has a significantly higher risk of danger attached to it, without us mentioning the fact whatsoever. However, let's keep things in proportion, statistics show there is a far greater chance of being killed on the roads." He spoke in a very matter of fact manner. "Everyone in this room has been there and yes, some of us have exciting stories to tell our grandchildren. But we are all sitting here because we knew how to avoid or extricate ourselves from difficult situations." Zvi was trying desperately hard to get things back on track. "We want you to help us and it's our responsibility to make sure you have all the tools you could possibly need. There is nothing to worry about as we keep repeating, this job is not like the movies portray and it's very boring." He stopped talking and refilled his glass with water hoping to get some sort of response, but Jerry remained silent. "Should we move forward together, we would want to train you in Israel where you would stay as a guest of our government," he finally said.

There was still no response from Jerry. "As I stated at the beginning, Jerry," Chaim repeated, "We would obviously like you to help us, but it's your choice."

"How long do I have to consider?" Jerry enquired.

"Do you really need time to mull over things?" asked Avraham looking quite surprised.

Jerry, thinking about the repercussions and having quickly visualised himself as James Bond in several life threatening predicaments finally replied, "What if it goes wrong, I screw up? I could be putting Rochelle's life at risk and who knows, maybe a family at some stage."

"You won't screw up as you say, and we, with our British and American friends will be with you all the way. No one can predict what will happen which is why it's our responsibility to teach you the skills you need and how to look after yourself. We aren't talking about petty theft here, we're looking at the safety of each and every Jew and Gentile in whatever country they choose to live," Shimon replied, trying to reassure and convince Jerry.

"You'll teach me everything I need to know?" Jerry attempted to confirm.

"By the very best in the world," Samuel quickly replied.

"I need time to think it through. You surely can't expect me to give you an answer to such a big decision without having time to consider it properly. I also have a business to take into account, not forgetting a life," Jerry stated firmly and out of the blue a question came to mind, "And how long would this training take?"

"I'd imagine you would probably be away for around three months," Chaim answered. Keen to try and get things moving he asked,

"When do you think you would be in a position to give us an answer?"

"I don't know, I just told you that I need to give it some serious thought," Jerry repeated, annoyed that they kept pushing, expecting him to drop everything there and then. "If I have to give you an answer now, it certainly won't be the answer you want to hear. I'm sure I'll have a million questions to ask, how do I reach you?"

Chaim handed Jerry a business card. "You can get me anytime on the bottom number," he said, "And please, not a word about our discussion to anyone."

"You'll hear from me next week some time," Jerry said as he took the card and stood up, hearing the click from the door as it was being remotely unlocked whilst Chaim walked towards it. "I'll see you out, Leon should be waiting for you in the lounge," he finished, adding, "And thank you for your time."

Nineteen

The journey back to Jerry's office was made in silence, Leon dropping him off then immediately continuing on his way.

As Jerry made his way to his office he passed Rochelle who gave him a look as if to say, "Well, what was it all about?" Without stopping, Jerry simply said "We'll talk about it later," and continued to his room where he closed the door, something he rarely did.

Jerry spent the remainder of the afternoon replying to his emails and then using the web, researched as far as he could, the Mossad, Shin Bet, the Arab-Israel conflict and international terrorism. After everyone else had left, Rochelle walked into his office.

As she stood in front of his desk in a similar fashion to a naughty child when summonsed to the head teacher, she waited for Jerry to talk which didn't take long. "They told me I mustn't speak a word about what was discussed to anyone, but as far as I'm concerned you're not just anyone and we promised each other a while back there would be no more secrets between us. Besides which, I can't do this without you and you're partially involved in their game in any case. But please if asked, you know nothing and whatever you do, don't mention to anyone that we've discussed anything, particularly Leon. I know you can keep a secret far better than I can and I need to talk this thing through with someone,' he finally said as if getting it off his chest. He had already spent a while contemplating the comment regarding Rochelle's involvement.

Rochelle, not knowing quite how to respond, "You know I'll keep it between us, but if you don't want to tell me then I quite understand."

"They want me to be a spy," he blurted out, not being able to restrain himself any longer. "Have you ever heard anything quite so ridiculous?" he said, but Rochelle just continued to stand there listening. "It was the Israelis who attacked the A&E system to help us win our first contract. I'm sure that's why there was no follow through on that address of the perpetrator I gave Leon if you remember?" Rochelle didn't answer and Jerry wasn't sure how to approach the next question. He loved Rochelle. "It was their way of financing us. Did you know about it? Please answer honestly; at the very least I deserve the truth."

Rochelle looked genuinely stunned by Jerry's remark. "Jez, I promise you I had no idea and I don't believe Leon did either, the way he acted at the time. I can believe he told them about you, but that's as far as he would have been involved, I'm sure about that. I could swear to it. I thought he would be our first punter, not A&E or the Milky Way."

Jerry laughed for a moment. "They also said you had no knowledge of anything and I believe it. You're probably right about Leon as well, he wasn't involved at the beginning, he was also probably unknowingly used like we've been just pawns in their game. I'm not sure how much he told them unwittingly though. But the main culprit was Dr Fog. He's been working for Mossad for many years. He once asked me to join his team which must have been on their behalf."

"How did he get involved with the Israelis?" Rochelle asked.

"It's a long story, but his parents were killed helping Jews during the war. I was told that some of our clients he introduced are fronts for terror groups. Your friends have been playing with us since the beginning and now they think its pay back time."

"I'm sorry, I had no idea," she said reassuringly whilst making her way around to him and pushing his chair a little way back from his desk, she perched on his lap, placing her arms around his neck.

"I'm not implying you did. If you say you didn't, I promise I believe you. I've already said that," Jerry told her again, reassuringly.

"So what exactly is it they want from you?" she asked lovingly.

"They didn't go into detail, but the essence of it is that they want me to infiltrate terrorist groups via some of our clients. Before that, they will teach me to become a spy and train me to look after myself, using their own words," Jerry replied, feeling somewhat calmer now he was discussing it with Rochelle.

"What do they mean by looking after yourself?" she asked.

"That's precisely what I asked. Apparently things can occasionally get a little out of hand and possibly verge on the dangerous side, so they'll teach me how to take care of myself, which I imagine is learning how to fight. All the training will take place in Israel as a guest of the government, whatever that means other than I won't need to pay for it. They said it would last about three months, but again we didn't go into any detail. That's all I know," Jerry said, beginning to feel excited at the prospect of playing out his childhood dream.

"And what was your response to them?" Rochelle enquired.

"I told them there was no problem and to book me on the next flight over," he said, the excitement draining away as quickly as it came, being replaced by anger at such a ludicrous question. "What do you think I said?" he asked her in an irritable tone.

"I don't know, that's why I asked, I wasn't trying to wind you up," Rochelle answered, realising that she had upset him.

"I told them I had to think about it, I had a business and girlfriend to consider and maybe at sometime in the future a family. They were somewhat put out by my request for time to consider the offer, expecting me to say yes there and then," Jerry stated. "I informed them I'd get back to them next week, probably with loads of questions," he added.

"And what do you want to do?" she asked.

"I'm actually not sure. At first I thought the whole thing was a joke, I even checked to make sure it wasn't the first of April, with Leon doing an April Fools thing on me. Then on the way back I started to think it through properly and maybe it might be a lot of fun. You know how much I love James Bond and other spy films and enjoy reading espionage books, look how many Tom Clancy's you've bought me recently. When I was a kid I used to wonder what being a spy would be like and I must admit curiosity got the better of me when the government announced the doubling in size of MI5. I was one of the many thousands that checked out the criteria on their web site. But I have to consider the business and of course you," he said thoughtfully.

Rochelle gave him a kiss on the cheek. "As far as I'm concerned, if you want to go you have my full support. After all it's for the good of the community. I can also assure you the business will survive in your absence, there is a good management team in place and your technical people would love you out of the way for a while, that I know," Rochelle told him, trying to make him smile. "And most important, I'll be here waiting for you."

"Thanks for the vote of confidence," he said, this time kissing her. "It feels great to know how much I'm wanted here, but it doesn't end when I return from three months training, that's just the beginning. Who knows what they'll ask me to do afterwards and I'm also concerned that you could be put at risk which is totally unacceptable."

"If you want to play out your childhood fantasy then do so, I'll be with you all the way. But I'll back you just as much if you decide you don't want to get involved. Did you discuss it with Leon on your way back?" Rochelle asked.

"No, on the way up he told me he had no idea what they were going to discuss and he didn't say a word on the way back. Since I was warned not to say anything, I kept quiet," Jerry answered.

"What did he say during the meeting?" Rochelle enquired.

"He wasn't in it, it was six Israeli pensioners, or so they looked to me. Leon thought there were only going to be four of them, so he really has been kept in the dark," he said.

"It's your choice," Rochelle repeated affectionately. "If you want to discuss it with me again then just say the word, if you don't, I'm just as happy. Do as your heart desires, but don't make your decision based on the business or me, it's what you want to do," she said as her last comment on the subject. "I'm off now, see you at home, what do you want for dinner?"

"I'll collect Chinese if you fancy it," he said.

"I fancy you, but Chinese will be fine to eat," she replied smiling.

First thing the following Monday Jerry dialled the number on the business card. "Chaim?" he asked as the call was answered.

"Yes, this is Chaim," was the reply from the other side.

"Jerry here," he said. "I have considered our discussion and decided you can count me in, but you need to give me time to sort things out, business and personal. I assume I can't tell anyone what I'm doing."

"Survival in this business is based upon one word alone, that word being compartmentation which operationally translates to mean the need to know basis. The less people who know, the less they can mention inadvertently, or have extracted by force and the more secure your cover remains," he said. "Let's meet up and discuss everything, but a trip of this length does need planning and is not something that can be keep quiet until the last minute."

"What do I tell people around me? Questions are bound to be asked. People at work, family, friends, they'll wonder why I'm going off for three months and without Rochelle," Jerry asked.

Chaim replied, "Let's say we leave the details until we meet, when we will create a complete cover story for you, but start to give it some thought," he suggested. "Depending on the length of your stay with us, which I should be able to confirm more accurately when we get together, maybe we can arrange a holiday or two for Rochelle which will help with your cover. With regards to others, think of something along the lines of travelling around, say Europe, for work and maybe even a break. I understand you've been under immense pressure recently and you haven't taken a holiday since you started university." There was some interference on the line and Chaim waited until it had cleared before continuing. "I'll call you shortly to arrange a meeting, but regarding dates, please let me know when you'll be ready and I'll make the necessary arrangements. You must give me about a month's notice so I can organise our side, as was said last week, we'll have the very best people to teach you and as I'm sure you'll appreciate it takes time to arrange such things. Having said that, the sooner the better," he stated.

"I'd say it'll take me about three months to prepare my side, I want to make sure the business is organised properly, but I'll keep you updated," Jerry replied.

They said their goodbyes and Jerry hung up.

Twenty

As they reached the tunnel to the entrance to London's Heathrow airport, the driver called to Jerry sitting in the back of the cab, "Terminal One, correct?"

"That's the one," Jerry answered.

When the taxi reached the departure building, the driver removed Jerry's case and bags from the boot, handing them to him.

"It's on the account, yes?" the driver asked, referring to the credit account Igloo had with the cab company since they used cabs frequently and the account saved the hassle of paying the driver at the end of each journey. "Please sign here," the driver requested, handing Jerry a docket and pen.

Jerry made his way to the far end of the terminal building where EL AL had their own sectioned off check-in area. As he approached the enclosure he counted a number of uniformed police officers carrying automatic weapons, both on the check-in floor itself and above him on a balcony overlooking it, vigilantly watching the hustle and bustle of the area, in particular that around the EL AL desks and the substantial queue of passengers quickly forming. He also identified a number of what he thought were Israeli security personnel milling around the area.

Jerry had been issued with a first class ticket which besides the usual benefits of first class travel also provided him with a fast track route through the security checks. He went straight to the allocated desk leaving the stream of passengers waiting patiently to go through the security controls that always precede an EL AL flight. He watched his luggage as it passed through an x-ray machine, a standard feature for travellers using Israel's national airline as far back as Jerry could remember, following which he endured a thorough interrogation from the security officers.

"Why was he going to Israel?" He had already sorted out a cover story with Chaim. "Who had packed his case? Had anyone given him a package to take out? Had he any relatives in Israel? How long was he staying in Israel? Where was he staying?" The questions were endless, but Jerry had rehearsed sufficiently to be able to breeze through them. Eventually being handed his boarding pass, he was allowed to proceed through emigration to airside where he was directed to a comfortable first class passenger lounge.

Looking at his watch the time was 8am and Jerry figured Rochelle would already be at her desk in the office. Until he returned she was responsible for making all the decisions. He dialled her direct number from his mobile.

"Hi, darling," she answered, seeing his number on her telephone display.

"Sleep well?" he asked.

"Not really, I was lonely and already missing you," Rochelle replied, trying to hold back the tears.

"I'm missing you too," Jerry told her. After a short pause and not having given much thought to it, he decided to ask, "When I get back, how would you fancy organising a wedding?" thinking it seemed the right thing to say at the time.

"Whose?" she enquired, playing along with Jerry, but he chose not to reply.

"I've been into all the gadget shops several times already and I'm bored. What do you suggest I do for the next couple of hours before boarding? You know how much I enjoy waiting around with nothing to do," he said sarcastically, expecting some inspiration from her.

As Jerry had anticipated, Rochelle came up with an idea to keep him occupied. "Think of me," she suggested. "Do multiple re-runs of the other night in your mind, that should keep you more than occupied until you take off," she said. Jerry couldn't help smiling to himself and imagined the look on Rochelle's face. "Better go now, I have plenty of work to do," she said and trying to add some humour to the atmosphere: "The boss has gone off on some trip or other; he won't tell me when he's coming back and has left me in charge to run the place. Call me before you board, darling!"

"I will, not sure how many times though. I really wish you had stayed last night," he told her in a tone that assured her he really meant it.

"So do I. I love you. Don't forget to call me later!" And she hung up.

Twenty-One

The plane landed at Ben Gurion airport following a very smooth flight and the passengers made their way to the white buses waiting on the tarmac at the bottom of the boarding stairs. As each became full, it made the three-minute journey from the aircraft to the terminal building where the passengers joined the ever-growing queues for the immigration booths, mixing with passengers from a number of other flights that had recently landed. Jerry was fortunate; travelling first class he was one of the first off the plane and shuttled to the terminal building before the majority of other passengers from his flight had disembarked. As he entered the busy building, two young Israeli girls, dressed alike in tight jeans and white blouses, both with their hair tied back and carrying similar black handbags approached him.

"Jerry Freedman?" one of them asked, hoping they had the correct person.

"Yes, that's me," he replied.

"Please come with us," the same girl requested. Neither of the girls were wearing any form of identification that he could see, unlike every other worker in the airport and could easily have been tourists looking for a good time, except they knew his name.

As they came closer, Jerry could see they were probably somewhat older than he originally thought. "Excuse me, but who are you?" he asked, rather than just following them, having not been told of any rendezvous before he reached the main arrivals collection area.

Almost in unison both girls removed identical small leather wallets from their bags, opening them to display photo identity cards. Before Jerry had a chance to absorb their content, the cards had been safely returned to their appropriate bags. Believing they were sent to collect him as they said, Jerry decided to do as they asked and followed them, ending up at a closed passport control booth. One of the girls took a key from her pocket and proceeded to unlock and open the door at the back of the booth. She stepped inside and as the light illuminated the interior she asked in English, "Please, your passport and the immigration form you completed on the plane," holding out her hand to take them from him. Jerry handed them both to her through the gap in the protective glass. He heard more than watched her flicking through the pages of his passport as every immigration officer does whenever one enters a country, followed by the tapping of keys on a keyboard and the thump thump of the rubber stamp being used, his attention focused on the disturbance behind him. Within seconds of the booth being opened, a long queue had built up behind him and the second girl was desperately trying to direct passengers away, informing them the immigration point was about to be closed.

Once the necessary formalities had been completed, he was given back his passport and bottom half of the immigration form enclosed within it. "You'll need the remaining part of the form to escape," she said grinning as though she knew precisely what he was about to endure. Having finished, she stepped out of the booth, switched off the light and locked the door. The other girl gave up on the queue jumpers and returned to where Jerry was waiting. "Let's go," they said together and the three of them made their way to the baggage reclaim area.

"Your luggage should be one of the first through with the other first class passengers," Jerry was told and within minutes the conveyor belt sprang to life with a loud jerking noise, the second case venturing out to do its parade of honour being his. When it came close to where he was standing, Jerry bent forward and lugged it off the mechanical monster.

They then went through customs where the officials paid no attention to them, not that Jerry thought it would make any difference even if they had, having witnessed the immigration booth being opened specifically for him. The three made their way through the arrivals hall and out of the building into the early evening humid air, to a car waiting for them outside the main entrance despite notices to the contrary. "You'll be staying at the Sheraton Hotel in Tel Aviv for a few days to relax and acclimatise with the odd meeting thrown in," the girl that carried out the passport formalities informed him as the Mercedes started to move off. "I'm sorry, we haven't introduced ourselves, I'm Sara and my colleague is Debra," she said as an after thought, pointing to Debra sitting in the front beside the driver. "We work for the Office of the Prime Minister and have, with colleagues, been assigned to look after and supervise your stay. There will be a member of the team on hand at all times, twenty-four hours a day. Anything you need we'll organise for you, well within reason," she hastily added with a bright smile. "Since all the trainers involved in your course are operational personnel in their field of expertise, part of our role is to manage their availability with us. We'll explain in more detail later, once you've settled in." Jerry noticed she spoke almost perfect English.

"I just need to call home and tell them I've arrived safely," Jerry told her, removing his mobile phone from a zipped inside pocket of his sports jacket. Before he had a chance to switch it on, Sara offered him the use of a phone, one that she had been holding for a while, although Jerry hadn't noticed for how long.

"It's okay, I'll use my own," he said, "Besides, it has all the numbers in it and I would never be able to remember them."

Sara stopped him, politely giving him a set of rules stating they were for his personal safety. "You don't use your phone or credit cards. If you brought travellers cheques with you, then please don't use them either. All your valuables can be locked away for safe keeping including your passport and I certainly recommend you to do so since we'll be moving around quite a lot. I'll be happy to organise it for you when we get to the hotel. If you need cash for anything we'll provide it. No matter what you need from the shops, please just let us know and it'll be procured on your behalf. I don't want you to use anything that could identify your whereabouts whilst you are here. When you want to make telephone calls we'll lend you a mobile phone. Unfortunately we can't give you one to keep for the duration since we want to continually change the number you'll be calling from." Jerry listened, thinking the girl was suffering from a bad attack of paranoia and her recommendations were somewhat over the top, although he knew he had no choice but to let her finish and to go along with her suggestions. "A credit card transaction records the place, date and time of use and when a travellers cheque is cashed the date and place of encashment is recorded whilst a mobile phone call can be traced back to the cell from which it originates. So let's start as we mean to carry on, please use this phone."

Jerry realised Sara was prepared for this discussion, the reason she was holding the phone. Reluctantly he took the mobile and called Rochelle in the office. "Hi, it's me. I've arrived safely," he told her as soon as the call had been answered. He felt awkward using someone else's phone, particularly for a personal, international call. What made matters worse was despite his relationship with Rochelle, Jerry was still very shy and he now had to speak to his girlfriend with two other young women within earshot. How could he possibly tell Rochelle he was missing her, or how much he loved her? He continued his conversation, "The flight was okay, just very boring as you can probably imagine, about five and a half hours and they are two hours ahead here so it feels like I've been travelling all day." Without giving Rochelle an opportunity to say hello he just continued, "In the few minutes since arriving I've already been reprimanded for nearly breaking the rules. By the way, don't bother to call me since they're confiscating my phone so I'll call you as often as possible. Anyway, how's it going there?"

Rochelle replied in her most upbeat tone, "Usual stuff, nothing of any consequence, but it seems so weird not having you around, suddenly becoming even more so now you've told me you're not at the end of a phone whenever I want you. I had planned to call every night when snuggled up in bed cuddling my teddy pretending it to be you, it'll have to be a dumb teddy from now on," she said trying to make a joke to hide her disappointment. "Please call me as often as you can and darling, don't forget about me, I love you so much."

Jerry looked at Sara and Debra hoping they weren't listening to the conversation before whispering, "How could I possibly forget you, I've an image of you etched onto my heart and remember, you're partially responsible for me being here." He paused for a reply which never came and he reverted back to speaking normally. "Could you please let my parents know that we've spoken and I've arrived safely? I think I told them I was going to be in France for the first couple of weeks, down south near Nice. You have a copy of my itinerary so check before saying anything."

"Don't worry; I'll deal with it. Is there anything else you want me to do?" She asked, but Jerry didn't answer, knowing Rochelle was close to tears. "Please darling, take good care of yourself and don't do anything silly. Call me later if you can, bye for now," she said with a sniffle building up, quickly disconnecting the call before it turned into a stream of tears.

Handing the phone back, Jerry also gave Sara his passport, credit cards, traveller's cheques, his ticket for the return flight and the small amount of Sterling he had brought with him. He spent the best part of the next thirty minutes taking a note of his phone numbers, writing them on a sheet of paper Debra gave him for the purpose. Completing the task, he handed his phone to Sara. "That's everything for safekeeping as you suggested," he told her in a sarcastic tone whilst folding up the paper and sticking it in his pocket. He couldn't resist adding the comment, "Are you really sure this isn't somewhat of an overkill? I can't keep using your phone and have you buying everything I want, how do you think it makes me feel? I'm not a charity case."

"I appreciate your feelings but please humour us on this matter. In time I'm sure you'll understand why we're taking these precautions, until then I ask you to keep an open mind," Sara replied in a very calm tone. "I assure you we're not trying to cause you any embarrassment, so please don't take it that way. Use the phone and anything else as much as you like, think of it as being yours which it is other than the logistics of everything," Sara continued, hoping she was getting through to him. It wasn't the start she was hoping for; most people would have jumped at the chance of living for free for a few weeks. "If it makes you feel better, I'm sure we can organise repayment at some point when you are back home," she finally said having thought about it, although she knew it would never happen, certainly not in monetary terms.

Arriving at the hotel, the porter took Jerry's luggage as the two girls with Jerry followed him, the driver staying with the car. The group passed through the hotel foyer and made their way to the second floor, suite 207. "What, no registration?" Jerry commented as they approached the room.

"We've already taken care of it, don't worry," Sara replied. The porter knocked on the door and after a couple of moments it was opened from inside.

"Meet Moshe, another member of our team," Sara said. "Although I'm sure you were hoping we would all be girls," she laughed.

Jerry was quite relieved there was at least one male on the team but thought it would be good etiquette to laugh with Sara, particularly as he had already stepped out of line with his comment in the car. "Well, if I'm staying in places like this for the duration of my trip I can't complain," he said approvingly, taking a quick look around the room.

"Freshen up and sort yourself out, Moshe will stay with you. Let's all meet up for dinner downstairs in say an hour," Sara suggested.

"That's fine with me," Jerry replied after looking at his watch, it already being 7.40pm. He unpacked, showered and dressed in fresh clothes. He learnt from Moshe that Sara was their team leader and as he had been told by her, they worked for the Office of the Prime Minister explaining the department was basically responsible for special security duties including national security and special operations. He told Jerry that Sara would talk through the details of his visit over dinner.

Twenty-Two

The dining room was full when Jerry and Moshe walked in. To be allowed to be seated at a table Moshe had to confirm they had a booking. On giving the name, the manager looked down a list detailing the day's reservations. On finding the reservation they were shown to a table for four where Sara and Debra were already seated. Judging by the number of empty glasses, the two girls had been waiting quite some time. Having carefully perused the menu, they each placed their order with the maitre d' following which Debra, speaking in a quiet voice, confirmed that Jerry's valuables had been locked away securely and re-confirmed that whatever he needed was just a request away. After a few minutes of exchanging niceties, Sara got down to discussing business. She started to list the key subjects which were to make up the core of his course, reiterating all the tutors were active in their various fields of expertise. "For this reason we can't give you a confirmed timetable since despite booking the specialists, their priority must remain the security of the nation and the very nature of their jobs means they occasionally get last minute calls forcing them to cancel anything they may have previously arranged." She then stated that one of her responsibilities was to ensure nothing slipped through the net for whatever reason and she would therefore juggle sessions around when the need arose. "At the end of each week we will issue a schedule for what we hope will cover the following week, giving you the best possible idea of what you will be covering," she added.

"Here in Israel our working week starts on a Sunday, the equivalent of your Monday, but Friday is a half day finishing at lunchtime, the afternoon and all day Saturday is free time for you because of the Jewish Sabbath," Debra informed him.

Beginning to review the subjects that would be covered, Jerry enquired on several occasions why particular activities were being included, believing them to be irrelevant in his case. Sara went to great lengths to explain the course had been based on a core curriculum used many times before and from that, particular elements were then added or removed depending on the region in which the agent would operate and to a lesser extent, on the type of operations anticipated. "Your programme has been compiled by very senior people following consultation with some of our best field agents to ensure you are taught everything you may require," she stated. "Although you may not appreciate the reason for certain classes at this stage, there is a rationale for each subject to be included," she insisted, adding, "It's obligatory for every would-be field agent to be taught the art of self-defence as a prerequisite for working for us." Becoming annoyed by Jerry's on-going argument, Sara wanted to make things perfectly clear, albeit in a friendly manner. "With respect, it's not for you to question the content since you have no experience in this area which is precisely why you are here."

Feeling the tension quickly rising, Debra attempted to change the topic of conversation. "You'll be expected to work long hours every day, starting early in the morning, with lectures often continuing well into the night. Additionally you maybe given homework which you will be expected to complete after that." Jerry assured everyone that he was not afraid of hard work, reciting for them a few typical days when he was developing the Igloo project from the time at university until fairly recently. Debra could see he enjoyed talking about Igloo; his attitude suddenly becoming more relaxed again, putting an end to the previous argument.

Also having calmed down, Sara continued to detail the arrangements for the remainder of the week. "Tomorrow is completely free and you could play being a tourist for the day in and around Tel Aviv with Debra as your guide." Before getting an answer she continued with the schedule. "I apologise for a statement I made earlier, on the way here when I said we would be staying in this hotel for a few days. Unfortunately the meetings planned will now have to take place in Jerusalem so we will be driving down there on Friday morning in preparation for Sunday."

Debra cut in, "Can I suggest I show you the sights of Tel Aviv tomorrow and then on Friday afternoon I don't mind doing the same in Jerusalem. If we stay at a hotel near the Wall we can go there on Saturday morning, something I always think is an experience not to be missed." Jerry knew Debra was referring to the Western Wall, the only surviving remnant of the Holy Temple and the most holy place in the world where a Jew could pray. There were always numerous Sabbath morning services taking place with different Rabbis.

Sara continued to provide Jerry with useful information on the way the course would run. "Some subjects will be taught on a one to one basis, for others you will be put into small groups, mostly with IDF recruits." The IDF, she explained was Israel's Defence Force. She warned him, "Whilst mixing with other people, you must always stick to the cover story we have created for you," and she handed over to Debra to take him through it, a task repeated several times followed by a further ten minutes of testing. Wishing to move onto other issues, Sara concluded the subject by suggesting they continue to practice over the coming days since he had to be completely fluent with it by Sunday. Sara's final words on the course itself for the evening were: "We are attempting to cram a great deal into a very short period of time to enable you to return home as quickly as possible. It is also designed to put you under immense pressure to see if your reactions change under tough conditions."

Apart from the few questions Moshe asked Jerry while testing his cover story, he had remained silent until Sara had finished. "There will always be a team member on hand if you encounter any problems or issues," he said, handing Jerry a piece of paper with two emergency contact numbers written on it. "Please memorise these rather than carrying around the paper," he requested and then went onto suggest: "It's probably a good idea to give them to Rochelle in case of an emergency, they'll make her life far easier than enduring the ordeal of attempting to use the embassy communication network, something I wouldn't wish on my worst enemy," a comment Jerry found far from reassuring. "We have no issues with you keeping in touch with her, but would prefer for you to call her rather than the other way around, for which we will provide a phone. She should only use these numbers in an emergency." He repeated.

"Everything you will learn, although you may not believe it now, is for your long-term benefit and is included as a direct result of many years experience and at a cost of several lives," Sara summarised.

"You must be exhausted," Debra observed, "So to finish this evening on a pleasing note, I'm sure you'll be thrilled to know we have included a number of free days where we would be happy to show you some of the sites of Israel. We are also hoping to organise a long weekend in Eilat, our Southern Red Sea resort, for you and Rochelle, probably sometime around the mid point of your stay." With everyone finished, they left the dining room and Jerry headed for his bed.

Before falling asleep, Jerry called Rochelle, having been given Sara's phone, passing on the emergency contact numbers and checking that no problems had transpired in the office and she was alright. Content in having spoken to her, he closed his eyes.

At 6am on Jerry's first Sunday, the telephone beside his bed rang, waking him abruptly. "Breakfast in the hotel restaurant in forty five minutes please," the energetic female voice on the other end of the line commanded. Jerry quickly showered and dressed in jeans and a T-shirt and made his way down to the restaurant. Although a lover of meat, always having enjoyed an English breakfast whenever the opportunity arose, over the last couple of days he had started to enjoy the typical Israeli breakfast, an infinite banquet of dairy products. As he made his way around the buffet, he spotted Sara and Moshe sitting at a table for four in the far corner, furthest away from the majority of guests enjoying what he considered an early start to the day. He completed his acquisitions and made his way towards them.

"Good morning, Jerry," Sara said.

Jerry returned the greeting whilst placing his tray on the table. He felt quite refreshed, having enjoyed the last couple of days sightseeing in Tel Aviv and Jerusalem. Sara waited for him to start eating before saying: "When you've finished breakfast we'll take a short drive to meet some of your instructors. You'll then need to prepare for a long drive north after lunch, as we're going to what will be your home for the next few weeks. Starting tomorrow you need to be in the gym by six-fifteen for an hour of physical training. The first week, until Friday, you'll be eased into the regime, training with new army recruits. As time progresses, you'll move to tougher groups. Your overall physical training is under the responsibility of Dani." As she mentioned the name, a tall, wide, bald headed, hard looking man appeared at the table. He was wearing a dark blue tracksuit and carried a face which looked as though it had been through a mangle on more than one occasion. "Jerry, meet Dani," Sara said. They shook hands and Dani sat himself at the table.

Dani turned to Jerry. "I'll teach you everything I know so should you ever meet someone in a dark alley that resembles me in any way, you won't be afraid," he smiled. "And if you are worried about my handsome features, you should have seen the condition of my opponents once I had finally finished with them."

Sara butted in: "Dani instructs many groups in hand-to-hand close contact fighting, including our elite forces. He has seen action on many occasions and is single handily responsible for, shall we say, giving a number of terrorists a very good hiding."

"We will learn the art of Krav Maga," Dani carried on. "Roughly translated into English it means street fighting. You will learn to be aggressive, but also how to control and manage your aggression. I'll teach you to use cold weapons such as knives and sticks, poles, chains, anything like that, using them to your best advantage in addition to learning how to counter them without any weapons other than your body and anything you can find around you to use." He patted Jerry firmly on his shoulder. "You'll find out that a fight should only last a matter of seconds. We're not interested in long drawn out brawls as in a ring where points are awarded by the judges. It's also important to understand when you have defeated an enemy," he continued, staring at Jerry. "You must remember to never under estimate your opponent, even when they're down they remain a threat until their last breath has been drawn. It's at that point you can relax a little in the knowledge the fight is over and you're the victor." Dani noticed Jerry failed to react, something he found unusual. Most students at least managed a gasp when he indirectly instructs them to kill. Dani promised, "I'll turn you into a lean, mean fighting machine, you have my word." He then smiled, helping to make him look even scarier. "You'll start tomorrow although unfortunately I won't be around for a few days, but the instructors have been fully briefed. I'm sure you and your body will enjoy the exercise. Shalom," Jerry remembered that this meant goodbye and on that note, Dani stood up and walked out, taking a bread roll from Jerry's plate with him.

Moshe advised Jerry, "From tomorrow I suggest you eat breakfast after gym. Whenever we're in a rush to go somewhere I'll take something for you to eat in the car."

Looking at her watch, Sara said, "It's time to make our way to Police Headquarters." Together with Moshe she stood up, Jerry lagging moments behind, scrambling to finish as much of his breakfast as possible.

At the headquarters building, the three of them were shown to a sparsely furnished room with four hard plastic chairs positioned neatly around a square wooden table. Paint was flaking off the walls onto the tiled floor which probably helped to keep it cool from the heat of the summer. After about five minutes, a police officer dressed in civilian clothes entered the room, slamming the door shut behind him as if annoyed by something. He joined the others, sitting in the unoccupied chair beside Jerry. As he did so, he spoke in Hebrew to Sara and Moshe for a couple of minutes. The conversation seemed to be very much one sided and as he spoke, Jerry could see disappointment in Sara's expression. The officer, moving his chair to a position where he was facing Jerry started: "Jerry, my apologies for speaking in Hebrew to your friends here. It's just much easier for me, but I will repeat for your benefit what I have told them. It is good to meet you, I have already heard a great deal about you, all very positive I hasten to add and I'm pleased to have been given the opportunity to spend time teaching you over the coming weeks," he said smiling, although Jerry could see he wasn't really the gentle friendly type. "I don't wish to cause you any worry, so please relax a little. The techniques I hope you learn from me and my colleagues, I pray you'll never need to use," he said. "But the knowledge and experience we'll attempt to pass onto you should be treated as if it were an insurance policy." He paused to ensure Jerry understood his broken English. "You hope to never make a claim on it, but it's there just in case you need it." He smiled again. "My speciality is interrogation. It's my job to get people to talk and I use a number of techniques to achieve this. What I am going to teach you is how to conduct yourself when undergoing an interrogation, should you ever find yourself in the unfortunate position of having to contend with a counterpart of mine." He stopped and again spoke to Sara and Moshe in Hebrew.

Returning to English and focussing his attention back on Jerry he carried on, "Just before I stepped in here this morning, I was informed that the colleagues I had hoped to introduce you to have unfortunately been called away on urgent business. They have asked me to relay to you that they also look forward to working with you. We had hoped to spend the morning going through the key areas which we are going to cover as a team, but it will now have to remain a surprise," he said, trying to be humorous, something which didn't suit him at all. "You have my assurance; we will all work closely together in the hope that by learning the various skills in a combined manner you become far more proficient across all our disciplines. I understand we start properly later this week." He spoke a few more words in Hebrew, said "Shalom" to Jerry, and then the three Israelis stood up and prepared to leave, quickly followed by Jerry.

Following the meeting, Sara took Jerry and Moshe to her office, which was located in a ten-storey office block a few streets away from the police headquarters. It looked like a typical government style building constructed from large brownish stone. Her office was on the third floor and rather than waiting for the lift, she made Moshe and Jerry climb the staircase, telling them that it was good exercise. From the speed Sara managed to reach her floor it was obvious she regularly chose the stairs as opposed to using the lift. Leaving Jerry and Moshe to struggle on their own, she patiently waited for them on the landing, Moshe reaching her quite some time before Jerry who was thankful the office was on the third floor and not the tenth. When they finally seated themselves on the hard wooden chairs in her office, Sara allowed Jerry time to catch his breath and compose himself before going through a number of other important issues that needed to be dealt with.

Having completed everything she needed too, Sara suggested eating lunch before setting off on the long and tedious drive to Bezet. She raced them down the stairwell with Jerry again taking third place and led them to a bistro she frequented, where the tables and chairs were sprawled across the pavement, providing a fantastic view of the Judean hills on which Jerusalem is built.

When they had finished their meal, Sara used her radio to organise transport and within a couple of minutes a car had stopped almost alongside them. Settling the restaurant bill, she joined the others already seated in the back of the Mercedes to start their five-hour journey towards Bezet, a small town just south of the border with Lebanon. During the uneventful drive, they spent the majority of the time testing Jerry on his cover story until they eventually reached the town, continuing north east to the large military base which over the years had provided Israel's primary response to attacks emanating from within Lebanon and Syria. Sara informed Jerry she would stay the night, ensuring he settled in; whilst Moshe would remain on camp until the following Friday when he would be replaced by Debra who she hoped had remembered to forward his belongings from the hotel. On arrival they were shown to their respective quarters, Moshe and Jerry sharing a dormitory with four army cadets, whilst Sara had her own room in the officer's quarters. They sat together in the canteen for dinner and as they finished eating, Sara wished Jerry luck.

At 5.45am the following morning, Jerry was woken by the bright ceiling lights and noise of everyone dressing around him. Looking around he realised he was the only person still in bed; even Moshe was up and prepared for a session in the gym. Sitting upright in the contraption someone the previous day had tried to convince him was a bed, Jerry felt the fresh morning air hit his face. He ached from the uncomfortable mattress which was far worse than sleeping on his parent's couch. It finally dawned on him that he was now in a world a million miles away from the one he had left just a few days earlier. Jerry realised he had to accept and quickly become accustomed to his new accommodation for the time being. He remembered the comment one of the six elders, as he referred to them, had made in the first meeting. "You will stay as a guest of our government." With that thought he hurriedly dressed and followed the others to the gym, surprised Moshe had decided to participate. At the end of the fifteen-minute warm up, Jerry was already exhausted, but together with the other cadets he managed to endure a further hour learning initial combat moves of forward and back punches, followed by head and body blocks. He was partnered with Moshe and quickly realised that despite Moshe's slight build and lack of height, he was more than capable of holding his own in a fight should the need arise.

A shower and hearty breakfast followed the morning exercise after which Jerry was taken with a different group of cadets to the firing range where he was shown the workings of a pistol. He learned how to dismantle, clean and then rebuild it before being given the opportunity to fire a number of rounds. After lunch at the base, Jerry sat through a very welcome classroom session, learning to remember and recognise individuals. Following dinner, Moshe told him to spend the evening watching the film Exodus, chronicling the rebirth of a people and a nation, along with a few cadets. Set in Palestine in 1947, the film portrays the desperate attempts by settlers to reach the Promised Land and the efforts of the Israeli underground to defeat British and Arab opponents in its struggle to create the State of Israel. Although virtually asleep by the end of it, Jerry managed a short conversation with

Rochelle before settling in for the night.

Tuesday took on a similar format: gym before breakfast, followed by a classroom lecture. A trip to the firing range took place in the afternoon with another history lesson after dinner, which included Arab Israeli relations over recent years. The remainder of the week started with what had become the norm, spending a little over an hour in the gym before breakfast. By Friday, although Jerry was beginning to acclimatise, his body ached in places he never knew existed, with more bruises than he had managed hours of sleep since his feet touched Israeli soil. He had learnt the principles of a large number of fighting moves and was beginning to string them together quite well. He quickly realised that to be the victor of a fight in hand-to-hand combat had nothing to do with physical strength, size or body weight. It depended entirely on speed, agility, concentration, technique and the element of surprise. He had watched petite girls take out large, seemingly tough guys in a matter of seconds. Both the instructor and Moshe were surprised and delighted with the speed of Jerry's progress. He had also satisfactorily completed three sessions on the firing range and many hours in a classroom working on memory, recognition, description and the first principles of surveillance and interrogation.

On Friday afternoon, at the end of his first week, Moshe returned home and was replaced by Debra. "How's it going?" she enquired, despite being briefed by Moshe and all the instructors that had been involved with him during the week.

"Please could you explain one thing to me again?" Jerry asked Debra. "I know I've been told several times but I need reminding. Why I'm learning to fire a gun? You do know it's illegal to own and carry guns in the UK unless they are licensed? That's one law I'm certainly not going to break for anyone," he said.

Debra was slightly taken aback by the question, believing he had finally accepted things as they were after she and Sara had gone to great lengths explaining it. Eventually she thought of a suitable reply. "As I'm sure you found out when you shot your first few rounds at the beginning of the week, firing a gun, whatever size, is not as simple as the movies make out. Should you find yourself in a position where a gun just happens to become accessible and you have the need to use it for personal safety, at least you'll know how too. I'm sure you're fed up with being told; much of what you are learning hopefully will never be used. What we are teaching you is how to protect yourself if a situation should ever transpire, that's all."

Jerry decided not to pursue the argument, at least for the moment. "So what's my first week's report like," he enquired of her in a light-hearted manner, changing the subject.

"So far everyone appears happy with your progress," she smiled. "Although a couple of your instructors have suggested you learn a little Hebrew whilst you're here. Since I'm around for the weekend, I'd be happy to teach you rather than trying to cram yet another subject into what is already a very busy and strenuous week," Debra suggested. "I can arrange as many weekends as required. That's of course if you want me too. I appreciate Friday afternoons and Saturdays are the only time you have to relax and unwind a little. So the choice is yours," she said.

Jerry cut in, "I'm not sure why I need to learn Hebrew but I suppose it can't do any harm. I don't care much for weekends anyway, I've always worked seven days a week back home," he told her.

"That's great," Debra replied. "They do an excellent Friday night here on camp which I think is worth participating in. After, we can find a quiet spot somewhere and start. Let's see how it goes this weekend. If it works for you, I'll organise something more formal for the coming weekends," she said cheerfully.

"Where should we meet?" Jerry asked her.

"Oh, don't worry; I'll be in the canteen for dinner. I know a number of the senior officers here, having spent quite some time on base whilst serving in the army." The memories brought a grin to her face and provided Jerry with yet another small piece of evidence demonstrating Sara was responsible for quite an elite team.

Jerry enjoyed the experience of a communal Friday night service and dinner and as promised, Debra followed it with the two of them spending several hours learning Hebrew before settling in for the night. Debra, like Sara, had been given her own room in the officer's quarters.

The following morning Jerry slept until seven-thirty and after dressing made his way to the canteen for breakfast where he found Debra waiting for him. Once he had satisfied his hunger they went off to learn more Hebrew, a task which lasted the whole day, besides a short break for lunch.

Twenty-Three

The following three weeks continued very much as the first, although Jerry felt sure he was being pushed somewhat harder than the cadets he'd started training with, although it was difficult to confirm. On reflection he realised he had only been with any one group for a matter of days, being pulled out once he had mastered the basic techniques being taught. On one occasion, whilst taking a well earned break after a fifteen-minute full contact spar, he thought about it for the first time realising the groups he'd left spent far longer practising each move whilst he was continually learning new techniques. Over a period of four weeks, Jerry had learnt numerous moves and was able to string them together reasonably fluently in a fight. On several days each week, his schedule now included two sessions a day in the gym and his body remained in a constant state of being battered and bruised, patched up with plasters and bandages which did nothing to ease the pain. Whenever he moaned, Sara reminded him they were trying to cram the best part of a two-year training course into a matter of weeks and working under such pressure was all part of the experience.

Jerry's shooting skills had also developed quite well. Although he would never reach the level of a sharpshooter, he had become sufficiently accurate with a number of weapons to protect himself in a worse case scenario. Practising for many hours, he was pretty fast at changing magazines and adept in stripping and rebuilding various weapons even when blindfolded, although he still failed to understand the need and made his opinion known to everyone that mattered.

Several sessions were taken up learning about explosives and IEDs, improvised explosive devices. He learned who used them, how they were built and how to defuse them. He was taken to a location where he experienced from a distance, the blast and affect of different types and amounts of explosive materials. He was also shown a number of IED's that had been retrieved over the years, from very sophisticated bombs built into briefcases and virtually undetectable, through to crude, nail filled pipes designed for maximum carnage. Jerry heard horrific stories of how terrorists used primary and secondary devices for the utmost effect, the first to attract the targets, the second to inflict the greatest bloodshed. Knowing his expertise in electronics, he was allowed to have fun using his knowledge to design and build trigger and detonation mechanisms which were then hooked up to explosives, enabling him to experience the results.

Jerry learnt to master the art of retrieving items from his subconscious memory, minute details which enabled him to remember and recognise individuals, objects and facts. He also started to learn the knack he had always lacked, being able to approach a complete stranger and start a conversation, enabling him to subtly obtain information from individuals. Jerry began to enjoy the sessions and looked forward to turning his textbook knowledge into practice outside the classroom, a task scheduled for the forthcoming weeks.

At the end of the fifth week, Sara carried out a formal review with Jerry and gave him the stock answer to his usual questions of "Why this? Why that?" which they both knew parrot fashion and had almost become a joke between them.

On this occasion she added an additional comment: "As I understand it, the intention is for you to predominantly work alone rather than as part of a team and therefore it's of paramount importance that you are able to carry out your role without unnecessary fears," she told him.

"Such as?" Jerry enquired.

"This job is tough enough for even the most experienced agent. Everyone is naturally afraid of being caught and that's when silly mistakes are made. I'm not referring to you in particular," she quickly added, not wishing to be antagonistic. "It can happen to anyone placed in such a situation," she explained. "If you're confident in looking after yourself whatever the circumstance, you'll start the task feeling self assured and therefore be less likely to make stupid errors," she said as if she were talking from experience. "I watched the look on your face when I introduced you to Dani. If you had met him in a dark alley a few weeks ago you would have trembled in your boots to put it politely," she smiled. "It's only natural and I would have been worried if you didn't feel that way, but now you have the confidence to go up to someone like him and ask to borrow money for a phone call. Isn't that true?" she asked.

Jerry thought about it. "I suppose there is something in what you're saying," he reluctantly agreed.

Sara went on, "I'm delighted to tell you everyone is pleased with your progress. We all agreed that you have earned yourself a long weekend which I hope can be organised for next week," she told him. "I'm trying to book the Sheraton in Tel Aviv from Wednesday evening through to Sunday morning when we have to move to another military base."

Jerry thanked Sara. He was elated at the prospect of a few days off from what had become a very strenuous and mentally gruelling schedule, giving him a chance to recover. The thought he was progressing well in their eyes helped him maintain his spirit, particularly since his improvement wasn't something he could monitor himself. The likelihood of a break encouraged him to push himself even harder over the following few days, knowing he would shortly be able to relax for more than seventy-two hours.

They arrived at the Sheraton at 10pm, having put almost a full day's training in before the long drive south, only stopping for a quick meal. Sara walked him to the lobby and handed him a plastic card, one slightly larger than a standard credit card, which she informed him was the room key. She also gave him some cash and a mobile phone. "If you want transport please call me. We can have a car here within a few minutes." She then did an about turn and walked out of the foyer.

Jerry followed the porter with his luggage to his room. Using the card Sara gave him; he opened the door and switched on the lights. As he entered the small hallway he glanced around, his eyes immediately landing on an image of a beautiful body draped in shining white silk lying on the bed, the golden hair gently merging into the soft flowing material which seemed to end just below the buttocks revealing a pair of long slender legs. It took Jerry a moment to come to his senses; at first he thought he was seeing a mirage, or his brain was playing games with him. Quickly turning to the porter and taking the luggage from him, Jerry pushed the door closed with his foot, dropped his case and bags where he was standing and took another, much longer look at the stunning vision now standing just inches in front of him.

On a low coffee table between two armchairs sat an ice bucket containing a chilled bottle of Champagne with two glasses standing beside it. Rochelle, seeing Jerry's eyes rapidly moving between her and the bottle, asked in a very sexy voice, "Do you want to open it before or after you say hello?"

Jerry's eyes quickly returned to the exquisite body having confirmed it was just covered by a thin white silk wrap around dressing gown that struggled to reach the thighs, loosely tied around a thin waist. "Let's sip it whilst we say hello," Jerry replied, his face alight with joy.

"I bought this robe especially for you," Rochelle whispered in his ear as he was running his hands down her body having felt her breasts and moving towards the knot holding the gown together.

"And it's doing wonders for me already," Jerry struggled to reply, not wishing to break away from a kiss. As the garment parted, he uttered, "I need a shower; I've come straight from a training session. Why don't we open the Champers afterwards?"

Between kisses, Rochelle without speaking a word, slowly undressed him as she had done on the very first night they spent together, although this time his clothes looked a little worse for wear.

Having silently examined his body with her eyes for several minutes, she then took his hand and led him to the bathroom as if he were a small child, turned the shower on and allowed him to slip her gown off as they stepped into the cubicle together.

"Remind you of anything?" Rochelle asked quietly while she rubbed her soapy hands over his body.

"As if," he replied with a grin, remembering the words he used on their first shower together, whilst trying to kiss her body all over, "But the wrong order of events. I seem to recall the last time we did this in a hotel it was just before checking out time rather than just after checking in. But if the rest of the events are as memorable I shan't complain in the morning," Jerry managed to say, despite mouthfuls of soapy water.

"You look very well, somewhat leaner and fitter than you were a few weeks ago and even more moorish," Rochelle managed to mutter.

"Moorish?" he asked.

"Yes," she said. "Something you just can't stop nibbling at," she explained, before adding, "By the way, Igloo's doing fine thanks for asking."

Jerry, noticing she was upset he hadn't enquired replied, "I know it's doing fine, I have every faith in you. Besides I get frequent reports and not only from you," he said smiling. Remember I'm being trained to be a spook." He wondered if he would ever understand how women think and what he should and shouldn't say.

"What's a spook, surely not a ghost?" Rochelle asked, thinking she had only ever heard the term used in the Scooby Doo films.

"I don't think so," Jerry managed between chuckles. "It's the industry term for a spy," he informed her. "I've been trained to extract information from people through casual conversation, they shouldn't even be aware of divulging anything to me," he boasted. "And you know how much I love testing things thoroughly," he told her.

Rochelle muttered a "Yes," as if to ask where the conversation was leading. She was now only interested in him concentrating on her and was upset she had even mentioned the subject in the first place.

Carrying on, Jerry told her, "Well, I tested it out the other day and I must admit I was surprised how well it works." Jerry really was beginning to enjoy himself. "I found out you spend every Friday evening with my parents and something else," he said making out that he was having trouble remembering, "Oh yes, you went out for a meal with Mike a week or so ago, you..."

Rochelle cut in, "It wasn't like that, he's a friend and we had things to discuss," she stammered, having forgotten all about it. "Why, are you jealous?" she asked in a mocking tone.

"I'm jealous because he took you out and it should have been me. But I trust you if that's what you're referring to," Jerry reassured her in a serious tone.

They dried each other and led by Rochelle, they went to bed having opened the chilled bottle, spending the night making up for lost time.

A loud knock on the door at nine-thirty the following morning woke them both. "Room service, can I come in?" was shouted through the door in Hebrew.

Jerry took one look at Rochelle and called back in fluent Hebrew, "Can you come back a little later please?" His response came as something of a shock to Rochelle knowing foreign languages had never been Jerry's stronger subjects.

He then asked Rochelle, "Do you want to go out and about today? There's a car and driver at our disposal."

"Why not, it's been several years since I've been here and if we stay in we're unlikely to get out of bed," she replied. "Don't worry; you don't have to tell me anything you've been up too. I'll brief you on the office tomorrow. Let's forget about everything today except having a good time," she said kissing him again. "You really do look great though. You have lost a lot of weight and developed muscles in places not even I knew existed," she continued whilst feeling various parts of his anatomy. "You're becoming quite a hunk, I could really fancy you if I saw you walking down the street or on the beach," she finished, nudging him in her normal jovial way.

Jerry, in his best Parker from Thunderbirds impersonation tried to say, "Let me organise our transport m'lady," which made them both laugh.

By the time they had finished breakfast, Debra was waiting for them in the hotel lobby. "Your regular driver Adom is outside and has instructions to take you wherever you wish." She handed Jerry an envelope. "Here's some more cash in case you need it, we couldn't give you too much last night without ruining the surprise, but don't feel obliged to spend it all." She also handed him a mobile phone for the day to allow them both to call home, taking back the one Sara had given him the night before.

"If we ask Adom to take us around, will he do a good job, or do you want to brief him on what to see? Rochelle hasn't been to Israel for a long time so I want her to gain the most from it," Jerry said, quickly adding, "Of the sites that is."

"So you had a good night last night," Debra said winking. "If I were you I'd do the Tel Aviv area today. You, Jerry, have already been to many of the places I'll suggest he takes you, so you should be able to do the guide bit for Rochelle. If you manage to start earlier tomorrow and I realise you haven't seen each other for a while," she said smirking. "I'd go down to Jerusalem. Let me know and I'll book you into a hotel for the Sabbath, returning here Saturday night after stopping off for dinner at a great steak restaurant in Netanya. It's a bit of a drive but see how you go, I'm sure I can get a room fairly easily if you want one."

"Sounds a great plan," Rochelle replied. "And thanks for looking after him so well for me."

"Don't thank us; we need to thank you, both of you from what I hear. If only there were more people like you two, who knows, maybe the attacks against us and to an extent the Western World would be dramatically reduced," Debra spoke with real conviction. "Come on," she called to them, "You're wasting valuable sightseeing time. Jerry, is there anything else you want or need?"

"No, I don't think so." He looked at Rochelle and added, "I have everything I want, thanks."

They spent Friday in Jerusalem visiting Yad Vashem, a vast complex of tree-studded walkways leading to museums, exhibits, archives, monuments, sculptures and a memorial built on the Mount of Remembrance as a reminder of those that perished during the

Holocaust. Adom then took them to the Western Wall in the evening and they returned the following morning, with Jerry participating in one of the many Sabbath morning services taking place. It reminded him of his Bar Mitzvah and for the first time in many years he remembered what it felt like to be a real Jew.

Having had one of the best steak dinners they could both remember at the restaurant Debra recommended, Adom returned them to the Sheraton late on Saturday evening, informing Jerry he and Moshe would be waiting with breakfast in the car at 7am the following morning.

The two love birds returned to their room in the knowledge that it would be their last night together for several more weeks.

Twenty-Four

The military base to be Jerry's home for the next few weeks was close to a town called Ashkelon, almost due south of Tel Aviv, along the coast.

The facilities were very modern compared to those at Bezet, with only two people to a room, providing Jerry with far more privacy than he previously had. He and Moshe would share the room and Jerry was hoping that when Moshe wasn't around he would have the room to himself.

Training was to commence immediately on arrival, there being just enough time for Jerry to leave his luggage in the room, the task of unpacking having to wait until the evening. The first lecture was photography, where over the following few weeks he would learn to take high quality photographs with a range of equipment, from special miniature surveillance devices to conventional cameras. He would also learn to develop the negatives and print the pictures, already knowing the procedure to download and manipulate electronic images, possibly better than his tutor.

A briefing for two field exercises covering topics completed in the classroom over the previous few weeks followed the lesson. Debra explained to Jerry he would be taken to a shopping mall in the centre of town; on the way he would be shown a photograph of a target. For the first exercise he was to determine the accuracy of information obtained, which stated the target would be in the shopping mall at a certain time. He was to assess the validity of the information by attempting to locate the target and if successful, noting the precise location and time. He was also required to provide photographic evidence of visual contact. The second exercise involved selecting a store, which he would then be required to establish who owned it, details of staffing, weekly turnover, what happens to the daily takings each night, the security measures in place and to sketch a plan of the store. Two days were allocated for the second exercise due to the amount of information required.

Jerry chose to eat lunch at the base rather than at the mall as he enjoyed the food at Bezet and hoped the army fed all its troops in the same fashion, rather than Bezet being a one off.

Leaving empty plates from yet another excellent meal, Moshe and Jerry made their way to the shopping centre, leaving the car at the quieter, far end of the car park. Before vacating the vehicle, Moshe showed Jerry the photograph of the target whilst informing him: "When we walk in, I'll give you the opportunity to select the store you want as your objective. After that, I'll leave you alone and we will meet back here at 6pm. If you need me for any reason you have the numbers." That said, Moshe took back the picture and handed Jerry a mobile phone and some Shekels.

"Can't I keep the snap with me for confirmation?" Jerry asked.

"I'd rather you didn't," Moshe replied, starting to put the photograph back in its envelope, "I know this is your first attempt, but let's see how you do from memory. After all, in the field you wouldn't be able to take it with you; if you were caught you would have serious difficulty explaining it."

Jerry pleaded with him, "One more look, please!" Managing to win Moshe over, he spent several minutes studying the image and recording as much detail as possible, storing it in his memory as he had been taught.

Choosing what appeared to be a busy little toy shop for the second exercise they then went their own ways, although Jerry felt Moshe was never going to be far away, watching his every move. He decided to sit at a café which gave him an excellent view of everyone entering and leaving the mall. By coincidence it provided him with a clear view of the entrance to the toy shop and he was certain it would be a good position from which to plan his infiltration of the store. On route to the café, Jerry purchased a copy of the previous day's Daily Telegraph, his favourite newspaper, one of the many overseas papers available in Israel, but due to transportation and like all other international papers on sale, it lagged behind by at least a day. Jerry believed he could still use it to provide the cover he wanted. Having ordered a large hot chocolate, he sat at an empty table in the main thoroughfare, found the crossword page and started to complete some of the words. Although he enjoyed doing such puzzles, the real reason for selecting that particular page was to enable him to write down any information he wished to record, figuring people would not question someone completing a crossword, whereas writing on any other page could raise questions. To enhance his story, Jerry asked a woman sitting at a nearby table one of the questions, making sure anyone watching him could see he was merely trying to complete the crossword.

After sitting at the table for over two hours, Jerry began to believe he had either missed the target, or his report would have to state it was fictitious information, since the time given for the target to be in the vicinity had passed some fifty minutes earlier. Just as he was about to concentrate his mind on how best to obtain the necessary information about the shop, rather than continuing to focus on finding the target, he happened to peer over the top of the paper, only to make eye contact with what he could swear was the person in the picture he was shown. The target was looking at the toy shop window and Jerry, checking his watch, made a note of the time and place, adding a brief description of the woman and in particular, what she was wearing. He also managed to take a couple of quick snap shots using the miniature digital camera he was given. He continued to maintain his position for a further half hour whilst consuming a second hot chocolate as a celebration and to help maintain his cover.

Finally building the courage to launch his plan to infiltrate the store, he wondered if a relationship existed between the target from the first exercise and the shop. In his head he ran through the process used to choose the store and was satisfied he was not influenced by Moshe whatsoever, his selection was completely random, he could easily have picked any other unit in the mall.

Jerry entered the store and mooched around, appearing to take an interest in several products. He noticed three closed circuit television cameras and on a mental plan he marked their positions. He also kept a note in his mind of the location of the two Cash and Wrap counters and a white painted door at the back of the sales area, leading to what he thought would be the stock room. Assessing personnel, Jerry was aware both cash points were manned by women, guessing each of them to be in their mid thirties, with another fit young girl, probably in her late teens and wearing an assistant's uniform, working amongst the shelves. He looked to see if there were any other workers and was eventually happy they were the only members of staff on the shop floor. Realising there were no visible screens displaying the images from the cameras, Jerry deduced they were likely to be in a back office, possibly watched over by a security officer. Having considered the most likely place for the room, he concluded it had to be on the other side of the white door and realised there was a need to see precisely who and what was lurking behind it. Deliberating on how best to achieve that goal, he decided befriending the young assistant would be the easiest way to further his knowledge.

Looking for what appeared to be a reasonably complicated toy he could use to start a conversation by asking questions relating to it, Jerry hoped he would then be able to steer the conversation to more general things. He eventually selected a remote control model aeroplane and with it in hand he approached the young assistant. "Excuse me," he said attracting her attention. "Do you speak English?" he asked despite the fact he was already quite fluent in Hebrew thanks to Debra.

"Yes," she replied.

Without further hesitation, Jerry launched into a barrage of questions relating to the product, all of which he was surprised the girl was able to answer. "Do you know the 'ins' and 'outs' of all the toys on sale?" He couldn't help but ask, relieved the assistant gave him such an opportunity. The question was so natural; he knew she wouldn't give it a second thought.

"I've been working here for three years but living it for eight, when my mother bought the shop after my father died," the assistant replied, immediately feeling the tears swell up in her eyes. She was about to explain how she had started to work there and learnt about the toys, but Jerry didn't give her the opportunity.

Seeing the look on her face and change in her voice, Jerry jumped in. "Oh, I'm sorry, I didn't mean too…," stopping suddenly as though he meant it.

"That's all right," the girl said. "You weren't to know." He pulled out a handkerchief from his pocket and offered it to her. "Don't worry," she said, "I have my own out the back." She walked towards the door Jerry had thought led to the stockroom, with him following close behind, hoping for an opportunity to peep inside.

As the girl unlocked the door with her key which she kept on a chain, the other end fastened to her outfit, Jerry repeated: "I'm really sorry." And without hesitation he followed her into a small hallway with three doors leading from it, two of them open. The first door was to the office and as the owner's daughter went in, Jerry heard her speak to a man. Understanding the conversation, he was able to confirm the presence of a security guard and from the glare emitting from the small gap in the doorway to the dimly lit office she had just entered, he knew the location of the closed circuit TV monitors. Whilst on his own for a moment, he stuck his head around the other door that had been left slightly ajar, finding it led into the stockroom. He carefully studied the layout and in his mind calculated the proportion of the two rooms in relation to the sales area he had measured earlier by pacing it, knowing each of his paces was approximately one metre. He noted the position and number of windows, the overall height of the building, the position and dimensions of the back shutter to the loading bay, the location of the cameras and the arrangement of the shelving. The girl came out of the office apologetically, asking Jerry for his handkerchief before walking the few paces towards the third door, which once opened, revealed a small kitchen with the bathroom at the far end of it. Jerry followed her in and again took note of the layout and security measures.

"I'm sorry," she said, returning his handkerchief. "My father was killed in a terrorist ambush and whenever I think about it, I just seem to burst into tears."

"I've upset you and would appreciate the opportunity to make it up to you. What do you say to us meeting for coffee or dinner tonight?" Jerry asked in his most polite English adding, "I want to apologise properly for causing you this distress."

She sniffled and agreed. "Coffee would be nice," she said. "I'm working until 9pm but would be happy to meet outside the front of the shop then, if that's not too late? We could go to the coffee shop across the plaza which is open until at least midnight," she suggested.

"I'll be here," Jerry confirmed, squeezing her hand affectionately. He then released it and making his way back into the shop said, "See you at nine."

Leaving the store, Jerry couldn't believe how simple it had been for him to obtain a complete layout of the building, allowed without question into the stock room and office area and this in Israel where security is meant to be so tight. What if he had been a burglar, or worse still, a terrorist? Checking his watch he realised he still had forty-five minutes to kill before he was due to meet at the car. Deciding to peruse the shopping centre in search of presents for people at home, he remembered the need to be careful since everyone other than Rochelle thought he was in Europe. He made a final mental note for the day, to ask Sara how to deal with the issue of buying presents.

Jerry was waiting beside the locked car when Moshe slowly sauntered up to it. He used the time to contemplate his achievements of the afternoon, repeating the events in his mind as if watching a recording of it. He found it difficult to believe it was him, since for the first time in his life he had approached a girl, a complete stranger and managed to chat to her as if they had been friends for many years. What was even more incredible to him was that he had arranged to meet her again that evening, a sort of date and he felt no embarrassment throughout the discussion. Jerry reflected on just how much he had changed since meeting Rochelle and was delighted he was beginning to acquire the qualities he had longed for from a very young age. At the same time he was very aware not to allow himself to become overconfident; having seen it happen many times and always disliking such a person, who he felt eventually fell by their sword.

Whilst driving back to the base Jerry asked for the use of a car for the evening to which Moshe informed him such a request had to be approved by Sara, whilst jokingly reminding him that he was as good as spoken for. Arriving at the base, Sara debriefed him, confirming the correct target had been identified and after listening to Jerry's justification for a vehicle and a cover story he had created for the operation, she sanctioned the use of a car on the proviso it had to be from a hire company. When questioned on her reasoning, Sara explained only a hire vehicle would fit Jerry's cover. He would tell the girl that his stay in Israel was only temporary. With that in mind, it would be unlikely he would have access to a locally registered vehicle that wasn't from a rental company. Sara added jokingly that it was solely to be used to take the girl home and for no other purpose whatsoever. To ensure Jerry didn't lose his way, it was agreed he would follow Moshe, at least on the way over; the return would have to be played by ear. Cover, in as far as where he was staying would be arranged in time for the evening, organising something with a local hotel. Overall, everyone was astonished by his success and the way he managed to utilise a situation he inadvertently stumbled upon to such advantage.

Before dinner Jerry endured a further session in the gym. He then showered, dressed, ate and practiced driving on the right hand side of the road as opposed to the left, something he would be competent with if he had been driving in Israel for several weeks as he was likely to lead the girl to believe. Moshe sat beside him whilst he drove around the local roads. "By the way," Moshe suddenly remembered, "Rochelle asked me to tell you she arrived home safely and all is well at the office." He then gave Jerry details of a nearby hotel in case he needed to mention it.

He arrived at the shop a few minutes early and was immediately approached by Shoshana as soon as he stepped into the empty store, asking him to wait the few minutes until they closed. Jerry watched her secure the premises and he replaced the duty security officer escorting her with the daily takings to a night safe a few minutes walk from her shop, just past the café where Jerry sat that afternoon, which was now closed. They then walked across the concourse to a coffee shop. "Are you sure you don't want anything to eat?" he asked, hoping she would say no since he had already eaten dinner.

"No, thanks," she replied in excellent English. "I had dinner earlier this evening." They ordered drinks and sat in the more comfortable chairs in the dimly lit rear of the café where the candles on the tables provided a sensuous glow. Asked what he was doing in Israel, Jerry explained he was attempting to find his uncle on his father's behalf, since his dad was unwell and wanted to be reunited as a family before it was too late. Shoshana then told Jerry her life history and he easily encouraged her to talk about the shop, managing to find out everything he needed and a lot more. The time passed quickly and they were the last two customers in the shop, only leaving at the request of the owner as the time approached 1am.

"Do you have a car or can I drive you home?" he asked her.

"My cars in the loading bay, but thanks for the offer," Shoshana informed him, adding: "I really enjoyed myself."

"Maybe we can do it again before I leave?" Jerry suggested.

"That would be nice," she replied and they walked out the main entrance into the humid night, kissing each other on the cheek before turning in opposite directions towards their respective vehicles.

Jerry made his way back to his car noticing Moshe parked beside it. He chose not to acknowledge him exactly as he had been trained. Jerry started the engine and waited for Moshe to pull out. A few moments later he followed the blue Volkswagen.

Sara was eagerly waiting his return at the base, keen to find out how her protégé had performed. "Brilliant," she said excitedly after he provided all the information during the debrief session.

"How do you know I haven't made it up?" he asked.

"We know," she replied and quickly moving on said, "Don't forget that you have gym at six-thirty this morning, don't oversleep." She then paused for a short time, followed by, "Since you have saved a day in completing the exercise, we'll see if we can put it towards another break. Well done again."

They then all made their way to their respective bedrooms, Jerry ecstatic having achieved something he had never believed he could, although he kept the true success a secret from the others.

Twenty-Five

Over the following three days, the majority of time was spent teaching Jerry how to plan a major surveillance operation, broken up by two gym sessions each day and one on the firing range where Jerry learnt to deal with moving targets. He had his first run in an action packed exercise where man made targets in the shape of humans; men, women and children, randomly popped-up around the student who is required to make a quick decision whether they are goodies or baddies, the baddies holding a machine gun. Points are gained when shooting a baddy, with some being deducted if they are not blasted away, or worse still, a goody shot in error. With only a second to identify a pop-up and make the decision whether to fire before the subject disappeared, Jerry found the game fun and scored well, achieving points for hitting four out of seven baddies and only losing one out of ten goodies. Assured it was an excellent result for a first attempt, he enjoyed the praise despite his feelings for the subject.

It didn't take long for Jerry to appreciate tremendous resources were required to mount an around-the-clock surveillance operation. Covertly following a car involved four or five others at any one time, possibly supported by motorcycles, each continually swapping the tail, ensuring the target was never followed by the same vehicle for too long, providing the opportunity of it becoming identified. To achieve this, each member of the squad had to remain in close proximity to the vehicle being shadowed and in constant communication with the remainder of the team. A similar process was required for following a subject on foot. Jerry was also taught and shown electronic tracking devices, how to use them, their benefits and limitations. The lecturer organised for him to participate in a live surveillance operation with a team from a specialist police unit. On completing his stint on the operation, Jerry started to learn how to detect even the most experienced observation teams.

In the gym Jerry was starting to learn how to deal with stick and knife attacks and the many methods such weapons are used by both experienced and inexperienced opponents. He was taught how to disarm someone holding a gun at his head or back, something Jerry didn't believe possible until he proved it for himself. Both Debra and Moshe joined the sessions when they were free, allegedly to brush up on their skills which Jerry observed was completely unnecessary. He enjoyed being partnered with either of them since it continually reinforced for him the fact that strength and size had nothing to do with the ability to win a fight, at least not when using the art of Krav Maga. However hard he tried to hit them, they were always able to block and counter attack, never failing to 'down' Jerry on every one of their attacks, despite him being somewhat taller than both of them.

Need necessitated Jerry to remain focussed whilst in the gym, however on one occasion, for no reason whatsoever, his mind wondered to a comment Leon once made when they were discussing Rochelle, although he couldn't remember when. "She can handle herself if she needs to." He now for the first time pondered whether she was trained in the art of Krav Maga. His mind immediately followed this thought with a vision of scenes from the Pink Panther films where Inspector Clouseau found himself continually being attacked by his manservant Kato to keep Clouseau on his guard. Jerry replaced the images of Kato and Clouseau with Rochelle and himself and he couldn't hold back a grin. "Life could get quite interesting," he chuckled, being quickly brought back to reality by a steel bar being thrust at him.

Jerry was put through further recognition and simple infiltration exercises where he continued to surpass expectations, mastering a good technique in extracting information from people. More than anything else, he was pleased with his newfound confidence, overcoming his shyness and the problem of forever being embarrassed whatever the situation. Completing all the sessions on learning to interrogate, he was then taught the other side of the coin, being the person questioned, both under pressure and in a more subtle manner, similar to the way he had obtained the information from Shoshana.

They taught Jerry a number of key rules to obey whilst working alone and as part of a team, often referred to as the rules of survival. Having far more confidence in himself, he constantly argued with his lecturers regarding scenarios they discussed in the classroom, the new Jerry was not one to hold back on making his opinions known; doing it in a pleasant manner and to his surprise the lecturers enjoyed the banter between them, much of it in Hebrew.

One evening during the twelfth week of the course, Sara arrived in time for dinner, bringing an Israeli girl with her, one that looked to Jerry to be no older than twenty. "Meet Ruti," Sara said, introducing them. "The two of you will be working together for a while, I therefore suggest you get to know each other this evening and let's all meet up after gym tomorrow." The three of them continued to chat whilst eating, Jerry managing to make a pig of himself he enjoyed the food so much, although his body needed to replace the energy burnt during the day. Ruti complemented him on his grasp of Hebrew and the conversation continually swapped between English and Hebrew allowing them both to practice. Sara, finishing her meal first stood up. "I've an urgent meeting to attend so I'll leave you both to it," and she walked out of the dinning room.

"Do you know what Sara has planned for us?" Jerry asked Ruti once they were alone.

"No, I've absolutely no idea," she sheepishly replied as if she should have done.

In an attempt to find out a little more about Ruti, Jerry bombarded her with questions. Despite her answering each without any hesitation, Jerry was left with a nagging doubt about the validity of her answers, as if she was trying to hide something from him. He attempted to trip her up on several occasions, precisely as he had been taught, but it was as if she had been sitting beside him in the lectures, always managing to pre-empt his every move. After a mentally exhausting evening, he concluded Ruti was possibly another exercise Sara had managed to concoct. Treating it as a reality check he gave himself a pat on the back for not being embarrassed. The thought crossed his mind that if he weren't so in love with Rochelle he wouldn't hesitate in asking Ruti out on a date, she was certainly his type, both physically in as far as her figure and intellectually, she was definitely a smart cookie. Thinking about it a little more, he realised she was not the first girl he could recall that had attracted his attention since arriving in Israel, putting it down to missing Rochelle. He then hoped she wasn't missing him in the same way, eyeing up other guys, or worse still, taking it a stage further.

Despite regularly phoning Rochelle, most of the time they just discussed Igloo. Jerry constantly wanted to tell her how much he was missing her, but regardless of his increased confidence he just couldn't make himself say the words for fear of bringing Rochelle to tears, something he knew he wouldn't be able to stomach. The best they ever managed was a quick "I love you," and blowing kisses over the ether to each other. Both Ruti and Jerry were tired and with an early start the following morning they went to their respective bedrooms at around midnight, Jerry calling his parents, his weekly check-in call and then a fairly lengthy chat with Rochelle, secretly searching for reassurance before he was able to fall asleep.

In the gym the following morning Jerry found himself paired with Ruti and realised she must be on a similar course to him. Due to the pain she inflicted on his body, he could tell she was somewhat more advanced in Krav Maga than he, who despite many attempts, failed to inflict any pain on her, even with the advantage of having sticks, knives and chains to use.

Following the gym session they both freshened up, enjoyed

breakfast together and sauntered to one of the small briefing rooms on the base which had been transformed into a classroom for his stay. On opening the door, Sara, Debra, Moshe and a couple of new faces were waiting for them, somewhat impatiently judging by their stance. As soon as the latecomers were seated, following the quickest of "Good mornings" and a comment from Sara saying, "We have some changes to our plan for the next few days," but offering no further information on what they were, she asked Debra to dim the lights and switch on the slide projector. The first picture was of a multi storey office block; a quick count showed there were twenty floors.

Sara started to speak, at the same time pointing to the image: "This is the headquarters of the Histadrut, the trade union," for Jerry's benefit, glancing at him to ensure he was paying attention. "As most of you are aware, there has been substantial unrest within the union over the last year or so, with a number of one day general strikes, on each occasion succeeding in bringing the country to a standstill. It's now believed a small group of militants within the organisation could be behind these actions and a view beginning to form in some circles is that they have a specific goal, possibly originating from outside our borders." It was clear Sara was being very careful in the words she used, before pausing for questions or comments from the assembled group. Not being any she continued, "At the moment we have no specific information to substantiate this, although various reports have been received that union members have dug up some kind of dirt on the Chairman." Stopping momentarily to moisten her throat, "We're speculating here but believe a bunch of sour grapes maybe blackmailing him, there being no other reason we can deduce for the Chairman's radical behaviour, a complete change in his style. He has thrown his full support behind these actions, to the extent of exerting enormous pressure on the management committee to ensure the rank and file members voted in favour of all these crippling strikes. Historically the Chairman has always been very reasonable with whichever party is in power, taking the time to attempt to resolve issues before the word strike was even mentioned. Over the last year, ever since this current round of action commenced, he hasn't even contemplated sitting around a table to discuss a solution and no one outside of the union actually understands what they are demanding, it appears as if it is simply strike, strike, strike for the sake of causing disruption."

As Sara was speaking, Debra flicked through a number of slides of the Chairman and other members of the management committee with Sara annotating each slide as they appeared. They also viewed several images of individuals believed to be some of the activists involved, although she repeated for everyone's benefit, "there is no confirmed intelligence on anything I've said, everything is pure supposition."

"We need to determine the facts quickly. If this trouble continues the government could topple, taking with it the current peace talks in addition to the agreements already in place with some of the mainstream Arab groups, which has for the moment at least resulted in fewer attacks against us," Sara informed her people before sitting down.

"I'm sure you all appreciate the gravity of the situation Sara has just described," announced one of the new faces, a man in his early fifties who had been listening intently until then. "It's therefore of paramount importance to find out the true situation," he stated, repeating Sara using slightly different words, probably in the belief it would add credence. From his mannerisms, Jerry assumed the man was a senior officer in one of the many Israeli security agencies, possibly even Sara's boss. "Only once we have a full understanding of the situation will we be in a position to deal with it in the most appropriate way," he continued, stopping for a few seconds to look around the room. "Consideration has gone into how best to obtain this information, with discussions having taken place in various government departments over the last forty-eight hours. We have decided, based on recent successes of quickly obtaining high quality intelligence, Sara and her team, with some additional support," at which point he looked directly at Ruti, "are probably the best chance we have of finding out exactly what is going on in time." He then directed his next comment to Sara, "You will naturally have access to whatever supplementary resources are required to achieve our goal in the fastest, safest manner." Jerry sat there bewildered, the only thought he had was his appreciation to Debra for teaching him Hebrew so well, otherwise he would not have understood a word of what had been said.

Sara took the floor again. "Another strike has been organised to start in ten days from now and it's believed this strike is designed to cause maximum chaos, pandemonium far worse than we have experienced to date. The situation, if one does exist, has to be dealt with before then, enabling best endeavours to be made to avert the strike." Sara spoke with an air of authority in a manner Jerry had not witnessed from her before, now realising many of the comments she had made to him over the period must have been spoken from experience as a field officer, immediately increasing his respect for her. "We'll move to a more suitable location later today which will be our operational base, somewhere closer to the field of action. Our first objective is to quickly agree and implement a plan." She told them to prepare to leave whilst arrangements were being made to secure appropriate accommodation.

Within the hour they were on the road heading north towards Tel Aviv, the journey being made in silence. Jerry spent the time contemplating the story, was it for real or just another Sara fairytale. He couldn't believe that he, not being an Israeli citizen and a novice to boot, would be included in a live operation on home territory. He had read about the strikes in newspapers, so part of the story was certainly true. Mulling over the facts, he eventually came to the conclusion it was yet another exercise, one Sara was intent on making as realistic as possible, it could even be his passing out examination, he thought.

They arrived at a Kibbutz, Shefayim, a few kilometres north of Tel Aviv, off the main road heading towards the holiday resort of Netanya. Turning into a tarmac covered path, being the main access into and out of the Kibbutz, they drove up to the guest house where the car stopped and Sara entered the building, Jerry watching her walk towards the reception desk through the glass doors. A few minutes later she returned to the car and they slowly drove further along the road, following it around the back of the hotel. "We have a group of chalets for our use and I've been promised we won't be disturbed," she announced. As they slowly continued along the path, they came to a sharp left bend followed immediately by a right fork. Taking it, they could see a relatively isolated complex of what looked like huts. "We have sufficient rooms for us all to stay on-site without the need for anyone to share, whilst being able to retain a meeting and operations room. Jerry, you'll be pleased to know we don't have use of their gym either," Sara said, emphasising the word don't as she issued the keys to each door. "Five zero seven will be the planning and briefing room and five zero eight the ops room. I'll take five zero six if you need me. Let's get ourselves sorted out and meet in five zero seven in say thirty minutes." She then handed out the remaining keys.

The remainder of the afternoon was spent examining all the data that had already been collected by Sara's team and others over the last twenty-four hours including details on the previous strikes. Sara encouraged the group, which included Moshe, Debra and Yakov, another member of her team Jerry had not previously met, as well as Ruti, to put their ideas into the melting pot for consideration. After breaking for dinner in the hotel restaurant during which everyone refrained from discussing the mission, they reconvened in the planning room where each of the ideas were evaluated, until they retired to their respective rooms at two-thirty the following morning, having failed to come up with a suitable proposal. Keen for everyone to be fresh, Sara told them: "Breakfast at seven and back here at seven thirty," hoping a break would allow them all to be more productive.

After the ideas had been discussed, dissected and analysed again, Jerry asked if he could take a physical look at the building to get a feel for the case, an idea Sara agreed with, suggesting Yakov take both him and Ruti. Not wishing to have a vehicle close by, potentially attracting unnecessary attention, it was agreed that they would call when they wanted to be collected.

Yakov dropped them at the end of the street in which the Histadrut building was located and they walked up the road together like old friends on a stroll. Jerry stopped at a convenience store where he bought several chilled cans of soft drinks, crisps and chocolates for the two of them to nosh and newspapers to read whilst observing the building from a bench in sight of the main entrance.

They watched the building for two hours, noting and photographing all the comings and goings. They had been issued with cameras, Jerry with a high resolution digital single lens reflex, which despite being a little on the bulky side produced high quality images that could quickly be downloaded to a computer. The camera also had an inbuilt Bluetooth wireless interface allowing it to connect to a mobile phone to transmit the pictures anywhere in the world. Ruti had selected a miniature camera built into a brooch with a small cable running inside her sleeve to her hand allowing her to snap away without anyone knowing a thing about it. She had also been issued with a miniature-recording device, allowing her to make verbal notes rather than having to scribble things down, a spy's Dictaphone Jerry thought.

Whether from boredom or wanting to do the job properly, Jerry decided to take a walk around the perimeter of the building, checking for other entrances and exits in addition to CCTV cameras and anything else he considered useful to know. Other than noting the many cameras providing a complete circle of vision, the only real points of significance were two identical green wooden doors at the back of the building, one at each end, leading to the car park. Jerry noticed that neither door had any means to open it from the outside, meaning they were specifically exits and not entrances into the building. From a brief examination, since he was sure his movements were being recorded for prosperity by a vigilant security guard, the doors appeared to be secured in the middle and he assumed it was via a push bar locking mechanism. Looking at the wall immediately above both doors, Jerry could see there were windows at regular intervals all the way up to the top of the building, both sides looking identical. Jerry assumed they were to allow daylight into a stairwell, the windows being on the landing for each level. He made the assumption the doors were emergency exits.

Returning to the bench, Ruti was about to organise their collection when the Chairman emerged from the building. Without hesitation Jerry told her, "I'm going to try and have a word with him," and quickly thinking aloud, "My cover will be an English student doing a thesis on trade unions around the world." He looked at Ruti for approval, adding:

"I don't think we have anything to lose and although we agreed earlier not to make contact until a plan was agreed, we didn't expect an opportunity to present itself so early on," he tried convincing her. She remained silent, the look on her face saying everything Jerry didn't want to hear. "Organise transport and I'll meet up with you at the drop off point in a few minutes," he commanded her before running off calling out to the Chairman, "Excuse me sir, excuse me, do you speak English?" as if he had no idea who the man was.

The Chairman looked in Jerry's direction wondering what the commotion was about, stopping on seeing Jerry rushing towards him while Ruti looked on from a distance. They seemed to be talking for ages before the Chairman resumed his walk towards the rear of the building, probably to the car park, Ruti thought, continuing to watch Jerry in step with him until they were both out of sight. The next time Ruti saw Jerry she couldn't believe her eyes and had to look again before accepting the fact that he was sitting in the passenger seat of the Chairman's car on route to who knows where? The two men seemed to be in deep conversation as the Chairman drove past her position.

Twenty-Six

Ruti was collected from the same location she had been dropped off just hours earlier and was driven back to room five zero seven where Sara thoroughly debriefed her, furious with Jerry for going off on his own and to a lesser extent with Ruti for allowing him to do so. "Why didn't you stop him from taking off like that?" Sara demanded to know. Combined with her anger was a deep concern for his safety, despite her confidence in his ability to take care of himself should the need arise. She knew he was now as competent in self defence as most of her team. The issue playing on her mind was that they had no idea who they were dealing with. "Was it just a group of militants? If so, how ruthless were they? If they caught Jerry would they tear him apart?" What concerned her most was the possibility of there being more sinister evils at play and if so, would they be satisfied in just roughing him up a bit, or would he be finished off completely? She was duty bound to call her superiors and inform them a field agent was missing whilst involved in an operation.

Debra and Moshe had significantly more confidence in Jerry's abilities, convincing Sara to delay raising the alarm too quickly by reminding her of his performance in all his exercises. She finally agreed to allow him a little more time before calling it in, but she did start to consider the potential repercussions, Jerry being British with all the issues it adds, on top of everything else. Only pleadings at the highest levels of government could have any chance of avoiding a major international political crisis. She was advised of the sensitive nature of his training before he arrived in Israel, thus the reason for being so strict about his personal security and confiscating anything that could prove he was actually there.

Unable to concentrate on the operation, they decided to take a break and went across to the dining room for an early meal, but it quickly became obvious no one was really interested in eating, neither were they in the mood for making polite conversation, they just sat at the table for half an hour in complete silence. Even Ruti, who had only known Jerry for a matter of hours, had taken a liking to him. It was something about his character; he seemed to give out an aura which attracted people to him. Since his arrival, everyone who had come into contact with him had mentioned how they had been drawn to him; he was good natured, thoughtful, considerate and very conscientious, there was not a single person who had a bad word to say about him. On the occasions he disagreed with something, he somehow managed to argue his point whereby one seemed to enjoy arguing with him. The thought he might be in some kind of trouble sickened them all, the fact he had brought it upon himself had been forgotten, at least for the time being. Jerry had put himself at risk for others, people he didn't know, for a country where he wasn't a citizen. Everyone around the table that evening had a lump in his or her throat.

The group returned to the chalet complex, pacing between the ops and planning rooms as the minutes and then the hours ticked by. Finally, after checking her watch, Sara said, "That's it," with tears in her eyes. "I can't delay the inevitable any longer; I should have called in hours ago. I've now broken as many rules as he has. My record commanding an operational team has until now been unblemished, certainly never losing an operative and today, in a single moment of madness by one individual, I have lost someone that had the potential of being one of the best operatives we've ever had," she added, thinking of all the weekly reports she had read from his lecturers and written to her superiors, in addition to having watched him in action on numerous exercises. From the first time he went on the streets, it was clear he was thinking as an experienced field agent and even demonstrated it earlier in the day not forgetting to use a cover story, coming up with something suitable without hesitation, one, which on analysis from what she knew of it, should not have failed him. "So why has he not returned or at least made contact?" Just as she started to key the digits for her commanding officer into one of the phone on a table, the emergency mobile phone rang. Thinking it would be Jerry, she answered it sounding very relieved.

"Hello, is that Sara?" the voice on the other end asked.

Sara recognised the voice but couldn't place it. It was certainly not the voice she was expecting to hear, this one belonged to a woman. The anxiety immediately showed again, her disappointment visible to everyone. "Sara speaking," she replied hesitantly.

"Hi, it's Rochelle," Sara heard through the earpiece.

Suddenly recognising the voice and name, she felt a horrible feeing in her stomach. How was she going to explain they had no idea where Jerry was? Worst still, whether he was safe? "Rochelle, how are you?" she said in the most upbeat tone she could muster.

Rochelle wanted to get straight to the point. "I'm fine thanks. Look, I'm sorry to be calling you, I know you don't like me phoning, but I'm concerned, having received what can only be described as a very worrying call."

Sara couldn't believe contact could have been made with Rochelle so soon and immediately started evaluating the information she had just received. "How much pain had they inflicted on him to make him crack so quickly? And if he did talk, he knew to give out the emergency number, not a personal one." Which led onto "Had they recognised him?" She was aware that his picture had frequently appeared in British, European and American newspapers. Before he was selected, Sara knew the publicity he had received in the media had been taken into consideration, deeming it to be of benefit for the future role he was to have. She suddenly realised the cover story he made up on the spur of the moment hadn't taken his public exposure into account, anyone doing their homework would immediately see through it and be able to identify him. "Why make their demands through his girlfriend and not direct to the authorities and why by phone?" she asked herself, unable to understand the reason for it.

Rochelle continued, "I've had a very strange conversation with Jez. Firstly, he referred to me as Sara and then babbled on about something to do with his thesis; he has a great story for it and wanted to check that he could use it. That was about it, which was unusual in itself since I'm normally cross-examined several times on what's happening with the business and he has never failed to end a conversation telling me how much he loves me. Is he all right? I think he's flipped, gone crazy or something," she said, having quickly recounted everything.

Sara breathed a sigh of relief, her initial concerns were unfounded and she could probably scrape through the call managing to alleviate Rochelle's concerns. It dawned on her that Jerry had not divulged any information whatsoever and Rochelle didn't call to speak to him. As Sara was thinking, Rochelle remembered she had omitted to mention her reaction and a crucial part of the conversation. "At first I thought it was a wrong number, but I could swear it was Jez's voice. Why call me Sara? At the time I couldn't think of anyone with that name and then I thought maybe he had dialled me by mistake meaning to speak with you." Not giving Sara an opportunity to comment, "The strangest and most worrying thing was he didn't even recognise my voice and ignored everything I said, appearing to be having a conversation with some imaginary person. I think the guy has gone doo lally."

"It's a long story which I can't go into now, but I assure you there's no reason to be alarmed by the call, he's just trying to prove something to me. How long ago did you speak to him?" Sara asked.

Rochelle looked at her watch, "About an hour or so, I was out and didn't have your number with me."

"That's fine, thanks for letting me know. I'll get Jerry to call you tomorrow if you want," Sara suggested in an effort to prevent her from asking to speak with him.

"Yeh, that would be great, but please make sure he remembers who

I am first, the call really upset me. Well thanks and bye," Rochelle said before hanging up.

"I take it you all understood the gist of that call? Why he didn't phone here I really don't know," Sara said to the others after reflecting on the conversation, repeating verbatim what Rochelle had said whilst Debra transcribed it.

A slightly relieved Debra said, "Well at least we know he's alright."

"Up to an hour ago," Sara quickly replied. "But we can't leave him out over night, not without knowing where he is. I'm still going to have to call it in and take the consequences."

"I think we have managed to buy a little more time. After all, he's demonstrated that he has the integrity to make contact with us even if it wasn't the way we expected. Knowing him I'm sure there's a good explanation for contacting Rochelle rather than us," Moshe argued, trying to convince Sara to hold off a little longer from doing anything. "Let's just analyse the way he thinks for a minute. Remember when he asked the woman in the café for help doing the crossword puzzle purely to enhance his cover, or the way he created and maintained a story on the toy store exercise. I believe he knows precisely what he's doing and although he lacks operational experience, he has demonstrated on many occasions he can think quickly on his feet even when under pressure and like you, I believe he'll make an excellent operative," he said referring to an earlier statement Sara had made. "I'm sure if we analyse the call using his mindset, we'll find a message in it somewhere. The one thing we immediately know is he's okay and I don't buy the argument he's gone insane, he was fine this morning. Right or wrong, there's a good explanation for him phoning Rochelle rather than us. There is also a reason why he asked for you and why he pretended to be talking to someone else, totally ignoring what Rochelle was saying. I haven't figured it out yet because he's very clever, maybe too clever for us, but I'm convinced there are rational answers to everything he did and it doesn't include the word mad anywhere," Moshe insisted, adding "Other than going off on his own in the first place."

"You could have a point Moshe," Sara replied referring to Jerry having a good reason for his actions, which she may not have initially appreciated. "I accept we're all worried and that's affecting our judgement, or at least mine. Let's consider the information again," she suggested, beckoning them to sit around the main table rather than continually pacing from one end of the room to the other. They evaluated numerous possibilities over the following couple of hours, the time passing as if it were minutes, whilst consuming several litres of coffee and smoking a sufficient quantity of cigarettes to cause lung cancer in an elephant. "It's now a little past eleven o'clock, he's been absent for over nine hours and the last contact was more than three hours ago," Sara informed them all, having kept an eye on the clock. "If something has happened to him it could have enormous repercussions, not just for this operation, but for international diplomacy as well, you do all realise that?" Everyone except Ruti nodded. She had been seconded from Shin Bet for this operation, being one of their best field agents. All she knew about the mission before meeting Sara was that her orders originated from the top brass of her organisation and stated she would be working closely with an English agent. Other than that, she had no idea who Jerry was and knew better than to ask either her superiors, Sara or Jerry directly whilst they were getting to know each other the previous evening, despite the many questions he had asked her.

"Who fancies a cappuccino from the café?" Debra asked. "If we still haven't heard anything when we get back, then I accept it would be time to report in," she suggested.

"I think we're just putting off the inevitable, but I need another cigarette so I'll go along with you," Sara replied.

They walked across to the café opposite the guest house, catering for both tourists staying in the hotel and the Kibbutzniks, the name given to residents of a Kibbutz. As they were making themselves comfortable at the only available table large enough to seat them all, they spotted Jerry sitting in a secluded corner under the leaves of a palm tree, in deep conversation with another man, someone in his early twenties. He had seen his colleagues enter the room and casually lowered his head signalling them to ignore him. Understanding the message, the team continued to sit where they had originally chosen and ordered their drinks. Sara's mind was in a state of confusion, unsure whether she should be elated on knowing he was safe and well, or annoyed he had broken almost every rule in the book in terms of personal security, compromising not just himself, but the whole team.

They sat drinking coffee for about an hour until Jerry and his new found friend stood up to leave. The two of them shook hands and Jerry walked him to the adjacent car park after which he returned to the café, approaching his colleagues as if nothing was wrong, "I suggest we go to five zero seven," he said and without another word being spoken, Sara settled the bill and they left.

Once seated around the table Sara started: "I hope you've got an excellent excuse," in an angry tone, having had sufficient time to convert her anxiety into temper.

"Give him a chance to explain," Debra butted in. Jerry spent the following two hours being debriefed on the information he had obtained throughout the day, but providing only very briefest of explanations as to why he acted as he did.

"Jerry, you appear to have obtained what I sincerely hope transpires to be very useful intelligence. However, I'm unable to condone the manner in which you went about acquiring it," Sara told him angrily. "Over the last three months people have gone out of their way to teach you about personal security, but it would appear from your actions today that you just haven't absorbed one word of it and everyone has wasted their valuable time, or worse still, you don't think it applies to you," she reprimanded him. "Firstly you take off on your own with someone who maybe involved with undesirables at the very least. You then call Rochelle with some nonsense, but in essence, acting an idiot and more importantly, putting her at risk. If that weren't bad enough, you complete the day by bringing an unconfirmed source back here, where your colleagues are based, potentially compromising the operation and putting everyone's lives in danger. What were you thinking of?" Sara shouted.

"I don't believe I've caused any harm whatsoever and I resent such allegations. Neither do I believe I have compromised the mission or the safety of any member of your precious team for that matter. With respect, you were not on the ground and therefore have absolutely no idea what was evolving," Jerry stated in a very calm but assertive manner. "Before you have a heart attack over this and write me off in the process, may I suggest you listen to my reasoning behind what you believe were foolish actions, then and only then will any of you be in a position to determine whether I acted inanely or not," he finished as though he had completely ignored Sara's reprimand and that he had done nothing out of the ordinary.

Without giving anyone an opportunity to comment he continued, still in a very forceful tone, "An opportunity presented itself this morning whilst Ruti and I were carrying out the reconnaissance. If I recall your briefing, time was of the essence and I chose to take what I thought might be a lucky break and see where it would lead. None of the cover stories we had discussed this morning, or yesterday morning in actual fact," he corrected himself after checking his watch, "In my opinion would have worked for this particular situation. I came up with an idea and I passed it by Ruti, although I probably didn't give her a fair chance to comment on it, there just wasn't the time."

Jerry was on a roll and not prepared to let anyone comment until he had finished. "Fortunately, the cover story I quickly devised and the manner by which I introduced myself to the Chairman were successful and he bought the story I recounted earlier. As the afternoon progressed, I was asked more and more questions about my course and my research, since my questions to him and his children became more searching as time progressed." Jerry paused to ensure everyone was paying attention. "I was forced to elaborate on my basic cover to fit the questioning, maintaining their confidence in me whilst allowing my objectives to be achieved. I was aware of the hours flying by and I correctly reckoned on you guys becoming concerned for my safety so I wanted to get a message to you confirming I was okay. However, I couldn't just stand up and say I need to check in with my operations controller since I'm really a spook and investigating you, so I came up with a story to speak to my tutor which I believe was a reasonable request to make, allowing me to make contact with you whilst keeping my cover intact," he explained, still not allowing any interruptions.

"The next problem to contend with was deciding on a number to call. As I've previously stated, I was an English student, University of London and all that, so I could hardly dial a number in Israel. I had to call London in case they checked, remembering your reasoning for using a hire car a few weeks ago." Again he didn't give anyone the chance to comment, "You Sara taught me, with others of course, to be as realistic as possible, so I was only going by the book, the same book you just accused me of not knowing or ignoring. I tried to think of the best way to get a message to you, one that I could get away with and you would understand, finally coming up with the idea of phoning Rochelle and calling her Sara. I knew she was sensible enough to realise the message was really meant for you and would relay it for me, from which you would know I was safe. The rest of the conversation was primarily for the benefit of the people in the room at the time. Roch obviously played her part correctly," he said in a tone accusing Sara of not being on the same wavelength and therefore implying that she must be pretty stupid.

"Finally, why come back here with someone?" he threw out the question knowing he was the only person able to answer it. "Mordechai, the Chairman's son wanted to talk to me. A good chunk of the information came from him and I believe he is an excellent source to continue to work with, I'm sure Ruti can nurture him and obtain far more." He smiled for the first time since returning to the room although there was still some aggression in his voice. "He wanted to talk to me in private. He suggested coming back to my hotel, it certainly wasn't my choice. I couldn't call you to organise something with another hotel and yet at the same time I wouldn't be able to walk into one where, should it be necessary, proving I was a guest would be impossible and potentially blow everything. The idea of staying on the Kibbutz played nicely for me, being relatively cheap compared to a proper hotel, an ideal haunt for a student," he stated, "I figured at the worst you would move us on again, but I'm getting used to the nomads life you're giving me. I made a judgement call that the information he was providing was worth another move if it were deemed necessary."

Jerry paused for a moment to allow his reasoning to be appreciated by the others, completing the explanation with: "That's about it except Sara I accept your apology for all the insinuations you made earlier." There was perspiration on his face from his excitement.

Besides a smirk appearing across most of their faces from Jerry's final comment, no one spoke for several minutes, each trying to place themselves in Jerry's shoes and wondering how they would have reacted in the same situation. They were also attempting to assess the consequences, Jerry thought.

Sara was the first to speak and ignoring Jerry's closing statement, "We are a team and meant to work as such, which means not taking decisions to operate alone."

"This morning was all about the urgency of this situation," Jerry reminded Sara, maintaining anger in his voice despite the long explanation and forgetting it was already well into the next day. "I admit, when I started on this operation and at the time I took off with the Chairman, I wasn't sure whether it was for real or just another one of your exercises. However, having experienced what I have, meeting the family and so forth, I don't believe even you guys could find actors able to put on a performance with such sincerity that Mordechai and his sister have, despite all your resources. As the day rolled on, I realised my original thinking was flawed and this thing really is for real at which time I admit I wished you were with me the whole day," he said looking at Ruti. "As we drove past you, the thought did quickly cross my mind whether I would ever see you again." But his tone had still not changed even with this admission. "You guys could be right about there being a real threat here, something far bigger than you initially believed and which I sense could undermine the stability of the region," Jerry finished with.

"We have all had another long and exhausting day," Sara stated. "On reflection, it's been fairly successful thanks to Jerry, despite him taking unnecessary risks," she said thoughtfully. "Fortunately for us all he has come through the experience unscathed and we have a good opening into finding out what's going on. I'm not sure how much to congratulate you, Jerry, because I nearly smoked myself to death this evening and I wasn't alone. Everyone here was very concerned for you, we're your friends as well as colleagues, remember that you're part of a team, please be a team player from now on," Sara repeated, staring at him. "Let's all get some rest now and meet for breakfast at say, 7am." Everyone got up and as Jerry started to make his way to the door for a well earned three hour sleep, Sara stopped him for an affectionate hug, the others queuing behind her.

As Jerry finally managed to leave the room Sara called out, "You need to call Rochelle later this morning without fail. Besides the fact I promised you would, she didn't interpret the message quite as you thought, it actually upset her and she thinks you're having a mental breakdown, you called her by mistake and that you didn't even recognise her voice. Please don't forget."

Twenty-Seven

The morning started with a review of the information Jerry had obtained the previous day, assessing its reliability as far as possible, Jerry providing a short brief on each of his sources. He informed them: "Mordechai is the Chairman's son who had just finished university and is now looking for a job in corporate communications whilst his daughter Madi, who I believe is about eighteen, is preparing to start her conscription in the IDF." In Israel, Jerry found out, higher education was something Israelis undertake after they have completed their obligatory three years national service making Mordechai a year or two older than himself. The team recognised Jerry had accomplished a lot, the only person in the family he hadn't managed to speak with was the Chairman's wife. He had also remembered who had contributed what, allowing the information to be considered both on an individual basis and then validated against each other's, looking for contradictions. None could be found!

It was agreed Jerry would continue to use the cover story he had formulated. It seemed to be working and he could probably run quite a lot further with it, despite the fact it would be impossible to change at this stage, although Sara was very concerned that he would be recognised, leading to a whole host of problems and certainly blowing him out. Meanwhile, he was required to tell Moshe the precise details of it to allow all the supporting evidence to be put in place should anyone attempt to substantiate any part of it. Fortunately the story was relatively simple with minimal checks available, the major ones being his stay in Israel, an easy task for Moshe to organise and the UK side, ensuring Jerry was enrolled at the University of London on the course he had stated, a breeze of a job for Dr Fog. The other important point to organise was the tutor he had called from the Chairman's house, another item for the doctor in London to organise. Moshe was also given the responsibility of finding and briefing Jerry with as much information as possible regarding trade unions, enabling him to talk with knowledge of the subject rather than risking the chance of being caught out.

To gain the confidence of both Mordechai and Madi, Jerry told them his thesis included an analysis of the effect on the family where one member of it holds an influential public position and able to influence local or national politics. Jerry used the example of the reaction of friends affected as a direct result of a strike, asking if any blame was pointed towards either of them.

Despite the success of day two, time was of the essence and it was clear there was insufficient time for Jerry to continue to work all the sources alone. Somehow they had to get others into the families' confidence. With that in mind, Jerry thought it would be useful to categorise the sources in order of priority. "Of the three, top of the list is obviously the Chairman, but I'm not convinced he knows exactly what's going on. Then there's Mordechai, who has taken more than a casual interest in the business calls and meetings his father has hosted at home," adding, "I just can't figure out why he's taken such an interest. Finally, with the least ability to assist us is Madi who claims to have only seen and heard snippets, although I sense she knows more than she's letting on. The wife is keeping schtum, I don't think it's even worth the time attempting to speak to her."

Thinking for a minute Jerry announced, "Whilst we were chatting yesterday, I sensed that Mordechai was unattached and in search of romance. I think we could play on that if Ruti is willing," he turned his attention to her. "You're very pretty and from what I've seen, you have a great bubbly personality, an ideal catch for any man and I'm sure Mordechai would jump at the opportunity. I'm sure you can quickly worm your way into his affections, rapidly gaining his confidence. As I found out yesterday, once he starts talking there isn't anything that will stop him and I'm sure you'll be able to draw additional information from him. With a little luck he'll take you home where you'll be able to see and hear everything." As he finished, he noticed Ruti nod her head and smile and as if accepting the role.

Jerry suggested he concentrate his efforts on the Chairman although he wanted to meet with Madi one more time. If after that meeting he felt she had more to offer, they would have to consider introducing a third person.

Everyone contemplated Jerry's suggestions and Sara eventually agreed to it after reconstructing the seating arrangement of the previous evening, where it was proved that at the very best, Mordechai could only have seen Ruti's back and that was unlikely. Sara felt it would be disastrous if Mordechai recognised Ruti from the café, believing it wouldn't take him long to realise he was being set up. The next task was to plan how to introduce Ruti to Mordechai.

Debra eventually came up with the most workable idea and was roped into participating in it. The scheme required Jerry to invite Mordechai to a bar or café, where the introduction would take place. Yakov was tasked with creating a cover story for Ruti and to avoid any further sagas of losing agents, Sara requisitioned two surveillance teams to cover both Jerry and Ruti for their protection. Based on the intelligence already gathered, they were sanctioned immediately and without question.

The first action on Jerry was to arrange the chance meeting between Mordechai and Ruti. He called his new friend and organised lunch at a café in the centre of town. Aware that things needed to progress at a faster pace, he planned to meet with Mordechai's father again, managing to get a window in the Chairman's diary for mid afternoon, giving him ample time to match make Mordechai and Ruti. Following that meeting, Jerry planned to see Madi, but not knowing how long he would be with her dad, he decided to wait until he was finished before calling her.

As the designated time to meet with Mordechai drew near, Ruti made her way to the café with Debra whilst Jerry found his own way in a rental car requisitioned for the operation. The girls arrived as planned, half an hour before Jerry, who on arrival, found Mordechai already seated at a window table near the entrance, some way through a bottle of Maccabi beer. The café was full, mainly of young people, Jerry guessed between the ages of twenty and forty who, judging by the noise level, loved the sound of their own voices. Sitting at a table close by, were two good looking girls enjoying lunch whilst deep in conversation. A waitress handed Jerry a menu and waited to take the order as if in a rush to clear them out as quickly as possible. Having dealt with the waitress, the two lads continued their conversation from the previous evening, Mordechai showing real interest in Jerry's research, something Jerry found surprising, not believing he could be so convincing on a subject he knew virtually nothing about. Everything he'd spoken about so far to both Mordechai and his father was based on information he remembered from various media items and for the first time Jerry was pleased he had always taken an interest in global news and current affairs, reading the daily papers and listening to the bulletins on TV. At least today Jerry had the additional benefit of the briefing Moshe gave him.

Whilst eating, Jerry changed the topic of conversation to girlfriends and during the discussion boasted to Mordechai he had never had a problem pulling a girl and good looking ones at that. In his mind he knew it to be a lie, but of course he couldn't let on. Mordechai, with a hint of jealousy in his voice, remarked on how lucky Jerry was, explaining he had always been shy, forever having to pluck up the courage to ask a girl out. Jerry couldn't help smiling to himself on hearing Mordechai's comment and was pleased to know he was not alone in being intimidated by the opposite sex. Mordechai continued to tell Jerry that despite having had a few girlfriends, he was still a virgin, quickly adding it was not by choice. Jerry thought he was hearing more than he needed about Mordechai's sex life, but was relieved to know that Ruti would be safe in his company. Continuing the game with Mordechai, Jerry bet him he could pull any girl in the café and even find a spare for Mordechai who laughed and agreed if Jerry succeeded, he would pick up the tab for lunch. Jerry directed his head in the direction of two girls sitting a few tables behind Mordechai. "Don't turn round like that," Jerry quietly rebuked him. "Once the waitress has cleared these plates I'll ask them to join us," Jerry said and keeping to his word, when the table was cleaned, Jerry approached the two strangers, Mordechai trying to subtly watch his every move.

Jerry stood beside the girls' table for a few minutes and now Mordechai could just hear them giggling above the background noise. Shortly after, Jerry returned to Mordechai, "Failed, did you?" he suggested, delighted Jerry was unable to live up to the reputation he gave, although at the same time disappointed he was unsuccessful.

"I wouldn't put it exactly like that," Jerry replied.

"Well they haven't come running into your arms, have they?" As Mordechai was finishing his sentence, the two girls made their way over to where Jerry was still standing. Jerry beckoned to Debra to sit beside him and Ruti naturally sat beside Mordechai, who was more than surprised and very pleased he had succeeded.

"We are about to order dessert," Jerry said to the girls after encouraging everyone to introduce themselves. "What would you like?" He asked them whilst calling over the waitress to take the order.

Conversation between the four of them started very generally, each person stating what they did for a living, the girls sounding very convincing whilst regurgitating their cover stories. They were both dressed appropriately for the hot sunny day it had become, wearing short skirts and loose tops and Mordechai couldn't take his eyes off Ruti's exposed, well tanned thighs, something that annoyed Jerry. Seeing Mordechai and Ruti were starting to get on well together, Debra turned her affections towards Jerry, leaving Ruti and Mordechai to talk together. Having finished their desserts and looking at her watch, Debra announced she had to get back to work. Jerry stated he also needed to move on, as much as he would have loved to stay a little longer, but pointed out with a smile that three's a crowd. Ruti asked Mordechai not to rush off since she was enjoying herself and didn't have to be anywhere, to which Mordechai agreed. "You'll get the bill won't you Mordechai," Jerry said winking at him with a smile across his face. Once outside the café, Debra and Jerry kissed on the cheek, in clear view of Mordechai before going their separate ways, Ruti and Mordechai almost unaware the others had left, since they were deep in conversation.

Jerry entered the Histadrut building for his appointment with the Chairman. Once again the discussion started with the organisation in general, this time concentrating on the management committee. Jerry then decided to chance his luck by throwing in a few 'What If' scenarios. Initially they were non-specific situations, with him showing a keen interest in the Chairman's responses, even to the point of cross-examination. He then posed more probing questions, maintaining the same matter of fact tone, asking, "What could happen if militants were able to gain control of a trade union?" purposely not mentioning any names. A number of possibilities were discussed with Jerry making notes and taking time to talk through several hypothetical situations, both men clearly enjoying themselves. The Chairman eventually asked how such issues fitted in with Jerry's research, to which he received an immediate honest response: "To be honest, I'm not quite sure yet. I have examples from various countries where unions have managed to topple governments, particularly non socialist ones, but I want to consider the question of their ability to do far greater damage to a country, if that were possible."

The Chairman thought for a minute and Jerry believed he was about to speak, only for silence to prevail. Jerry finally said one word, excitedly, as though it had just sprung to mind, "Blackmail."

"What?" the Chairman asked with a look as if a bolt of lightening had hit him. "What do you mean by blackmail?"

Jerry, remaining excited asked, "What could happen if the leadership were being blackmailed? Is it a scenario worth considering?"

Jerry noticed the Chairman stuttering for the first time. "Yes, I suppose it is," he answered. "But how could the payment of money have an adverse affect on either the union or the country?" he asked sheepishly as though he had something to hide.

"As part of my course I've had to consider the way in which policy is made, for instance; who decides on a call for action? Who decides on whether a vote should take place? Who has the authority to agree terms and settle a dispute? And so on. Following through on that concept, what if the blackmailers were not interested in money but had some sort of hold over the union, making it carry out their demands and thereby controlling policy or decision making. I don't know, is such a situation feasible?" Jerry asked.

The Chairman failed to address any of the issues Jerry posed as if in some kind of trance. Finally he said, "I'm sorry, I need some fresh air. Can we continue another time?"

Jerry, not wishing to break off at this critical stage suggested, "Let's go for a stroll outside, I could do with some exercise."

They walked around the area for the best part of an hour, the whole time discussing the Histadrut. Finishing, they slowly made their way back to the office and Jerry thanked the Chairman for his time. They shook hands and Jerry, just about to walk off, quickly added, "If I need anything else, I'll give you a call and thanks for everything, you really have been a great help." The Chairman then disappeared inside the building.

Jerry returned to the Kibbutz as quickly as he could, reporting back to Sara. "Let's see what Ruti has found out and take it from there. You've done well, but we still don't know what organisation is behind it," Sara told him. Jerry was amazed at how calm she remained throughout his debrief.

Ruti returned a couple of hours later, although it was only a flying visit on the pretext of freshening up and changing into something more suitable for the evening, since she and Mordechai were dining out together. The information she managed to extract was minimal, it wasn't easy to start discussing such subjects in the first few hours of a date. She was still in the let's get to know you phase of the relationship. Jerry concluded the two of them were already getting on well together, noticing a couple of red marks on Ruti's neck that he could have sworn were not there before she left for lunch. The little she did find out concurred with Jerry's information and she was tasked with trying to identify the militants and if possible the group controlling them.

Twenty-Eight

The following morning, having had an early breakfast, the team met up in the operations room and again analysed the information. Mordechai had unknowingly been somewhat talkative during the evening, naming people that had recently become frequent visitors to their house. "It's amazing the special properties booze contains," Ruti laughed.

Sara tasked the remainder of the team with finding out everything they possibly could on the names supplied whilst Ruti was to continue working Mordechai which she didn't mind whatsoever and Jerry was still trying to catch up with Madi, having failed to make contact with her following the meeting he had with her father the previous afternoon which lasted far longer than anticipated.

Before Ruti went to meet Mordechai, Sara decided it would be prudent for her to brief her boss on the information already obtained, whilst she did the same, both making it clear that at this stage the information had not been substantiated and therefore not to be considered as confirmed intelligence.

Ruti then returned to the loving arms of Mordechai, a budding romance as far as he was concerned, they were really getting on well together despite the short time they had known each other. Ruti was slightly concerned as Mordechai had passed a comment over dinner the previous evening stating he thought she was taking an unhealthy interest in his father's occupation, but judging by the number of times he called her that morning, she was relaxed in the knowledge he had obviously accepted her response.

Jerry used all the charm he could muster to arrange lunch with Madi, during which she claimed not to have overheard any telephone conversations, although admitted noticing a number of visitors to the house over the last year or so, commenting that until then, her father had always refrained from bringing work home. She admitted that some of the men frightened her, even though she had nothing to do with them; all the meetings taking place in her father's study behind closed doors. Madi had frequently heard shouting and whenever her mother asked about the arguments, she was always told to not get involved and that it had nothing to do with her. On the occasions she persisted in her questioning, it inevitably ended in terrible arguments, so Madi made a point of keeping out of the way.

Jerry repeated his reason for asking such questions since Madi constantly enquired why he was so interested in her father's private meetings, asking questions such as: "What do my dad's meetings have to do with your research?" Obviously suspicious of him, Jerry was not sure how he was going to extract descriptions of the visitors from her, something he really wanted as he felt she would be able to describe them in detail, having demonstrated a meticulous manner about her. By matching images to names, Jerry believed it would help in identifying the individuals involved.

Jerry backtracked a little, reminding Madi she mentioned how scared she often became and how the problem was affecting her parent's relationship. "From what you've said, the trouble is certainly having a significant negative impact on the family and therefore very much within the remit of my research." Whilst enjoying a pizza, they chatted about the effect it was having on her and how she was actually looking forward to getting away from it all whilst in the army.

"Just out of interest, nothing to do with my thesis whatsoever, I'm fascinated to see how our perception of things differ. It's something I covered as part of a philosophy module in my first year at university," Jerry said, completely out of the blue. "Two people can look at the same image and see very different things. That's what art is all about, different interpretations of the same subject." For a reason that eluded Jerry, all of a sudden Madi wanted to tell him everything she knew, as though a safe in her head had just been unlocked. She was immediately far more relaxed talking to him and Jerry decided it was an opportunity he wasn't going to lose. Without further hesitation, Madi spent the next forty-five minutes graphically describing several of the visitors.

Jerry stated he would also be in fear of the individuals as she had described them. "Putting that aside," he started as a summation, "Returning to my research, it's clear the family unit can be severely affected when a member of it is in a prominent political position as in your case." He then thanked her for taking the time to meet with him. "I'm here for a while longer," he said. "If you think of anything else that might be useful, you know where to find me, just leave a message for me if I'm not around."

The additional information both Ruti and Jerry had gained throughout the day was passed to the rest of the team during the evening debriefing session and the task of researching all the individuals continued through the night by a support team Sara had created in her office. In all, there were more than sixty people working on identifying the various individuals. By breakfast, full names, addresses and various other details had been found for several of the descriptions and one of the largest surveillance operations ever instigated in Israel had already been implemented.

The Prime Minister was briefed early the following morning and it was decided he should attempt an off the record meeting with the Chairman, without mentioning anything which could compromise either Jerry or Ruti. The objective was to stop the strike, which it was believed in itself would lessen the affect of any attack if the security forces were unable to prevent it entirely.

The Chairman managed to avoid a meeting with the Prime Minister for two days, which again was completely out of character. Aware that strike day was quickly looming, Sara finally decided to send a car to collect him, taking him directly to the Prime Minister. Ruti's decision to continue her relationship with Mordechai, despite the fact that everyone thought she had already bled him dry of information, ensured that Sara knew the whereabouts of the Chairman to enable the collection to be made.

The Prime Minister was never a man to mince his words and not about to start now. He immediately informed the Chairman he was aware things were not quite as they should be within the Histadrut. He tried to cajole the man into revealing all, thereby creating a route to resolving the issue, however, the response was constant denial to the various allegations the Prime Minister put to him. Beginning to lose patience, the Prime Minister stated he was aware Hizbollah terrorists had infiltrated the Histadrut, linking up with a small group of militants and he went on to explain the plan combining the next strike with a major terrorist attack against Israel. Sara had been able to confirm the involvement of Hizbollah the previous day from the descriptions Madi had given Jerry. Sara's team, having managed to locate and detain two of the terrorists involved, had extracted by interrogation, the proposed offensive. Following this intelligence, all checkpoints between Israel and the Palestinian Territories had orders to stop and hold every fuel tanker trying to pass into Israel. Roadblocks were also quickly established on the minor roads used by Palestinians entering Israel when wishing to avoid the lengthy delays that existed at the checkpoints and border patrols were substantially boosted. All military and police leave was cancelled, effective immediately and an order was given to stop and search on site all civilian fuel tankers within Israel.

The Prime Minister informed the Chairman that fuel tankers laden with explosives were to be driven onto petrol station forecourts across the length and breadth of the country with the explosives being detonated simultaneously. "The terrorists anticipate the strike will create large queues at garages due to the fear of fuel shortages and when the tankers explode," he paused momentarily, "Well, I'm sure you can imagine the resulting scenes," adding, "To make matters worse, our emergency services will be delayed in reaching the blast sites due to the additional municipal disruption caused by the strike." He stopped to allow the full extent of the potential carnage to be digested.

"The long and short of it is the strike must be called off immediately," the Prime Minister instructed the Chairman. "Tell me what hold they have on you and I'll do my best to protect you." The information available on the blackmail was pure speculation on Jerry's part, following the stroll he had taken with the Chairman.

The Chairman pondered the situation for a short while and finally provided the Prime Minister with the full story, going into great detail, but tried to assure the Prime Minister he had no knowledge of any terrorist activity. He suddenly had a look of fear on his face, having suddenly appreciated the full extent of what was happening. He concluded the meeting by assuring the Prime Minister he would do his utmost to reverse the strike call.

By the ninth day of the operation, the IDF had seized fifteen tankers laden with explosives, with a further twenty-seven held at checkpoints, although only two of them had explosives found on them.

A further vote for strike action had been scheduled for late afternoon that day, with a recommendation to abort from the full management of the Histadrut. At 9pm the result came through. It was close, only three percent difference between aborting and proceeding with the action. Fortunately, the three percent was in favour of aborting. Within minutes of the result, seven militant union members and a number of suicide bombers found in possession of, or driving fuel tankers, were arrested.

Twenty-Nine

On route to the airport for a week's break with Rochelle, Jerry and Sara stopped off for a short meeting where he was introduced to the Prime Minister. Eager to be with Rochelle, Jerry thought he would have rather been making his way to Ben Gurion than sitting listening to a politician, even if it were only to be for a few minutes. The Prime Minister had wanted to personally thank Jerry for his part in aborting what could have been the worst terrorist attack in Israel for many years. "Your efforts have averted bloodshed on a scale I can't even pretend to contemplate," the Prime Minister told him, continuing, "We have a policy not to disclose the names of our country's heroes, but suffice it to say you will be commended for your efforts in averting this attack," the Prime Minister stated. "You should be very proud of yourself, Mr Freedman." With that comment the meeting concluded. Back in the car Jerry had to admit he was impressed the Prime Minister had taken the trouble to meet with him and imagined the memory of the occasion would stay with him forever. They continued the journey to the airport where he would finally be reunited with Rochelle and together they would catch a flight to Eilat for a well earned week's holiday.

He was taken to the departure lounge in terminal two, the terminal for internal flights, where he found Rochelle who had already been there for several hours, having arrived from London much earlier that morning. Sara handed Jerry an envelope containing a bundle of Shekels, details of the Eilat Princess, the hotel they were booked into, vouchers for excursions including Scuba Diving and Swimming with the Dolphins, the phone number for a taxi driver that would drive them around wherever they wanted and of course their boarding passes. She also handed him a mobile phone. "Just call if you need anything," Sara told them and looking at Rochelle: "He deserves a lot of love and pampering this week, he's worked very hard." She paused. "I'll leave the two of you to it. See you in seven days. Have fun!" With that said, she left Jerry and Rochelle hugging and kissing.

Rochelle told Jerry how much she had been looking forward to being together again and how she was concerned the trip may have been postponed due to talk of yet another general strike in the country. She had endured more than enough of them being separated and was now definitely ready to start planning the wedding he had intimated whilst waiting for his flight at Heathrow airport many weeks earlier, all that was necessary was for him to propose properly. Having been given his cue, Jerry managed to tell her just how much he was missing her and the week was going to be about them and them alone, no talk of the office whatsoever. His words brought tears to her eyes, which, completely out of character had the same effect on him. They spent the rest of the time whilst waiting for their flight, hugging and kissing.

Forty five minutes later, which to Jerry and Rochelle seemed like just a few minutes, they were led out with around 70 other passengers to board what looked like a fifty year old bucket with wings attached. It was painted bright yellow and had rust marks over the entire fuselage and the propellers on both sides looked as though they had seen better days. "Are they serious?" Rochelle asked Jerry, referring to them boarding the plane.

"I'm sure it's quite safe, but you can hold onto me as tight as you like. I don't think we'll have the opportunity to join the mile high club on this flight though," he said smiling.

The journey lasted a little over an hour and turned out to be very smooth, although the hum of the engines was somewhat on the loud side. After they collected their luggage and walked through the small arrivals hall of Eilat airport, they spotted a board being held up with Rochelle's name on it.

"I'll take you to your hotel, it's the Princess I believe," the driver said.

"That's the one, is it nice?" Jerry asked.

"One of the best hotels in Eilat. You could spend your whole vacation there without leaving the grounds and you would never be bored," the driver replied.

"We could do that in the worst hotel here," Rochelle butted in, nudging Jerry in her normal way, immediately noticing how much firmer his muscles had become.

They settled into their suite, not having to check-in and agreed to have a late lunch in the room, they had a lot of catching up to do. Rochelle reminded him it had been nine weeks since they had been together and then only for three days. Despite the fact Jerry couldn't tell her how much he was missing her on the frequent phone calls between them, he continued to repeat it now they were together. Rochelle had not changed whatsoever, she still looked stunning, even more so in his eyes now, since he hadn't seen her for so long. Jerry on the other hand had lost more weight since the last time they were together and his physique had continued to develop. He was now looking like a slim version of a competitor in the TV contest The World's Strongest Man. Her only comment as she slowly removed each garment of his one by one, was that she didn't want him to lose any more weight or develop his muscles further, he was now butch enough for her. Stopping for a candle lit romantic dinner for two on the beach, they finished the evening as they had started it, showing each other just how much love existed between them.

Most of the following day was spent on the private beach belonging to the hotel, Rochelle looking as though she was modelling the bikini she chose to wear that day. Following a light lunch at the beach bar, they found a quiet area and went skinny-dipping and after drying off by lying on the soft sand, taking turns to rub sunscreen lotion over each other, they took a romantic stroll through the town, returning to the hotel having just enough time to make love again before dressing for dinner. They spent the evening dancing at the hotel's nightclub, retiring to their suite early, Rochelle not believing she had fully fulfilled her promise to Sara of pampering and smothering Jerry with love. The rest of the week was spent doing the usual tourist things, excursions, Scuba diving and various boat trips as well as spending time on the beach where Rochelle ensured she made the most of the sun, creating an all over tan, whilst Jerry enjoyed rubbing the lotion over her whole body. The only excursion they couldn't do which appealed to them both was a trip into Egypt, since it required passports and Jerry didn't have his, it wasn't needed for the internal flight. Throughout the holiday, Rochelle had been careful not to ask Jerry anything about his training and to compensate, she gave an almost minute by minute account of what she had been up to since they were last together, excluding the business, keeping her word they wouldn't discuss it.

The week passed far too quickly for both of them and before they knew it they were on the plane returning to Tel Aviv, where Rochelle was catching an interconnecting flight back to London and Sara was meeting Jerry. "How much longer do you think you'll be here?" she asked Jerry as they heard the landing gear locking into place.

"I really don't know. I hope not too long. I'm told I'm progressing well, but who knows what they have planned," Jerry replied. "I seem to recall that they were initially talking about three to four months and its now coming close to four so hopefully it won't be much longer," he said on reflection. "But they also told me that the break would be around the half way mark, although I think they were only planning one break at that time and this is the second," he added. "Have they organised any more flights for you?" he asked.

"No, but they only informed me about this trip around two weeks ago so no clues there," and she leant over and kissed him. "I love you darling and I can't wait for you to come home," she whispered in his ear.

"Me too, on both counts. I have to admit I've enjoyed the change and learnt a lot, but I've had enough and want to be home with you again," he replied as they felt the thump of the wheels hitting the ground.

They disembarked, had one last hug and kiss and went their separate ways.

Thirty

Sara met Jerry in the arrivals hall and immediately greeted him with, "Hi Jerry, I trust you enjoyed your break and are well rested," as she motioned him towards the exit where a car was waiting to take them to the Sheraton Hotel in Tel Aviv. As they arrived, she informed him, "You'll be based here again for a short time, but don't think you're still on holiday. There's a session on the range this morning, then onto a gym since I realise just how much you've missed both over the last couple of weeks," she said smiling. "Dani is going to work with you on a one to one basis so you should enjoy yourself," quickly adding, "I did tell him that both you and your girlfriend are happy with your facial features the way they are and he assured me that he would try his best not to modify them. So sort yourself out and get changed quickly, we're already late."

"Nothing changes here does it? Except that I must be going up in the world, I've got a suite this time." Jerry observed looking around the bedroom.

"You'll notice that the lounge area will be converted to a classroom by the time you get back, so don't get too excited by the suite, it was cheaper than booking two rooms," Sara replied before changing to a much softer tone, saying "I'm not sure I congratulated you on the great job you did the other week, even if you were a little reckless. I'm very proud to be responsible for you and I also speak for Debra, Moshe and all your trainers. Even Ruti, who's a very experienced field officer couldn't praise you enough." Sara said with real sincerity. "The people of Israel, although the majority of which will never know, are forever indebted to you and I assure you there will always be a home here for you and your family. Now let's get on with the job in hand, you have more training sessions to complete." Having finished what she wanted to say, Sara gave him a kiss on his cheek.

The next three hours were spent playing Shoot The Baddy, Save The Goody, as Jerry named the fun packed game, this time playing it inside a building where the lighting conditions kept changing, as well as outside in the bright sunlight. They then took a short drive from the range to a gym where Dani was waiting to rough him up a little, demonstrating how to use the body as an excellent fighting machine.

Jerry hadn't noticed until now, but the aches and pains he had sustained from the previous training sessions had subsided whilst he had not been in the gym. Despite the shock to his body on using certain muscles again during the strenuous warm up exercises and the constant blows he sustained from Dani, he was surprised how much he enjoyed the session and looked forward to the next.

Sara was correct, by the time they returned to the hotel the suite had been transformed to look like a school with a bed at one end. Even the television had been changed to one with a larger screen and a Video and DVD player had been connected. The best part was the installation of a computer linked to the Internet, the only device Jerry had really missed. Sara was concerned from a security angle about him collecting his emails, but he assured her he could do so without leaving a trace and she finally bowed to his greater knowledge on the subject, fully aware of his background. She then informed him they were entering the final phase of the course which would continue to concentrate on teaching him to protect himself; from recognising he was under surveillance, to handling himself under different types of interrogation. On most days there would be two sessions with Dani in the gym and three sessions a week on the range which he still considered a complete waste of time and told Sara so. The rest of the time he would cover theory in his bedroom, or practise on the streets of Tel Aviv, carrying out exercises based on what he learnt in the classroom. Having been taught the intricate techniques of surveillance, he would practice detecting if he were being watched, including how to force a team into the open. He learnt to use peripheral vision, enabling him to sense things at the very edge of what the eye can see, data that is normally dismissed by the brain. What Jerry found most reassuring was being told the majority of organisations didn't have the resources or capabilities to run a proper shadowing job, thereby making it far easier for such an operation to be exposed. He enjoyed learning the various tricks to flush out anyone pursuing him whether he was in a vehicle or on foot.

Over the three weeks following his return from Eilat, Jerry completed several street exercises where at the end of each he had to state whether he thought he was being followed, which on some occasion he was, others not. The exercises were carried out in both busy shopping areas and open spaces, whilst walking and driving, where he had to be careful not to be distracted from the road, but at the same time carrying out his checks, knowing he wouldn't be able to lose the opposition by crashing the vehicle. He learnt to select locations that would provide him with the best opportunity of viewing the surrounding area whilst not appearing suspicious, such as shops with large windows which provide excellent vantage points, particularly corner shops allowing him to monitor all directions. They taught him to always purchase something, thereby having a reason for entering the shop. He could use a call box for the same purpose, again ensuring he made a call in case it was checked. The trick he enjoyed the most was in a car, practicing driving at night without lights and dropping into parking spaces. Tutors demonstrated how to detect whether anyone had disturbed his belongings, opening doors and removing or planting additional items for a potential set up. Jerry happily passed on his knowledge of detecting intruders in electronic data and protecting against such intrusion using Igloo's standard sales demonstration.

On one occasion, during the third week whilst on an exercise, Jerry was in the process of checking whether he was being followed by subtly looking through the windows of a convenience store located on the corner of a busy crossroads, appearing to be browsing the various Israeli newspapers and magazines, holding one in his hand. Whilst surveying the area, he spotted a white four-door saloon with a magnetic blue strobe flashing on its roof, heading towards the store, coming to a screeching halt outside the entrance. Three large men jumped from the vehicle, one waited outside with the car whilst the other two burst inside and headed in Jerry's direction. "Who are you?" the lead man shouted at him in Hebrew, at the same time as quickly showing his badge. Jerry thought for a moment, caught off guard and in a state of confusion. Trying to think of the best response, he made out he didn't understand Hebrew, forcing the man to repeat the question in broken English, giving Jerry time to consider his response. Jerry immediately replied with his name. "You will come with us," the same man shouted. His partner had positioned himself in such a way so Jerry couldn't move, although no physical contact had taken place, grabbed the magazine Jerry was holding and then secured his hands behind his back using plastic wire ties, followed by pulling a hood over his head before he was marched out to the waiting car.

Prior to being shoved into the back of the vehicle and made to lie on the floor, he was frisked to ensure he was not carrying any weapons. The three men kept shouting at Jerry in Hebrew, calling him a terrorist whilst Jerry maintained he couldn't understand what they were saying. "English, English," he continually repeated, the words muffled by the hood. He felt the engine start and the car sped off at high speed with the siren blaring.

Eventually the siren went quiet and they came to a stop. Jerry heard the doors open just as he was grabbed under the armpits, dragged from the car, then frog marched into a building and along what he thought must be a stone walled corridor into a dingy smelling room he deduced to be a cell. The door was slammed shut behind him, although he could clearly hear constant chatter from a two-way radio and its operator close by. Speaking in Hebrew, one of his captors asked him to empty his pockets and again Jerry made out he didn't understand. A minute or so later, a new voice with an American accent spoke to him in English. Not having heard anyone else enter the room after the door was closed, Jerry assumed the new voice must have already been in the room when he arrived. The voice appeared softer, friendlier and politely asked:

"Jerry, please empty your pockets."

"How can I," Jerry replied. "My hands are tied behind my back, his voice still muffled by the hood.

"My apologies," the voice replied apologetically and Jerry thought he was about to lose the uncomfortable hand restraints. "That's not a problem, I'll empty them for you," the person said and removed everything from Jerry's pockets using as much force as he could get away with, followed by another complete body search from head to foot, pushing Jerry against the wall several times as hard as he possibly could for no apparent reason.

"Please release my arms and remove this cover from my head," Jerry pleaded with him.

"All in good time," was the reply as if they were the best of friends. "For the moment, please just do as I ask." There was a fairly lengthy pause followed by, "I think you need a little exercise having being cramped as you were in the car, so show me how high you can jump," he asked Jerry who immediately complied without question. "Not just once, keep jumping," the voice ordered, this time in an angry tone after the first jump. "That's very good," the man said, Jerry having jumped several times. "Please continue to jump until I tell you to rest and if you stop before I allow it, or I don't think you are jumping high enough, I will signal to you like this," and at that moment Jerry was struck across the back of the knees with a baton. "Can I assume we understand each other?" the voice asked.

"Yes, I understand you," Jerry managed to stutter as he continued jumping, ignoring as best he could the pain that shot through him. His wrists were quickly becoming raw from the continual rubbing of the plastic ties caused by the movement and although he couldn't be sure, he thought he felt a trickle of blood running down his left hand. He endured numerous whacks from the stick, not just making contact with the back of his knees, thighs and calves, but also across his back and kidney area and he wondered what Dani would do in this predicament. Having no idea how long he had been jumping, he was finally commanded to stop. He heard the door being opened and was then pushed out into the corridor and led to another room where he was thrown into a chair before quickly being pulled back up to a standing stance. To Jerry's relief, his hands were released and he was shoved back into the hard wooden chair, almost toppling over backwards.

There were a couple of minutes during which Jerry could sense no movement or sound in the room and then, as if by magic, his hood was removed. "So what's your name," the same voice said from across a desk enabling Jerry to put a face to it.

The man was not one of the two that entered the shop, but Jerry was unable to tell if it was the third that waited outside. Like those that arrested him, he was of substantial build, wearing a long sleeve dark blue shirt with the top two buttons undone and his sleeves neatly rolled up his arms above his elbows, similar to the way Jerry had often seen soldiers dress. His skin was a dark tan and his head and face cleanly shaven. Using his periphery vision rather than moving his head, Jerry was aware of two other men standing almost behind him, one on either side of the chair.

"Jerry Freedman," he replied

"Your real name?" the interrogator asked.

"That is my real name," Jerry stated in a timid voice, still very confused about the situation, not knowing if he was participating in yet another exercise, or he really had been arrested. Following the error he initially made with the Histadrut briefing, this time he wasn't prepared to jump to any hasty conclusions. The only thing he was sure about was the intense pain he felt over almost his entire body from being hit so frequently whilst jumping. He thought: "Surely they wouldn't have inflicted so much pain on me if this were merely an exercise, not even Dani would go this far, it must be some mistake."

Not believing him, the interrogator asked, "Where's your passport?"

Jerry considered the question carefully. He remembered handing it to either Sara or Debra the day he arrived to keep safe with his other valuables. After trying to analyse the various options open to him, he believed his best option was to use the cover story he had manufactured for the Histadrut operation rather than revealing the truth, certainly at this stage, just in case Sara was behind it, he didn't want to be seen to be giving up so early on. He knew the story inside out, having gone over it so many times in his mind since the operation and whether this was for real or not, the details could be substantiated; he remembered Sara making Moshe do everything necessary for the mission itself.

"It's in my hotel room," he replied, realising after he had said it, what the next question was going to be.

"Which hotel would that be Jerry?" the interrogator enquired sarcastically.

Before it came Jerry had already started to contemplate his response. Should he state the truth or use the hotel Moshe registered him in when providing the cover for Shoshana and the toy shop exercise which suddenly seemed so long ago. He was constantly advised to keep a cover story as close to the truth as possible, so he finally decided to do so, answering "The Sheraton Tel Aviv."

"And what's the reason for your stay here in Israel?" Jerry was asked.

Trying to stick to the story, he found he had difficulty remembering the detail for some reason and then recalled a lecture where he argued the point of one's brain shutting down when under immense pressure or when in shock, now realising the lecturer knew precisely what he was talking about. Jerry finally managed to respond, "I'm doing research for my degree thesis on International Trade Unions and with the recent general strikes here, I was interested in the Histadrut." As soon as the words had left his lips Jerry felt a sudden shiver rush through his body with the thought: "If the guy knew about the terrorist attack and this is for real, then he could easily assume I had some involvement and not believe a word I've said." Since it was too late to change the story, Jerry continued. "I've had several interviews with the Chairman," which he knew could easily be verified, but he completely forgot about the subsequent meeting with the Prime Minister, which would have brought this stupidity to an immediate conclusion. He just couldn't get his brain into gear.

The interrogator ignored Jerry's reply, "And you call yourself Jerry Freedman. Tell me Mr Freedman, why don't you carry any identification? You have no credit cards, no traveller's cheques, no passport, just a few Shekels and a prepay mobile phone with no record on who owns it, one of the advantages of such a call plan, which combined with the lack of other papers, for me adds up to someone who wants to conceal their identity. What's more Mr Freedman, I've never met anyone that peruses a magazine rack full of Hebrew journals and then claims he doesn't understand the language."

That was a very observant point Jerry thought, suddenly realising how such simple errors can be made leading to disaster. "Didn't Sara warn me to be careful during one of our arguments?" he thought, wishing he could turn the clock back.

"Jerry, you were seen peering out of a shop window, who were you looking for?" the officer demanded, "Or who are you trying to hide from? What is the real reason for you being in Israel?" he shouted aggressively.

"I don't know what you're talking about," Jerry insisted, becoming more frightened as time progressed.

The interrogator persisted, "What organisation are you working for, Jerry? Tell me and I can help you. If you don't, there is little I can do except promise you more trouble than you could ever imagine."

"I don't know what you're talking about," Jerry repeated.

"Tell me, Jerry, what's your address in England?" the interrogator asked, sounding as if he were beginning to get somewhat fed up with Jerry's replies.

Jerry had to think for a moment, finding it difficult to remember his address. Trying to regain some sense of reality, he eventually managed to provide the correct information.

"What's your room number?" he was quickly asked, the interrogator changing his line of questioning.

"Room number?" Jerry repeated in a confused voice, still thinking of his home address.

"I thought you said you were staying at the Sheraton Hotel, so I naturally assumed you are staying in a room," the interrogator replied sarcastically while speaking in a quiet friendly voice again, as if he had never shouted.

Having to think again since he had stayed in several rooms and hoping he remembered it correctly he answered, “Oh sorry, its room three two seven.” He then heard and understood the interrogator tell one of the other men to take a team and search the room. Hearing that, Jerry now realised this was no exercise and tried to think as rationally as he could the best way to proceed.

“Please start telling me the truth Mr Freedman. We have been keeping an eye on you for some time before we decided to take you off the streets and throughout the period you have been acting in a very suspicious manner,” the interrogator stated, almost pleading with Jerry to start talking.

Jerry tried to replay in his mind the events of the last few days until the point of his arrest. He couldn’t believe he had not spotted any sign of being watched, he had become quite proficient at recognising when he was under surveillance, considering himself to be a professional at it and rightly so. If the interrogator was speaking the truth and there was no reason for him not to be, Jerry thought it must have been a major operation to avoid detection, something he had been told only a few organisations in the world had the ability to pull off. With this in mind he failed to understand how such a job could have been sanctioned, since the people responsible for authorising it must surely have been at a level where they would have known of his existence. He thought about breaking cover, giving out the emergency phone numbers, but on reflection he didn’t think he would be believed now.

The interrogator changed tact again, shouting angrily. “All I want is the truth. Who are you working for? What is the target? Is the attack planned? What’s your role?” The American relentlessly bombard Jerry with questions.

“I’m telling you the truth,” Jerry kept repeating, the questions and answers just going backwards and forwards without change.

A few minutes later a woman entered the room and spoke to the interrogator in Hebrew, Jerry understanding verbatim what was being said. “I have spoken to the Sheraton Hotel. Room three two seven is occupied by a Mr and Mrs Cohen of New York. They arrived last week, booked in for thirteen nights. The girl on reception said they’re a nice old couple. A team will arrive at the hotel shortly to confirm.”

Jerry thought to himself "That can't be." Then he remembered that Sara had organised all the bookings, he had never had to check-in and had no idea what name the rooms had been booked under. What he couldn't understand was how reception managed to identify the room's occupants. "It is three two seven, I'm sure of it," he thought to himself, terrified to the point he could feel his legs trembling, "God, what mess have I got myself into here?" The interrogator repeated the news in English for Jerry's benefit.

"The receptionist must be mistaken," Jerry blurted out, having had time to consider his response before the information was repeated for him in English. He was now more than ever thankful for Debra's Hebrew lessons, although they were unlikely to get him out of this predicament.

"Well, shortly my men will arrive at the hotel and then we'll know for certain, won't we Mr Freedman?" He waited a moment, then "I ask you again, although I'm getting somewhat fed up repeating the same questions over and over, just tell me the truth and make your life easier," the interrogator pleaded, still choosing not to believe Jerry.

"I've told you the truth," Jerry insisted, not sure what else to say. At that moment he had a vision of Rochelle in her bikini in Eilat. "Was he ever going to see her again?" he wondered. He asked himself if he should mention the trip to Eilat as he was sure it was booked in her name, deciding: "I would only be getting her involved and that certainly isn't fair."

"When and how did you arrive in Israel?" the questioning continued, although Jerry wasn't sure how much he actually heard.

"I arrived about four months ago, by plane, EL AL, from London to Ben Gurion and planned on returning to England in the next few weeks," Jerry said, not being able to think straight.

Another knock on the door interrupted the questioning. "No Jerry Freedman at the Sheraton, no Freedman staying in any hotel or hostel in Tel Aviv. Furthermore, there is no entry for a Mr Jerry Freedman on immigration records going back six months." The report being made by what sounded to be the same female voice as before, but with the door behind him, Jerry couldn't see the face.

After the interrogator repeated the information for Jerry to understand, he added, "So, Jerry, you don't seem to exist in Israel, you carry no identification, you only use cash. Surely you can see things from my point of view and agree it's somewhat unusual?" not expecting a response he continued, "I'd also like to point out to you there is absolutely no way you can avoid immigration at Ben Gurion airport. I'm not going to ask you nicely again, so please just tell me the truth, this is your final opportunity."

Jerry wondered what Sara and Debra did when they stamped his passport. "Did they stamp it?" They returned it to him closed and he never bothered to check, he had no reason too, he had heard it being stamped and was sure he also heard his details being keyed into the computer. He was so confused; he couldn't remember whether it was Debra or Sara that took care of the immigration paperwork whilst the other was doing something else. "What else?" His memory was failing him badly and his mind uncontrollably focusing on the wrong issues. "After all, what difference who dealt with it?" He asked himself. "How could I have been so trusting of them, but then why shouldn't I have been? The fact was they obviously hadn't entered me on the computer, but why not? They had mentioned something in the car whilst on the way to the hotel," but again Jerry couldn't recall what. All he could remember was handing them everything that identified him and could be used to prove who he was. It suddenly dawned on him the interrogator was right; he really didn't officially exist in Israel. All he knew was he had to focus his full attention on getting out of this mess thinking he should have told the truth immediately, now he was just digging himself a deeper and deeper grave as time passed.

"I promise you I've been telling you the truth. I keep my valuables locked up in the hotel. They must have made a mistake," Jerry decided to say, trying to sound confident.

The interrogator stood up and walked over to Jerry's side of the desk, grabbed him by the collar lifting him out of the chair and threw him against a wall. "Don't play games with me, boy," he shouted at Jerry. He then took another baton and hit Jerry across the stomach. Jerry managed to tense his muscles in time to only be slightly winded.

Then another came, and a third. "Now tell me the truth, who are you working for?" he shouted at Jerry, clearly having lost his temper.

Jerry tried to remain calm and suggested they go to the hotel where he could prove he would be recognised.

"You maybe recognised, but what's your real name? And who are you working for?" the interrogator yelled once more, holding Jerry by his collar with one hand, the baton in his other, pushed under Jerry's chin in an upwardly direction.

"I've been telling you the truth the whole time," Jerry cried out again. He wondered how long he had been there and if Sara had sounded the alarm. "Surely that would bring an end to this nightmare," he thought, followed by "I obviously wasn't being followed by her team on this occasion since they would have stopped this mess when they saw me being arrested."

"Throw him in the cell and get him in front of a magistrate tomorrow morning before I do something to him I might regret," the interrogator ordered the other officers.

"Yes sir," one answered and within moments he was marched off to a cell, after his hands had again been secured behind his back and the hood replaced over his head. He heard the door slam shut and then locked.

For what he thought was several hours, Jerry sat on the bench that was his bed, listening to the chatter on the radio. He knew he was in some sort of specialist police station, guessing it must be anti terrorist, but failed to understand why they kept his hands secured and his head covered.

Eventually he heard footsteps close to the door followed by the sound of it being unlocked. Jerry had no idea of the time, with the hood he couldn't even determine whether he had been there overnight or not, although he thought he had.

"Your final chance to tell the truth," It was the same American again.

"I have told you the truth!" was Jerry's only reply. He was then swiftly dragged out to a waiting car, forced to lie on the floor in the back and with the siren blaring he sensed being driven off at high speed again.

The car finally came to a halt where he was pulled out and marched into a building. He couldn't be a hundred percent sure, but thought he recognised the feel of it. That was until he was dragged up several flights of stairs, having no idea how many, then dragged along a corridor into a room where he heard the door close behind him. The only encouragement he had was the feeling of standing on a soft carpet rather than the hard stone floor.

The hand restraints were removed and the interrogator's voice announced, "Your honour," in English. The hood was removed and as his eyes adjusted to the bright daylight, Jerry found himself standing before Sara, Debra and the policeman that had spent many sessions teaching him how to react when being interrogated, his abusers standing either side and behind him.

Sara spoke first, "Sorry about the pain. Dani told us that you wouldn't notice it, but it did look ruthless. We'll take you to hospital and have you checked out just to make sure you haven't sustained any serious injuries." Debra had some antiseptic cream ready and gently rubbed it into his very sore wrists, before covering them with bandages. "It had to be realistic, I hope you appreciate that," Sara told him with a look as if she had felt every blow.

"I assume I passed and can I please eat before we go to the hospital, these animals didn't even have the courtesy to offer me a drink, let alone something to eat," Jerry replied having worked out for himself he had spent the best part of twenty four hours under arrest, missing out on lunch, dinner and breakfast.

"You passed with top marks," they all said together.

"And no, we will have a decent meal after the hospital, just in case you need any treatment. Come on, the sooner we go, the sooner you can eat." Sara added.

Thirty-One

Apart from receiving treatment for the superficial wounds to his wrists and back, Jerry received a clean bill of health from the hospital, after which Sara and Debra took him for a slap up meal as promised. "Once again you excelled in your performance over the last twenty four hours, although I must admit we have come to expect such accomplishments from you and would be very disappointed if you failed to do well. Strictly between the three of us, ever since you arrived, you have exceeded our expectations in every aspect of your training," Sara told him. "You are causing quite a stir within various agencies here, some have even considered asking you to stay in the belief you can do more from here than in England and want you to work full time for them," Sara finished telling him, with a tear of joy in her eye. She knew her protégé would be leaving shortly and the thought upset her. Never before had she felt so much for a trainee or fully fledged agent she had been given the privilege of being responsible for, throughout her seven years of being a commander.

Jerry, who had only once before seen Sara show her feelings, the last time being on his return from Eilat declared: "You know I can't stay, my life, my home and my family are in London, including a fabulous girl and a fantastic business. You guys have helped me develop my character in areas you'll probably never appreciate, suffice it to say I was very shy and completely lacked confidence in myself before arriving here," he explained. "I must admit, generally I've enjoyed myself over the last few months, much of it down to the two of you who have looked after me well beyond the call of duty, even when I've done things in a slightly unconventional manner and I want you to know I really have appreciated it. However, whenever I found the going really tough and there have been many occasions, thinking of home and what's waiting for me there is the only thing that's kept me sane. I'm no James Bond and never will be. Anyone thinking the contrary is making a huge error of judgement. I was extremely lucky in achieving the results on the Histadrut operation; I went into it believing it was another of your exercises as I said at the time," Jerry continued to tell them. "Obviously I'm as pleased as you are with the result, but fortunately there was no need for '007' heroics to be involved for the mission to be successful. To be honest, I feel that my time here is up and I now need to return home."

Sara was taken aback by his frankness. She was aware he used to be very shy and embarrassed and he was far from fit, having been briefed prior to his arrival, probably one reason she was so pleasantly surprised at his rapid progress and achievements in areas she assumed he would find difficult. Feeling a need to respond to his final comment: "I understand how you feel about home, I just thought you would appreciate knowing the impression you've made here, particularly with the people that count. No one will keep you unwillingly, that I can assure you, just don't be surprised if you're approached although I have given them my view as to what your response would be." she advised him. "The course will shortly be completed and I want you to know that Debra and I will miss you, having become so used to you being around," Sara said looking at Debra, checking she was speaking for them both. "Don't start packing just yet though, there's still a little more learning to be completed and we also want you to spend a few days in either Egypt or Syria, to understand the Arabic mentality, a culture very different to ours. After that we will party and then you can go home. What they have in store for you in England I really don't know."

Jerry, trying to remain upbeat despite not really wishing to stay any longer answered "Let's get on with it and finish as quickly as possible." Whilst having a chance to relax, he thought about certain elements of what he had endured and to returning home, wondering what and when his first operation would be. "Whilst we're chatting, there are a couple of minor issues which have come to mind. The first relates to yesterday's affair," he stated. Without considering a need to phrase it diplomatically, he asked, "Do I exist in this country?"

Sara had been waiting for the question since the morning, surprised it took so long in coming. "If you want me to be completely truthful then the answer is; no you don't. There is absolutely no record of you being on the flight coming over here, or of entering the country, no stamp in your passport, no hotel bookings in your name, basically no record, electronic or otherwise of you being here whatsoever," she confirmed. "Your interrogator and his team were correct, but don't worry, they have no idea who you are or what you're doing here, when they brought you back they were told you emigrated here a few years ago and are being trained to carry out special operations. They believe Jerry Freedman is a cover name and we have given them another name, which if they ever bother to check will concur with the story, including photographs, Israeli passport and ID numbers, everything that a citizen requires," she said smiling. "Part of our job is to look after and protect you, ensuring your security isn't compromised in any way whilst you're here, which will also protect you from prying eyes when you get back, that's why we have been so careful. We will destroy the lower part of the immigration form when you leave, just as we did with the top part on your arrival and your name will again be removed from the passenger list once your return flight lands in London. It must be listed during the flight should anything untoward happen on the flight. We had to play things properly in as far as going through immigration when you arrived since we knew you had been on holiday here when you were younger and possibly remembered the procedure and of course for the benefit of anyone watching," she finished explaining, "We could have just collected you from the aircraft."

"So, where have I been for the last four months or so?" Jerry asked, talking quietly so that no one could possibly overhear.

"As I understand it, the cover story you created before you left England had you travelling around Europe for work and a well deserved rest," Debra stated, looking for confirmation from Jerry which was given. "Passports are no longer stamped and records of the movement of European citizens across most European countries are no longer maintained, enabling you to cross from one border to another without trace unless you use something that identifies you," she continued, looking at Jerry. "It just so happens that you have left a trail of electronic records during your travels, for example using your mobile," she quickly added. "But fear not, we're settling the bills, same with your credit cards. You have also been thoughtful enough to have sent postcards to your parents, Rochelle's parents and your office from various European cities; we'll go through a virtual tour of your trip before you leave."

Jerry looked surprised, he could understand their ability to play with records in Israel, what astonished him was the trouble taken to place him in Europe for the whole period. "That leads nicely to my second point," he said, but noticing Debra had more to say he waited.

"I'm sorry, let me just finish. You'll get to keep some of the entry vouchers for various sites you visited and we even have photographs of you there. Don't worry, all your belongings will be back here by the time you leave," Debra said, thinking she was pre-empting his second point.

Before another word left his mouth, Jerry thought about Rochelle's trips, choosing not to ask anything for fear of hearing something he wouldn't like. "But hotels require passports for ID," he suddenly remembered.

"That's correct, but if you recall, we have your passport which is sufficient," Sara reminded him.

"But the photo in it...No, don't tell me, I don't want to know." Jerry decided he had heard enough. "Thanks for sending the postcards which does lead nicely to my second question. How do we deal with presents?

I can't exactly return home empty handed. Not after this length of time."

"We were planning to ask you who you wanted presents for so that we can procure appropriate items from various countries across Europe that you've visited. We still have a couple of weeks, but please start giving it some thought. I assume you want something extra special for Rochelle, which, before you say she knows you're here; if others were to see it, they may well ask embarrassing questions. So, to avoid any problems, her present will also come from one of the European countries you allegedly visited. I'd be happy to suggest something if you want." Debra offered and then thought it worth mentioning, "But, please, whilst we're on the subject, you mustn't take anything back from here, including the clothes you bought to replace what became too large. I know you mentioned replacing much of your wardrobe again since a lot of items have been ruined and we'll happily do that for you, but only when you get back to London. I hope that's clear," Debra said firmly, a tone he rarely heard from her.

Over the following fortnight the training continued as Sara had suggested. He and Debra then prepared for a short stay in Syria. Whilst there, they would attempt to gain information on a certain terrorist cell known to be active along the border, although the collection of information was a low priority, a bonus if possible, no risks were to be taken. They were merely a couple on holiday and would spend their time sightseeing and mixing with the locals as far as possible, so Jerry could gain some understanding of the way Arabs live and think.

Debra was a good officer, more than able to act the part, whatever was required. She appeared to enjoy hanging off Jerry's arm and even the occasional passionate kiss when the job called for it. Jerry carried out his role with perfection, although he felt guilty when they were forced to embrace each other, demonstrating to people around them they were a couple very much in love. He was also perturbed at having to share a bedroom, no longer through embarrassment, despite having twin beds rather than a double. "Please, don't tell Rochelle," he kept pleading with Debra.

"Don't worry, I won't. But I will say she's a very lucky girl," Debra replied on every occasion, only to hear him argue it was he that was the lucky one.

The trip lasted just under three weeks when Jerry started to appreciate the stark differences in the way Arabs lived, worked and thought, the extra week due to a bad stomach he contracted, blaming the local cuisine. They obtained a small amount of information, nothing significant, but at least a token contribution, before returning to Israel.

Jerry endured a final few days of summation in addition to practising his cover story for his return, but his mind was well and truly back in London. The trip concluded with a celebratory dinner attended by most of the key people involved with his training. He even received a call from the Prime Minister thanking him again and wishing him luck for the future.

Having had all his valuables returned in addition to the presents he requested, a pile of photographs and other items he had apparently collected whilst travelling around Europe, Jerry was finally in a car with Sara, Debra and Moshe being driven to Ben Gurion airport to catch a flight to London. This time they avoided passport control and escorted him onto the plane, boarding before the other passengers. They all hugged him and wished him luck for the future, his stay of five months having come to an end.

Thirty-Two

Rochelle met Jerry in the arrivals hall of Heathrow Airport's Terminal One, Jerry being one of the first from his flight to pass through the large glass doors signifying the end of the customs hall and entering the United Kingdom at just after one o'clock in the afternoon. Having given him a very affectionate but public welcome home, they walked arm in arm to the car and headed in the direction of the penthouse.

"Have a rest when we get in this afternoon; we're celebrating your return with both our families tonight. They have apparently missed you," she told him, seeing he was somewhat exhausted.

"I'd rather celebrate with just you," he replied, with a naughty grin. "Like we did in Israel."

"Those were good times which of course I'd love to repeat tonight, just you and I, but no one has seen you for over five months and if we don't meet with them they'll only come over to us, you know what your mother's like," she told him. "I suggested a restaurant rather than either of our mums cooking which was the original idea, this way we can slip away earlier. I'm sure you can put on a great act of being exhausted. Don't forget they think you've been in Europe all this time."

"I know, I've had a virtual tour of the continent before I left and had to learn my itinerary and what I did where. What a bore it was, although I now know all the sites and stuff. Remind me to show you some photos of me at all the big tourist attractions, I certainly got around," he told her, although she didn't appear too surprised. "I even have an entry voucher for Euro Disney and a photo of me posing with Mickey Mouse. I understand I also sent a number of postcards. You're a good girl for sorting it so that we're at a restaurant rather than my parents, I don't think I could hack that tonight." As he was talking, Rochelle watched his eyes slowly close and within minutes of sitting in the car he had drifted off into a deep sleep, leaving Rochelle to drive him home.

Besides waking for a few minutes to transfer his body from the car to the apartment, Jerry slept for the remainder of the afternoon whilst Rochelle washed the few items of clothing he had returned with. "Looks like we have a wardrobe to fill, you haven't brought back any of the clothes you wore out there and those you left here won't really fit you now," she said as she heard him stir, listening carefully to the quiet response.

"According to Sara, they'll pick up the tab for replacing everything as long as I'm sensible about it. I know it's an opportunity you wouldn't miss for the world!" he muttered.

Both Rochelle and Jerry started dressing for the evening, despite struggling with his clothes, which were now far too large. Whilst Rochelle was brushing her hair, Jerry asked, "Have you started organising the wedding yet?"

"Wedding? What wedding might that be?" Rochelle asked, moving over to him and kissing his lean muscular body.

"Mine," Jerry replied, continuing to dress, trying to ignore Rochelle's intimacy.

"And can I ask who too?" she quietly asked.

"You can ask, yes. I can't stop you from asking anything, we live in a country with free speech," Jerry replied, trying to play Rochelle at her own game, knowing he couldn't.

"Well," Rochelle asked again, trying to bite his very tight stomach, unsuccessfully.

"Well what?" Jerry continued.

"Who too?" she repeated, undoing his trousers he had just put on.

"I didn't say I'd answer, did I? I just said you could ask." He pulled her up as if she were as light as a feather and standing together with their bodies making contact; they stared into each other's eyes for several minutes.

"Yes," she said. "Yes I'll marry you," she confirmed, adding "in case you thought the yes was my answer to your original question." Having finished the sentence with another passionate kiss, she finally managed to pull herself away from Jerry's grasp and opened the middle drawer of the dressing table, removing an envelope. Holding it out to Jerry, she suggested, "Take a look."

Jerry opened the unmarked envelope and removed four sheets of typed notes. He read the heading on the first page: "The Wedding of Rochelle Levy to Jerry Freedman."

He grabbed hold of her and they kissed again, this time as if it was their first time. "I don't want you to have any affairs and use the excuse it was for the good of the country now that you're a fully fledged secret agent," she said, only half jokingly.

Jerry got down on one knee, "There's only one girl for me, I promise you." Standing up again he said with a voice full of elation, "I suppose I got that a little bit messed up, but I think you got the general gist."

"You can do it again properly," she replied, this was one moment she had dreamed of her whole life and it was going to be just as she imagined it.

Jerry got down on his knee again and taking her hand. "Rochelle," he started, "I've missed you so much these last few months, please do me the honour of becoming my wife." He waited there looking up at her sparkling face with an appealing look, patiently waiting for an answer.

Looking down at a guy who had completely changed in almost every aspect of his being over the relatively short time she had known him, she wasn't sure whether to play him along a bit despite the notes she had just given him. Eventually she couldn't resist responding, "Mr Jerry Freedman," she said. "There is nothing more I would love than to become Mrs Jerry Freedman," and she helped him off his knee, gave him another kiss before looking at her watch and realising the time. "Come on, finish getting ready, we're late. By the way, I'm not sure I mentioned I finally gave up my flat a few weeks ago," she called out to him as she walked towards their en-suite bathroom.

"You didn't, but I thought there seemed to be more stuff around here compared to when I left, but that's great, maybe I'll carry you over the threshold when we get back tonight," Jerry replied, glancing around the bedroom suddenly noticing it contained even more of her bits and pieces than before he left.

Both families met up at Jerry's favourite restaurant, the star of the evening arriving slightly late for which Rochelle apologised using the excuse she couldn't wake him. Whilst going around the table greeting everyone and giving each their present, his mother's first comment was to ask if he had been eating well, since he looked as though he had lost far too much weight. Everyone remarked on the length of his trip, asking how he could have stayed away for so long? "It really hadn't been fair on Rochelle," his mother kept repeating before remembering to thank him for all the postcards he had sent. It was Rochelle's father who commented on the change in Jerry's physique and the noticeable increased confidence, but having glanced at Rochelle, he decided against asking any questions.

They drank Champagne and toasted Jerry's return. Whilst waiting for desserts to be served, Jerry tapped his spoon three times on the table, not too hard, just sufficient to attract the attention of his family and a few tables close by, bringing to a halt the conversations everyone seemed to be enjoying. "You have all complained I've been away far too long and maybe you're right. Although you'll argue it's not immediately obvious from the photographs I've shown you, most of the time was work related, which I hope will transpire to be very beneficial and in any case I spoke to Rochelle almost every day. Whilst being in a different environment I found the time I desperately needed to make some serious decisions about my life," he announced, having first apologised to the people on the adjacent tables for the disturbance. He then removed the envelope Rochelle had given him from the breast pocket of his jacket and opened it, removing the sheets of paper as though they were a prepared speech. As he unfolded them, he looked at Rochelle's father and asked, "Sir, would you please allow me to marry your daughter?"

Slightly stunned at hearing the unexpected, Rochelle's father could only just manage to murmur, "Well yes, of course," quickly adding, "If that's what you both want."

"That's just as well," Jerry replied as he handed out Rochelle's plan for her wedding.

The toasts changed from welcoming Jerry back to 'the happy couple', whilst there were cheers, shouts of congratulations and clapping from the tables surrounding them.

A new topic of conversation which would last well past this evening commenced, certainly in the female quarter, being the design of Rochelle's engagement ring and planning what was immediately named 'A Wedding to Remember.'

Thirty-Three

Jerry had been back for a little over a month and finally managed to catch up with the ongoing projects and orders Igloo was working on when he received a call for a meeting at the Israeli Embassy. Not having heard from anyone since his return, he had wondered on several occasions when the call would come. He knew instinctively this would be the start of his clandestine activities, his extra curricula job as a spook. "Would I be working solely for the Israelis, or as originally suggested, in conjunction with the UK and US authorities?" He pondered, although he wasn't really bothered either way.

Having arranged to meet after completing an urgent task in the office, Jerry arrived at the Embassy a little after 3pm and endured the numerous security checks, for which he now more than appreciated the need. On this occasion he was not kept waiting long, being taken to the same room where everything had commenced some ten months earlier. After the knock on the door, there was the familiar, just audible click as the lock was released and the door opened.

"Please take a seat Jerry," one of two Israeli men seated at the table requested. Jerry noted neither the atmosphere nor appearance of the room had changed since his earlier visits and was certain he had never met either of the men previously, although from their greeting they tried to portray an impression of being life long friends. Jerry guessed one was probably in his late forties, whilst the other had to be well into his fifties. Without introduction, something Jerry had now become accustomed to, the younger of the two opened the meeting, speaking entirely in Hebrew. "Firstly, before we get down to business, please accept this small gesture on behalf of our President, our Prime Minister and government and the people of Israel." At this point Jerry was handed a polished wooden box, about four inches square, two inches deep, accompanied by a white envelope. "Please, open them both," the man continued and Jerry carefully lifted the lid off the base. Inside was a large, solid gold medal resting on a wooden stand. A Star of David, the emblem of Israel, occupied the majority of the space on the face of the medal, with the inscription: "For The Courageous Services Provided To The State of Israel" engraved around the edge. As he read the words, a lump formed in his throat as the memories, which he had managed to push to the back of his mind since his return to London, suddenly took over all his thoughts. Rather than examine the medal further, Jerry closed the box and moved onto opening the envelope to find an Israeli passport in his name.

"Thank you," Jerry said, somewhat embarrassed at being given such an honour, despite not being entirely sure what medal it was. "I was pleased I could be of some help. It seemed to make the investment in training me worthwhile."

"The Tzalash medal, often known as Tziun La Shevach translates in English to mean the Medal of Honour, the highest military award our country presents, whilst the passport proves you are an Israeli citizen, a requirement to receive the medal. There will always be a place for you in Israel whenever you want and of course citizenship extends to every member of your family should you wish," the man said. "Regarding the operation, it was never our intention to involve you in our internal security I assure you." The same speaker stated, "We were lucky you happened to be in the right place at the right time. Throughout history, the Israelites have been very fortunate to have God look down on them favourably, assisting in the defeat of their enemies despite improbable odds. This was yet another miracle bestowed upon our nation."

The elder man, who had remained silent until then continued, "Since your return we have allowed you to settle back to normality and catch up with your life and business and we wish you and Rochelle Mazeltov on your forthcoming marriage." He went onto say, "We have been asked to invite you to take your honeymoon in Israel, where I can guarantee there would be no gym, range, or classroom sessions unless you specifically request them." As he spoke, he wore a broad grin across his face suggesting he knew everything that took place whilst Jerry was out there. "It would be as a guest of our President. You have become something of a hero, with your name regularly brandished about in certain prominent circles. What you achieved for our country, in comparison far exceeds all the financial contributions we receive each year and our nation will be indebted to you for ever."

Jerry, slightly unsure how to respond to the offer, finally replied, "I'll need to ask Rochelle, but thank you for the invitation, I'll let you know, if that's alright."

The elder person continued: "Let's get down to the other reason we invited you here today which I'm sure you have already guessed wasn't just to award you with the medal and citizenship. We of course trained you to work for us and we now need to call upon your services." He paused to offer Jerry refreshments, which were already sitting on a tray in the middle of the table. "I know I don't need to remind you that everything we discuss here is confidential," which Jerry immediately thought was precisely what he was doing. "Since your first meeting here, the world of terrorism has moved on, like everything else it doesn't stand still. We have intelligence confirming several individuals have been trained in the use and operation of Inter Continental Ballistic Missiles, something I believe you were once shown photographs of." The speaker jogged Jerry's memory, he had completely forgotten about them. "We believe two trained individuals have recently been deployed into an active terrorist cell based in Lebanon and reconnaissance is currently being carried out to establish feasible targets."

It was the turn of the first speaker to continue. "This means the clock has begun ticking much faster, although we don't think they have taken delivery of any missiles as yet. What we can take as gospel is the time between receiving them and launch will be short and if you recall, they could be fitted with either nuclear or chemical warheads. We urgently need to confirm the targets being assessed. It's believed London is on the list since one member of their team has already made several trips here over the last few months, four that we are certain about and possibly more. Unfortunately, the UK authorities have not managed to keep tabs on the woman during these visits," he informed Jerry with disappointment in his voice.

Three photos were passed to Jerry, all of the same girl who looked around eighteen or nineteen years old and could easily have passed as the average American teenage princess if she had paid more attention to herself. From the surrounding detail in each of the pictures and with his newly acquired knowledge, Jerry deduced she was approximately one and a half metres tall and weighed around a hundred and twenty pounds with long auburn hair and a great looking body.

In all the photos, which had clearly been taken at different locations and without her knowledge, the girl looked as if her skin had not been in contact with soapy water for quite some time and her hair was screaming out to be introduced to shampoo, a brush and definitely a stylist.

"Before you suggest it, yes, she is American," the younger man confirmed, confident Jerry was about to propose it as an idea. "We are not sure how long ago she moved to Lebanon, or why and it's worth bearing in mind she could be a decoy, walking around as she does obviously attracts attention," he said stating the obvious. "We are particularly concerned since this terrorist unit has a number of smaller, yet horrifyingly deadly missiles which can hit Jerusalem, Tel Aviv and certainly Haifa with ease, whenever they wish. Jerry remembered the original photographs he had been shown and that it was something he had managed to confirm whilst in Syria with Debra.

"We have invested enormous resources in several failed attempts to penetrate the cell. We are hoping you maybe able to infiltrate this group through a link that already exists." The speaker paused as he handed

Jerry another photograph, waiting for him to enquire further, but Jerry remained silent, concentrating on the images. "Mohammed Hieddah, a name I doubt you have come across yet, is the money behind this particular terrorist cell. He has also been the single financier of more than half of the suicide bombers in Israel over the last few years. A brother and brother in law are two of the three company officers of DataLink Inc., a Delaware company." Jerry instinctively looked up from the photos when he heard the name DataLink.

"Of course you're already aware DataLink is a client of ours and one I have had personal dealings with. The three directors are American though," Jerry said with some confidence.

"They are American citizens when it suits them to be," the elder man stated.

"What's more important is all three have recently made numerous visits across the Middle East, allegedly on DataLink business. Neither we nor our American counterparts have been able to trace any company activities outside of North America and the United Kingdom so why the façade? What's become apparent is a definite connection between the girl and DataLink, but we don't know how or why," the younger guy told Jerry in an attempt to start tying things together. "Phase one of the operation is to asses the overall situation and determine the potential targets, allowing decisions to be made on how best to protect our country and those others that maybe at risk." He held his hand out for Jerry to return the photographs. "Finally," he said, "A friend of yours requested operational responsibility for this phase and thinking you wouldn't object, I've authorised it." Without further delay he picked up the handset of a phone and punched in a couple of numbers. On hearing it had been answered he simply said, "Come in please." Moments later Jerry heard the door behind him automatically unlock and open.

Glancing over his shoulder wondering who this person was, his emotions immediately got the better of him. "Sara," he called out excitedly and jumped out of his chair almost knocking it over. "It's great to see you again," he said in English, giving her a long tight hug.

"Mazeltov on your engagement, Jerry, and on being awarded the

Medal of Honour," she said. "I hope you're happy to work with me again?"

"There is no one I'd prefer to work with," Jerry replied, "Although I only really know you and part of your team so not many to choose from," he added smiling, still somewhat surprised at seeing her again.

The younger Israeli finally took it upon himself to conclude the meeting. "Sara is fully briefed and has access to all the necessary resources back home. Why don't you both stay here?" he said looking at Sara. "Bring Jerry up to scratch on everything." The door clicked again and the two men made their way out of the room calling out: "Shalom and the very best of luck," leaving Sara and Jerry to start the job of planning the operation as the door closed behind them, the lock clicking once again.

Thirty-Four

Sara shared all the intelligence available on DataLink, its officers and the company's activities, at least those that Jerry was not aware of. She followed on with reviewing the sparse details that existed on the girl, for which they hadn't even a name and then Mohammed Hieddah, including information on a number of recent attacks he had funded.

It was well after seven o'clock by the time the two had finished and Jerry, remembering Rochelle mentioned she would be working late in the office, called her to arrange for the three of them to have dinner in a popular kosher Chinese restaurant in Golders Green. "Rochelle will be pleased to see you again," Jerry said. Sara was not over keen on the prospect since the last thing she needed was a jealous fiancée causing unnecessary distraction, something that had once happened to a colleague. She argued she was tired but Jerry ignored her and having spoken to Rochelle, made a table reservation.

"Where are you staying?" Jerry asked out of interest.

"Initially at the Ambassador's residence somewhere near the Swiss Cottage area so I'm told," she replied, "I only arrived at lunchtime today and was brought straight here."

"I know where his place is, not that I've ever been there. How long are you over here for?" he enquired.

"That really depends on you," she answered. "This is a very big operation, the type that says you've made it in this game. It needs to be planned meticulously," and after pausing, she sort of ordered him, "And I don't want you disappearing on me this time, you understand?"

"I understand, ma'am," he said, saluting her.

"This is no joke, Jerry, I'm being serious. We could be talking about hundreds of thousands or even millions of lives at stake here, including yours and mine," she said firmly. "Not that I'm trying to put you under any pressure or anything," she stated in a more relaxed tone.

"I'm not treating it as a joke I assure you," Jerry replied. "But I'm sure you told me once, we must have a good sense of humour and some fun whilst doing the job to prevent us from going crazy, or at least it was something like that."

"I may well have said that and I hope we do have fun whilst working together, but I also believe I mentioned every job must be treated with the utmost respect which includes being taken seriously. If you fail to play by the rules this becomes a very dangerous game and one I don't wish to be involved in," she continued and then with a lot of excitement in her voice she finished, "But enough of that now." They then made their way to Jerry's car which was parked a short distance from the embassy.

By the time they entered the restaurant, Rochelle was already seated at a table with a drink in her hand. Following the usual greetings and the congratulations on the engagement, Rochelle quickly established that Sara's trip was not a holiday and she knew better than to ask any further questions. Besides, she was aware Jerry met her whilst he was at the embassy. She could only assume the rest.

"I don't believe I've told you," Sara said during a short break in the conversation. "I was promoted just after you left," she stated looking at Jerry." Apart from a slight raise in salary, it means I have a larger and more comfortable office and I'm now responsible for five teams rather than one, so five times as many problems," she said jokingly, "And it's entirely thanks to you."

"How is your promotion down to Jerry?" Rochelle butted in.

"You haven't mentioned anything?" Sara asked Jerry.

Thinking Sara was referring to the award, Jerry answered, "No, not yet. When have I had the chance? "I've been with you all afternoon."

Sara realised that Jerry had not discussed his trip whatsoever, then, glancing around the fairly full restaurant to make sure no one was paying any attention to them, continued "You can show her the item now if you wish, do you have it in your briefcase?"

Jerry looked around, not sure whether to listen to Sara or wait until they were home. "What are you both talking about?" Rochelle demanded to know.

Jerry looked at Sara who gave him a positive nod. He bent down to his briefcase and carefully opening it, he removed the envelope and box. Handing the envelope to Rochelle first, she took the passport from it.

"Why have you been given an Israeli passport?" she innocently asked not understanding why they were both talking in riddles.

"He, with his family which includes you of course, have been given Israeli citizenship for the work he put in whilst with us," Sara informed Rochelle. "And to enable him to be awarded something else," she said excitedly.

"And this thing you've been awarded, presumably it's what you're holding? Would it happen to have anything to do with your promotion Sara?" Rochelle enquired for either to answer.

"Show her," Sara said impatiently.

Jerry handed the box to Rochelle who carefully removed the lid.

"Wow," she exclaimed and studied it for a minute before asking, "But what does 'For the courageous services provided to the State of Israel' mean exactly?"

"Ah," he exclaimed then shushed her to talk quietly. He looked quickly at Sara and then into Rochelle's sparkling eyes. He whispered, "That's an excellent question." He paused a moment, more for effect than anything else. "A large part of my course consisted of exercises, putting into practice the theory they were teaching me. One such exercise transpired to be a live operation. Fortunately it was successful and they gave me this for my part in it. Nothing more than that," then looking at Sara, "And don't worry, I haven't told her anything about what I learnt or did, only that there was a mix of theory and practical. It wasn't too hard for her to guess I did a fair amount of training and Krav Maga though."

Sara cut in, "You confirmed that for me just now. I must admit I thought you would have said more, I wouldn't have blamed you. If we didn't trust either of you we would never have organised the trips for you both and I certainly wouldn't be sitting here now," she reassured him. "And about the medal, Rochelle," she continued. "It's the Medal of Honour, the highest award we bestow on anyone and no, I haven't been presented with one before you ask, you should be very proud of him, as I am." she said, smiling at her protégé.

"Did all this take place when you phoned and called me Sara?" Rochelle asked, beginning to remember certain details.

Before answering, Jerry looked at Sara for reassurance before continuing, "Yes, I needed to get a message to the old battleaxe over there," Jerry replied, smiling back at Sara, not quite sure what to say after her comment, which suddenly brought everything into perspective, realising probably for the first time exactly how important his role had been. "I thought you would relay it for me, understanding what I was wanting of you," he told Rochelle, referring back to the call. "It was no big deal, really it wasn't," Jerry tried to reassure her.

"No big deal, but they gave you the highest medal in the land for your courage. Doesn't that mean you risked your life or something?" Rochelle asked, not knowing whether to be ecstatic or very concerned.

"As if I would be so foolish as to risk my life. Just remember, I didn't even have the courage to ask you out on a date," he replied, trying to laugh it off.

Rochelle took another good look at the medal and then closed the box handing it and the passport back to Jerry. She topped up all three wine glasses and trying desperately to hold back the tears, she lifted her glass and toasted him, before giving him a kiss and whispering "I love you" quietly in his ear, followed by a more stern "We'll discuss the medal later."

At the end of the evening Sara paid for the meal in cash, which triggered Jerry's memory on all the personal security training. From the one single act, he guessed the operation was being carried out without either British or American knowledge, let alone cooperation. Not wishing to ask, he also presumed Sara's presence in the UK would never be traceable.

Jerry and Rochelle drove Sara to the Ambassador's residence and then returned to the penthouse. With them both preparing for bed, he approached Rochelle speaking slowly and quietly. "I'm going to need to concentrate a fair amount of time to DataLink, but alone. Is that something you think you can organise without questions being asked in the office? I know it's very unusual for me to work single handed on a client project these days." When he had finished he placed his arms around her waist.

Work was a taboo subject in their bedroom so Rochelle knew something serious was up. She just as quietly answered, "I'm sure we can come up with a reason why the project should only involve you," she added, "As I've said before, I shan't ask any questions. I just want you to remember I'm always here for you if you want to talk about anything, whether you're looking for a dialogue or just a sounding board. She placed her arms around him, pulling him closer to her, kissing him on the lips. Without raising her voice she carried on, "Please also remember you have an appointment in just over eighteen weeks, one you must attend," she reminded him.

"Appointment in eighteen weeks?" Jerry repeated in a questioning tone, pulling away from her, completely unaware of what she was referring to.

"Yes, one you certainly can't cancel," Rochelle repeated, now in her normal wind-up manner.

Jerry looked confused. "You're playing co-star," Rochelle replied, to which Jerry looked even more confused, all his thoughts focussed on the operation.

"A wedding! Your marriage to me, remember?" Rochelle finally said loudly, beginning to get upset.

"I'm sorry darling; I thought you meant something work related. Our wedding never entered my mind as something I could possibly forget," he said trying to pacify her. "This little task I've been given will be completed well before then."

"Oh, yes, this little task, thanks for reminding me," she repeated in a sarcastic tone. "I believe you asked earlier 'How could you have possibly been involved in anything dangerous when you didn't even have the nerve to ask me out?' So they give these medals, the highest medal they have, to anyone, do they? Just for being there!" she exclaimed, continuing the conversation from dinner.

"Come on darling, it was nothing, I promise. I'm here aren't I?" he said with his most appealing look he knew she found irresistible.

"Don't put that look on now, it's not fair," she smiled. "The point is, I always want you here. I'm concerned for your safety, that's all. I'm not annoyed as in being annoyed if you understand what I'm trying to say. I know the old Jerry probably wouldn't have done anything, but we now have a new one, a leaner, fitter, confident Jerry who eventually emerged from a holiday in Israel and one that I love more and more each day," Rochelle told him trying to recall as much detail of the incident as she could. "Wasn't that weird call you made to me just before our week in Eilat, around the time there was going to be a general strike? I'm sure I read somewhere something about a major terrorist attack being foiled, but at the time I didn't put the two together. I don't suppose you know anything about it, do you? Mr Bond," she said pulling him towards her again.

"Mr Bond?" Jerry repeated questioningly, his mind elsewhere again.

"Not only have I caught a real electronics genius, but also I've got my own '007' thrown in as well, Mr James Bond. I'm very proud of you." As she finished her sentence she gave him a tight hug and kiss. "As I warned you before. You had better not make love to another woman on the pretext it's for queen and country," she smirked. "Come on, let's go to bed and celebrate your medal. I'll fetch the Champagne," she whispered after finally releasing him.

Sipping the Champagne in bed, Jerry quietly spoke in Rochelle's ear, "I know you left arranging the honeymoon to me but I need to ask you a couple of questions to ensure I deliver to your expectations. After all, we'll only have one honeymoon and I want you to have the very best."

"Umm," was the only response Jerry heard from Rochelle as if to say, what's coming next.

"Do you want to be treated like royalty with guides taking us on the sightseeing bit and having to dress formally for dinner and all that jazz, or just do the hotel and beach thing?" he asked.

Without having to think about it, Rochelle answered, "Treated like royalty would be nice."

Jerry then asked, "And would you be upset if it were a country you may have visited before?"

Once again Rochelle needed no time to consider an answer. "I don't mind the destination as long as it's hot, exotic and I'm by your side."

Rochelle then spent the next few hours showing Jerry just how proud she was of him.

Thirty-Five

Over the following days Jerry spent all his time reviewing the paperwork from the project he completed for DataLink many months ago, well before his trip, following which he re-examined all the available intelligence with Sara. Together they evaluated a number of alternatives which could potentially be used to initiate a new relationship between DataLink and Igloo and in particular between Jerry and the company's owners. The main problem to overcome was that once a handover of an Igloo system had been carried out, not even Igloo personnel can gain access to the system its protecting.

Jerry finally came up with a plan which he felt gave him some chance of being able to penetrate the organisation, providing him with the freedom he required to access their data systems, the only downside being the time it would take to conceive a product that would be of interest to them, build a basic prototype of it and after having completed all the work, there was still a chance DataLink wouldn't be interested. "How long would it take?" he wondered, but it was a question he couldn't answer. The only thing he was certain about was that neither Sara nor her bosses would welcome the delay; they were keen for contact to be made soonest. Reflecting on his previous mission, it seemed to Jerry that the job of espionage was always against the clock. Sara tried to think up a faster route to reach the same objective. Failing to do so, she reluctantly agreed to go along with Jerry's proposal, who's scheme relied on him approaching DataLink with a concept for a new product, something he hoped would interest them sufficiently to accept an opportunity of becoming involved in defining the specifications and then carry out alpha and beta testing. If they went along with it, Jerry would be required to spend a lot of his time with them, accessing their systems and generally getting close to the people that mattered. His only remaining problem was to come up with something that would whet their appetite.

The product would need to relate to the activities Jerry officially knew nothing about. "I'll have to approach DataLink as if it were a cold call, give them an overview of our idea and say we are looking for clients to work with us," he told Sara. "And with luck they'll want to be involved. Once I'm taken into their confidence, it should be reasonably easy for me to probe around. If not, it's going to be back to the drawing board for us."

The next three weeks Jerry worked day and night trying to think of a product which would open the DataLink door for him. For each idea that came to mind, he examined the feasibility of being able to create such a product. The time he was investing in it reminded him of what his life was like before Igloo became successful. Rochelle, understanding the importance of his work, buried herself in organising the wedding with the help of her mother and forthcoming mother in law.

Jerry was excited when he finally came up with something he considered to be his key to DataLink's door. He quickly built a prototype with assistance from two of his technical team, telling them he was playing around with an idea which he wasn't sure would be commercially successful, but wanted to determine its technical viability at the very least. To speed things up, he also enlisted the support of Dr Fog as it involved areas of technology that Dr Fog excelled in.

Following minimal testing, Jerry telephoned the DataLink's

technology officer, Igloo's main contact. "We are considering the introduction of a new product into the market, one that secures data such as general radio and video signals" he explained. "We are approaching clients to become involved in working together with us to finalise the functionality and trial it. I was wondering if it would be of any interest to you?" Jerry enquired.

Listening to the details on the capability of the product, the technology officer replied. "I would like to see what you have and hear your views on the contribution we would be expected to make. Then, if I feel it would be something of interest, we can discuss the finer points."

The response was the best Jerry could have anticipated given the circumstances. He didn't expect them to commit without more information and by the time the conversation was finished a meeting had been arranged. In his mind he thought, "The key fits the lock, I now just need to turn it carefully."

Remembering a comment made during his first meeting at the embassy and fortunate Rochelle insisted from the very beginning that the source of each enquiry was recorded, Jerry checked through Igloo's customer files to discover who introduced DataLink and if they in turn had introduced other clients, following the line as far as it would go. He created a chart showing each connection, the list starting to take on the look of a family tree. To be sure DataLink didn't suspect anything untoward; Jerry knew all the organisations on the list had to be approached with the same offer, lest one client mentioned it to another. He initially considered someone in sales could carry out the task on his behalf, but there wasn't room for even the slightest mistake to be made and it was his responsibility to ensure this. Having finally managed to whittle the list down to seven clients in the chain, Jerry had similar conversations with each. Two additional meetings were arranged which Jerry knew he would have to attend for the benefit of his cover story.

Enlisting the assistance of Rochelle in preparing the presentation, he carefully listened to her comments and suggestions on how best to sell the idea, knowing there would be only one opportunity to convince

DataLink. Together, the couple worked over several evening to create what Jerry hoped would be a convincing case. The dates of the presentations happened to pan out so that DataLink's was the last, giving Jerry two dress rehearsals to perfect it.

All three presentations were successful, with two of the companies wishing to be involved in the project, the third asking to be informed when it became commercially available. DataLink was one of the two that relished the idea of being part of the development process, producing a product to meet their precise requirements. Jerry made a mental note to inform the other organisation they weren't required, but to thank them for their interest and time. "I've unlocked the door, now the fun starts," he thought to himself. "What happens from here will determine whether I'll be successful or fail in this business." An agreement was quickly reached where DataLink would work with Igloo to specify the final requirements and for their assistance, they would have the opportunity to purchase the solution at half the sale price when it becomes available. When Jerry notified Sara she was overjoyed with the news, despite the time it had taken.

During the negotiations, one of the directors approached Jerry, asking if he would be interested in carrying out a small bespoke project for a client of theirs. "We do from time to time become involved in individual development work, but each assignment has to be approved by our acceptance board who make their decision based on the requirements and whether the necessary skills and resources are available at the time," Jerry replied.

"I appreciate that. Our client is currently travelling but will soon arrive in the UK. I will organise a meeting as soon as I know their availability and we can take it from there." the director suggested.

"Is this the client Sara is interested in?" Jerry couldn't help wondering. "If it is, I wonder if they would they have approached me even if I weren't currently spending so much time here?"

Having to keep up the façade, the project progressed with Jerry concentrating the majority of his time on it, tailoring the product to DataLink's requirements. One of the first tasks he completed was to build a back door into the Igloo system, enabling him to gain access to their existing infrastructure without trace whenever he wished, although he knew it would only remain open until such time that Igloo issued an update. During the evenings, Jerry connected to the DataLink network from his study examining all their files, but could find nothing providing him with any clues.

Finally DataLink, with Jerry's assistance, implemented the new product on a live system for a two-week trial. From the original briefing at the embassy to commencing beta testing had taken nine weeks and as yet, Jerry had no information to forward onto Sara. More disappointing to him was that nothing further had been mentioned about the special project since the first enquiry. Jerry desperately needed to know whether the client that had been mentioned was in fact the one he believed he was interested in and if so, were they really connected to the missiles in any way or was it just a wish that he should discount. He was very aware that Sara was beginning to become anxious over the length of time it was taking, as was Rochelle, but for a very different reason.

At the end of the first week of the trial, while Jerry was just finishing tidying things up for the afternoon, one of DataLink's other directors approached him. Expecting to be asked how the project was progressing, he prepared a quick statement in his mind.

"Do you remember sometime ago you were asked if you would be interested in a bespoke project for a client of ours?" the director asked Jerry, not mentioning anything concerning the current work.

"Vaguely," Jerry replied trying to make nothing of it and slightly taken aback, despite being more than interested in the question.

"Our client is arriving in London over the weekend and wishes to meet with you on Monday morning. Can you be here at eight o'clock?" Jerry was asked.

"Yes, of course," he replied.

"That's good; I look forward to seeing you then. Have a good weekend," the director wished Jerry who returned the sentiment before packing up and leaving the building.

When Jerry arrived at DataLink's offices the following Monday, he was met at reception by two of their directors, one being the person that spoke to him the previous Friday afternoon. "We have been asked to meet our client at their place," Jerry was told and then led out of the building to a car. Jerry assumed they were heading for a central London hotel.

Having driven across Waterloo Bridge to reach the south side of the River Thames, they slowly fought their way through the morning rush hour traffic, finally reaching the address in Bromley around sixty-five minutes later. As the younger of the two directors drove, Jerry realised the destination was well known to him since he appeared to know the route faultlessly, as if having made the journey on many occasions. The silver Lexus parked outside a Victorian Town house constructed on three floors. The exterior looked as though it could do with a makeover; the existing whitewash on the walls had either flaked off or, where it still remained, was a dark shade of grey.

The three men walked up the pathway to the green painted wooden front door and with a slight push it creaked open. Jerry was surprised it wasn't locked; the area didn't appear to be a crime free region from what he had seen as they neared their destination. Stepping into the hallway, the elder of the two directors called out, "Mohammed."

"In here," came a reply from an open door at the far end of the shabby, poorly lit hall Jerry found himself standing in.

Sitting on one side of the room was a man about forty-five years old, who looked as if he was of Middle Eastern origin and opposite him sat a young American girl. Jerry was introduced to Mohammed and Kavitah, but he had already recognised them from the photographs he had been shown. He shook their hands and repeated Kavitah's name to make sure he had it right, before sitting on the couch next to her. He realised he had hit the jackpot, but his training had taught him to remain relaxed and hide his excitement whilst his brain was trying to send Sara a message using extra sensory perception.

Kavitah immediately started questioning Jerry. "What experience do you have in dealing with data security for armed forces?"

Jerry specifically refrained from asking who they were representing, hoping it would come out naturally in conversation, knowing that if he enquired, the response would be of no benefit to him.

"Igloo has a fairly substantial contract with the UK's Ministry of Defence and armed forces of several other countries, but I'm unable to discuss any details with you," Jerry replied.

"Have you ever carried out work on intelligent munitions?" Kavitah continued to ask in an American Mid-West drawl that had a hint of Middle Eastern harshness attached to it.

"That's it," Jerry thought to himself. "If this plays out the way I think it might, then maybe we'll start to get somewhere." He tried to answer the questions to the best of his ability whilst attempting to find out whatever he could.

"Unfortunately as I've just said, I'm unable to divulge specifics on any client without their express permission, in the same way as I'm sure you wouldn't appreciate me discussing details of work we may do for you," Jerry replied.

"That's very commendable and I admit you come highly recommended. However, before we can continue, we must confirm you have the necessary expertise in the area we require," the girl said. "Otherwise we're all just wasting our time."

"There's no point going around in circles," Jerry stated with a hint of annoyance in his voice. "All I can tell you is we've implemented a number of solutions based on wireless data networks and wireless voice networks, if that's of any help to you," throwing ideas out to see if he could confirm what she was actually after.

"Can you elaborate on the wireless data solutions you have implemented?" Kavitah enquired.

"We have a number of derivatives of our core wireless product," Jerry told them and whilst he was speaking he opened his briefcase and removed a sales pack, quickly flicking through the literature until he came to the insert titled 'Secure Wireless Networks', which he removed from the batch and handed to Kavitah. "To date, we have not encountered a requirement we have failed to deliver against by using or modifying this core product," he said reassuringly. "I'm sure the datasheet answers all your questions."

Quickly scanning the document, Kavitah then spoke to the others in a language Jerry didn't recognise. Despite trying to the contrary, he couldn't help but stare at her whilst she appeared to be in a heated discussion with the three men. He tried imagining what she would look like cleaned up and at the same time, wondered how a young, good-looking American girl could get herself mixed up with a group of terrorists. His attention quickly returned to the meeting when Mohammed asked: "What would such a system cost?"

"It's difficult to give you a firm price at this point," Jerry replied. "It depends on a number of criteria including the amount of time we need to work on the project, which is directly proportional to the modifications required and the type of munitions it's going to be used with, whether it has inbuilt intelligence that we can add too, or if a separate Traffic Access Unit is required. Then it comes down to numbers," Jerry told him.

"Let's assume we are looking at a small trial, say five devices, each being an intelligent missile," Kavitah suggested as a base number on which to calculate the cost.

"Assuming a relatively standard transmitting device and receiver, I would imagine we are looking at around two hundred thousand pounds," Jerry replied. "But I would need to check with the sales team."

"That much?" Mohammed exclaimed, somewhat surprised. "Is there any room for discounts?" he asked.

"If we've already implemented something on a similar missile, we can probably reduce the price slightly. But I wouldn't have thought it would make a tremendous amount of difference. This is, after all, a very small trial. What we would normally do in such a situation is compensate on the rollout," Jerry explained, knowing that in this case there would be no roll out.

"And how long would it take you to implement?" Kavitah asked.

"I can't really answer that at this stage. Firstly I need to know precisely what we are looking at, both the munitions itself and your specific requirements. Then, as I've already mentioned to DataLink, the project needs to be approved by our acceptance board, when, if successful, it would be added to our development schedule.

Completion would be based on when work could commence and how long it would take." Jerry was attempting to show he was merely a cog in the process rather than being the main or only person involved. "I must warn you that only a small number of bespoke projects we are asked to undertake are actually accepted. If it is, financial terms are agreed and a projected completion date confirmed, based on the anticipated time required. To put a job forward for approval, I need to have access to the specifications and detailed circuitry of both the transceiver in the control unit and in the munitions." Kavitah was far from satisfied with Jerry's reply and pushed for a more precise answer. "From what you've told me and my knowledge of the kit, I'd imagine we could probably implement something within three to four months following receipt of deposit, but don't hold me to that timescale," Jerry informed them in an attempt to get a feel for the timescale.

"We and by that I mean my government, need it implemented much sooner than that. Launch tests are planned to take place within the next few weeks," Kavitah declared.

Before he replied, Jerry noted she cleverly made a reference to an authority. "Are they merely trying to gain credibility with me, or was the Lebanese Government involved? Assuming it is the Lebanese. Should I push the issue now or take it up with Sara?" he asked himself.

"Assuming the missiles are identical; if you can supply me with the necessary paperwork, I will be pleased to review it and prepare a full proposal within a couple of days, which will include a price and approximate timescale on the assumption that we would be interested in taking on the project," Jerry finally answered, having decided this wasn't the time to question anything.

Once again he listened to what sounded like another heated discussion lasting several minutes. Using his knowledge of Hebrew, Jerry tried to understand some of what was being said. He couldn't.

Eventually Kavitah confirmed all testing would be carried out using the same type of missile and DataLink would deliver the information to Jerry by the end of the day. The meeting was concluded and Jerry was driven back to DataLink's offices to collect his car.

Thirty-Six

Jerry called Sara from his car as soon as he had driven a few miles from DataLink's building. They met up at a coffee shop in St. John's Wood, close to where she was staying and on route to Igloo's office.

"I've finally managed to get some information," he told her excitedly.

"So, I'm listening," she replied after a pause, thinking he was going to launch straight into it, as he had always done in the past.

"Your anonymous American beauty answers to the name of Kavitah. I'd say she was from the Mid West but judging by her accent, has spent a number of years in the Middle East," Jerry stated.

"Is she back in London?" Sara immediately enquired.

"She certainly is," Jerry replied smiling, deliberately holding back for a moment the fact that he had actually met her.

"So the girl is in London again," Sara said out loud, although she was really thinking to herself rather than talking to Jerry. "Now we have a name, or at least part of one, we can search our databases and see what they reveal. I don't suppose there's a surname?" Sara asked.

"Unfortunately not, but we do have a mobile number," and Jerry passed over the slip of paper with Kavitah's contact details. "She mentioned she was working for a government but didn't say which and I chose not to ask. She appears to be responsible for co-ordination and logistics; and I wouldn't be surprised if she's one of those trained to launch the missiles. She's a very pushy woman and did most of the talking this morning. From what I learnt from your people," by which he was referring to his course, "Women are normally the underdogs in most Arabic countries but that is one particular characteristic she hasn't adopted. I can also confirm your friend Mohammed is Mr Money Bags behind everything. He tried to beat me up on the cost of an Igloo system," Jerry told her whilst smiling, casually revealing he had met them both.

"He's here as well?" Sara asked.

"It's either him or a very good double," Jerry replied, trying to lighten things up a little. "I think they are both staying at twenty seven, Burford Road, Bromley. That's where I met with them this morning and was told they were staying. But that's not all of it." There was no stopping him now he was in full flow. "They have up to five missiles and are looking to launch as soon as possible, possibly within the next few weeks. I hope to have the full specifications of the control unit and the missiles later today, so I should be able to confirm precisely what we are dealing with." He continued, "They want me to provide a system to lock out unauthorised access to the missiles. For that type of protection, they must have serious concerns that someone may attempt to change the coordinates after launch, whether that's the original supplier or someone further down the supply chain," Jerry said, providing his analysis for free. "I can't think of any other explanation for wanting to implement such protection. Unfortunately I don't yet know where the missiles are, or what the targets might be," he finished disappointedly.

"Nothing for weeks and then you manage to meet with people we have difficulty keeping tags on, following which you bombard me with information gained from the meeting," Sara said smiling, having taken time to digest everything she had just heard before she responded. "If Igloo is going to supply them with a system, presumably you'll be in a position to control the timescales. Can you push to delay your implementation for as long as possible?" Sara asked Jerry.

"This morning I provisionally quoted them three to four months with an immediate reaction that it was far too long. I have promised them a full proposal in which I will include timings, but I feel if I quote something too far in the future they will decide it's not worth the delay and cost, ending up proceeding without our involvement and closing the door behind us, so we need to settle on a happy medium," Jerry tried to convince her. "We maybe able to buy ourselves some extra time on actual installation but again it will need to be carefully managed," he said thoughtfully. "Oh, I'm also playing hard to get, telling them we may not be interested in the project, but don't worry, it hasn't put them off one iota."

"Once again Jerry, I've got to say that you've done well," Sara congratulated him, "You've been very patient and it looks as if it's beginning to pay dividends. Please continue to keep me posted and I'll let you know if anything comes up on the girl."

"Before we finish I have one quick question," Jerry stated as they were both preparing to leave. "Am I not obliged to report such an approach to the authorities here? After all, we are talking about weapons of mass destruction and would Kavitah not be expecting that in any case?"

"Two good questions," Sara said thinking it through. "I suppose technically you should report it but that could blow everything. See if you can sound Kavitah out and let's play this one by ear. If at the end of the day questions are asked, my government would sort it out with yours. At this point in time, gaining as much intelligence as we can has to be the overriding priority for everyone."

Satisfied with everything, they said their goodbyes and Jerry returned to the office spending the afternoon on tender hooks, waiting to see if any documents would emerge as promised and if so, how he was going to deal with it. Knowing he had a meeting, Rochelle asked if his morning had been successful, to which Jerry responded that he would know by nightfall. As the afternoon progressed with nothing arriving, he became more and more despondent.

At 6.15pm, as Jerry was writing replies to the latest emails he had received, the front door buzzer sounded. "Parcel for Jerry Freedman," a courier's voice informed the receptionist. The office officially closed at five thirty but reception and support had been manned until 9pm Greenwich Mean Time for some time now, a benefit purely for their growing list of American clients. Before allowing the deliveryman in, the receptionist called Jerry to check he was expecting a package and on confirmation she allowed the motorcyclist into the foyer. After he explained his instructions were to hand the parcel to Jerry Freedman personally, the young girl on the evening shift contacted Jerry again who, following their conversation, reluctantly made his way to the front desk. Under the tinted visor of the crash helmet Jerry thought the courier looked familiar, someone he had seen around the DataLink building on several occasions, but he couldn't be certain.

Returning to his office with the package in hand, Jerry locked his door and placed the sealed padded envelope in the middle of his desk. Sitting down he spent several minutes just staring at it. Finally, using a pair of scissors kept in his desk drawer, he held the padded envelope by the taped end and cut it open. Lifting the envelope by its sealed end, Jerry held the opened parcel facing downwards, allowing its contents to fall out. Not being quite sure what to expect, he found five thick manuals all with white covers and red titles lying on his desk. He could only describe their condition as being well read. He picked one up and flicked through it, then placed it back on the table and repeated the process with a couple of others. Leaving the remaining two untouched, Jerry sat back in his chair and took in a deep breath, continuing to study the contents of his desk for about five minutes before punching some numbers into his mobile phone, using a prefix he had been given in Israel.

"Sara?" Jerry enquired

"Yes, is that you Jerry?" he heard from the person on the other end of the call.

Jerry knew he had to be careful with what he said over a public telephone system, even with the knowledge the call would be difficult to monitor and trace. "Yep, just to say that I've received a parcel." Jerry then hesitated and as Sara was about to speak, he added, "But I believe it's the wrong items."

"What do you mean? How could they be wrong? Surely you stated precisely what you needed." Sara asked in a distressed tone.

"I assume they've sent me the samples I requested but I can't really tell." He told her with a nervous chuckle before adding, "Because the instructions are in a foreign language, one we are not familiar with here and I would have thought they know that."

Understanding the message Sara informed him without hesitation. "I can get them translated for you."

Jerry thought for a moment. "I'm sure they are aware that we would be asked some embarrassing questions by anyone we contracted to translate for us," he finally replied, willing Sara to understand what he was getting at.

Appreciating Jerry's problem, Sara responded, "That's true and well thought through. I was merely considering the practicalities. Let me mull over this properly, I'll call you back in five." And with that, she hung up.

Jerry continued to concentrate his eyes on the manuals in disbelief, wondering what Kavitah expected him to do. He was contemplating how far they had delved into Igloo's resources, "Did they know Igloo had no Russian translators? Were they waiting and watching to see how I'd react? Do they expect me to take the manuals to British Intelligence? Or are the expecting me to get them translated privately?" he thought, the ringing of his mobile phone interrupting him.

"Jerry, it's me," Sara said, knowing he would recognise her voice. "I'm sorry it took a little longer to call back than I suggested. I've discussed the issue with colleagues. The general consensus is that you call Kavitah and tell her your problem, try and gauge her reaction which I know is difficult over the phone but see how it goes," Sara said, "It could be that they simply didn't give it a second thought, such groups have been known to make serious but genuine mistakes in the past." Sara paused, waiting for a comment that didn't come. "I was once involved with a terrorist unit where they had obviously prepared for an attack by removing the firing pins from their grenades, a difficult task to carry out quickly whilst in the field. They then cleverly stuck tape around the levers to stop detonation until the required time when they would simply remove the tape when throwing the grenades, a task much easier and faster to carry out than removing the pin. Fortunately for us they forgot to remove the tape rendering the grenades as useful as cricket balls. They realised their mistake when our boys kindly returned them with the tape removed. So who knows? Call me back with the response. Bye for now" and the line went dead.

"Bye," Jerry said to an earful of static before rummaging through his wallet for the slip of paper that Sara had returned to him after noting Kavitah's details. He dialled the mobile number scribbled on it.

The phone rang for a couple of minutes and just as Jerry was about to cancel the call it was answered. "Hi, it's Jerry here, Jerry Freedman from Igloo," he said.

"Oh hi Jerry," Kavitah replied, "How can I help you?"

Jerry continued, "I've received your package and reviewed the contents of it, thank you. Unfortunately I can't progress with anything since nothing is printed in English. Everything is in the same language, possibly Russian."

"Are you sure?" Kavitah asked sounding quite surprised, "I didn't see what they sent you. I take it you don't know anyone that can do a translation for you?"

"I can certainly guarantee they're not printed in English and almost certain it's Russian. As far as getting them translated, I don't know anyone off the top of my head who could translate them," Jerry answered. There was a lengthy pause where Jerry could hear mutterings in the background and he assumed she was either at the DataLink offices or with their directors.

Finally, Kavitah got back to him, "I'm sorry, apparently the person who dealt with it just carried out a direct instruction to get the items to you as quickly as possible. Do you want to see if you can find someone to translate them, or for us to get a set in English to you?"

"This is it," Jerry thought, "I must think this through carefully before I answer, although I do think she sounded a little surprised. Of course she may have been expecting this call and rehearsed it." He finally responded, "I'm sure I could probably find someone to translate them, but I don't believe it would be a very clever thing to do, besides the time it would take. I'd imagine whoever I contracted would be likely to question what we are doing with such products and report it to the authorities leaving us with a lot of explaining to do, which would then take up unnecessary time, so if you can get me the information in English it would be a great help," he finally said.

"Are you in your office tomorrow?" Kavitah asked.

"Let me see," and he waited a moment as if he were checking his diary. "I have an all day training session with some of the guys here which I can probably change around if necessary," he finally said.

"We will get you the English versions and collect what we sent today; it will probably be sometime late afternoon again. Please accept my sincerest apologies for the inconvenience," she replied as if there was nothing untoward other than a simple error in not checking what was being sent.

"That's fine. I'll start the ball rolling here by checking if it's a project we are prepared to take on as I mentioned this morning, but nothing formal can be completed until I have written a report for which I need the information. On the surface though, it does sound as though it is well within our capabilities so as long as we have available resources it shouldn't be a problem." He was still hoping Kavitah would believe there was a chance Igloo would not accept the work and put her off any possible scent. "Once the project is authorised, I can quickly prepare a full proposal," he finished.

"I hope you don't have problems getting the project passed at your end and can get me the proposal as quickly as possible. You know the timescale we need to work too," Kavitah said, adding, "We will no doubt speak in the next couple of days or so. Goodbye," and she disconnected the call.

Jerry packed the manuals back in the envelope and re-sealed it, placing the package in the safe which was conveniently located in his office. He was fortunate only two people in the company had access to it, the other person being Rochelle, therefore no one would inadvertently come across the envelope and ask questions, although thinking about it he realised it no longer mattered since it was about to become an official Igloo contract. Whilst closing the safe he received a call on his mobile phone. Within two rings, before Jerry had a chance to answer it, the call had disconnected and the display showed that the number was withheld. As he was leaving the building about half an hour later for what he hoped would be a relaxing evening at home, the receptionist stopped him. "Have you spoken to an Arab sounding gentleman within the last half hour or so?"

"No, why?" Jerry asked.

"Someone phoned for you, wouldn't give his name but said you were expecting his call. As I was trying to put him through, the call seemed to get lost somewhere in our system which is unusual and he hasn't called back. That's all," the receptionist explained.

"Okay, thanks and goodnight," Jerry said, feeling quite pleased with himself.

"Goodnight," the receptionist called back to him as he walked out the front door heading towards his car.

Pondering the aborted calls, "I'll call Sara later," he decided, "I wonder if they were trying to check whether I contacted anyone immediately after speaking to Kavitah. If that were the case, explaining the two calls, it would confirm they have no listening equipment in operation around me. Did they think I was reporting to someone? It was a very crude and inaccurate method to use, I could have accepted or made another call to anyone, totally innocently, which would then possibly been misinterpreted and provide them with incorrect information. Perhaps I should call someone just to confuse them," he thought with amusement as he sat in his car. Jerry started the engine and headed out of the office car park on his homebound journey. He decided it might be prudent to take the long route to the apartment, just in case. He stopped to fill the car with petrol which it didn't really need, but the procedure provided an opportunity to check if he was being followed. He started the manoeuvre to pull into the petrol station located on the opposite side of the road, forcing him to cut across the lane of on-bound traffic, just what he needed to allow him to legitimately stop the traffic behind him as he waited for a break in the flow allowing him to cross safely. As he did so, he spotted a motorbike headlight heading in the same direction as he was travelling, move from the middle of the road to the kerb some fifty metres or so behind. The bike was obviously waiting for something and ready to move off at any time, rather than pulling in and stopping. Jerry deduced this since the engine remained running, something he could determine by the intensity of the headlight.

Having filled his tank with petrol and then paid, he returned to his car, started the engine and made his way back onto the road. When he had finally managed to cut across the road once more, heading in the direction for home, he took another look in his rear view mirror and watched the bike pull out, resuming its journey whilst maintaining a steady distance behind him. “Those Israelis really do know their stuff,” he thought, “Their counter surveillance procedures actually do work. It’s exactly as they taught me,” he remembered, thinking back to his surveillance lectures and exercises.

Thirty-Seven

Jerry waited until later that evening before calling Sara to report on the subsequent conversation he had with Kavitah, inform her of the aborted calls and tell her about the excitement of his journey home. He had noted the single headlamp following him the whole way, continuing past his apartment block as Jerry drove into the underground car park. "We'll just have to wait and see," Sara said, "Carry on as though you were not aware of anything; but I'm sure I don't need to remind you of that, or to keep your eyes open. I think you gave them the correct response and we can only hope they deliver tomorrow." They then said their goodnights.

Rochelle spent the evening running Jerry through the preparations for the wedding, although she could tell his thoughts were thousands of miles away. "Come on Mr Bond," she finally said, giving up on him, upset he wasn't sharing in her excitement; "It's time for bed."

The following morning Jerry again decided to drive the long route to the office, stopping off to buy a newspaper on the way. Fortunately Rochelle regularly drove herself to the office so she had her car available if she needed it during the day, giving her the freedom to do as she pleased, besides being able to leave earlier than Jerry, something she frequently did. He often thought it was a waste taking both their cars, but on this occasion he was pleased and made a mental note never to argue the point with her again. He carried out a reasonably thorough check from the newsagent and although he couldn't see anything to validate it, he had a nagging feeling someone was watching him, confirming to himself that it was far easier to detect such things at night rather than during the day, another thing he remembered he kept arguing about. "Those Israelis," he chuckled to himself again.

Jerry occupied his time checking through the details of all the projects they had in hand, a task he normally carried out once a month in an evening, as a double check on the sales and technical teams and to keep him fully up to date on everything. He also responded to the technical issues forwarded to him by his engineers, items they were not completely sure about, most of them being pre sales questions. He then looked at the first set of results from the DataLink trial which had been emailed to him, after which he reviewed the questions received and answered by the support team, noting new ones which he would add to the web site's Frequently Asked Questions section.

At 4pm he called Sara and just said: "Nothing" in a very frustrated tone and without speaking another word he disconnected the call realising he never even bothered to check it was her. An hour later, Rochelle, seeing how restless Jerry had been all day, suggested he went home. As he thought about the idea his phone rang. It was reception informing him there was a courier delivering a package that required his personal signature and he apparently had one to be returned. Jerry informed her he would be straight down; he then removed the envelope from the safe and made his way to the foyer. It was the same courier as the previous evening but Jerry was still unable to confirm the identity through the tinted visor. He also wondered if it was the bike that followed him home.

Jerry politely exchanged packages and returned to his office. He locked the door and was tempted to phone Sara to tell her the news but on reflection decided to leave the call for a while. He started to open the envelope in the same manner as he had a little less than twenty-four hours earlier. About to cut the edge open, his mobile rung twice and disconnected with the display showing the caller's number was withheld. He called down to reception and enquired if someone had just tried to reach him. The receptionist confirmed she had received a call which disconnected before it went through to him. She mentioned she recognised the voice, possibly as being the same as the one the previous evening.

Jerry deliberated over the calls. He walked to his window which overlooked the main road outside the office and the entrance to the building. Peering through the blinds without disturbing them, he could see nothing that appeared to be out of place. Returning to his desk he picked up his phone, pressed Rochelle's extension, and knowing she kept everything, he asked her to call the emergency contact number he had given her whilst he was in Israel which included the special prefix to provide additional security to the call.

"Please ask them to contact Sara and ask her to call me at the Chinese restaurant we went to the day she arrived, say same time as we spoke last night," and he then remembered to tag on for Rochelle's benefit, "How do you fancy Chinese tonight?" at the end of the sentence.

"I'll make the call immediately and yes, it would make a nice change to eat out together, I'll book a table as well," she replied, which only added to Jerry's guilt for using Rochelle and also potentially putting her at risk, but he knew she would be upset if he ate out alone leaving her at home. Another thought went rushing through his mind. If she hadn't wanted to join him, she would be alone with someone possibly outside the building watching her, a thought that made him shudder. He suddenly remembered the image and joke of Inspector Clouseau and Kato and considered running through a few moves with Rochelle, only dismissing the idea due to it being too close to their wedding day, should she be injured by accident.

Clearing his mind, Jerry finished opening the envelope and tipped out its contents. From the manuals laying face up, he could immediately see the titles were in English. Lifting each one individually, he flicked through them to confirm it was not just the titles printed in English. Once satisfied they were all readable, he replaced the manuals in the envelope, folded over the open edge and placed it in his briefcase, having to lean hard on the lid to force it closed.

He walked across to Rochelle's office. "I'm sorry about tonight darling, but it will give you an opportunity to update me again on the wedding plans. This time I promise to listen," he said.

Rochelle looked at him. "Jerry, you don't need to apologise for anything and besides; we haven't had Chinese since we went with Sara. You know how much I like it. But please don't use the excuse it will give us time to discuss the wedding. I know you'll be sitting at the table in body but your mind has been elsewhere for some time now, ever since your visit to the embassy and tonight you'll be anxious until you receive Sara's call. I'm not going to ask any questions, you know that, I'm just reminding you I'm here for you whenever you want," she told him quietly, adding, "The message has been forwarded and a table booked," pausing for a moment before saying, "And I love you more than anything," as she blew a kiss across the desk.

Notifying the waiter of a possible call when they walked in, they ordered and were partly through their meal and wedding arrangements when Jerry was told his presence was requested on the phone.

Jerry walked over to the bar where the telephone was located and taking the handset from the barman said, "Hello"

"Jay its S"

"Hi," Jerry said, careful not to mention any names and coming straight to the point, "I now have the correct details and a repeat of yesterday's calls. I also had an idea on the way here but admit I didn't action what I should have done, due mainly to being with the wife and you know how she gets when I start with business around her," he told Sara realising the barman could hear every word he spoke and was therefore careful to disguise the conversation as far as possible in the hope Sara would understand he was trying to tell her that he thought he had been followed again, but couldn't be sure.

"Thanks for letting me know, I'll see if I can find out anything that might help you, meanwhile do the paperwork they're waiting for and when we next meet you can provide me with any additional details you have," she replied. Saying, "Goodbye," Jerry handed the handset back to the barman thanking him for its use.

Returning home after the meal, Jerry spent most of the evening reviewing the manuals and considering various ways to integrate the TAUs, Rochelle having a reasonably early night leaving him to it.

Believing it would not be difficult, he started work on the proposal, basing it on a standard Igloo template originally created by Rochelle. At 3.30am she woke and realising the other side of the bed was still empty, despite being half asleep she made her way to the study in search of Jerry.

"Come to bed darling," Rochelle said quietly. "You'll be fresher in the morning," and without giving Jerry an opportunity to argue, she saved his work on the computer, placed the manuals back in the envelope and took him to bed. Within seconds of his head hitting the pillow, Jerry was in a deep sleep.

Rochelle woke at her usual time, dressed and went to the office leaving Jerry in bed. When he finally woke up, he continued working on the proposal from home, completing the final sentences as Rochelle returned that evening. He priced the project as he had originally estimated, providing discounts based on volume, knowing the numbers would never transpire, but none the less playing his part in the game, setting the first discount break at twenty five units. Having reviewed the specifications in detail, he couldn't find any significant hardware or software modifications necessary to adapt a standard product to meet this particular requirement. There were always amendments needed when undertaking such a project, but this one looked no different to many others they had completed. Jerry calculated the changes would take no longer than a week or two to complete, however he was going to quote six weeks to carry out the required changes. He felt it was an acceptable timescale which Kavitah and her crew would agree too, whilst providing him and Sara time to try and ascertain the targets. He then hoped to be able to add a further two or three weeks attributing it to implementation problems if the need arose.

Having calculated the dates, Jerry felt the necessity to test the strength of his relationship with Rochelle. During dinner he casually asked her, "Would you mind postponing the honeymoon for a few weeks after the wedding?" citing it as a fairly common phenomena these days, "I promise a delay would ensure it would be that much better." He then prepared himself for an outburst of abuse.

"Jerry," she said pausing momentarily. "I know you're involved in something major and since its business too, I fully understand, all I ask is that you don't keep making excuses, you know I don't appreciate them. Just ask or tell me things as they are. If you feel we need to wait a while before taking our honeymoon despite your assurance a few weeks ago that everything would be finished in time, then I'll accept it since I value your judgement and know you understand how to prioritise your commitments." Rochelle spoke in a very relaxed manner as if she had been expecting the conversation and had taken the time to prepare her response. "To make up for it though, you really will have to ensure we are treated like royalty when we go," remembering the words he had used when asking about the destination.

"Thank you for being so understanding," he replied in a very appreciative voice whilst making his way over to her chair. He slid one arm under her thighs, placed his other under her arm and carried her through to their bedroom. "I'm sorry I haven't really been myself recently," he whispered before kissing her. "It's not that I don't think you can't keep a secret because I know you can," he kissed her again. "It's probably hard for you to understand or appreciate this, but I don't want to say much to you for your own safety and it hurts me keeping things from you, that I promise." As he finished whispering, he laid her down gently on the bed and started to slowly remove her clothes, garment by garment, both forgetting about everything else until the following morning.

Early the next day, having had Rochelle check through it, Jerry sent the proposal by courier to DataLink and awaited their response, something which didn't take long in coming. A call from Mohammed offered two hundred thousand United States Dollars for the trial system. After quickly checking the current exchange rate using the Internet, Jerry refused the offer. Following several minutes of negotiation, they finally settled on two hundred and fifty thousand dollars, paid in full on signing contracts. Mohammed also pushed on the timescale and Jerry promised to do his best to complete earlier, although he said the contract would state the six weeks as documented in the proposal, but that work would start on receipt of funds.

Believing this was the time to push the issue of reporting the contract to the British authorities, Jerry considered the best way to approach the subject. "I need to know the name of the organisation that will be party to the contract, allowing the paperwork to be completed, which will then have to be submitted to the relevant government department due to the nature of the equipment we will be interconnecting with." Jerry informed Mohammed.

A silence followed, Jerry could almost hear the cogs turning in Mohammed's head. "Would reporting the job cause a delay? Do you have to await authorisation?" Mohammed finally asked. Before Jerry had a chance to reply, Mohammed offered: "I'll ask DataLink to look into the matter bearing in mind you're not supplying a weapon, or a component that makes up a weapon, just a security system. Can I suggest that for no reason other than time, you push ahead with the project whilst DataLink confirm the situation? If it transpires that you should have submitted the information, then I will financially compensate you for any inconvenience caused." Mohammed paused before adding, "And for your trouble, I'll add a bonus to the basic price." He then confirmed that for simplicity sake the contract should be in the name of DataLink, which would ensure that Igloo were not exporting the system and therefore even less likely for the need to report anything.

Following the conversation, Jerry took the proposal with his handwritten notes of the amendments to the sales and administration people and asked for the paperwork to be sent by hand to DataLink as quickly as possible. He marked the project as a priority job for himself alone. The contract and invoice left the office just after lunch. Jerry thought to himself, "Well, this is make or break, based on their response, I'm either home and dry or, if I'm very lucky, at best I'll be spending the rest of my life looking over my shoulder." He brought

Sara up to date during the evening in-between more wedding arrangements from Rochelle. For the first time since accepting the operation, he was able to put it to the back of his mind and really relax in the knowledge there was nothing further he could do at this juncture. He had, despite being careful, not detected any additional surveillance attempts on him.

Whilst Rochelle was talking him through the wedding, he stopped her for a moment and again apologised for being so pre-occupied, not appearing to have taken an interest in much else, particularly their wedding. He assured her that he was as excited about getting married as she was, if not more so. Rochelle, in her very calm manner confirmed she understood, as long as he was there on the day.

At just after 11am the following morning the contract was returned to Igloo's offices marked for Jerry's attention, duly signed with a note that the funds had been transferred to Igloo's bank account. Jerry checked with the bank to find that three hundred thousand dollars had been deposited, at which time he opened the necessary files. As far as the office was concerned, this was just another bespoke project.

Thirty-Eight

Jerry worked tirelessly on the project, enabling the interconnection of TAUs to the necessary equipment, which proved to be a relatively simple task, exactly as he had envisaged. Once the hardware design had been completed, he considered for the first time the implications of what he was supplying and suddenly realised he was assisting a terrorist organisation to potentially cause unmitigated devastation to a significant part of the western world, particularly if nuclear or chemical warheads were to be used. "If it were just meant to be threatening, why would they require such sophisticated security? They are obviously planning to launch them," he thought to himself. On reflection, he could see he had acted like a robot, programmed to carry out a particular task which he completed without question or thought. Igloo had received a handsome fee for his effort, but there probably wouldn't even be the time to enjoy it. He realised he had made a huge mistake in going along with everything, but believed it was now too late to change direction. He should simply have told Kavitah that Igloo was too busy to take on the job, thereby leaving the missiles open. Even if he had not become involved, his brain told him: "They would still have the missiles to launch." Frustrated, the thoughts continued: "There must be something that can be done about it, otherwise we're just sitting ducks." He desperately attempted to focus on what was now needed, trying to formulate an idea in his mind. Eventually a seed started to germinate which caused him to examine line by line the software built into the TAUs. The task had suddenly taken on a new dimension, one he kicked himself for not considering earlier. The project had suddenly become far more complicated than he had originally anticipated.

To stand any chance of success he needed to provide features Kavitah or the DataLink boys would be unable to detect, whilst ensuring there would be no compromise in the protection being provided against other intruders. Consulting with Dr Fog and Igloo's internal specialists on a number of issues relating to the wireless element and in particular aspects of micro switching, it didn't take long for Jerry to realise the kit Igloo used in this area only operated over a short distance. The final solution he was configuring in his mind required long range communications and therefore Igloo's test equipment would be unsuitable. The more Jerry delved into it, the more it dawned on him an electronic communications expert would have to be involved to resolve certain issues beyond his scope of knowledge in this particular field. He remained annoyed with himself for not assessing the situation correctly from the beginning. Taking all his errors into account he admitted to himself he had been a complete idiot.

Having passed on the bad news to Sara and explained in some detail the type of experience he required, she arranged for the relevant expert to be sent over from Israel. "It will take a couple of days for him to arrive due entirely to your concerns regarding the calls and potential surveillance a few weeks ago," she told Jerry. "For that reason he won't be taking a direct flight, instead he will enjoy a tour of the northern hemisphere before arriving in London."

Jerry finally met up with Sara's specialist, David, in his hotel room two days later and initially went through a detailed, non-technical explanation of his proposed solution, followed by a summary of the requirements. David listened intently for well over an hour without comment until Jerry had finished. "It sounds as though your idea could actually work. A very out-of-the-box solution to the impending problem," he remarked. "What you need is possible, but I don't believe it's an off the shelf product. The equipment necessary would need to be modified to achieve your objective," he informed Jerry, concluding with, "You will also require an extremely powerful transmitter and receiver, or transceiver and to the best of my knowledge Israel doesn't posses that type of capability, so we need to consider involving our American friends."

Having agreed in principle the solution was workable and certainly worth a try, David phoned Sara to confirm the availability of resources for the work and very quickly it appeared he was more than happy with the response he received. Since David would have to return to Israel to manage the development of his part of the solution, Jerry wasted no time in proceeding to discuss the technical details with him, followed by debating every possible scenario and issue that could arise, ensuring the fastest possible design and build of a working device. The result of the day's deliberations was for David to build a generic adapter able to connect to almost any transceiver and one way or another, gain access to whatever communications equipment would be required. The other key feature required of the adapter was the ability for it to be controlled via a standard PC connected to the Internet.

The final topic they covered was housekeeping, where Jerry noted he would have to supply the frequency range of the weapons in addition to a TAU with an authorised code. Fortunately, for some reason he could recall ordering an extra TAU to be built when completing the internal works form, marked as a test unit for the project, ensuring it did not appear on any client paperwork.

It was agreed Jerry would keep hold of the spare until they knew where the device would be located, at which time it would be sent by diplomatic pouch to the relevant destination. David informed Jerry, "I'll immediately put a team on the project and hope to be in a position to commence testing in around ten days. Despite the urgency, for security reasons I'm staying in London for a further day or so before taking another indirect flight back to Israel. Sara has arranged for me to appear to be having several other meetings just in case."

There was suddenly far more work required than Jerry had

accounted for and he was no longer comfortable it could all be completed in the timescale to which he had committed. What irritated him most was on this occasion the extra work was not at the request of the client as was normally the case. He started relatively simply but as Jerry continued to develop his ideas he felt a need to provide more and more exclusive features, hopefully allowing them to make the difference between life and death for what could be millions of people. Developing these enhanced functions gave rise to a number of technical issues and delays, all of which had to remain secret from the client. He started to be haunted by the indoctrination he endured from many of his lecturers: "Never underestimate the enemy, always presume you are dealing with the best." The problem was that he had no idea of their level of technical ability.

He wrote and rewrote the code until it provided him with the functionality he desired, often working throughout the night. This project had a completely different feeling to all others, one he had never experienced before. If he made an error, however small it might be, the potential outcome was beyond comprehension. No other project he had undertaken had such consequences attached to it. The pressure maintained the adrenalin rush, keeping him going day after day, testing, retesting and testing once more, in the hope of finding and then eliminating even the most insignificant of programming bugs.

The task was further complicated since some of the functionality Jerry was looking to obtain was specifically related to the missile's intelligence and nothing to do with the capabilities provided by a TAU. For everything to work as he planned, additional logic was necessary in the missile's own hardware and software and that was something he knew he would never be able to do. He eventually devised a workaround to achieve the required result which necessitated building a second electronic circuit into the casing of the TAU and connecting it in such a way it would behave as if it were part of the missile's own circuitry. He hoped this would enable the missile to interpret a third coordinate rather than just the standard two-dimensional longitude and latitude it was designed to accept, being the key to Jerry's plan. Without it very little else was relevant. Since obtaining an identical

Inter Continental Ballistic Missile was out of the question, he could only test everything by simulation, using a programme supplied by David. The thought that the most important component could not be field tested and in affect being left to chance created an unsavoury taste in Jerry's mouth.

Whilst working on the project, Jerry kept in constant contact with the directors of DataLink and Kavitah whom had shown up in New York for a few days following a long weekend in Paris.

"We are nearly ready to discuss implementation," Jerry told her on one such call. "Where is the hardware located at the moment?" he asked, using the guise that the information is required to consider the logistics of physical installation.

"The control and launch station is a mobile unit in Lebanon and two missiles are currently stored with it. The other three are being delivered imminently," Kavitah replied, not giving the question a second thought.

"Who's connecting the TAUs to your kit? I didn't include overseas travel in our pricing, particularly since we have almost given the system to you," Jerry told her, referring to the price that had finally been agreed. "But it is a relatively simple task. I can train a member of your team here if you wish," Jerry said.

"That's probably the best idea. When do you think that could take place?" Kavitah asked.

"We're in the process of final testing at the moment, so it shouldn't be too long now. I'll keep you posted, but I don't envisage any significant issues to be thrown up at this late stage," he replied reassuringly. Appearing satisfied with the progress, Kavitah concluded the conversation by telling Jerry she looked forward to hearing from him.

Sara arrived at Igloo's offices at Jerry's request, although she made a point of telling him it wasn't her preferred location for a meeting. "I'm working solidly on this project and haven't the time for day trips at the moment," Jerry told her, confirming, "It has nothing to do with the embassy being out-of-bounds for us both," which had been the case ever since the plan had been hatched, a point in time which now seemed as if it were centuries ago. Sara had the added inconvenience of having to find accommodation where no identification was required, since it was imperative that no one could possibly link her with anything to do with Israel, she was just another tourist in London if anyone enquired. "Several things to go over," Jerry started, "Opening with the most important. Roch has accepted to delay our honeymoon so your bosses better keep to their word or I'm dead meat here," he told her smiling despite meaning it as a serious comment.

"I'll pass the message on, I'm sure they'll give you a honeymoon of a lifetime." Whilst speaking, Sara was suddenly overcome with jealousy. She had grown very fond of Jerry and more recently, working so closely with him, she wished on numerous occasions the relationship was far more than being his boss regardless of being more than ten years his senior. The one drawback of her job was that it didn't allow her to have a lasting personal relationship. But Sara was a professional and had always managed to keep her feelings to herself, ensuring they never affected her judgement.

Jerry continued to brief her, "There are currently two missiles in Lebanon, stored with a mobile control unit. The others are due to be delivered as we speak. The potential targets are New York, Paris and probably London. Kavitah is currently on tour."

"You have been busy on top of building the device itself haven't you?" Sara suggested. "And thanks to you obtaining Kavitah's name, we have also been able to track her presence in Tel Aviv and Jerusalem," she quickly added.

"I've also been working closely with David. If these are the targets, we need access to certain American facilities for an idea I've been trying to implement into the system. Is that a possibility?" Jerry asked her, although he could anticipate her answer having discussed the option in length with David. But things had to be done officially.

"If we can demonstrate New York is a potential target, I think we will get all the co-operation we need. Since 9/11, you only need as much as a slight hint and every security organisation is mobilised," she said. "The only problem we have with our colleagues over there is they immediately try to take over the operation, believing they can do everything better than anyone else, irrelevant that all the ground work, the hardest part, has already been completed and I, like many of my colleagues, begrudge that."

"Surely it's not possible on this operation since somehow it now revolves around me, not that it was intended to be that way in the original brief if I recall correctly," Jerry reminded her.

"Very true," Sara agreed, responding to the comment that Jerry seemed to be in control of the situation, feeling slightly better with the idea. She then went onto say: "But that's because once again you've gone beyond your original brief. Phase one was simply the collection of information. How to deal with it was never discussed and officially remains unallocated to any team." Sara did not mean it as any form of rebuke; she was very pleased with the direction in which things had moved, as were her bosses. "So what is it you're trying to implement? David told me he has been developing some kind of adapter for you but nothing more than that other than you're both satisfied with the initial test results. He thinks your idea is terrific," she told him. "My concern as always is time, I know I don't need to remind you two thirds of your six weeks has passed, or that you originally anticipated the project would only take a couple of weeks from start to finish." She seemed to take delight in saying.

Somewhat annoyed with her implication that he was unable to deliver on time, Jerry quickly retorted: "The quoted job was completed in three or four days. I then did some thinking, leading to additional features being added to the system." His composure then changed, becoming very serious as he talked Sara through every detail of the plan, including the extra functionality and the benefits he hoped they would provide.

"Do you think you can really pull it off?" Sara asked once he had finished, being just as serious and extremely impressed with what she had heard, despite her lack of understanding of the technology. "I apologise for the insinuation just now, it was meant more as a joke than anything else. You should know by now I'm one of your biggest fans and I can see you have put an enormous amount of work into this project in an attempt to achieve your goal," she quickly added.

Jerry wasn't sure how to reply. "All the tests I have undertaken here and with David look promising. But unless you can get me an ICBM to allow us to test it properly, until we try it in a live theatre of action, well, we can only hope. If I was a more religious person, I'd probably have added weeks of praying time into the development schedule."

Knowing an ICBM was out of the question, Sara had difficulty thinking of a suitable response. "I understand what you're saying about the testing. Let me have words with my people, perhaps we can get you access to research facilities and better simulators than David gave you. I wouldn't hold your breath for a missile though," she said jokingly, "but I think we can probably wangle it to keep you as number one," and then completely changing the subject. "Oh I nearly forgot, your number two fan Debra sends her best wishes and says keep up the excellent work." With that, she stood up and made her own way out of the office still in deep thought.

Jerry and David continued to test everything repeatedly until they were both satisfied. At David's request, Jerry had a further two TAUs built and forwarded to him through the Diplomatic Postal Service, where they were installed for what was hoped to be the final and most conclusive test of all. One was fitted to a Missile Launch and Control Unit, the second to an intelligent short range missile that Sara had managed to procure from the IDF following a briefing with her bosses. Having explained the plan to them, the procurement became a matter of just signing a few forms.

The adapter David had built was connected in the manner the two had agreed a couple of weeks earlier in his hotel bedroom. "The missile is set up in the Negev, the dessert area in the south of the country where we carry out a lot of military hardware testing," David told Jerry on a secure telephone connection. "If you're ready, so am I," he added.

"Let's go for it," Jerry said without hesitation, checking he had the correct documentation open on the relevant pages.

David then called out a set of coordinates and commands specific to the missile being used. Jerry recognised the instructions, not being that dissimilar to those he had learnt almost parrot fashion from the manuals received from DataLink. "The coordinates I've given you are about fifteen kilometres south and five kilometres west from the ones I'm going to use. We have around five minute's airborne time from launch to target," he informed Jerry. "I'm keying my coordinates in now," he finally said and Jerry could hear David typing away at a keyboard.

Jerry watched his computer screen and mobile phone, which he had placed alongside his keyboard. Sixty five seconds after David started to enter the coordinates Jerry received a text message, which he read and immediately deleted. He waited a further ninety seconds and then keyed into his computer the information provided by David. Shortly after he received a second text and once read, he again deleted it. Both men eagerly waited to hear from the people in the Negev.

Thirty-Nine

Jerry confirmed the date of the training day for a representative of DataLink which was to take place at Igloo's offices. He created a user manual, taking a basic draft and making the necessary amendments, mainly addressing the physical interconnect with the missile and control unit.

He then met with Sara for a pizza, the main reason being to discuss a particular concern that had dawned on him. "I have the green light to approach our friends at any time," she told Jerry, having congratulated him on the successful Negev test with David, adding that she understood it wasn't a conclusive test as the missile used was not the same as Kavitah's.

Jerry, sitting opposite her wasn't interested in being congratulated for anything and wanted to get straight to the reason for requesting the meeting. Taking the opportunity of a pause in Sara's dialogue he quietly said with a morbid look on his face, "I've come up with one very big hole in the plan that neither David nor I thought of before and even if we had, there wouldn't have been anything we could do about it since it's not a technical issue."

"What is it?" she enquired, her face turning white as if a pot of paint had been poured over her, just from his look. Up until now she had been ecstatic with the progress, believing it could save an unthinkable number of lives, besides earning her another promotion and she couldn't even contemplate what it would do for Jerry's credibility internationally. "I've talked your idea through many times now with some of the best brains in Israel and elsewhere," she informed him. "Not one person has identified an issue, quite the reverse, everyone is extremely impressed with the plan and the technology built to carry it off."

Jerry remained silent as the waitress served their pizzas, staring blankly at Sara as if a romantic statement was about to follow, her face remaining unchanged. "There are only two possible permutations by which the missiles can be launched," he started as soon as they were alone again. Sara immediately realised from his tone and expression this was going to be another of his long drawn out speeches. "The first is where all the missiles are launched together, although in reality they'll have to be a few minutes apart since they only have one launch control station. Basically an all or nothing situation, probably a surprise attack similar to 9/11, no warning, no nothing, just bang." Sara nodded as if to agree. "In that scenario, we can roll out our plan with absolutely no problem at all," Jerry said with confidence, before reverting back to his worried appearance. "However, that scenario is highly improbable, since from what I recall you taught me, they are more likely to threaten verbally and when the threats are ignored, they launch missile number one against the least significant target, increasing the stakes as each threat is ignored until either the global powers give in, or are wiped out."

Sara sat in her chair desperately trying to understand what difference the two launch procedures made as far as Jerry's solution was concerned, although she had to admit she agreed with his analysis.

Jerry continued since Sara remained silent. "The problem is simple and so obvious now I can't believe I missed it." He took a bite of his pizza, swallowing it before continuing, noticing from her reaction she hadn't deduced anything yet. "Let's assume missile one is en-route to target A, we take the appropriate evasive measures as planned and they work. If a miracle happens, Kavitah and her crew may think some kind of technical fault occurred, but unlike many, I don't believe in miracles and my assumption is that she will immediately know someone has been playing around with things. Surely you accept they will have one of those two thoughts?" Jerry waited and finally observed a slight affirmative nod from Sara. "Assuming they are stupid, when missile number two performs exactly the same trick as its predecessor, even the most ignorant of terrorists, including those that forget to remove the sticky tape before throwing a grenade at their enemy, will realise the idea of it being a fault was beyond the realms of chance and probability. Don't you think?" he asked, but in his usual way he just continued. "That leaves missiles three, four and five, each being relieved of their TAUs, thereby removing our ability to carry out the action we have planned, allowing them to launch their attacks without hindrance. I trust you're with me on this. I haven't mentioned it to David yet, I think it would destroy him," Jerry finally stated.

There was a long silence before he heard a very timid "Yes, I understand exactly what you're saying and have to agree it is a possibility but not a technical issue and there is absolutely no way you could have addressed it." The expression on her face remained.

Sounding as though he had accepted defeat, Jerry just said, "What it amounts to is that all our work over the last four months has been in vain, except for the profit Igloo has made," trying to make some light of the situation. "I have booked a training session for one of DataLink's people for next Tuesday. I suggest a surveillance team be put on him, Kavitah and Mohammed, allowing us to identify the launch site in advance, destroying it before anything happens. If we can't find it first, we will get the coordinates when they launch the first missile and then someone is going to have to move pretty quickly to get there before they launch the second."

Sara wasted no time in telling him, "You know that's an impossible task, not only could we not do it, but the Americans couldn't either. It's much too big an operation, particularly as it's cross border, in countries that none of the potential targets even talk to."

"So you're telling me everything I have done over the last few weeks is totally wasted then?" he just repeated.

"No. I'm not saying that at all. Firstly, let me remind you we were only tasked to identify the targets, the additional work you took on since then is a tremendous bonus if it's successful," she said in an upbeat tone. "Thanks to you we fortunately have a good idea of the targets, and if your worst case scenario transpires, we are where we would have been if you hadn't taken on the additional role," she said trying to console him. "Furthermore, as you just stated, we will have the coordinates of the control unit once the first missile is launched, which will be a significant advantage in many ways."

"And what's the plan when we know I've failed?" Jerry asked, still very despondent.

"We will know as soon as they are ready to launch, since we can assume it's when your friends take delivery of the TAUs. We can assume they won't hold onto them for long. The first thing we do is inform the target countries who will immediately step up their national air cover and with the advanced warning and knowledge of the origin and destination, there is a significantly greater chance of destroying the rockets well before they reach their intended targets," she said reassuringly. "And who knows, we may even be fast enough to get bombers to the launch position quickly, after all we already know it's somewhere on the Lebanese border."

"Increasing the probability of success and being successful are a million miles apart, but I hope you're right," was all Jerry could find to say.

Trying to cheer him up a little, Sara remembered, "I followed through on a comment you made to me a while ago, although I'm not sure if it offers us any benefit. Early on, you suggested that Kavitah and her little group must be nervous of someone interfering with the missiles. We have tracked the supply chain as far as we could," she continued, although it was apparent Jerry couldn't really care less, he was trying to figure out a way he could destroy the missiles before they were launched if everything went wrong.

Unperturbed, Sara continued, "The Russians originally supplied the missiles as we already know. However they were not purchased directly from the state, a second link, we believe to be an arms dealer, sold them to the Russian mafia. From there and where we feel the source of Kavitah's concern rests is the missiles spent some time under the ownership of an al-Qaeda unit, before having been sold on again, eventually finding their way to Lebanon. We know there are conflicts between al-Qaeda and some Arab fundamentalists. What's more, if al-Qaeda obtained cash for the hardware and still manage to take control of the missiles for their own use, they're in a win win situation, filling their coffers to fund further attacks whilst obliterating their chosen targets." Having watched Jerry throughout her report she considered stopping at that point, but something urged her on. "Without your system, there is a chance that al-Qaeda get to hit their targets, ones we have not identified and are paid for doing so, gaining additional funds to finance further attacks. By installing your system, you can prevent them from gaining control of the missiles, so at least we'll know the intended destinations."

"I think they'll be relatively pleased with the targets selected in any case," Jerry replied.

"But they won't get the recognition and respect that they would if they carried out the attack themselves, which is what they would really want."

"I don't know anymore. You're far more familiar with inter terrorist politics than I am and as you so rightly pointed out, it doesn't make any difference, or not that I can see," Jerry said, immediately continuing, "Once I've trained their man and deliver, it becomes a waiting game. I think we should bring the Americans, Brits and French in now so that they can be prepared. We mustn't forget there are five missiles and only three or four likely targets at the moment, or do you think they will hit both Jerusalem and Tel Aviv?" Jerry asked, his tone continuing to show his feelings.

Sara, trying to regain a positive note and already considering how this information was going to be received when passed up the line of command, answered, "I can't say at this stage. Maybe there are only three missiles after all and before you jump in, I agree, three is almost as bad as five. All we can do is wait," she suggested, adding, "I'm inclined to agree with you regarding the notifications but at the end of the day it's not my decision. I can only provide the intelligence and put forward my recommendations. It's down to others to decide what action is taken, if any. I take it you have had no more strange calls, or been followed?" she asked, truly concerned.

"Not that I've been aware of and I'm still carrying out anti-surveillance techniques," Jerry replied. Finishing their meal, they paid and left the restaurant.

As they reached the doorway, Sara stopped Jerry, "You have to take the downs with the ups in this job, Jerry. You kept telling us you're not James Bond, you're right, things never go as smoothly as in the films and we are not always successful." She then kissed him on the cheek before heading off in the opposite direction.

Forty

Two students arrived at Igloo's offices for the training session, one being Kavitah, confirming Jerry's initial suspicion she had been trained to launch the missiles. The other was a young Arabic boy whom Jerry believed could only be in his early twenties if that. Compared to Kavitah he was clean and smartly dressed, wearing a suit and tie. Jerry, looking at the boy's facial features, height and build, believed he could well have been the courier that had delivered the documents and the bike that had followed him.

Both had a tremendous amount of knowledge relating to the operational detail of the missiles as though they had designed them themselves and Jerry added to their skills by teaching them how to install the TAUs, step-by-step. The manual he prepared read like one of the 'For Dummies' series of computer training books, this one he thought would be appropriately named 'Installing A TAU To An ICBM For Terrorists'.

Jerry again gave consideration to what he was doing: "I can't believe I'm supplying a system to a known terrorist group, assisting them in destroying some of the world's major cities with only a limited assurance of being able to prevent the impending carnage." The conclusion he reached was based on his system not having been tested on the missiles being deployed, his lack of confidence in the ability of the individual nations air defence systems to avert such a strike and his concern that they would quickly learn of his mischief during their first couple of launches and negate his access for the remaining ones. He couldn't stop thinking, "I suppose there is some credence to Sara's argument that at least we have a good idea as to the potential targets and therefore a small chance of causing such an attack to fail. I hope the missiles aren't launched on my wedding day, Roch would kill me!" He smiled to himself that he was almost more concerned about his wedding being ruined than the world destroyed. For some reason he subconsciously focussed on the subject of his wedding. "Perhaps it would be prudent to instruct someone else what to do when the missiles are launched. But whom could I trust and who would have the capability, wouldn't screw up and could keep the secret? I don't think I know anyone with all three attributes."

The training day progressed well, Jerry could see both participants felt very competent in carrying out the installation, which they practiced several times on a mock-up built for the occasion. He made a joke that he had ordered a real ICBM for them to practice on, but it had unfortunately been held up in customs. Judging by the questions being asked, Jerry felt he needed to provide them with some reassurance that everything would fit together as they had just been taught and operate in the manner he had explained during the day, providing the security measures they had specified at the start of the project. To put their minds at ease, he showed them a number of diagrams and other information from the manuals and made sure they understood how the system functioned. He finished off the day by reminding them to change the access code once the units were installed, as he had shown them to do, locking out anyone at Igloo accessing the system, either on purpose or inadvertently. This statement was standard in all training sessions and manuals and was a task always carried out on handover in situations where Igloo undertook the installation. He also provided them both with a copy of the user manual he had written.

As they were packing up their belongings, Kavitah asked, "When will we be able to take delivery of the TAUs?"

"A natural question to ask at this stage of the project," Jerry thought. He took them both into the Lab as he referred to the technical unit, a large room partitioned into three sections, development, construction and testing. They made their way to the testing area where he pointed out to her the boxes going through their final paces. "Would you like to see the video of the complete testing procedures?" he asked. "We have an electronic recording which I would be happy to show you." For quality control purposes, Igloo recorded the complete build and testing cycle for every unit they produced. The two students followed Jerry to his office where he swivelled the screen so they could both see clearly and then selected and downloaded the recording for their devices from Igloo's electronic library, which they watched together with interest. As soon as the video had finished, Jerry printed a copy of the test results to date and handed the sheet to Kavitah, who after studying it appeared to be impressed. "To answer your earlier question, I would hope by the end of the week, early next week by the latest," Jerry said. "How do you want them shipped?"

"I think it's best if we collect," Kavitah said looking as though she had quickly considered a number of alternatives in her mind. "Just let me know when they are ready. You've done well Jerry. Thank you."

"Not at all, it's our job. I'm sure you checked us out thoroughly before you took us on," he replied.

"You knew we would verify you properly the first day we met. We have contacts within a couple of your clients, which is why we decided to approach you in the first place. They both told us if anyone could provide a solution it was you," she said smiling. "Well thanks and goodbye," and Kavitah left the building with the lad as if they were a couple, leaving Jerry even more concerned for the safety of the world.

Forty-One

Kavitah arranged for the collection of the TAUs and Sara organised the additional one to be forwarded to its final destination by diplomatic pouch. Jerry was relieved that despite all the additional work, he had managed to complete the project by the agreed date and quickly reached the conclusion there would be no benefit in trying to delay the delivery, an idea he had originally discussed with Sara. As far as he was concerned, despite all his efforts and those of many others, there was nothing more that could be done to stop Kavitah from carrying out her mission. The very best anyone could possibly hope for was the TAUs to be fitted correctly, the missiles launched in close succession of each other and everything to work as planned, but control of the outcome had now passed into the hands of the terrorists. The only alternative to everything working precisely as anticipated and he knew how unlikely that to be, was for Kavitah and her mob to be so inept or nervous when it came to the real thing, they found themselves unable to programme the coordinates into the missiles, or forget to attach the war heads, both the latter options as equally unlikely as each other.

Unable to do anything further for the operation except sit and wait, Jerry spent the next week catching up on office work he had allowed to build up, in between visits to a tailor for a morning suit which Rochelle insisted had to match both fathers and his best man. He also found time for a haircut and everything else he needed to do for the wedding. During the evenings he drafted his speech, knowing it would sound a whole lot better if he allowed Rochelle to tweak it, but then he wouldn't be able to surprise her, something he very much wanted to do.

Anthony, his best man, Jerry's one very old school friend, tried on several occasions to organise a stag party, but Jerry always managed to find excuse after excuse for not having one. They eventually agreed on the two of them going out for a steak dinner, Jerry's favourite meal, Jerry making it perfectly clear that it was to discuss the rules of engagement for the day, what he wanted and didn't want Anthony to do. Unknown to Jerry, Rochelle had already met with Anthony and taken him through the order of the day and had, as far as Anthony was concerned, answered all his questions.

Jerry also took the time to pick what he thought were a selection of the best photos of Rochelle and himself together, which he had somehow managed to find by going through her fairly large photograph collection. He had two sets enlarged into 10x8's by his friends at the embassy where they had a photo processing lab and were able to produce what he required within hours, a job that he had been quoted three weeks from the local processing shop, despite explaining he only had a couple of days in which to get them done. He then mounted each set in a smart leather album he had inscribed with a personal message, one for each set of parents. Remembering Rochelle had put presents for the bridesmaids on his list of responsibilities, he spent almost a full day on the task having consulted with his mother first; he didn't want to make any mistakes with them. The final task he had to organise was to buy a special present for Rochelle. Not being clued up on purchasing such items, he eventually selected a heart shaped platinum locket on a neck chain, for which he found and placed a photo of Rochelle on one side and one of himself on the other having had them reduced in size. He gave everything to Anthony to bring on the day, along with all the other regulatory items such as wedding rings, which he collected at the same time as purchasing the locket; checking the engraving he had secretly asked the jeweller to do for Rochelle's ring, which read, 'Rochelle, my one and only love, forever. Jerry' followed by the date of their wedding. Having chosen the rings together several weeks earlier, he had called the jeweller afterwards to organise the engraving. He wondered if Rochelle had the same idea but decided to wait rather than sneak a preview in order to be genuinely surprised and have that 'first time feeling' on the day.

The remaining few days before the wedding passed without Jerry hearing anything from Kavitah. He considered calling her to make sure everything was satisfactory, but thought better of it. He decided to talk to the technical manager at DataLink, apologising for the delay in writing up the results of the beta test, explaining he had been working flat out to complete the job for their client, although he knew the manager was aware of the reason. "I'm getting married this weekend," Jerry informed him. "But assure you I will pick up on it afterwards." Jerry was certain the fact he had made contact would be forwarded on.

Rochelle and Jerry agreed to spend the weekend apart, from the Friday evening until the wedding on Sunday, each staying with their respective parents. They also decided not to communicate until they were together in the synagogue, except in the case of an emergency. Jerry took a few papers home from the office to review over Friday evening and Saturday, stopping boredom from setting in, knowing he would miss Rochelle. He also had his laptop computer and of course his mobile phone with him. Most of Saturday he lounged around feeling quite content, his mind predominantly thinking of Rochelle, except for an hour during the afternoon when he met with Sara as arranged.

Wishing his parents good night on the final night of him being a single man, as he made his way to his former bedroom which he still considered to be his, Jerry reminded them to wake him at around eight-thirty. He had arranged for his best man to arrive at nine-thirty, the photographer due at the same time with another dispatched to Rochelle's parents if he remembered correctly. He planned to leave the house shortly after eleven for the fifteen minute drive to the synagogue, arriving forty-five minutes before the ceremony was due to start.

As he lay in bed, despite it being the second night, he still found it strange to be in his old room and on his own, having become so used to having Rochelle lying beside him. He couldn't help feeling an extraordinary sensation, one he had never experienced before, it was not one of doubt or nervousness of any kind, but genuine excitement for the following day and of spending the rest of his life with the girl of his dreams. He stretched out to switch off the bedside light when his foot felt something at the bottom of the bed. Griping it between his toes, he pulled out an envelope which had his name written in script on the front, with the scent Rochelle knew to be his favourite.

He sat up and carefully opened the envelope, immediately noticing it was hand written. "Rochelle never hand wrote anything," he thought to himself, even notes were keyed into her palm pilot or computer, virtually every written communication he could ever remember her creating, beside signing a cheque, was typed on a computer or her palm and printed on the nearest infra red or Bluetooth enabled printer. Impressed by the trouble she went too, he slowly started to read the words, beginning with the following day's date.

"My darling Jez,

Since we first met that fateful Thursday evening two and a half years ago, you have always been in my thoughts.

In those early days you were just a young, shy, incredibly clever teddy bear that lacked confidence in everything except your project; with just a handful of people you could call your friends. I remember as if it were yesterday, the first time I saw that twinkle in your eye, neatly blended with the embarrassment shown on your face when you asked me up to your bedroom.

Today I am marrying the only true love of my life and my best friend. As you know, over the last few years there have been a number of boys that have tried to beat you to it, all having failed miserably, now only left watching the dust settle in the wake of your boots. Not only has your body changed so dramatically for the good and I'm proud to hang off your arm for that reason alone, but your mind has changed even more so. I have never before seen anyone beaming with so much confidence and yet so modest at the same time, the only one thing having not changed by your success is your good nature and thought for others.

You are a true knight in shining armour, a man that lacks sufficient hours in the day for himself, but at the same time is prepared to drop everything and devote all his time to literally saving the lives of others, complete strangers, if necessary by placing his own life at risk.

My darling, lover and best friend, there are no words that truly do you justice; you are like a character that has jumped out of the pages of the very best fairytale, as if you were but a dream.

Our romance has been a whirlwind, albeit short lived, only to move onto longer and even better things if that were at all possible, but I know the time we have been together has served as an advert for our future, a future that I am longing to start and pray never comes to an end.

By the time you read this, it will be just hours before the start of our new life together and I want you to know that I'm looking forward to it more than anything in the world.

I want you to remember, I will always be here for you.

All my love, forever.

Your very best friend and lover.

Roch"

Returning the note carefully to its envelope, Jerry wiped away the tears of joy that had formed. His excitement seemed to increase continuously throughout the night and he barely slept, maintaining a tight grip on the envelope, holding it close to his heart. There was no need for him to be woken by his parents as he had requested, he had showered and dressed by seven and had phoned his best man before eight, reminding him of the various items requiring his attention, then requesting him to purchase a couple of additional items from a general store on his way over, bits and pieces Jerry found he suddenly needed.

The day as planned was to be a religious service at midday in the synagogue where Jerry's family had been members since he was very young, followed by a luncheon and tea dance for nearly three hundred relatives and friends. The day was to finish with an intimate dinner with their closest family and friends, fifty three in all, the other guests being scheduled to leave by six.

As Jerry watched Rochelle walk slowly down the aisle arm in arm with her father, it was as if she were an angel, looking more beautiful than he could ever have imagined. Not only was she blessed with stunningly good looks, she had a perfectly shaped body, one that could easily be associated with a world famous catwalk model. His perfect dish was then garnished with intelligence to complete it. Jerry really did consider himself the luckiest man alive and the lingering thoughts of everything else going on in his life at that particular moment just evaporated as soon as his eyes fell upon her.

There were a number of faces he was surprised to see, not that he didn't want them to share in his special day, it was just that he would never have thought to invite them. He was overjoyed to see Sara, Debra and Moshe, the three people probably most responsible for the majority of moulding him into the person he had now become, besides of course his bride. Debra and Moshe had brought Ruti with them, she having moved from Shin Bet to a team commanded by Debra during the series of promotions that followed the Histadrut operation. They had come over especially for the wedding, or at least that's the story they told, something Jerry had doubts about despite being very pleased to see them. Leon, Dr Fog, Peter and many other faces he recognised from the barbecue were also guests, but although Jerry didn't know many of them that well, he was well aware they were all good friends to Rochelle and there for her whilst he was off gallivanting. There were a large number of people from Igloo and Jerry even spotted a few clients and the company's professional advisors. Besides both his and Rochelle's family which appeared to make up the majority of the guests, there were many Jerry first labelled as Rochelle's friends, but quickly remembered they had also become good friends to him.

During lunch, Rochelle made him mingle with the guests, which brought back his memories of the day they first demonstrated their feelings for each other at Igloo's party, something he made a mental note to add to his speech.

The hall, although large, was decorated exquisitely with the brightest of flowers, balloons and other novel ideas and with the help of a large band; an aura of joy and happiness was created that no one present would ever forget.

The speeches followed the usual toasts, the first delivered by the best man, which everyone found highly amusing. With the help of Rochelle's and Jerry's parents, he had managed to obtain photos of the couple, dating back from birth to the present day. He had them converted to slides and projected on a large screen for all to see, whilst providing a commentary that compared their parallel paths in life almost year by year, intertwined with a number of highly embarrassing stories of their childhood that had obviously been extracted without force from their respective parents. The stories were of the type one tries to keep out of the public domain, but everyone other than Rochelle and Jerry were thoroughly enjoying the tales, laughter being heard from all four corners of the room.

The best man finished his speech and the Toast Master handed the microphone to Jerry to a round of applause. Once silence prevailed, he started in a tone far more serious than his best man, speaking in a manner Rochelle had never heard from him before, with genuine emotion, bringing tears to her eyes. As she glanced at her mother sitting on an adjacent table, Rochelle could clearly see tears running down her cheeks. Whilst listening intently to Jerry, since he had refused her a private preview, she looked around the hall to see he had unwittingly managed to achieve the same effect from many of the guests, despite the numerous jokes he had included. Rochelle was comforted in the knowledge the tears were of joy and happiness and not of sadness or grief.

Having almost completed his speech, Jerry called his best man to assist with the traditional presentations. Before continuing and a break from convention, he also asked Rochelle to join him, he wanted the presentations that were about to be made to be seen to be from them both rather than him alone. As Rochelle approached Jerry, the first thing she did was kiss him in front of everyone, something that produced a further round of applause intermixed with the odd wolf whistle. Continuing with the task in hand, Jerry first called up the three bridesmaids followed by the pageboy and Rochelle handed them each their gift, presents she knew to expect since she reminded him to organise them.

Believing Jerry had finished, Rochelle started to walk back to her seat, stopped by Jerry quickly grabbing her arm. The best man handed her a large bouquet of flowers, Jerry being given another by the toast master whilst calling up their mothers, each presenting a bouquet to their respective mother-in-laws. Keeping the women at the podium, Jerry then asked both fathers to join their wives as the newly weds presented them with the photo albums. Rochelle didn't pay too much attention to them at first, until she flicked through them more carefully, when she was suddenly overwhelmed, realising the time, effort and thought that had gone into producing them and once again tears of happiness formed in her eyes whilst she whispered a quiet "Thank you" and gave him a peck on the cheek.

"And finally," Jerry said into the microphone once the photographer had finished with their parents and they had returned to their seats. "Mrs Freedman," he called, as his best man subtly handed him the locket after removing it from the box. "You know when you agreed to marry me you made me the happiest man on earth." To which everyone could see Rochelle nod. "I didn't think there would be a day where I could possibly be any happier than the day I came back from my European trip and you said 'I will' to my asking you for your hand in marriage. Rochelle, I've searched and searched but can't find any words to describe how I feel today. Not only am I even happier but also prouder than I ever thought possible; simply knowing you're finally my wife. You've been there for me whenever I've needed you. When I had to travel, indifferent to the country I was in, you turned up as frequently as you could, surprising me each time. You leave me alone without moaning when you know I need time to myself and you've done a magnificent job planning and organising this wedding whilst I've been preoccupied in the office. Please accept this memento as a very small token of my love and affection for you." He showed her the open locket, allowing her to see the photographs of their two faces staring at each other before closing it and stepping behind her. He then carefully placed the chain around her neck, fastened it and turned her 180 degrees so that her eyes were gazing into his, before finishing the presentation by giving her a kiss to remember, before leading her onto the dance floor for her first dance as Mrs Rochelle Freedman.

They spent the night in the honeymoon suite of the hotel and whilst sharing a bath together, Rochelle told him how moving she found his speech. "As I said in my note, you have changed so much since I first met you and all for the good," she said and they spent the remainder of the night demonstrating their love for each other.

When she woke the following morning she found standing on the dressing table the note she wrote for Jerry, framed and in the bottom right hand corner was Jerry's favourite photo of her.

Forty-Two

Leaving the hotel for the first time as Mr and Mrs Freedman, they spent the day holding hands whilst running between both sets of parents, neither of them having any contact with the office. During the day, Rochelle reminded Jerry several times that their honeymoon was temporarily postponed, certainly not written off, to which he agreed, kissing her each time. Jerry managed to slip away from her for an hour or so, to collect his mobile phone and laptop from Sara who took them when she had visited the previous Saturday. He hid the computer in the boot of his car, a place he never kept it for fear his car maybe stolen, but on this occasion there was no choice as he went back to Rochelle who was, for about the hundredth time, recounting the events of the previous day with her mother whilst noshing wedding cake. He was well aware if Rochelle had known that either device was close to hand the day before, he would already be on his way to the divorce courts. However, with there being a high risk of an imminent attack, he had to have the tools to hand if he were to stand any chance of being able to deal with it. Quite what would have happened if Sara had given him the prearranged signal during the service or luncheon, he didn't wish to contemplate?

They both went into the office on Tuesday and worked as usual except taking lunch together, an activity Jerry still often chose to ignore. In the evening they arranged to have dinner with Sara, Debra, Moshe, Ruti and a couple of other close friends from overseas, formerly Rochelle's friends, which turned into another late night enjoyed by all.

The following days passed without incident, Jerry continuing to work on the project with DataLink, amazed and very pleased with what started life as bait for an anti-terrorist operation was evolving into a potentially highly profitable product for Igloo. At one of the weekly management meetings where he finally decided to present it, Jerry was strongly criticised for progressing a product to beta test stage without having had sign off from the management team. He had agreed some fifteen months earlier, that before ideas were developed beyond an in principle concept document, the team would evaluate and make a joint decision on whether work should continue beyond that point and until now, Jerry had always respected the agreement and gone along with the majority vote.

Looking at Rochelle sitting opposite him, Jerry realised he would have to apologise for pushing ahead on this project without the team's consent. "I know I agreed to the rules and have until now not broken them. I'm also not going to hide behind the fact that I own the company so I can do what I like." As he spoke he watched the relief on everyone's faces, they had fully expected him to use that argument if he ever broke the agreement. Rochelle smiled at him as he continued. "However," he added, "It didn't interfere with any scheduled work, mine or anyone else, which if I recall correctly was the sole purpose of implementing the agreement, since it was feared I would distract people from fulfilling orders on time. Furthermore, not that it is directly related to this project, but certainly due to it, we were in the right place at the right time to win a three hundred thousand dollar bespoke development contract." Jerry looked around the table to see if there was anyone that still needed convincing, concluding his argument with, "I do believe it has huge potential and I would ask you to consider signing off on it now." After explaining the product in more detail by request from the sales manager and detailing the technical resources to produce a production model, the project received its official management approval.

On the odd occasion Jerry attended DataLink's offices over the following few weeks finalising data from the trial, whenever he happened to bump into one of the directors he made a point of casually asking how Kavitah's testing was progressing, to which he always received the same answer: "It's going well."

Forty-Three

On a cold Wednesday afternoon, some six and a half weeks after her wedding, Rochelle and a member of her sales team were meeting with a new client, discussing the details of a bespoke project, a conference that Jerry had been requested to attend. While reviewing the requirements, Jerry's mobile phone alerted him of the arrival of a text message. Ignoring the phone, Jerry apologised for the interruption and continued the discussion. Within a few minutes of the first message, a second text was received. Being unable to ignore two alerts, Jerry read the second message before reviewing the one he had previously neglected as the blood immediately drained from his face. He jumped up from his chair knocking it backwards, excused himself from the meeting and looking as though he had just seen a ghost, he left the room, quickly making his way to his office as a third message arrived. Wondering what was happening, Rochelle apologised to the client and ran after Jerry fearing the worst, although she had no idea what that was. Jerry entered his office and quickly closed the door, locking it to ensure privacy. Rochelle reaching it seconds later started knocking impatiently, repeatedly crying out "Jerry" until he finally allowed her in. "Rochelle" he said firmly. "Go straight back to the meeting.

Apologise to your client and explain I have an urgent issue to deal with and that you are able to conclude the details. Take a technical guy with you just in case there are any further technical questions," he commanded her. He had never spoken with such authority before and although she didn't like his tone, or the look of fear on his face, she felt on this occasion it was probably better to obey than argue.

Jerry immediately called Sara from his mobile phone, plugging in his hands free kit, whilst opening various applications on his computer that he had specifically written for this one occasion. As he was doing so, he received a further text.

When Sara answered her phone, Jerry calmly said, "Four missiles launched, the first about ten minutes ago." He then called out, reading from one of the open windows on his screen, the destination coordinates of all four missiles followed by the launch coordinates which not surprisingly were the same. Whilst doing so, he received a fifth notification and an additional set of destination and origination coordinates appeared on his screen, which he also read aloud for Sara's benefit.

"We'll keep this line open for as long as we can, I suggest you power your phone using the mains if you have an adapter," she advised him, but Jerry had already thought of that and had been carrying a spare adapter in his briefcase ever since the TAUs were collected. Concentrating on his screen he could hear Sara making calls on another line. Jumping between the various programs, Jerry focussed for a moment on the one that translated the coordinates into named locations and he slowly read them aloud in order for Sara to hear, "New York, London, Paris, Rome" finishing with "Jerusalem." His eyes returned to the application that continually recalculated the time to target for each missile based on its current position and speed, the position being constantly recalculated using a Global Positioning System built into each missile. It didn't take him long to realise the tracking and forwarding of data was utilising a very powerful transceiver, something David confirmed Israel didn't possess. "So the Americans are involved," he muttered to himself. "Which means the TAU and David's adapter must have been sent to a US monitoring facility."

Opening one final program, Jerry started to quickly tap away at his keyboard. He was entering commands that he had practiced thousands of times over the last few months, sometimes blindfolded, a trick he had learnt on the firing range, so he could do it in the dark if the need arose.

Whilst his fingers constantly bashed at the keys, Jerry's thoughts meandered to a vision of fighter pilots rushing to their aircraft, fuelled and ready for immediate takeoff. "Even if they manage to hit their targets, there was still a chance that a nuclear explosion in mid air could have devastating results if it occurred over populated regions. God, the human race needs you now, make this work," he found himself pleading.

The first missile to reach its target would be the last to have been launched, having the shortest airborne time, its destination: Jerusalem. Jerry keyed in a code he had preset when building the TAUs, but he failed to get a response on his screen. He tried again and again to no avail. He was sure there was a connection to the US transceiver since he was receiving real time updates on the progress of each missile to their respective destinations. He was also certain that neither Kavitah or anyone else for that matter could have changed the code, it was burnt into a Read Only Memory chip inside each TAU, all of which were sealed with vast amounts of epoxy, only leaving the battery chamber accessible. Attempting to tamper with the electronic circuitry would mean destroying the TAU beyond repair and if that were the case he wouldn't have received the text messages in the first place. Jerry noticed there was only fifteen minutes airborne time remaining before the first missile heading towards Jerusalem reached its target. If they were fitted with either nuclear or chemical warheads as suggested, the population of Jerusalem at the very least was about to be wiped out.

"Jerry, Jerry," he heard through the earpiece.

"Yes," he called back to Sara.

"All countries have launched evasive measures, how are you doing?" she asked him in a very calm voice.

"I'm not," he mumbled, his voice filled with fear. "I'm not getting a response from any of the TAUs. I need to speak to the people who are tracking the missiles for us, the people with the extra TAU and David's unit. I need to speak to them now," he shouted down the phone out of frustration rather than annoyance, whilst continually attempting to send the commands. "We only have a few minutes, please get hold of them quickly, my office line is free, use the direct number." As far as Jerry was concerned, speed was the foremost importance, security was now secondary.

Sara didn't answer but within the minute his desk phone rang. Jerry placed the call on loudspeaker so he could continue with both hands to work the keyboard and mouse. A male voice with a strong American accent announced, "I believe you wanted to speak with me, sir."

"Do you have some of my kit connected to your equipment?" Jerry asked in a considerably calmer tone than when he had just spoken to Sara.

"I have a device attached to a transceiver and another to a computer, if that's what you're referring to, sir. They were fitted about two months ago." Jerry had some difficulty understanding him due to the strong southern accent.

"That's a good start. Listen to me carefully please, because something is wrong and we don't have much time to sort it out," Jerry, begged. "It's sending data to me as it should, but when I try and talk to it, I'm not getting a response as if it's not seeing me," Jerry told him.

"I don't know sir, I'm just a radio operator here," the American replied, in no apparent rush.

Jerry thought for a moment analysing the description of the fault as he had just described it and asked, "The computer to which the adapter is connected, is it stand alone or connected to a network?"

"I believe it's connected to our network, it has shared files so I guess it must be. Yes sir," he answered, still with no urgency.

"Do you know whether you are behind a firewall?" Jerry asked, his fingers still attacking the keyboard at a rate that would make the best touch typist proud, still unable to obtain the expected reply. Sweat was dripping from his head and hands onto the keys, whilst he was trying his utmost to maintain a calm voice.

"It must be sir," was the reply. "This is an NSA listening post."

"NSA?" Jerry repeated in a questioning tone. "What is the NSA?"

"We're the National Security Agency. Our main activities are to protect national information systems and produce foreign intelligence and you ask if we're behind a firewall," the American laughed.

Jerry was more than frustrated which he did nothing to hide. "Please listen very carefully because we have no more time for niceties. I don't care what you have to do, what rules need to be broken, just get me access to your network now," and he gave the IP address of the computer he was using.

"I can't do that sir, you need authorisation to access our systems," which was the stock answer.

"If you don't allow me immediate access, millions of lives could be lost. Can you live the rest of your days knowing you could have easily prevented such a massacre, but decided to stick to protocol and do nothing?" Jerry asked in an attempt to pile on the guilt to get a result. "Sara, Sara, you there?" he called down his hands free microphone.

"Jerry, I can hear everything and I'm already on the case, just stay calm," she told him.

Whilst talking to both of them, Jerry retrieved the emails which had earlier been converted to the text messages using some code he had written for the purpose. He opened the first email and examined its header information. There he found the originators IP address which he hoped was the address of the computer at the NSA that he needed to access. He opened the second email and then the third. They all showed the messages had originated from the same address. "They aren't that clever then, I hope," he thought, taking a deep breath.

His hands flew around the keyboard whilst sweat continued to pour off him. He checked the time to first impact, a little over eleven minutes. "I'm not going to make it," he said out loud.

"Where's my access?" Jerry shouted out so both Sara and the radio operator would hear, whilst his fingers continued working as though they were totally separate to the rest of his body, under their own control. Looking at the clock again, only seven minutes airborne time remained.

"It's being dealt with I promise you, but meanwhile do whatever you have to do," Sara replied calmly, knowing precisely what Jerry was capable of and the potential result if he just waited.

With less than six minutes to the first impact, Jerry's fingers were slipping off the wet keys as he continued to work the keyboard. "Come on, I've done this a thousand times before and always succeeded. Don't let me down now, Mr Brain," he said to himself. Looking at another window he noticed the time was quickly disappearing, with a little over four minutes remaining before the first missile would reach its target. "Bingo!" he finally shouted out with some relief in his voice. "I have access," he added quietly to himself. He then went back to his well-rehearsed procedure. He keyed in the code and this time received the expected acknowledgement. "Just under two minutes to detonation, it must be over Tel Aviv by now," he thought. "Bond would succeed and so can I. Just remain calm Mr Freedman," he kept repeating to himself.

Jerry's first function was to block the access code, locking out Kavitah and her friends, giving him sole control. He then entered new coordinates calculated after the final testing was completed. With the modifications that he had made, Jerry knew he should be able to send a third coordinate which would point the missile in a vertical trajectory almost at a right angle to the surface of the Earth, but he was well aware this was the one element that had only been tested in simulation exercises and on the missile procured by Sara and tested in the Negev. Finally, he accessed the self-destruct mechanism which was linked to a timer within the TAU, setting it for six hundred seconds before activating the self-destruct mode.

"That's it, no more I can do on this one," he thought, whilst watching the time to impact for the missile blank out from his screen. Within a few seconds, he received another text message on his phone which he ignored. Glancing at the wall clock opposite him, he knew if what he had just attempted failed, impact and devastation was imminent.

Trying to clear his mind and wiping the moisture off his hands and face using a handkerchief from his pocket, Jerry started to repeat the procedure on the second missile, then the third. As he was finishing with the third, he heard the radio operator announce that access was being authorised and it would not be too long until he would have two-way connectivity. "Too late," Jerry shouted back, having forgotten all about him for the last few minutes.

"Calm down, Jerry," Sara ordered, whilst he continued to work on the remaining two missiles.

"You have two way access sir" the American voice announced, but by then Jerry had already completed everything he could do. He received four more text messages on his mobile, but only read the last one.

"If the missiles changed direction as I've planned, they should all be heading away from the Earth," he said to whomever was listening, sweat still pouring off him. The position status program showed all the missiles as if they were hovering at the point of their last update, with the time to destination blanked out. Jerry hoped the information was correct since it would be the first indication the third coordinate had been interpreted correctly by the missiles, although he wasn't sure why the detonation time had disappeared. "A minor bug if everything else works," he told himself. He believed he only had moments to wait before he knew for certain.

"Sara, you there still?" Jerry called out.

"Yes Jerry, I'm still with you, I told you I won't leave that easily," she replied.

"What's the news from Jerusalem?" Jerry asked.

"The missile has been lost from radar but no reports of any impact. I'm doing your praying here," she said, referring to a comment he once made to her.

"Do you still need me, sir?" Jerry heard from the phone on his desk.

"You're not going anywhere either, just hold on tight, I assure you your bosses won't argue," Jerry called back. "Remember they gave me access to your network, even if it was too late."

"If you say so, sir," he heard in the now familiar accent.

"I do," Jerry stated in a tone indicating that the question should never have been asked.

Jerry glanced at his clock. The first missile should have detonated by know. "Sara, news please?" he called out to her.

"I've heard nothing yet, but communication channels are still open so that's a positive sign," Sara replied.

"Sara, please keep talking, I can't handle the silence. It's as if I'm on my own in the world with no one here to help me," Jerry requested, trying desperately to describe how he was feeling.

"Jerry, don't worry, I'm not going anywhere, I promise. I'll relay everything as it comes through but I don't have a very good singing voice," she said trying to relieve some of the tension. For the next two minutes not a sound was made by any of them, for Jerry it felt more like two years.

Finally the silence was broken by Sara's calm voice in his ear, "I've just received confirmation that all five missiles have disappeared from radar. I repeat, no one is showing any missiles on radar; Jerry," she called. "Hang on," and she went quiet before saying, "Israeli bombers have just blitzed the area surrounding the launch site coordinates. Images before and after are already being examined and from what I've been informed so far, I believe there were three targets, two male and a third, a female."

"What about Jerusalem?" Jerry asked anxiously.

"I haven't heard anything yet," Sara told him.

"What's this all about sir?" came the voice from the speakerphone.

"Your bosses will no doubt tell you shortly," Jerry replied.

"Jerry, I'm not sure how to say this," he heard Sara start, his heart immediately sinking as he focussed back to her voice.

"It didn't work," Jerry said slowly. "Jerusalem's been annihilated."

"Listen, Jerry, listen," Sara stated firmly. "Israel and America have recalled their fighters, the other nations are about to do the same. No country has taken any military action to intercept the missiles. I'm awaiting satellite data at the moment," Sara said.

There was a knock on Jerry's door. "Not now I'm busy," he shouted out.

"It's me darling, Rochelle." She called through the door in a very gentle voice.

"Rochelle, I'm busy," Jerry repeated loudly.

"Let her in, Jerry," Sara insisted, "I have just heard the President of

America will shortly be addressing the American people, so she's going to know all about it anyway. This one you won't be able to hide from her, she already knows enough to put two and two together," Sara said, hearing Jerry.

Jerry unlocked his door and allowed Rochelle in, before locking it again. "Jerry, you look as though you have just come out of the shower, besides appearing absolutely awful. What's going on?" Rochelle asked.

"I'd also like to know the answer to that question," the American radio operator stated.

Listening to the conversations taking place in Jerry's office, Sara interjected, "You can give them an overview, reminding them not to repeat anything you say, or that they have heard." As Jerry considered what he would tell them, Sara spoke again. "Jerry, please try and relax now, you've done your bit, there is nothing more you can do, the mission is over and it's been a great success. But I'm still with you don't worry." She could only imagine how Jerry felt, comparing it to her first successful operation which was nothing to what he had just achieved. "By the way, all nations have now stood down their fighters," Sara informed him, trying to provide a minute-by-minute update.

"It's like this then," Jerry started, planning to summarise everything into a couple of sentences. "A terrorist group managed to obtain a number of Inter Continental Ballistic Missiles. They were launched a short time ago targeting major cities around the world including London and New York." He paused, considering how best to finish the statement. "A speedy response and some good technology successfully neutralised the missiles before any reached their targets. The rest I'm sure you can work out for yourselves. Having said that, the only thing you know about this is what you hear officially. I trust that's clear to you both?"

Neither of them spoke for a while whilst they absorbed Jerry's words. "You're kidding me," the voice on the other end of the speakerphone announced in a tone as if to say I don't believe it! "And I heard you mention Jerusalem a little earlier. What were the other two targets?" he went onto ask.

"It doesn't matter now," Jerry replied.

"Jerry," Sara broke in. "I have some initial data through from the satellites. It appears that all the missiles self destructed successfully. From the sudden increased radioactivity count above the Earths atmosphere, it seems as if they were all carrying nuclear warheads."

"And we're safe?" Jerry asked.

"Yes. It certainly looks that way. I believe your plan executed perfectly despite your doubts. Mind you, our American friends aren't going to be too happy that you hacked into their allegedly secure NSA facility rather than wait for authorisation. You do know that don't you? They'll want to know precisely how you managed it," she said being very careful not to sound as if she was rebuking him in any way.

"What did you want me to do? You saw the time ticking away. The first target would have been destroyed before I received authorisation. I had to hack into them and besides which, you sort of suggested it if I recall correctly," he told her in an unquestionable but defensive manner.

"You hacked into us?" the voice from the speakerphone repeated as a question.

"Don't worry about it pal," Jerry replied, interrupting his conversation with Sara.

Over the speakerphone, Jerry heard a sudden round of applause and cheers. "What's going on over there?" Jerry called out to his American colleague.

"Your story has just been sort of confirmed here," the radio operator told him. "They have just made an announcement stating that one of the transceivers in the facility here has been used by a multi national team of security forces to avert the largest terrorist attack ever attempted. Sir, my colleagues around me and myself are standing saluting you, whoever you are," Jerry heard an even louder applause.

"Jerry," Sara called.

"Yes," Jerry replied in a very patient tone.

"A Scotland Yard Anti Terrorist team, along with Debra, Moshe and Ruti have just picked up four people in Central London, three of them are the directors of DataLink, the fourth has yet to be identified, but I think we know who it is, don't you?" Sara happily announced.

"All three directors of DataLink, I thought it was only his brother and brother in law involved?" Jerry questioned.

"Well, according to Debra all three have been arrested, Mohammed being the fourth person," she spelt out for Jerry.

"Sir," called the radio operator. "I'm being called by my managers and need to sign off. I'm sorry, but despite everything just now, I'm going to have to report that you hacked into our facilities. That's going to cause you a fair amount of grief I'm afraid, but there is nothing I can do. The last time it was attempted the guy was thrown in jail." And with that the connection was severed.

"Jerry," Sara called.

"Still here," Jerry replied, mimicking the way she had responded earlier when the situation was reversed.

"I've got some calls I need to make," Sara told him. "I must get together with you at some time though," she said as an afterthought, already thinking about debriefing him.

"We can get together later, maybe have a celebratory meal somewhere," Jerry replied. "That's assuming I'm not in prison for hacking into the Yanks."

"Don't worry about that, they already knew there was a strong chance you would at least attempt it. I told them that if it took more than a minute or so to get you access, they would more than likely see you in their system without sanction. What took you so long?" she asked jokingly.

"I'm not sure, maybe I'm losing my touch," Jerry replied whilst Rochelle sat there, still stunned at everything she was hearing.

"So what about that meal, I think you owe me after this one," Jerry asked again, pressing the subject. For some reason he felt the need to see her in person. It was as though there was suddenly a new bond between them, having gone through everything together and he felt that seeing her would provide some sort of reassurance that everything was really alright.

"Sounds like a lovely idea but let's see how the rest of the day pans out if that's okay with you," Sara replied, knowing that despite she being the commander of the operation, she would be well down the list of people he would be meeting with over the coming few hours. "I'll catch up with you shortly, but once again, well done."

"Bye," Jerry replied and cleared the call. Staring at his mobile phone, he flicked through the text messages from the original launch notifications all the way through to the final confirmation of the changed destinations. He was in two minds whether to delete them or keep them for prosperity.

"Jez," Rochelle said quietly, trying to appreciate what Jerry had achieved almost single handed over the last few months. "You look terrible. Why don't you go home, have a shower and then rest. By the sound of things you more than deserve it." She walked around to his chair giving him a small peck on the lips before standing behind him, draping her arms around his neck. She spoke quietly, "I don't know what to say," and for the first time in her life, Rochelle found herself lost for words. But she could see he needed her support, for some reason when he should be elated at his achievement, he seemed totally despondent. Thinking it through, Rochelle realised that he had spent the last six months concentrating on just one thing which had reached its climax and come to an end in a flash, leaving him exhausted and completely drained of adrenalin. Trying to cheer him up, the only words that came to mind were, "Did I hear correctly, have we lost a client and do I need to make room for a second Medal of Honour?"

Jerry just smiled back at her.

Forty-Four

As Jerry tried to pack his things together, he took a number of telephone calls. The first was the President of the United States, followed by the British Prime Minister, the French President, the Prime Minister of Israel and finally the Prime Minister of Italy.

Putting each on speakerphone for Rochelle's benefit, they each had the same message for him; congratulating him on the successful outcome of his mission. Every leader concluded their conversation by inviting both Jerry and Rochelle to stay as their guest, allowing him to be thanked properly. The American President even specified that Jerry would be awarded The Presidential Medal of Freedom, America's highest civilian award.

When Jerry had finally finished on the telephone, Rochelle gave him a passionate hug and kiss. "What's that for?" Jerry asked.

"Do I need an excuse to hug and kiss my husband?" she asked, although they normally kept their business relationship very professional and it was unusual for any affection between them to be shown in the office. "Besides, it's not everyday my husband speaks to the President of America and several European Prime Ministers after saving millions of lives, or is this going to become a regular event?" she enquired.

"I sincerely hope not," Jerry replied. "It's been a hard few months but I think we can now have a honeymoon," he told her, "There are several destinations to choose from, or hop from one country to another and by the sound of it, I've kept my promise that we'll be treated like royalty," being the first thing to enter his mind. "And you can kiss me whenever you like," he added.

Jerry quickly finished packing his belongings and with Rochelle, started making his way through to reception. The story must have already broken on the internet, since as he walked through the open plan sales and administration office towards the reception area, a number of staff asked if he had seen the news, "Was it the same DataLink that he was working with?" and "Did he know anything about it?"

Jerry, still soaking wet and looking the worse for wear from his ordeal, chose to ignore the questions and holding hands Mr and Mrs Freedman left the building for the day, Rochelle calling out to anyone listening, "I think he's come down with something so I'm taking him home." She led him to her car and drove the few miles to the apartment, leaving his car in the car park.

The news that evening and for the following few days concentrated on the foiled attack, detailing the history of the terror organisation, how they operated, where they sourced their weapons, how they were successfully infiltrated and the measures taken to defend the countries at risk. At no time was Jerry's name or Igloo mentioned and Jerry couldn't believe how far from the truth all the stories were.

Before they started their unbelievable honeymoon, Jerry was debriefed by a number of agencies from all the countries involved, whilst Rochelle was following up on government orders, the largest coming from the NSA.